PLANET

DREAMS

Planet Dreams

Michaela Carlock

Keswick House
Redding, CA

ISBN 0-9653024-2-3

Library of Congress Catalog No. 97-75467

First Edition
2 4 6 8 10 9 7 5 3 1

Cover art and design by Diane Morley
Special thanks to Candia Ludy

Additional copies are available. For your convenience, order information is included in the back.

For Richard

I would like to extend heartfelt thanks to the following people for their encouragement and support:

Richard Hardie
Lynda Lanker
Hal and Kim White
Cathy and Rob Cawthorne
Emily White
Constance Roach
Candia Ludy
Diane Morley
Tim Schoch
Deborah Schneider
George Garrett
Horace and Jane Kelton
Lucille Enix
George Linville

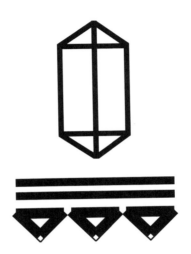

— ∞ ◯ ∞ —

"The world as you know it is a picture of your expectations. The world as the race of man knows it is the materialization en masse of your individual expectations. As children come from your physical tissues, so is the world your joint creation."

— Seth, from THE NATURE OF PERSONAL REALITY, by Jane Roberts

"Then we journey up and up through a long, black tunnel till we reach the Garden Angel ground, and then we sprout up through it like carrots, and there we are, Garden Angels now, not people—but the big, crooked, sad, new sort of Angels that haven't been there long. And our twin, who has disappeared in a little bright speck too small to see, passes through his shadow and comes here and gets in a lady's stomach and turns into a baby…Both worlds belong to both of us."

— Bill Bob, in THE RIVER WHY, by David James Duncan

— ∞ ◯ ∞ —

Planet Dreams

———— ∞ ◯ ∞ ————

ONE

Astrid settled comfortably into her favorite chair and flicked on her dreamviewer, eager to see what would emerge from a night of hazier dreaming than usual. She hoped she would have another dream from her recent series, which took place in some enchanting alien environment: Eight large and mysterious-looking moons hovered in the violet skies, each a different pale pastel, and massive canyons snaked through the planet's crust, colorfully layered in golden bronzes and teal grays, rubies and burgundies. The people she encountered in these dreams all treated her in a kind, friendly, interested way, and the plant and animal life on this planet was not only dazzlingly diverse, it was also sentient and telepathic.

Smiling with anticipation, she touched the video-record button. She always edited her week's dreams to put together highlights for her therapist, but she was also considering making an art video just for fun. Remembering she'd forgotten to put the tea kettle on to boil, she started to get up. However, the dream came into focus just then and she didn't want to stop it; so she stayed where she was, not quite confident enough, even yet, of her psychokinetic abilities to try to maneuver the kettle mentally.

She leaned back, curiously surveying the colors that were forming on the screen. Definitely not from the same series. Did she have a nightmare? Black swirled amidst dingy gray and beige; finally she discerned shapes. Blockish massive buildings loomed onscreen, reminding her of recent news clips she'd seen of the former South Bronx on television; the newly formed InterCity Boroughs Council had just decided to level it and rebuild, using the recycled materials. The graffiti-spattered dream edifices all looked filthy, and endless, stretching as far as she could see. A hopeless, menacing anxiety exuded from every aspect of the scene.

What did this dream mean? There were so many different kinds, Astrid still had difficulty differentiating between them. She really couldn't tell prophetic dreams from ones that presented everyday psychological and spiritual information in symbolic form or from ones that dealt with alternate lives, whether past, present, or future. She was learning, though. Her dream therapy had already helped tremendously.

Suddenly the point of view shifted, and Astrid observed a plump, pasty-faced young woman sleeping in a little cubicle. The entire cubicle was covered by what looked like a very thin, dirt-colored carpet and possessed no furnishings whatsoever. The woman slept in a slot in the wall, and Astrid noticed a teeny old-fashioned television screen embedded in the opposite wall as well as an ancient, stained sink. She watched the woman rise and put on one of three shabby dresses that were hanging on a peg. She fixed herself a bowl of what looked like oatmeal, except that she used water out of the tap. When the woman left the cubicle, Astrid's point of view faded out; then abruptly, the brightly striated canyons of her alien planet swept into the field of vision. Astrid breathed a sigh of relief and ran through the dream in fast motion to see whether any new developments had occurred, but they hadn't. That seemed rather odd.

She got up thoughtfully and put her kettle on to boil, then ambled over to the front porch to collect the fresh milk and bread that she had delivered every day. A man in the neighborhood provided the service, and very reasonably, too, in Astrid's opinion. She skimmed a little cream off the top of the milk to put into her tea and settled down to eat in her breakfast room. She had just taken her first bite and snapped open the paper to the comics when someone knocked on the door.

"Come in!" she shouted. Looking up, she saw her friend Robin breezing into the kitchen. Robin stooped to give Astrid a kiss, then seated herself across the table and poured herself a cup of tea.

"Where's Nate?" she asked.

"Working on the space dump."

Robin nodded, slipping the front section of the paper out from under the cartoons. "Going to work?"

"Yeah." Astrid blew on her tea to cool it, smiling over at her friend. "What about you?"

Robin shook her head, her red hair catching the sunlight that streamed in through the kitchen window. "No, not today. I put in six hours on toxic cleanup yesterday. I think I'll check to see if anybody needs a raft guide." Glancing down at the front page, Robin froze, her lips parted in dismay.

"What is it?"

"My god, someone in Castle Lake was stabbed in an argument! Can you believe it?"

Astrid frowned and reached for the paper. "Let's see."

Robin handed it over to her and flopped back in her chair, gnawing her bottom lip.

Astrid felt disquieted as she scanned the article. She hadn't heard of anyone using physical violence for about the last eight years, ever since the effects of the UFO virus had finally stabilized. No one knew for sure whether aliens had actually released the virus, but after the mysterious message about the virus had flashed on television and computer screens worldwide, right at the turn of the millennium, the media had dubbed it the UFO virus, and the name stuck. Astrid thought it more likely that a person had engineered and released the virus, since it certainly seemed the majority of elusive aliens that interacted with humankind were committed to noninterference. The persistent accounts of entities that appeared to engage in forcible hybridization and genetic manipulation of humans represented, in Astrid's view, the unpleasant minority. Even in those cases, the entities seemed more intent on interacting with individuals than with the entire globe, and of course, some of the remote viewing data indicated that these beings were actually working for a constructive genetic goal that included both races. Not ever having had any personal interaction with these entities, Astrid wasn't sure what to believe about them.

At any rate, the main effects of the virus, apart from a debilitating lassitude that lasted for months and brought global civilization to a practical halt, appeared to be endocrine changes that made violence and physical aggression a thing of the past. In addition, it unmasked the species' psychic abilities, which deepened empathy. War became obsolete almost overnight, and extreme altercations had become so rare that an account such as this one rated as big news. Puzzled, Astrid leafed rapidly through the rest of the section, but found it filled with the usual—world news, Northwest news, weather and gardening information, a toxic cleanup report for the local area as well as the world, notices for cultural and community events, ads for luxury goods.

"How…bizarre," she remarked finally. "Although, I see the perpetrator claims it was an accident."

"How do you 'accidentally' stab someone, I wonder?" mused Robin.

"Good question." Astrid reread the article, but found the account confusing. The argument had evidently started at a party where a few people had too much to drink and the person with the knife seemed to have gotten carried away. "Oh, well. Fortunately, it's an isolated incident. Cosmic rays must have zapped those two."

Robin laughed. "Yeah, maybe a hole in the ozone found them."

Astrid arose, stretching. "I should get ready for work. Feel free to stay if you'd like. The fridge is full, if you want to make yourself some breakfast."

"Thanks, but I need to get going myself. I'll see you later."

"Hey, maybe we can work out a raft trip together while Nate is gone."

"I'd love to." Robin gave Astrid an affectionate squeeze.

Astrid returned her hug fondly and then headed outside to her bathhouse, a pleasant, aromatic structure built from cedar and nestled among tall, smooth-barked manzanita bushes. She started to take her antifertility herbs, which she kept in the bathhouse, but then hesitated. She wanted a baby, and she felt sure the Birth Center would give the go-ahead. Especially since she possessed such a generous amount of psychokinetic ability. Besides, with all the miraculous medical developments in the past few years, most genetic damage could be repaired before the baby was born, a big difference from only a few years ago. Chromosome damage from the string of environmental disasters that had occurred right before the turn of the century had proved heartbreakingly widespread. Consequently, the genetic counselors at most local birth centers in just about every part of the world could not in good conscience issue many approvals for couples wanting to have children.

Compliance in the West Coast provinces wasn't required, it was voluntary, but the strong sense of local responsibility that had developed since the introduction of the UFO virus prevented anyone from going directly against the recommendation given. With so much human labor and so many material resources necessarily devoted to the cleanup of the planet for so long, communities couldn't afford to birth and care for grossly deformed babies. Everyone accepted this fact.

Now that the pace of cleanup had slowed, however, everyone could relax a little and devote time and resources to other areas. Genetic research had been one of them. Astrid counted herself fortunate that she was wanting to conceive at this much more auspicious time, even though mothers still risked a substantial mortality rate from toxemia related to childbirth, another common side-effect of the 20th century chemical spills and explosions of radioactive wastes.

In the end, she decided to forgo the herbs and to visit the Birth Center soon. Although theoretically she could become pregnant the day after she stopped taking birth control, the reality was that it would probably take her a while to get pregnant.

After showering, Astrid brushed out her hair, which was black, thick, and stylishly cut into three distinctive tiers; then she applied some metallic blue eye shadow that was almost exactly the same color as the freckles that dusted her nose, an apparently harmless mutation of her own that had expressed itself only after her bout with the UFO virus. She selected a burgundy tunic and deep blue leggings, then agonized over whether to wear her cobalt-blue boots or the yellow ones. Since she couldn't decide, she wore one of each.

She loved the feel of the garments against her skin, proud that she had been part of the research team that had engineered the plant responsible for about seventy-five percent of the community's clothing needs in the winter. It looked and felt just like thick, soft cotton, but had three times the warmth and insulative protection of wool. The fiber had caught on elsewhere, too. Shasta City grew and exported a great deal of it, helping to make the area a very prosperous one.

Astrid added a little air to the tires on her bike, then took a leisurely route to work. When she reached GenFarm, she dismounted and coasted on one pedal to the covered bike rack, where she parked. She noticed her friend Louise's bike as well as the one that belonged to Meagan, a local animal rights activist. The animal rights movement had grown so powerful in the Pacific Northwest that almost no medical research and absolutely no cosmetic research used animal subjects. In addition, fewer and fewer communities in the region were raising animals for food. No law existed against it—no laws existed, period, not in this part of North America—but the strong peer pressure acted as a powerful enough inducement to bring the practice out of favor. Many people had started to switch to plant substitutes.

Personally, Astrid didn't think the domesticated animals had it so bad these days. They led a healthy life pampered by loving caretakers, they were hand-fed special treats and housed in roomy pastures and barns. Most farmers even brought in an animal sensitive at slaughter time who conferred with the animals to determine who was ready to go. So, since she loved the taste of meat, Astrid decided to put her current efforts into engineering plants that produced meat-like fruits. And because, in a playful mood, she had decided to program the fruits to grow into little replicas of cows and lambs and rabbits, she had incurred Meagan's righteous indignation.

"I think that's sick," Meagan had blurted just the other day when Astrid's plants first began to develop in the greenhouse. "Those poor animals! And here you are, making fun of their butchery! What's wrong with you?"

"Hey, I just feel sorry for the apples and pears," Astrid had responded, not entirely fairly, since she knew that most fruits' reproductive strategy included being eaten and disseminated by animals. Biologically speaking, they wanted to be eaten. "You should see the callous look on your face when you bite into an apple."

When Astrid entered the lab, she knew, even before she saw the look on Louise's face, that something was up.

"How's it going, Louise?" Astrid greeted her.

"Not bad."

"Then, um, why do you have that look on your face?"

Louise sighed; clearly, she had been hoping Astrid would ask. "Okay, I'll tell you. I really think you're teasing Meagan too hard. She's young and very sensitive and very idealistic—"

"And has no sense of humor," Astrid interrupted.

"So fine—if you know that, why goad her? For Pete's sake, did you have to make your glycogenic fruits metamorphose into animal shapes? All they have to do is taste like and possess the texture of meat. When you cut them up and prepare them, they won't look different from an eggplant!"

"Well—they will if you cook them whole."

"Okay, fine." Louise glared at her. "At least stop taunting her, will you please? Now she's eating nothing but chlorophyll capsules, so she won't be hurting any living thing when she eats."

Astrid shook her head. She resisted blurting, "So where does she think they get the chlorophyll from? Rocks?" She didn't want to create dissension in her work place. "Okay, Louise," she said finally. "I apologize. I'll apologize to Meagan, too. Okay?"

Louise hesitated, then nodded, though observing Astrid carefully. "Don't screw it up."

"Don't worry!" Astrid laughed, then squeezed her friend's arm before heading to the greenhouse to find Meagan. She found her transplanting some feathery little seedlings into a richer bed of sand, murmuring to them as she worked. Astrid admired the girl's touch with plants— she just wished she weren't so touchy with humans.

"Meagan, how's it going?" she called, attempting to minimize her height so she wouldn't tower intimidatingly over her co-worker.

Meagan glanced up and frowned. "Fine, thanks."

"Hey, listen—I apologize for what I said the other day. And I'm sorry if my choice of fruit shapes offends you."

"Then why did you do that?" Meagan demanded, chin quivering.

"Well, look—I like animals. I didn't choose those shapes to bug you and make fun of animals. Didn't it ever occur to you that I eat animals because I like them? A wolf doesn't hate rabbits, you know—rabbits are his very favorite thing. Would you want to banish wolves from the universe?"

"Oh, and I suppose you'd like to be eaten!"

"No, but then I occupy the top of the food chain, don't I? I might feel differently if I'd chosen to be a prey species this time around."

Meagan made a face and jumped up. "You really are impossible!" She covered her ears and ran from the room crying, "Please don't apologize any more!"

Astrid exhaled heavily and dropped to the ground, finishing the transplanting for Meagan. She really operated on a totally different wavelength from that girl. Whenever she tried to lighten things up, it seemed, her tactic backfired and Meagan ended up even angrier than before. The tension was creating unease between herself and Louise, too. Maybe she should find a different place to work. But she liked GenFarm. She'd been one of the original group that had started this center, right after graduating from Humboldt State. It made her feel good to work here. Although lately it hadn't, she had to admit.

When she'd planted all the seedlings, she got up and strolled back into the lab, hoping that Meagan hadn't lodged another complaint against her. But Louise glanced up sharply from her scope when Astrid came in. And she looked very stern.

"Louise—I tried. I just can't seem to say anything right to her."

Louise didn't reply for a moment. "I didn't want to do this, Astrid," she said finally, "but you've really been creating a lot of dissension and conflict here. I entered the complaints against you in the central computer."

"Hey, wait a second!" Astrid protested. "Don't you think there might be two sides to this story? Meagan's not making me feel so great, either!"

"But you're older and therefore it's your responsibility to make peace. I tell you not to screw it up and you walk right in there and make an intolerable situation even worse. I'm requesting that you be taken off the meat-substitute project."

"Louise! You can't be serious."

"I am serious."

Astrid laughed in disbelief. "Look, I don't have any emotional commitment invested in the meat-substitute program. I don't care if I work on it or not. But I have to say I feel a bit ganged up on. Just because I haven't lodged formal complaints against Meagan doesn't mean she hasn't made my work harder and upset me, too. And she's an adult, though a young one, I admit. I don't know, I'm thinking perhaps I should work elsewhere for awhile."

Louise pursed her lips. "But—we have no other workers with your background."

Astrid nodded. "I know. I'm sorry."

"Well, it's up to you, of course. I didn't mean to chase you away. I like both you and Meagan and I would rather you could work together."

"I know." The article about the stabbing suddenly popped into Astrid's mind. Odd. Her difficulties with Meagan constituted a first for her. She had never experienced such friction with any other co-worker. "I tell you what, Louise—how about if I arrange my schedule so that our paths don't cross for a while? I have another project I'd like to work on anyway, if I can obtain approval."

"What's that?"

"I'll tell you if I get approval."

"Oh, come on! Tell me!" Louise pressed.

"Well, all right." Astrid grinned. "A baby."

"A baby?"

Astrid nodded excitedly.

Louise chuckled. Then her face changed. "But you know, Astrid—I've heard rumors that a lot of people have been turned down lately."

"Really? I've been hearing just the opposite, that they've been easing up. Do you know why?"

Louise shrugged. "No, not really."

"Hmm. I'll have to check into it. But I shouldn't have any problems with such strong psychic abilities, don't you think?"

"True. I hope so, anyway." Louise reached over and hugged her friend. "So when do you plan to start?"

"Soon. As soon as Nate gets back. He'll be home in two or three days."

Louise smiled. "Well, I wish you all the luck in the world."

Astrid beamed, happy to have Louise loosened up and friendly again. Louise was an old chum, one of the first lab workers—she hated to have her conflict with Meagan affect their relationship.

Astrid decided to leave for the day and give Meagan some space. She would come back sometime in the next couple of days when Meagan wasn't around. Instead, she headed over to work on the group sculpture that was going up in Black Butte Park.

Astrid hadn't conceived the design—someone else had—but she liked the concept so much that she'd volunteered to put some labor into erecting it. It was an abstract neon sculpture that stood fifty meters high, a jet black cinder cone serving as a backdrop. Because it generated so much light and used a substantial amount of energy, it would turn on only once a week when finished. The concept artist had programmed it so that no one would

ever know when it would suddenly flash on for an hour
or so. He wanted it to surprise people.

On her way, Astrid thought she saw the fleeting form
of an alien melting into the forest, but perhaps it was only
a deer. Sightings of aliens had risen in the last two decades.
A change in the earth's electromagnetic field had been
noted recently, and cosmologists speculated that this had
been responsible for bringing other realities closer to this
one, via the dimensional windows, magnetically
anomalous areas that created time and space vortices, or
"warps."

New Age devotees, who by now outnumbered
adherents of traditional religions in the area, believed that
they perceived and lived but one possible existence on
one version of Earth. Other versions existed at the same
time, although on different planes, or on the same plane
but at different times. This created the illusion of history
and the glimpsing at times of other worlds in dreams:
worlds that seemed quite familiar, yet different from this
existence, either subtly or outrageously. According to
current belief, a person's entity, or total personality, was
composed of several selves, all living different lives, some
of them appearing as "past" lives, some of them appearing
as highly evolved existences. A particular self, equipped
with an ego in order to perceive its experience consciously,
usually felt aware of only itself. And yet, through dreams,
through meditation and psychic practices, modern
spiritualists and mystics believed that contact could be
made with these other selves. "Aliens" might be alternate
selves of humans, a more highly evolved portion of the
total entity; or they might be unrelated inhabitants of other
alternate worlds, possibly alternate Earths that had taken
different evolutionary pathways.

When she neared the park, Astrid made a stop for a
glass of freshly squeezed orange juice at her favorite juice
bar. The canister of complimentary antifertility herbs on
the adjacent shelf caught her eye as she poured her glass.

Maybe I should take some, she thought guiltily, remembering what Louise had said about the Birth Center turning down people. But she didn't. She couldn't imagine being refused. Not with her body absolutely clamoring to bear a child.

TWO

Judy sat slumped in her bed slot, her eyes trained on the TV. She had just received a notice from the Ministry of Television that her hours watched had slipped below the minimum requirement, especially in the area of religious programming. Further disinterest could earn her unwelcome attention as a subversive, so she dutifully observed the preacher prancing in front of his audience, winking beads of sweat flinging in small droplets from his coiffed pompadour. He whirled and gesticulated. He crooned. Then roared. Then bleated in an insistent, anguished, mesmerizing voice, pleading for money from anyone and everyone who might be watching.

Ordinarily, Judy would have groped automatically for her credit booklet and sent some money. One reason she had stopped watching these programs was that she could ill afford to give away anything extra. But today she reached for her monitored channel-puncher instead. Somehow the program wasn't affecting her the way it always had in the past. She felt depressed. More depressed than usual. And this was making it worse.

She punched through several stations, running through the standard fare with disinterest. She lingered on the

"Disease of the Week" docudrama, this week's episode focusing on a new disease that softened the bones bit by bit until the victim turned into a bag of skin, a puddle of protoplasm, a limp sac of cellular mass fed by a battery of tubes and fluids and kept alive by a series of injections and excruciatingly painful medical treatments. In the docudrama, a young pregnant woman had contracted the disease, and the drama centered on whether to save the mother or the baby, who also had the disease.

She switched to "Litigation Court" and paused. Could it be? Good Lord, it was! It was her ex-boyfriend suing somebody else. Who was it this time? she scowled to herself, paying greater attention. She gathered, as she watched the contentious proceedings, that he had tripped on a crack in the sidewalk on his way to work. When he fell, he hit his head, and now claimed that the injury had befuddled his thinking.

"You never could think straight!' Judy shouted at the image on the screen, which certainly looked dopey enough to support his avowal of disability. He was suing the municipality, the concrete company that provided the cement for the sidewalk, the workers who had installed it, everyone who had been near him at the time of the accident and failed to prevent or cushion his fall, the two shopkeepers who owned the businesses closest to the crack, and the shoe manufacturer who had made the shoes he wore that fateful day.

That accident-prone jackass! Judy fumed to herself. Surely this time they wouldn't award him any damages. He'd sued so many times she was beginning to think he might warrant his own television show. If only she had known about this aspect of his before she had become involved with him. During this breakup scene, in his haste to get away from her pleading, he'd tripped on her shoes and toppled over. He managed to rip a ligament, which put him out of work for a long time. Moreover, he had incurred a lot of medical expenses which weren't covered by his health insurance. He'd sued her and won, his eighth successful suit. However, as she continued to watch in shock and disbelief, the jury awarded him $50 million. Of course, the lawyers' fees would amount to about $49,750,000, but that creep would still walk away from the whole thing with a tidy sum.

She exhaled heavily in disgust, more depressed than ever now. And what did she expect? Winning a lawsuit was one of the few ways a technodrudge could expect any sort of windfall. Perhaps, she brooded, she should come up with a case herself. But the more she thought about it, the more tired she became. She didn't want to sue anybody. She despised the whole practice and everyone who took advantage of it. Life was ugly enough without making it more so.

So she plowed through a few more channels, bored to nauseated immobility with the weekly "Trial of the Century," and finding "Lifestyles of the Savage and Dangerous" too depressingly bizarre: The program profiled the lifestyles of famous murderers. Since so many violent deaths occurred, it took a lot of effort to become a celebrity murderer, but the rewards were sufficiently enticing—movie deals, product endorsements, social prestige, and lots of media attention—that plenty of people pursued this route to stardom. In fact, a new show aired every week.

Finally she settled on "Rich People, the New Generation," although what was supposed to be so new about it she couldn't fathom. The same surgically and cosmetically altered actors and actresses (at least they looked like the same ones, but with their perfect, even and standardized features, who could tell the difference between them?) continued to steal each other's money, power, wives, husbands, girlfriends and boyfriends, and never left off sulking and languishing, strutting and preening, and performing petty cruelties out of pure nastiness.

Nevertheless, Judy decided to leave the channel there because at least she could derive some vicarious comfort from the simulated wealthy surroundings. The food looked so interesting—even though she didn't know what half of it was—the clothes so beautiful, the living quarters so spacious and bright. She had a window in her cubicle, but she lived far enough down the air shaft that little light penetrated.

Soon, though, a commercial for one of the thirty-seven different brands of all-in-one food powder flashed on the screen, and Judy switched off the TV in a fit of gloom. She supposed, as the government was so fond of telling her and everyone else, that she should be grateful for the amount of choice and variety she had available to her. In China, evidently, the people had only one kind of food powder. But she had tried all thirty-seven brands at one time or another and she had never been able to tell the difference between them. Only the packages were different. She wanted some of the things they ate on "Rich People, The New Generation." Little hope of that.

Little hope of anything, she thought, her melancholy deepening into despair. Little hope of love, of comfort, of change. She pulled back her blanket and sheet, fluffed her pillow as best she could, although it resisted all her efforts and lay flat and uninviting on her lumpy mattress. She undressed, taking care to treat her clothes and nylons as gingerly as possible in order to prolong their wear, trying not to look at herself before squirming into her ratty, modest nightgown. It was disheartening to look at herself after seeing those perfect specimens on television. She wished she could afford surgery. She wished she could be an actress. She wished, in fact, for anything to change, anything at all. Dear God, she started to pray, then thought again. She knew better than to ask for anything for herself. He wouldn't listen to her anyway.

And yet a small, intense voice intruded into her mind, surprising her: But if anyone out there is listening, anyone at all, she heard herself pleading desperately, please help! Change something—anything! Even if it kills me and everyone else on this godforsaken planet...

THREE

As Astrid rode the bike trail through the park, the fresh, sharp scent of the cedars and pine trees intoxicated her. The area around Shasta City had once been clearcut, but now a thick, healthy, young forest covered it, wherever the last volcanic activity from nearby Mt. Shasta didn't prevent trees from growing. The mountain hadn't erupted since the eighteenth century, but recently swarms of very small earthquakes had rumbled around the base of the mountain, fueling the ever-present speculation that the volcano might erupt one of these days. Mt. St. Helens had erupted in 1980, Mt. Rainier in 2001. Quite a few geologists predicted a period of renewed volcanic activity along the American edge of the Ring of Fire, the volcanic system encircling the Pacific Ocean. Astrid, among many others, often considered moving for this reason, since if Mt. Shasta blew, Shasta City would be history. And if the mountain blew in just the right—or wrong—direction, a lot of people would perish from the hot ash, including herself. But she never did anything about it. Astrid loved her community. And she enjoyed taking risks.

When she reached the sculpture site, she felt glad that she had made the decision to come over to the park. Her good friend Taro stood on some scaffolding, welding neon tubing.

"Taro!" she shouted delightedly.

He turned off his welding gun and tilted back his visor. "Astrid!" he retorted impishly. He clambered down from his perch and ran to meet her, giving her an enthusiastic, off-balance hug. "Astrid, my god, I think you've grown even taller since I left," he complained.

"Really? I think you've shrunk. What has Austin been feeding you?"

"Nothing but rice and beans," he glowered sulkily. "He's such a beast."

They both laughed. Austin worked as the sous-chef for the hottest restaurant in town; invitations to dinner parties at Taro and Austin's house were highly coveted.

"So—where should I work so that I don't get in your way?" Astrid inquired politely.

"Oh—anywhere. You never get in the way, you know that. You can help me weld these neon tubes if you'd like. I was delighted to see you pedal up. I feared Thumbs McGillicuddy might show up today."

"Oh, no. Is he working on this sculpture?"

"Yes, and I've just finished re-welding every joint he put in here yesterday. The kid's nice and all that, but I think he'd do better in recycling, where they need people to smash and crush. He's a walking entropy device."

"Don't I know!" Astrid shuddered, recalling the last project, a delicate one involving intricate polarized filaments, she'd worked on where Forest—nicknamed Thumbs McGillicuddy by Astrid and Taro—had tried to participate before finally being asked by all the other participants to select another sculpture. Astrid signed out a welding gun and a visor and joined Taro in putting together the topmost neon tubing, a wild, noodlelike conglomeration. When she needed three hands, Astrid took great satisfaction in trying out her telekinetic powers.

After a while, Taro slipped his visor back and took some deep breaths. Then he scrambled down the scaffolding, beckoning for Astrid to take a break with him.

"So, Astrid," he remarked casually, as they sprawled on the grass, "how have things been lately?"

"Oh, not bad, I suppose. I'm not getting along so great with one of my co-workers—Meagan."

"Big surprise."

Astrid laughed. "I have some sort of exciting news, actually."

"What's that?" Taro straightened up curiously.

"I'm going to start trying to have a baby."

Taro blinked, regarding her in amazement. "Tell me you're not serious. Please."

Astrid shook her head, chuckling. "No, I'm serious."

"What—with that giant partner of yours?"

"Well, of course. Not with you, certainly."

"Great. Just what we need. More giants."

"Hey—come on, be happy for me."

"I'm trying, I'm trying! Just give me a moment to get over the shock." He sighed. Then he brightened. "Come to think of it—this kid could turn out to be a midget. You know the law of the norm. It always ensures a return to the average to prevent unwieldy freaks. Two great big strapping things like yourselves—you'll probably send Mother Nature scrambling."

"You're so bizarre, Taro. Who cares how tall it'll be?"

"Spoken like a true tall person." Taro plucked a piece of grass and placed it between his lips. "But tell me— have you heard the latest rumors?"

"What rumors?"

He tossed the grass blade to the ground. "Have you heard about the sightings of—of weird creatures?"

"Well, the aliens, of course, but you know all about them, that's been going on for years."

"No, I mean unsavory creatures. Wraithlike things."

"Not that I know of," Astrid replied, chilled by his words. "Why?"

Taro sighed. "There've been some unexplained sightings around Mt. Shasta. A few hikers and climbers claim to have seen these…vaguely ominous creatures skulking around. But always out of the corners of their eyes, you know? When they look directly, there's nothing there."

Astrid shivered, remembering the elusive, fleeing figure she'd seen this morning in the forest. "Maybe… they're people's traveling astral bodies and with the increase in psychic abilities, they're becoming more visible."

"Maybe," Taro agreed uncertainly.

This news rekindled the worrisome unease that had plagued Astrid off and on all day. She decided, abruptly, to take the rest of the day off to relax and compose herself. She put away her equipment and took her leave from Taro, promising to spend some time with him soon. Her dream video from the morning drifted into her mind as she left the park. Good thing she had a session scheduled with her therapist tomorrow. That odd dream about that wretched character had really piqued her curiosity. And Louise's accusations troubled her. She realized that she often exhibited impatience and a playful—she liked to think—irreverence, but did that constitute a crime? Meagan could take some anti-sanctimonious lessons as far as Astrid was concerned.

On her way home, Astrid stopped by the market for some lunch items. She selected some kiwi fruit and grapes, along with asparagus and cheese. She had some puff pastries at the house that she had made the other day, and she wanted to make a cheese-and-asparagus filling. Normally she picked her fruits and vegetables from her own gardens, but her kiwi plants weren't bearing yet, and neither were her grapes. And her asparagus plants had only begun to nudge their ruby-tipped heads up.

When she coasted up to her house, she noticed that her front door stood open. She hopped off her bike and parked it under the overhang, then strode inside. When she spotted Nate coming out of the sauna, drying himself off with a towel, she gave a cry of pleasure and went running outside.

"Nate! You're back early!" she called happily.

"I was missing you, baby," he told her, sweeping her up with a lascivious grin. "And more volunteers showed than expected. So here I am."

"Nate—I'm so happy to see you! I've got some great news!" she told him excitedly, reveling in the kisses he was bestowing upon her neck.

"Really? And what might that be?" he murmured, as he slipped off her tunic and divested her of her leggings.

"I want us to get pregnant."

He froze. He took her face in his hands. "I can't say the idea doesn't excite me, Astrid. But are you sure? It's dangerous, you know."

"Of course I know. But I have a really good feeling about this."

"So—are you fertile now?" he inquired solemnly.

"Probably not," Astrid explained, starting to shiver. "This morning I didn't take my herbs, but more likely than not it will take a while. What about you—have you been taking precautions offworld?"

He shook his head and pulled her against him. "Astrid—what if I don't want you to take the risk? I don't want to lose you, girl."

"Nate, you won't lose me. Dying in childbirth is not my style. By the time I go, you'll be dying to get me out of your hair."

He laughed his deep, rumbly laugh. "Highly unlikely and you know it, you rascal! But I'll admit—it sounds like you know what you're talking about," he chuckled, looking down at her. "So what can I do? I can't resist you naked and I've already taken off most of your clothes." He scooped her up and ran inside with her, depositing her on the bed.

When they had finished with their love-making and play, they lay quietly, looking up at the ceiling.

"I take it you've cleared your plans with the Birth Center?" Nate asked.

"Uh—not yet, actually. I planned to go there this afternoon. Now that you've back, we can go together."

Nate sat up abruptly. "You haven't received clearance yet?"

His concern surprised her. "Well, I wasn't expecting you back so soon. And I doubt that I will conceive immediately. Besides, they've really eased up a lot."

"Don't be too sure, baby." Nate shook his head worriedly. "Rumor is that lately more people can't get approval."

"Yeah, Louise told me the same thing this morning," Astrid replied, troubled. "I guess we'll just have to go in this afternoon and talk to them."

Nate nodded and settled back against the pillows, his gaze returning to the ceiling. "Astrid—what's that?"

"What is what?"

"That brown spot on the ceiling." The roof and ceiling were both new, installed just last month, composed of a photosynthesizing, self-repairing organism that generated enough energy to heat the house and hot water.

Astrid frowned. "It looks like necrosis. That's strange. I'll have to check it out when I get back from the Birth Center."

"I'll check it."

"Thank you." She smiled at him and gave him a hug. "And thank you for coming back early. I missed you."

"Hey, I couldn't stay away."

She meant to get up and start lunch then, but couldn't resist indulging in more sex play with Nate. By the time they finally hauled themselves out of the bed, most of the afternoon had fled. So they decided just to have a leisurely lunch and enjoy each other's company and visit the center tomorrow. She glanced up at the ceiling, checking for more signs of necrosis. Funny thing, that.

FOUR

The minute Nate and Astrid walked into the Birth Center, they knew something was amiss. The people working there radiated a troubled, even harassed feeling. The two sauntered over to the nearest available genetic counselor and seated themselves, offering their hands in greeting. Astrid knew Sharon vaguely. Sharon was active in town meetings and whenever Astrid went—which wasn't very often—Sharon usually had something to say, propose, or discuss.

"So, how's it going?" Nate inquired.

Sharon sighed. "Could be better."

"Problems?"

"Yes. Lots. I hope you're not coming to talk about having a baby. Very few requests are getting approval."

"Why is that? I've been hearing rumors about that," Astrid asked, worried.

"Outbreaks of violence. We're afraid there might be back mutations from some undetermined source. Maybe some chemical dumps surfacing from the last century, undoing the effects of the UFO virus."

"So—what are you saying, everyone's supposed to stop having children until you figure it out?" Astrid knew her question sounded belligerent, but she couldn't help herself. This kind of pig-headed, generalized bureaucratic regulation of private, individual lives was exactly the reason the West Coast alliance had decided upon a more or less anarchic government. The confederation of town councils had drawn up some resolutions, but compliance was always voluntary.

Sharon sighed, a weary, long-suffering sigh. "What are your PIN numbers? We'll have a look."

Astrid and Nate gave her the numbers, then waited hopefully while Sharon scrolled through her records. A frown suddenly creased her forehead. "What's this about your workplace, Astrid?" she asked.

"Oh, Christ—listen, that's just a personality conflict. I can't even believe that Louise put that in. She's really protective of Meagan, I don't know if you know her or not. She's a younger worker at GenFarm. Meagan and I just don't like each other, that's all, but Louise has decided that I'm acting insensitively. But I've tried, believe me! I can't help it, the kid's a twit if you ask me."

Sharon sighed again, tapping her pencil on the top of her desk. She glanced back at the screen.

Astrid's lips parted in sudden comprehension and dismay. "You're not going to tell me this thing with Meagan might stand in my way, are you?"

Sharon laid down her pencil and massaged the bridge of her nose. "Aargh," she growled. She looked up. "I'm sorry to have to tell you this, but I've been given instructions not to give approval to anyone who's had serious enough social conflict to prompt someone into registering a complaint. But look, it's just for now. We're not saying no forever."

Astrid jumped up as if scalded. "You can't be serious! Just for that? Do you mean to tell me that Louise and Meagan are deciding whether or not I have a child?"

Nate reached for her hand. "Astrid, calm down."

"Calm down!" she exploded, jerking away from him. "This—person sits there with her bland bureaucratic expression, her fascist rules and recommendations, and tells me I can't get pregnant because two people are angry at me right now. And I'm supposed to take that calmly?" She whipped around to face Sharon. "For god's sake— don't I even get a hearing? I'm judged and found guilty just like that?"

Sharon's eyes became flat. "You know, Astrid, your behavior right now is not helping your case."

"Screw you! I don't need you to tell me how to run my life!" Astrid choked, so angry she could barely see.

Sharon shrugged, glanced at Nate. "Bring it up in Town Meeting if you feel so strongly about it."

"I will—don't worry," Astrid retorted hotly. She spun and charged out, surprised at the intensity of her reaction. Muttering an apology to Sharon, Nate rose and followed Astrid outside.

Astrid realized that Sharon had a valid point, of course—they couldn't let such a dangerous trait as violent behavior run unchecked throughout the population. It could destroy the community's fragile social structure, which was still evolving and struggling to succeed. But still, the measure seemed awfully drastic, out of proportion to the problem. She would definitely go to the next town meeting and bring up the issue.

"Jesus, what a little power monger," Astrid said finally, blinking back tears of anger and frustration.

Nate wound his arms around her and kissed her hair. "She's just trying to do what she thinks is right."

Astrid pulled away. "Why are you taking her side?" she asked, eyeing him testily.

"Astrid, I'm not trying to side with anyone. I'm trying to figure out what to do. Telling a genetic counselor at the Birth Center to get screwed is not exactly a solution, in my opinion."

Astrid shoved her hands through her hair and grimaced. "You're right."

"I think we should bring it up at the next town meeting."

"You're right, you're right. I know it." Astrid expelled a heavy breath, then looked around for their bikes. The interaction with Sharon had upset her so much, she'd forgotten where they parked. Spotting them leaning against a tree, she walked over to them, sniffling and wiping away tears. When she placed her hand on the trunk to steady herself, an electric shock of sympathy flooded through her, seemingly from the tree. Surprised and pleased, she mentioned this to Nate, who had come up behind her to give her another squeeze, and she took it as a psychic vote of confidence from nature. Things would work out. Perhaps the recent changes in the earth's electromagnetic field had put people's nerves on edge, the way cations generated in windstorms did; everyone would just need a little time to adjust. Perhaps that was the reason, not back mutations, that people weren't getting along as well lately.

Nate had work to attend to, and Astrid had other things to do, so they went their separate ways. Reassured by her lover and the tree, Astrid mounted her bicycle and sped down the shady street toward the pharmacy. She needed to pick up a few items, and she had some time to kill before her appointment with her therapist.

Astrid loved going to the pharmacy because it always smelled and felt so good. Today, as she coasted up to the open door, proved no exception. The pharmacy carried bath and massage oils, shampoos, soaps and lotions, homeopathic remedies, flower essences, and jars of fresh herbs and spices. Glossy dark blue ceramic tile covered the floor, lending a cool, sensual aspect to the place. Because he liked the color, the proprietor also offered dark blue crockery. Cloud sat at the counter reading a novel when Astrid breezed in.

"Hey, Cloud—how's it going?" she greeted him.

"Astrid!" He smiled at her, closing up his book. "What are you looking for today?"

"Oh, just some hand cream and a few herbs."

"I have some fresh chili powder in today," he said, "from Paula and Brent. And some dried flowers from Star Ranch if you're interested."

"Terrific!" Astrid moseyed over to the spice shelves, unscrewed the top to the pungent chili and peered inside. "Oh, man, they make the most beautiful chili powder," she sighed. "It looks like powdered rubies and garnets in there."

"It does, doesn't it?" laughed Cloud.

Astrid gathered up her purchases, dawdling over a display of bath pearls, creamy, perfumed hand soaps, and globe-shaped loofas, the latter a new product from her lab.

"How are these loofas selling, Cloud?" she asked.

"Great! People love them. They're a lot easier to get hold of."

Astrid nodded, pleased, and sauntered over to the counter where she handed Cloud her selections, bank card, and shopping bag. While he subtracted the credits and weighed her purchases, she perused the store. The ubiquitous container of complimentary antifertility herbs snagged her attention and she headed toward it guiltily, thinking she should take some before her evening with Nate. But the minute she screwed the top off the jar and inhaled the scent, she gagged.

"Gone bad?" Cloud asked, concerned.

"Uh, no—I just inhaled some powder, I think," Astrid replied hastily. Then she stood aghast as she realized that she had just lied—for the first time in several years. Because everyone possessed some degree of telepathy, and had since the turn of the century, bald-faced lying had become rather obsolete. She blushed, certain that he had picked up on her state of confusion. What if she was already pregnant? After being turned down by the Birth Center! Compliance with their recommendations was voluntary, sure, but community ostracism had replaced fines and jail sentences. She had no desire whatsoever to find out what that was like.

She snatched up her card and packet and fled the store, certain that Cloud suspected something. But most people respected and guarded individual privacy, so she also felt certain that he hadn't picked up on any particulars. He probably only knew that she was upset in some way connected to her fertility. She rode off to her therapy appointment shaken, and a little early, so she took the long way in order to compose herself.

When Astrid finally reached her therapist's office, a whitewashed stone cottage with a thatched roof squatting on top like a mushroom cap, she felt a little better, but not much. She grabbed her dream video out of her saddlebag and strolled into the cool, dark entryway. Last night she'd had another dream about that pasty-faced young woman in that dreadful setting. She hoped this wasn't the beginning of a new theme. It didn't appeal to her at all.

Apparently Maria didn't have any appointments before Astrid's, so she called out when she heard Astrid's steps, entreating her to come on into her office. Astrid did so, a bit reluctant and sheepish. Maria was so sharp — she'd know everything the minute Astrid even got near the office.

Maria turned her tiny, heart-shaped face up toward Astrid as she shuffled in. "Problems?" she inquired brightly. Maria had turned birdlike in her advanced years.

"Yeah, no shit," Astrid scowled. "In my dreams, in my life. Even in my new roof, for god's sake. It's got necrosis."

"Hmm." Maria observed Astrid closely. "Well, put your tape in the viewer and we'll get started."

First they ran through clips of Astrid's new planet, the one with all the colors and moons, then through a few problem-solving dreams involving work and relationships. But then that dreary environment flashed onto the screen, causing Maria to bolt upright in her chair.

"Interesting," she commented. "Another client of mine has had dreams in a similar setting."

Astrid glanced at Maria but didn't reply. She'd left these segments unedited, searching for any information that might clue her into the meaning of the dreams. She watched carefully as the scenes flickered, feeling almost sick as she did so. The first night she had dreamed about this place, she couldn't imagine anything worse than viewing that hopeless young woman in her drab little domicile. But last night she dreamed about the woman in her workplace.

The poor thing worked in a vast room filled with people at endless desks that were crowded with bulky, ancient-looking computer terminals. And paper. Paper cluttered everything—desktops, wastebaskets, even the floor. Astrid had never seen so much paper. Horrid fluorescent light buzzed overhead, and the noise from the printers and phones and shouting were deafening—even in a dream. Maria cringed and fumbled with the volume, then had to turn it up again as a new character made an entrance. Observing him, Astrid shuddered, thinking once again that she had never seen such a cruel-looking person. His smug, yet rather stupid expression, in addition to the tumors that disfigured his face, made him positively ugly. Had her superconscious created this person? She sincerely hoped not.

"Judy!" the man barked at the dream's point of focus. He carried a sheaf of papers in his fist and he shook them at her as she tried to wedge her bulk as far under the desk as she possibly could and still have two weak, nearsighted eyes peering up at him obediently. "This entire report is unacceptable!" he bawled. "Do it over again. And I want it on my desk first thing tomorrow morning."

He tossed the report at her, managing to strike the "Abandon File" key with the corner of it, destroying her last two hours of work. Astrid knew, in the dreamlike way of "knowing," as her protagonist knew, that the ugly man expected her to regenerate the report on top of the rest of her day's work. The woman's weak eyes watered as she bent wretchedly to her task, wishing that awful street gang had not stolen her glasses when she had returned home late last night due to just some similar harassment from her supervisor. She would have to go home late again tonight, braving the streets after dark. The horror of that fear bloomed so savagely into Judy's mind that there the dream ended, accompanied by sinister dream music replete with ominous tympani drums.

Astrid reached over and switched off the dream viewer, upset. She folded her arms. "So where did that come from?" she asked flatly.

Maria shook her head, her face grim. "I'm not certain. I'm wondering if it could be a nascent, unconsciously created group reality, born out of fears from our past."

"You don't think it's symbolic?"

Maria blinked, her eyes unfocused. "Hmm, I suppose it could be."

Astrid regarded her therapist and friend in surprise. She'd never known Maria to be so indefinite. "Well, symbolizing what, do you think?"

"Repression, maybe, or the threat of repression..."

Astrid tensed involuntarily, her mind turning to her interaction with Sharon at the Birth Center.

Maria gave herself a small shake, bringing her attention back to Astrid. "Whatever it is, it's certainly disquieting, isn't it? I might even use the word disturbing."

FIVE

Judy sat wretchedly in her uncomfortable chair, designed to keep employees awake and alert, wasting precious minutes while she allowed herself to wallow in self-pity. Why her? Why did the supervisor hate her so much, so specifically? Although he generally seemed to make everyone's life miserable in the office, she'd never observed him single anyone out so doggedly as he did her. It would be bad enough to struggle through three times the normal workload (and she did it), but he had to make things impossible. And put her at risk. She couldn't believe he regularly kept her late so that she would have to walk home after dark. Rumor had it that he'd been mugged five times—he must know what the streets were like. Maybe that's why he felt determined that someone else should share his misery. And he knew that she would always do as she was told.

Sighing, she absentmindedly pushed her non-existent glasses up, then fell all to pieces again as she realized she didn't have them any more. She'd have to replace them— she couldn't go on this way—but they would take half her week's meager salary. After taxes and benefits (a cruelly euphemistic term, in her opinion) were taken out, she had so little left over, especially considering what she had to pay for rent. She grimaced, remembering that she would receive even less this pay period, as her salary would include an additional garnishment since her creepy ex-boyfriend's lawsuit had finally worked its way through the anastomosing network of bureaucratic approval. Her chin quivered, although she tried as hard as she could to maintain her composure. This deduction from her salary came in addition to the other lawsuit that had gone against her. A burglar, attempting to break into her cubicle by smashing the glass in her window, had sliced a tendon in his hand, sued and won.

She didn't dare ask for a raise, either. The way the super felt about her, he might fire her. She felt lucky to have a job. At least she had a cubicle. The unemployed poor were invariably homeless, not only exposed to cold and rain, but also to street violence, in which women were routinely gang-raped, then hacked and dismembered, their body parts flung into gutters. She shuddered convulsively. She had an uncommon terror of meeting this demise. Although she missed her glasses, she suddenly felt grateful that was all she had lost.

She sighed again, straightened up, picked up the report she needed to rewrite. Two hours, at least. On top of the two hours of data she had lost from Mr. Egis' vicious toss. On top of the four hours of work that she should be producing while she redid the report and re-entered that data. Lord, she wouldn't get out of here until midnight! She wondered if she could spend the night at the office. It was against company rules and she could be fired for doing it, but the uncertainty of that risk might be preferable to the not-so-uncertain threat of physical violence that awaited her if she went home alone after midnight.

Judy felt her forehead to see if she had fever. She half-hoped most of the time that she would come down with one of the new incurable diseases that were always popping up. Cancer had been rendered less lethal around the turn of the millennium due to the accidental release of a genetically engineered virus, so no one died from that any more. But "benign" tumors and growths were common. High global radioactivity had resulted in the early 2000s from nuclear terrorism, meltdowns of nuclear reactors, and explosions of nuclear wastes. Nuclear weaponry and energy had finally become outlawed by the superpowers, all radioactive materials mined up and sealed away, heavily guarded to prevent more of the terror visited primarily upon the United States by countries housing drug cartels and extremist Muslims. Limited warfare, of course, continued unabated. By that time, however, vast areas of the United States, Latin America, and Middle East were uninhabitable, and it was too late to prevent the ensuing global Radioactive Period. Cancer no longer killed, as the by now endemic virus shut down uncontrolled cellular growth after reaching a certain threshold, but it achieved the irritating ubiquitousness of the common cold and new diseases cropped up annually, despite medical science's frantic and brilliant cures for the old ones. Often, due to the high mutation rate on the planet, old diseases became newly resistant within a matter of just a few years.

Nevertheless, the planetary population remained ruinously high—at least in her opinion—at twelve billion, due to the Malthusian effects of a high reproduction rate and base population. Birth control and abortion were illegal worldwide, and bonuses were given for children produced. The official reason for the emphasis on producing children was that so many died, with all the new diseases. But Judy suspected that the military needed lots of dispensable bodies and that the corporate government liked having huge labor pools, desperate for jobs, to draw upon and tax. Judy herself intended never to have children, no matter what kind of bonus they offered her. She couldn't imagine birthing a child to live in this odious existence, and viewed pregnancy with almost as much horror as she did involuntary disassembly by street gangs.

She worked for another two hours, then got up, massaging her eyes and forehead, and headed to the coffee room. One of the perks of her job, for which she was grateful, was that she received unlimited caffeine in the form of liquid or tablets. Caffeine was expensive, and she never could have afforded the quantities she consumed on her own. She had just sat down, nervously, to gulp a plastic cupful, when Mr. Egis stuck his head in the door. She jumped up, splashing hot caffeine down her front.

Mr. Egis slipped into the coffeeroom and shut the door behind him. He leered. "What's the matter, haven't I given you enough to do?"

"Oh, no, I have plenty, Mr. Egis. I, uh, just felt sort of tired, so…"

He crossed the room and grasped her arm. He hissed into her ear, "I know a way you can get in good with the super."

She froze. Oh, Lord, not this. She had hoped to avoid it, thinking he hated her so much he wouldn't want to touch her. Why her? she lamented once more. It wasn't as if she was attractive, for God's sake—she was flaccid from sitting at a desk all day, she was overweight from poor nutrition, and her color was bad—not that many people's looked very good. But she knew why. He'd impregnated just about every other female worker in the office—she was the last. He wouldn't care if anyone caught them, either. Although she could sue him for sexual harassment, she would then lose her job, and nobody else would hire her if she were dismissed.

He pushed her down on the table. "Now, you just hike up your skirt like a good girl," he instructed her.

Judy panicked. She did not want to get pregnant! And she did not want to have this repulsive leech so much as lick her feet. She twirled away from him with an adeptness that astonished her. For a minute, she felt almost strong. She wrenched open the door, panting from her exertion. Looking back, she saw that she had given Mr. Egis a bit of a start himself. An unfamiliar triumphant feeling surged through her, although she reflected as she scurried back to her desk that he would either try again or make her life even more miserable until she submitted.

Curiously, he stayed away from her the rest of the day. And when she went to give him the report he wanted rewritten, his secretary said he wasn't in. Probably off victimizing someone else, Judy thought bitterly. But he didn't show up after everyone left, either, with his revolver, as rumor had it he did often to force a recalcitrant employee. She dared hope that thwarting the initial impulse had made him decide he wouldn't stoop to taking advantage of someone as pathetic as she was.

She erred, however. He jumped her from behind when she finally left the office at midnight, deciding not to risk staying the night. She couldn't believe he'd waited so long. He tackled her just as she turned out the light, causing her to fall heavily onto the top step of the stairway. At first she despaired, and thought about yielding quietly and getting it over with. But some force deep within her bloomed up, flared outward. She managed to slither out of his grasp in the darkness. And although she fell painfully down the first flight of steps, bruising every inch of her body, she didn't break or wrench anything. She clattered down the remaining flights, her feet guided by adrenaline.

She was so glad to escape the clutches of her supervisor, she found herself out on the desolate street before she thought to prepare for the perilous walk home. She burst out of the building into the glare of one of the few remaining mercury-vapor lamps on the street. Gangs continually busted them, to give their activities cover, and the law-enforcement units continually replaced them. Not as quickly as they were destroyed, however. Judy winced in the glare, feeling like a pinned moth. A bad position. It would have been better to slip into utter darkness, not attract any notice. One could never be sure whether anyone was hiding on the street or not. The members of gangs trained themselves to walk like wraiths, to melt into the very cracks of buildings. They dressed entirely in black in order to blend into the darkness, and many of them had skin of the most peculiar, slimy texture due to chronic infection by a mutoid fungus that thrived in the sewer system, where many gangs lived and slept during the day.

A crumpled paper blew into the side of her face from the gusty wind, causing her to gasp. Behind the door, she heard her super—at least, she assumed her assailant was her super—making his way down the steps.

Don't hurry, she reminded herself, knowing, as everyone did, that running on the streets only served to arouse the sporting instincts of any lurking gang members, who considered any and all non-gang-members to be prey. As she fearfully picked her way among the shadows toward her cubicle unit, she thought that she might, at this point, welcome the company of her super. But she could have made him so angry by now that he might use her, then abandon her to the mercy of the gangs. Lord, she had certainly got herself in a mess. She couldn't put off her super indefinitely and still keep her job. He had absolute control over hiring and firing and she knew she could be replaced. Maybe she could get a black-market diaphragm. Her mouth twisted in misery and frustration. It would take her three months to save enough money for a diaphragm and by then she might be pregnant or jobless. She was debating the pros and cons of mutilating herself when she heard the scuff of a shoe on the concrete. She froze, knowing that this, too, was a no-no. Never freeze like a prey animal. Keep walking, she instructed herself. Obediently, her legs started up.

"Hey! Hey—stop!"

Never refuse a direct order, that was another unwritten law, whether it came from an authority figure or a gang member. Judy stood quaking, sweat popping out on her forehead and upper lip, drenching her hunched back. She heard running but couldn't make herself turn around. She cowered and waited; a hand seized her shoulder.

"Hey, I wanted to give you these." An extraordinarily handsome gang member sprang into focus as Judy's eyes flew open. He pressed something into her hand. Her glasses! Without thinking, she fumbled to put them on, eagerly. Then she cringed, waiting for the youth to smash her in the face with a bottle. He merely smiled.

"Well, that's that. Take care now." He moved off into the peripheral shadows, but she had the feeling that he watched her as she walked the last block to her unit. Dare she enter it, and let him know where she lived? She hesitated near the door, then looked behind her. She didn't see anyone. Well, to hell with it. She wasn't going to stay out all night. Or risk walking around the block, chancing an encounter with a gang member who wasn't nearly so nice. Or insane. She'd never heard of a gang member doing anything like this. She stuck her key into the electronic door and quickly stepped inside, whipping off her glasses to look for evidence of tampering, coating with some poisonous substance, perhaps, or a tiny injectable needle filled with some awful toxin. She sniffed them. They seemed okay. In the end, she placed them back on as she took the elevator to the fourth floor, which contained her cubicle. And that night she fell asleep to the most wondrous dreams she had ever experienced.

SIX

Astrid stared moodily at the ceiling while slouched in a chair, waiting for Nate to get dressed. They were going to Town Meeting.

"You been doing something about this roof, Nate?" she called into the other room.

"Yeah, definitely," he answered, appearing naked in the doorway, a soft pair of well-worn jeans in his hands. "It's not working?"

"Well, maybe it'll take a while."

"Right," he nodded. "It's a biologic process, you know."

"Right," she replied listlessly.

Nate's eyes narrowed in concern. He came over and dropped beside her chair. "You okay, baby?" he asked, stroking her cheek with his fingertips.

"Oh, sure," she sighed. "Basically."

"Astrid, if you really want this baby so much and there's a snag, we can just move. Other areas might not have this problem."

Her mouth twisted in a smile. "You're sweet. Thanks for offering. I don't know where I'd like to go, though, to tell the truth. I love our house, our friends, the climate, the mountains—and I really like the system here. Although it is odd, isn't it? I mean, here we have this supposedly voluntary anarchistic system and the Birth Center is deciding who's going to reproduce—just like the worst totalitarian nightmare."

"Well—hopefully it's not that bad."

Astrid sighed, sinking her chin upon her chest, picking nervously at the buttons on her blouse, a vivid pumpkin-orange one that she had selected to counter her present mood. It wasn't working. "I don't know, Nate. I just can't forget that mulish look on Sharon's face. Jesus, just like an old-fashioned bureaucrat."

Nate looked unhappy. He hated discord. "Maybe she's just under pressure, Astrid. We should give her the benefit of the doubt, anyway."

Chastened, Astrid uncurled herself and wrapped her arms around Nate. She burrowed into his neck, where wonderful soft clouds of beard and long nappy hair met and tickled her face. "You're such a nice guy," she murmured. "Why do you hang out with such a bitch?"

Nate laughed. "Because you're such a sexy one—you know that. We've had this discussion before."

"I know. I just like to hear it." She continued to hold onto him for a few more minutes, then drew back. For Nate's sake, she tried to adopt a more optimistic attitude. "Well, you're probably right," she said. "Everything'll work out. It always does, right?"

"Right," he grinned, clearly relieved. Then he reached over and lightly bobbed her nose with a cupped hand. He rose and finished dressing while Astrid returned to brooding. She didn't want to create a lot of negative expectation, but she had an uncomfortable feeling about the meeting they were going to. She sensed a subliminal anxiety in the community over the recent violence; people were starting to act a little differently. Louise, now that she thought about it, didn't strike her as the same old Louise. She considered, nervously, that Louise or Meagan might attend the meeting. In an effort to avoid any further conflict with them, Astrid had gone back to GenFarm only once in the last week, and then at night.

At least her dreams were faring better; perhaps that was a good sign. Last night she'd managed to appear in that dream series about that poor drudge character and to effect a positive act, which pretty much proved it was a symbolic problem-solving dream as far as Astrid was concerned. If she could have an effect in the dream world, chances were good that she could affect her own world in regard to this strange new situation. That bolstered her up a bit. And this weekend, she was going on a raft trip with Robin, to which she looked forward eagerly. The raging, thwarted child lust her body was experiencing right now made interacting with Nate somewhat painful.

She could, of course, choose to ignore Sharon's recommendation, but she supported the idea of voluntary cooperation passionately and preferred to go through the proper channels if at all possible. Astrid had taken a pregnancy test and found out she wasn't pregnant yet, so apparently her body's vehement reaction against the fertility herbs had a primarily psychological origin. Nevertheless, she couldn't bring herself to ingest them, so Nate took them.

What a good man he is, she thought, suddenly feeling guilty for wanting to get away from him. He wouldn't say so, but Astrid knew he was upset by the outcome of their trip to the Birth Center, too.

When Nate finally emerged, handsome in thick, soft leggings and a multi-layered assortment of T-shirt, vest, and jacket, Astrid walked over and hugged him hard. She beamed at him, tangling her fingers in his beard. "You're a nice man," she said finally.

"I try." He flashed her a grin.

"You do better than that."

"I'm glad."

Astrid glowed inwardly and buried her face in his chest, forgetting her pessimistic premonitions for the moment. It felt wonderful to be loved so well, to be able to trust a love so completely, without reservation.

"So, I thought we could stop by the Korean deli on the way to the meeting," she said, leaning back and smiling up at him. "I haven't had dinner yet—have you?"

"No, I haven't. The Korean deli sounds terrific."

They took their bikes, although a fine mist filled the air that night. Their clothing kept them warm even if it became wet, and Astrid bundled her glossy hair up into a rain hat. The unbroken quiet of the night and the pulsing of insect voices in the forest nourished her heart; she drew strength from her environment. And when they piled their plates with food at the deli, she took pleasure from the beauty of those surroundings, too. Under a glass dome, diners sat scattered among delicate blossoms and fallen petals, a carpet of nobbly, knurled mosses, well-tended small trees, and a gently bubbling stream that had been allowed to run through the room.

Astrid gazed around as she ate, contemplating the fact that everything in her environment conspired to calm and please her. Everything except that poisonous undercurrent, that subliminal tension. And her own thwarted desire. As she reflected, a curled brown leaf floated to her plate. She glanced up for its source and paled as she realized that the tree above her had sickened. It was infested with white fly. Somehow it seemed like an ominous harbinger of things to come.

"Oh, man, Nate—look at that tree." She nudged him and pointed up.

He took in its condition, but shrugged. "So?"

"Well, do you think—do you think this is a bad sign?"

Nate studied her curiously. "What—happening to sit under a tree infested with white fly?"

"I know. It sounds paranoid. I just have a bad feeling."

Their eyes met; Nate looked away uneasily. His hands lifted and dropped in a helpless gesture. "I know," he responded softly. "I have it, too."

Astrid shivered at his words. "So," she said brusquely. "Let's go. I don't want to miss any of this meeting."

They bussed their dishes, scraping uneaten food into the compost bin provided before stacking their plates, glasses, and silverware on the window ledge to the kitchen. They dropped their paper napkins into a recycling box.

When Nate and Astrid finally emerged from the restaurant, the mist had turned into a thick, billowing fog that obscured the road. Astrid asked Nate to lead, since he had a more keenly developed sense of direction. They clicked slowly through pools of light from the street lamps and then into dusky wells of darkness as the fog damped all vibration, light and sound.

The fog so effectively blanketed everything that Astrid and Nate coasted right up to the doors of the town meeting before they heard the shouting. They exchanged grim glances before parking their bikes and hurrying inside to the brightly lit interior.

Astrid couldn't believe it; everyone had their faces shoved into one another's, and they were positively screaming.

"Hey!" she yelled. But no one noticed. "Hey!" she shouted a second time, her voice cracking like a shot around the room. "What the hell is going on?!"

Everyone froze, then huddled ashamedly when they realized what they had been doing. A tense silence fell.

"So." A middled-aged man with a garnet-colored mohawk and elaborately pierced ears stood up. "Do we want to postpone the meeting?"

"Nah, I think we should get this over with," a teenager responded.

"I agree," Astrid seconded hastily; she couldn't bear to put this meeting off another minute. "May I ask what was going on here before we arrived?"

More silence. Finally Sharon spoke. "We're having a conflict between community policy and individual desires." Her voice sounded crisp and dry.

"Well now, that's something I want to discuss, too. To be honest, Sharon, I don't think it's right to suppress the rights of the individual."

Several voices murmured in assent.

"Even when those desires threaten the common good?" Sharon demanded, and here other voices swelled even more. Astrid looked around at their faces. She spotted Louise and Meagan among them.

"Look, individual and community good are one and the same. Any conflict between them is illusion, misunderstanding."

"In theory, that should be true, Astrid," replied Dane, an older man with a handsome beard, a man she liked and, in fact, had occasionally shared a bed with before she met Nate. "But in practice, it doesn't seem to be working that way. I'm afraid the introduction to this meeting is a case in point."

"So, what do you mean exactly, Sharon?" inquired Nate. "What is the specific conflict here?"

"We don't think people should be reproducing right now, not until we've figured out what's happening with the recent violence," Sharon informed him earnestly. "There is a distinct possibility that we're dealing with atavistic chromosomal arrangements."

"But yet you're asking everybody, whether they possess this atavism or not, to refrain from having children until the Birth Center figures out what's going on?" pressed Astrid.

This time it was Meagan who spoke. "It's just for a short while, Astrid."

"But I agree with Astrid," Robin interjected. "A lot of the conflict here has to do with the Birth Center deciding what's right for everybody. I don't see any reason why anyone who doesn't possess this mutation can't have children."

Sharon looked annoyed. "Look, it's just not that clear-cut. We're not entirely sure what we're dealing with or what we're looking for. We're *requesting*—we're not *telling* anyone anything—that people refrain for now. For god's sake, what is the hurry? Shortsightedness in a community strikes me as dangerous."

"And a group-think mentality strikes *me* as dangerous," Astrid retorted. "Don't you think that those of us who want to have children now have the community's interest at heart as well as our own?"

"That's true," added Carly, a fairylike wisp of a young woman. "I want to have a child myself. How many back-mutations have you found in community members who want to have babies, Sharon?"

Sharon shifted uncomfortably. "Well, none yet, but—" Here several agitated people interrupted. "But," Sharon sliced through authoritatively, "it's like I said, we're just not sure how the atavism might express itself genetically. There's been a significant new increase in genetic disease recently, too. We don't want to give birth to defective progeny."

"Of course not," Carly agreed. "But still, I think the decision as to whether to bear those babies should be our own. We've had to sacrifice our wishes a lot in this respect for a long time now. I really think it's time to take some chances."

"Hey—like I told you. We're not law. Individuals can do as they please. How the community then responds to them is their problem."

Meagan jumped up, trembling with passion, her eyes sparkling with righteousness. "Oh no," groaned Astrid softly to Nate.

"I can't believe anybody is even thinking about having children when we have this crisis at hand," she cried. "I think people have been way too concerned about their personal desires here!' She glanced significantly at Astrid. "It's selfish to want a baby now. How can anyone think their individual needs outweigh the good of a great many others?"

"Damn it, Meagan," Astrid shouted, furious at having her words twisted. "I never said the good of the individual outweighs the good of everyone else. I only said they're not in conflict!"

Meagan burst into tears, and her friends glared at Astrid. "I can't talk to you without arguing, Astrid—so please, let's not even start."

Louise grasped Meagan's hand to calm her and shot a warning look at Astrid.

Astrid felt at a loss for words. Was she the only one who perceived Meagan's manipulativeness? "I just didn't want to be misunderstood," she muttered sulkily.

"We understand your position, Astrid. Thank you," Louise responded primly. Astrid regarded her in surprise. Since when had Louise taken to sniping at her in Town Meeting?

Taro spoke up for the first time. Astrid hadn't even known he was here. "I think anybody who wants to birth a child should have their head examined, but I also agree with others who feel that true solutions lie where the good of society and the individual aren't in conflict. Everyone seems pretty hepped up over this issue, though, that's obvious, so I say we shelve it for later. We all graciously accept the recommendation of the representative of the Birth Center" —here he smiled winningly at Sharon— "and individuals must act according to their own conscience. What does everybody think about that?"

Tired murmurings of assent rippled the room, reminding Astrid of wind in a grass field. The meeting moved on to other issues, minor ones, like community projects and celebrations, apportionment of resources and work credits to art works and civil works, a discussion of what fruits and vegetables were coming into season and how various crops fared.

Astrid and Nate didn't stay until the end. Astrid touched Nate's arm and they slipped out silently into the night where the fog had condensed into snaking tendrils.

It twisted about them as they mounted the hill toward their house, cannily searching out thin places and gaps in their garments to chill and disturb them.

What *does* my conscience tell me? Astrid asked herself over and over again as she pedaled home, troubled when she received nothing but confusion for an answer.

SEVEN

Somehow energized by her beautiful dreams from the night before and feeling more daring than she had ever felt in her life, Judy called in sick to work. She had already used up her one annual paid sick day, but she decided to do it anyway. Normally she would have gone in despite yesterday's events, taken whatever abuse her super planned to rain upon her, and probably given in to being raped. And with her luck, she'd get caught in the act by one of the members of the Right Hand of God who worked in the office. The Right Hand of God was a vigilante civilian group of religious extremists. Their activities included the public flogging and/or stoning of women suspected of extramarital sex, even if she had been raped. Gays—or presumed gays—the Right Hand of God castrated. On the other hand, the members occasionally saved people from the street gangs.

The government leaders issued official denunciations of some of these activities but never made serious efforts to stop them. They had their hands full fending off hostile countries and terrorists, in addition to making their own attacks on these countries—and on half a dozen others scattered over the globe that still possessed some dwindling natural resources. In addition, they pointed out, the war on drugs required enormous expenditures, resources, and manpower, and law-enforcement officers couldn't be everywhere at once. Unofficially, however, Judy knew the government leaders condoned the actions of the Right Hand of God, since they believed the group contributed to law and order overall. And in fact, right-wing religious extremists had organized and mounted extremely effective political campaigns over the years, so they comprised a large and powerful sector of the government.

Once she phoned in sick, Judy felt nervous and restless. Probably her super couldn't do anything to her in her cubicle, but she didn't trust him. Through his tactics he had achieved superhuman status in her eyes, and she nursed a paranoid fear that he could do anything he wanted. So she decided to go out for a walk, something she usually did only on Sundays, her day off and, in fact, everybody's day off except for the Preachers. No business besides church business could be conducted on Sunday, which, since everyone except the wealthy and homeless worked all the other days of the week, made shopping difficult. The consumer economy had collapsed shortly after the turn of the century when the combination of enormous population pressures and wasteful consumption patterns used up most of the stuff there was to go around. These days, stores—what few there were of them—opened for the lunch half-hour, and then again after work for as long as it was light, because street crime kept people inside after dark. In the summer, that meant several hours; in the winter, none at all. However, the inconvenient hours didn't rankle as much as they would if anyone had much expendable income or if anything worth buying existed. Although expensive relative to most people's salaries, the goods available to the middle class were carelessly made from cheap materials and rarely lasted until a new one of whatever it was could be purchased.

Once out on the street, Judy looked around, trying to make up her mind where to go. All the streets looked basically alike, bumpy and hilly, lined with residential grids that rose thirty to forty feet high, with some retail space on the ground floors that housed pharmacies, regulation clothing and shoe shops, food stores, insurance agents and lawyers' offices, television outlets, small, unappetizing restaurants and bigger, even more unappetizing bars, regional police departments, clinics, and military recruiting centers. The military offered a substantially higher wage with all sorts of fringe benefits to its volunteers, but the losses of troops were often so heavy that the military commonly resorted to shanghaiing passers-by. This also tended to discourage pedestrian traffic.

Rumor had it that the ocean lay five miles to the west, and although rumor also had it that a wall built to protect the wealthy from the other classes obscured the view, still, she might be able to hear it or smell it. This would entail a ten-mile walk (no public transportation existed; it was too costly) and although she had never walked so far in her entire life, she resolved to do it.

After Judy had walked one mile, her thin pumps began to rub sore places. After two miles, they rubbed blisters and the concrete was beginning to bruise her feet. Three miles, and she was having trouble breathing, as she had inhaled more than the recommended daily dose of street air. Cubicles and workplaces all contained recirculating filtered and processed air. Her eyes burned, her legs shook, she needed to pee and of course no public facilities existed; but with a determination that astonished her, she pressed on for another two miles.

She passed few people, since most everyone was either at work or in their cubicles. Street gangs were active only at night; they slept in the sewer systems and subterranean tunnels during the day. She noticed a few winos and some bag people shuffling around with their carefully guarded garbage-can liners full of trash, many of whom probably wouldn't last the night. The street gangs used the other, more helpless street people as playthings in their glue-inspired games.

Hopelessness hung in the air around her as thickly as the dank chemical atmosphere, and Judy shivered, wondering what propelled her so single-mindedly towards a mythical body of water that she would probably never see. When the last two miles were up and still she observed nothing except the ubiquitous grids, she almost turned around in despair. But an unusual scent in a sudden breeze wafting past caused her to perk up. Some strange, vitalizing property lay in that breeze, and she wondered whether she had just caught a whiff of the ocean. Eagerly she dragged her aching feet another mile, at which point she was rewarded by a smooth, unbroken concrete wall that went as far as she could see in both directions. But there also came billowing around her a tangy, rich scent that filled her entire being with wonder and awe, and a gentle surging noise that sounded more alive than anything she'd ever heard in her life.

Judy collapsed at the foot of the barrier, exhausted but happy, perhaps even a little delirious. While she rested, a scurry of motion on the wall of the cubicle grid opposite her snagged her attention. She strained her eyes, blurry from irritation. When she focused upon a brilliantly colored lizard, half-green, half-blue, she let out an exclamation of astonishment. She had never seen anything so beautiful! She had never seen another living creature, save humans, roaches and rats.

As soon as her cry died upon her lips, she cursed herself, thinking she would probably scare the lovely little creature away; but he only turned his skinny head in her direction and trained his black eyes upon her. This startled her as well. She had never encountered such an intelligent gaze, either. Most people she knew, if not born close to half-witted with chromosome damage from all the pollutants, poor medical care, or substance abuse, usually grew up mentally impeded from poor nutrition and lack of stimulation. Judy herself possessed much greater intelligence than normal—a freak side-effect of a birth defect that weakened her respiratory system and heart. But she thought this lizard looked twice as smart as the combined intelligence of all of Earth's twelve billion inhabitants.

When it didn't move, Judy became emboldened to approach it and take a closer look. She crossed the street and advanced one step at a time, murmuring to it that she meant no harm, she only wanted to observe it, please stay, please, please stay. It remained rooted to its spot until she decided to try to pet it and stretched out her hand, at which point it bolted, throwing her off balance. She tumbled forward into the crumbling cinder block wall and dislodged one of the blocks as she fell, gashing her ankle. Tears started into her eyes until she noticed a package protruding from the hole the fallen cinder block had left. Glancing swiftly up and down the street—she saw no one—she plucked it out and peered inside the plastic bag. At first she didn't know what she was looking at, but gradually it dawned upon that she was holding a sackful of black-market contraceptive devices. Her wild elation at her crazy good luck quickly turned to fear, however. What she was holding would probably fetch thousands of dollars. Such a valuable cache should be under some kind of watch, even if sporadic.

Realizing that she was risking her life by doing so, she shoved the bundle down her dress, hoping that her figure would disguise the packet as just another unsightly bulge. Although her feet screamed in affront and her heart gave warning palpitations, not to mention the fact that she had to pee so bad that every movement was painful, she hurried back in the direction she came, waiting to feel at any moment the tearing thud of a cinquefoil (one of the popular current weapons) in her back, courtesy of the punk she had just ripped off. He wouldn't necessarily have offed her as soon as she discovered her prize. Gangs liked to stalk their prey, hunt them, toy with them. Most gang members had so utterly destroyed what meager gray matter they possessed from inhaling glue, propellants, and teflon sprays that little remained, she knew, except primitive bestial instincts, usually eating, fucking, and killing. Not necessarily in that order.

On her way home, a squad car made a desultory cruise down the street on which she walked, quickening her pulse. Citizens could be searched thoroughly at any time by the police or military, this power granted to them by popular vote of the citizenry, who loathed and feared the street gangs. In theory, the law was aimed at street thugs. In practice, however, police searched honest citizens more frequently, since they were easier to get hold of and not nearly so dangerous.

Judy quailed as they slowed to give her a scrutinizing glance. At times such as these she felt thankful for her unappealing appearance, since it seemed that the more shapely, attractive women fell prey to random searches more often than the likes of her. But if they felt bored, nothing could save her. They passed, after what seemed like hours, leaving her to scurry even more quickly home.

Once inside her cube, she gratefully relieved herself and then collapsed onto her bed slot, her heart hammering so alarmingly that she thought she might have a tachycardia. No such luck, however. She gradually recovered her breath, her heart slowed. She sat up and spilled the contents of her bag onto the floor, unmindful of the observing eye that inhabited her (and every) television (mandatorily installed by popular vote in an effort, supposedly, to prevent burglaries). Although a surveillance official could peep into her apartment at any time of the day or night, she knew that the sheer staggering number of cubicles to be observed prevented continual surveillance.

In fact, as a statistician, she knew that the odds of anyone checking in on her cubicle at this exact moment were remote. Especially since she led a particularly boring, docile life, even for a member of the middle class. Anyone assigned to pry into her space had probably given up in hopeless disgust a long time ago.

Her gleeful joy dimmed somewhat when she realized that diaphragms came in several sizes and she had no way of fitting herself properly. But, she figured, use enough foam (of which there were only three precious tubes, unfortunately), and she'd be safe. Maybe she was sterile, anyhow. God knows her last boyfriend had tried his best to impregnate her, she pondered. Maybe some justice existed in the universe besides that of the God who blessed all (and only) human reproduction, according to her religious instruction—another god who listened to her pleas for barrenness, although she knew such thoughts were heresy and likely to be punished somehow.

Judy felt primarily fear toward God, and in fact, He fell into her catch-all category of violent entities, which included the gangs, the law-enforcement agencies, the military, and the media producers. She wavered between furtive suspicions that God was nothing but a fabrication of the power structure—a nonexistent entity used to manipulate the masses—to thinking He had to exist. After all, everywhere she looked she saw proof of His existence: a baffling, angry, vengeful deity, with man wrought exactly in His image.

She sometimes wondered if she represented an entirely different species from these people, since she had no desire to perform violence or acts of vengeance. Even upon that slimeball louse of an ex-boyfriend who had sued her for his own clumsiness. What seemed ironic and hopeless, however, was that people like her—whom she privately considered more highly evolved—seemed at the mercy of those intolerant, heavy-handed others. And given the way power was structured, how could things ever change? Those people had all the cards stacked in their favor: They had the money, the weapons, the information, even God on their side. How on Earth could she hope to oppose them, powerless little technodrudge that she was?

Nevertheless, she resolved, with the illogic of the desperate, to find a way. She would find a way never tried before, a way that only a madwoman would entertain. One that couldn't possibly succeed. Yet one that, by its very impossibility and imaginative absurdity, might have a breath of a chance at confounding the unassailable.

EIGHT

"Pass the butter, will you, Nate?" Astrid requested, for the second time. She reached over and tugged on his sleeve, her gray eyes sparkling with amusement. "Nate? Have you left for space already or are you still with me?"

Nate frowned and laid down the daily paper. "Sorry, Astrid. It's just that the news is bizarre today."

Astrid tensed, her playful mood gone. "What is it?"

"Okay—people disappear every now and then on Mt. Shasta, right?"

She nodded slowly. Several theories for the disappearance existed, but one that had gained increasing popularity, along with an increase in alien contactee reports, was that a powerful dimensional window was located on Mt. Shasta. Reports of strange lights, sighting of strange beings and UFOs had always existed. Some people believed that the dimensional windows on Earth had become increasingly active recently, although no one knew why for certain. The most widely accepted hypothesis postulated that the recent change in the Earth's electromagnetic field affected the windows. The originally conceived structure of the atom, with its nucleus of protons and neutrons and its highly elusive electrons, had changed to a conceptualization of projections of multi-dimensional matter into a three-dimensional world. The windows were thought to be anomalous areas in the Earth's magnetic structure where the unusual energy fields set up a resonance effect in the probability functions of certain individuals; these anomalies affected the molecules of people's bodies in such a way that as a unit, they had greater access to the dimensions visited individually and non-consciously by the body's subatomic components.

Nate remained silent for a moment, mulling over the article. "Lately, it seems, a lot more people are disappearing."

"Really?" Astrid stood up and walked around the table to peer over his shoulder. She frowned, too, as she read. "Do they think this is related to any of the other stuff?"

"It doesn't say."

She sighed. "Christ, what is going on? Why isn't anyone talking about this?"

Nate hesitated. "Perhaps—they're afraid, Astrid. I know I am."

Astrid's hands clenched where they rested on Nate's shoulders. Fiercely she whispered, "I still want this baby like crazy. I don't care what else is going on."

He twisted in his chair so that he could put his arms around her waist and gazed up at her longingly. "I know," he murmured. "We'll have it. I promise you."

She sighed again, thinking back on the conversation she had shared with Robin on their raft trip. Astrid couldn't help herself. As they went through their preparations before setting off down the river, she had rattled on and on about the town meeting that had proceeded so contentiously.

"The thing is," she had insisted feverishly, "none of us is ignorant or stupid. I'm a geneticist myself, I understand the implications of the effects of a back mutation. But I really think the Birth Center is acting a bit hysterically. And authoritatively. Meagan talks about threats to our civilization—what is authoritativeness if not a threat to civilization?"

Robin sighed and put down her waterproofing sealer. "I agree with you, Astrid. But—and please don't take offense to this, you know how much I care about you— right now you strike me as a bit obsessive."

Astrid opened her mouth. Nothing came out, but a painful expression crossed her face and she abruptly broke into tears.

Robin gave a little cry of dismay and put her arms around her friend. "I'm sorry, Astrid."

"I know I'm being obsessive," she wept. "I just can't seem to help myself. You can't imagine what I feel like. It's terrible to want a child and not be able to have one. It gnaws at me all the time!"

"No, you're forgetting—I know how you feel. I wanted a child with Joshua, remember? But he didn't want to have one."

Astrid wiped her eyes in an effort to calm herself. "I haven't forgotten. I'm sorry, Robin."

"And you know, when we finally split up over the issue, that was even harder."

Astrid nodded tearfully.

"At least you still have Nate," said Robin, an earnest, comforting expression puckering her forehead.

"Right."

"And who knows—this thing may blow over sooner than you think."

"Sure."

But Astrid didn't think so. Her torment didn't come solely from frustration; a large amount of foreboding figured in, too. She couldn't say exactly what she feared, but the amorphous shape of it hung ominously in the back of her mind.

Returning to the present, Astrid kissed Nate abstractedly on the top of the head. "I guess...I should get over to Maria's for my appointment," she said, lingering to ruffle his thick hair with her fingers. Then she hurried off to get ready for the day's activities.

Since she had decided to take an official leave of absence from GenFarm, she needed to find another workplace. She planned to check out a few. And she was having tea with Taro. Luckily, she had stored up enough extra credits that she could take her time finding something she really liked. And temporary work always existed.

Maybe she could deliver dairy products for a while, like the man in her neighborhood, she mused as she coasted down her quiet, tree-lined street, dappled with glimmering, dancing ovals of sunlight. It could be fun riding around with a delivery cart, bringing people bottles of cold milk or crocks of butter, visiting with friends and enjoying the outdoors. She could do that even up until the last minute of her pregnancy. As usual, riding peacefully through the cedars, pines, and Douglas firs calmed her. But when she arrived at Maria's house, tension seemed to emanate from the very walls. Astrid entered cautiously.

"Maria? You okay?" she called.

Maria fluttered into view from her office. "Yes, dear—come on in."

Astrid obeyed, setting her video on Maria's desk apprehensively. "Has work been strange?" she asked.

Maria glanced up sharply. "It's that obvious?"

Astrid nodded.

Maria covered her face with her hands for a moment, then gingerly picked up Astrid's video. "Let me guess—more dreams about that depressing place?"

"Yes, but with some positive developments."

Maria shot her a curious look and shoved the tape into the dreamviewer, flicking it on. She watched in silence to the end. In fact, she stared at the blank screen for a few minutes before she stirred. Then she switched it off, commenting, "Interesting, the thing with the lizard."

"Yes!" Astrid responded eagerly, waiting for a word of praise. Encouraged by her success with the glasses, she had decided to go a step further and fabricate some contraceptives for Judy, as well as a means with which to draw her attention to them.

"Rather striking gang member."

Astrid nodded and smiled. "Yeah."

"Remind you of anyone?"

"Well, me, of course. Good idea, huh? You know, I'm really starting to feel good about how I'm taking control in my dreams. It really does make me feel more powerful."

Maria fidgeted, avoiding Astrid's gaze.

Astrid raised an eyebrow. "Isn't that one of my objectives in this therapy?"

"Ordinarily I would say yes, if this represented a normal dream series."

Astrid grew solemn, chilled by her words. "But...it's not?"

"I don't think so, no. Since I saw you last, several of my clients have come in with these dreams. Now, imagery can be shared between dreamers, but normally the details differ from dreamer to dreamer, carrying the stamp of their individual minds. But these dream locales—they're all the same! Down to the very last detail. I'm thinking that what we're dealing with here is another physical probable reality. One just as valid as our own."

"What does that mean?"

Maria leaned forward intently. "Astrid—it's a material reality. It has its own lessons to learn, its own fate. We mustn't tamper with it! Who knows what kind of damage we could do, no matter how well-intentioned our efforts might be?"

"Wait a minute. You're telling me that when I'm dreaming I'm doing something, I'm actually doing it somewhere in another physical reality?"

Maria nodded. "That's exactly what I'm saying."

Astrid leaned back in her chair, laughing. "Excuse me for saying so, Maria, but I find that just a little hard to believe."

"You do, huh? Haven't you been paying attention to the disappearances?"

"You mean on Mt. Shasta?"

"Precisely."

"Sure I have, but—"

"It must be anomalous molecular electromagnetic activity resulting from some stimulus. With the windows, it's an anomaly in the Earth's magnetosphere. With dreamers, it must be induced somehow from particular brainwaves generated in the dream state. For all we know, it could be an after-effect or a side-effect of the UFO virus."

Astrid shook her head. "Gee, I don't know. Theoretically, I might agree with your hypothesis, Maria, but it's just a little difficult to swallow personally. I mean, it's one thing to think about technologically superior aliens coming through the dimensional windows, or to imagine people somehow stumbling across an electromagnetic vortex on a hike, but, Christ—it's another thing to believe that I'm blithely tripping the light fantastic while I'm asleep."

Maria regarded her sharply, her black eyes beady and bright. "Do you believe in astral projection?"

"Sure. But that's different. The astral body isn't physical."

"Some people believe our material bodies aren't as physical as we're used to believing."

"Well, that might be so, but—I don't know. It just sounds like science fiction to me."

"In case you haven't noticed it, dear, we're living in the middle of science fiction."

Astrid's lips twisted into a smile. "This is true." She leaned forward, resting her forearms on her thighs. "Okay. Say this is all true. Are you suggesting that I shouldn't have given poor Judy a new pair of glasses? And that I should just let her get impregnated by that hideous abomination in her office?"

Maria placed her fingertips together, splaying them in a characteristic gesture. "That reality has its own laws. We don't understand them. Perhaps the result of that sexual union could grow up to provide the woman great comfort. You don't know enough to know."

"But she doesn't want it!"

"Then she will find a way to prevent it from happening."

Astrid stared at Maria in amazement. "Maria, I can't believe you're advising me not to help someone because she inhabits a different probable reality, assuming that is, in fact, what's really going on. I don't see how it's different from helping someone—or oneself for that matter! —in a dream reality or this one. That world is so out of balance, the power structure is all warped. How can she protect herself indefinitely? He has all the power—she has none!"

"Perhaps she's stronger than you give her credit for. Astrid, she *must* live her own life. You can't be there all the time."

"Well, maybe I can be there when she really needs someone," Astrid muttered stubbornly.

Maria eyed Astrid thoughtfully. "You're being awfully hard-headed, young lady."

Astrid flopped back in her chair belligerently. "But my intuitive sense of what to do is so out of kilter now, Maria. It seems like everything I want to do all of a sudden is frowned on by somebody. Things did *not* used to be this way!"

Maria settled back in her chair too, pondered, then rose with a weary grunt. "Tea?"

"No, I have to check out some job possibilities."

Maria shook her head as she filled her tea kettle with water. "These are difficult times, Astrid," she remarked, bringing the kettle to boil instantly with a laser heater. "Perhaps, because there is so much dissension and so many conflicting opinions now, we should try harder to listen to the common sentiment."

"I don't know, though, seriously, Maria. Maybe it's all the more important to listen to our own inner voices. Just because more differing opinions exist now doesn't necessarily mean they're wrong. Does it?"

Maria pursed her lips. "I suppose not, no."

Astrid rose to her feet, pleased at having reached an agreement on something.

"But I want you to promise me one thing," Maria insisted, shaking a finger.

"What?" Astrid regarded her warily.

"That you refrain from acting in that other reality. Observe it. Get to know it better before jumping in with those big feet of yours, will you? I mean it when I say you could be setting into motion a dangerous sequence of events."

Astrid stretched, unhappy with the request. "Okay," she finally agreed. "If I can. I don't know that I can keep from it."

"If you want to, you will." Maria patted Astrid on the back as she escorted her to the door. Astrid plodded glumly. Maria even followed her to the bike rack, a beautiful one fashioned from bronze and thick bubbles of clear glass that ordinarily delighted Astrid. But her therapy session seemed to take the pleasure out of everything. Maria laid a restraining hand on Astrid's arm.

"I don't mean to frighten you, dear, but you should also consider one other thing."

Astrid looked down at her, puzzled. "What is that?"

"Travel to other worlds is something we have no experience with."

"So?"

"So we don't understand the parameters yet. You should probably give yourself suggestions before you go to sleep that if you dream about Judy's world, you won't actually travel there. If you continue to visit that world, you could set up undesirable probability frequencies. You could become trapped in Judy's reality."

"Now there's a lovely thought."

"That's right. You should proceed with extreme caution. And don't forget what man almost did when he acquired the power to split the atom without the wisdom to use it."

"Oh, thanks a lot, Maria."

"Now off with you—go get a job, for God's sake."

Maria's parting attempt at levity mollified Astrid somewhat, but not much. She couldn't help but reflect that she had never experienced so much unwelcome conflict in her life—first Meagan and Louise, now Maria. And Sharon. Was she herself the problem or was something else more profound and insidious going on? Once people started telling other people what to do, she believed, that's where trouble began. Or were her beliefs fallacious? Did one have to sacrifice the individual will in favor of the majority after all? Was it naive and unrealistic to think that the common good and the good of the individual were one and the same?

Soberly pondering these questions, Astrid decided to go to the local dairy to check out job possibilities and to take the long way so that she could have a chance to sort out her thoughts. She chose to follow a fairly remote stretch, one that tended to be shunned, since rock slides so often tumbled onto the road. Even now some good-sized rocks lay strewn about.

At one point Astrid spotted a lone figure walking ahead of her on the road. Yet when she crested the next rise, she saw no one. She began to doubt her senses as she continued to pedal along and never overtook anyone. But as she passed a particularly knotted clump of manzanita bushes, a feeling of being observed, coupled with a stronger, viler, more predatory sensation, assaulted her. Propelled by blind panic, she shoved her bike into as high a gear as she could manage and shot away, almost pitching herself off an unguarded drop in her haste to leave the area. She took the first cross trail to the main road, only then slowing down enough to wonder whether her wrought-up emotional state had created the whole episode.

Safely surrounded by the bucolic pastures and pastoral cottages, quietly grazing cows and sweet-smelling clover, she suddenly found the idea of such a thing as she had imagined on the trail to be impossible. Now I'm creating bogeymen and malevolent beings, she chided herself. Nevertheless, the first thing she did when she strode into the dairy was to drink a glass of ice-cold milk to soothe her nerves. She turned away from the counter when she finished, lingering to gaze at the sumptuous profusion of blossoming lilac bushes that grew along the nearby fence. A small creature scurried along the edge of the lawn and she turned her attention to it, curious as to what it might be. Upon closer examination, it looked like an ugly little thing—furtive and scuttling, with a menacing sort of sinuous shape. She glanced away, discomfited, and turned to the man working the counter. "What *is* that?" she asked.

"What's what?"

"That little scuttling animal out there in the grass. It looks almost like a rat, but not like any rat I've ever seen."

"Hmm—I don't see what you're talking about."

Astrid twisted back around to look. "Well—that's strange. It's gone."

NINE

Astrid turned the brass knob on the indicator post to "occupied" and trod quietly through the aromatic pines and hemlocks that lined the path to the traveler's booth. Recently, small booths had been built and scattered throughout the community for the use of any passersby needing to duck in out of the rain, to steal a few impassioned kisses, to change clothes, or to rest. Each booth was different, artfully constructed from wood, stone, or glass. This one had six walls fashioned from lead-paned glass and a slate roof, with wild, tangled honeysuckle enveloping half the structure.

The minute she walked inside, a sudden cloudburst drenched the glass; clear, cold water streamed in crystal rivulets down the sides. Astrid paused, savoring the sight before reaching into her bag for her dress. She hadn't wanted to wear it all day, because it weighed a lot. It was a beautiful new lustrous silver chain mail, and even though it was made from a new recycled ultralight metal, it still had a heft to it. She dusted her hair with a few silver sparkles, slipped on a mint-green necklace and a few bracelets fashioned from a cool incandescent material akin to that of fireflies. Thus attired, and soothed by her pleasant interaction with the core group that constituted the dairy, she brightened up considerably. When she stole back out through the trees, which were now enshrouded in a tingly, clinging mist from the brief shower, she felt magical, as if she could accomplish anything. She walked her bike the rest of the way to the teahouse, using her telekinetic powers to ward off the last few sprinkles. She stashed her bike in the covered bike rack; then, pleased and excited by the prospect of a thoroughly decadent afternoon with her friend, she quickly mounted the marble staircase. She spotted Taro lounging under the awning.

"Hey, Taro!" she called. "Been waiting long?"

"Nope—I just got here myself. You look fantastic." He stood on tiptoe to give Astrid a hug. "How the hell are you?"

"Right now, fantastic. I can't wait to sink my teeth into one of their scones. I'm glad you chose this teahouse, Taro. But I'm surprised. I would've thought you'd go for the Kenyan teahouse."

"Oh, it's just that I love the pretensions of the English." He opened the door and politely motioned her ahead of him. She breathed deeply upon entering, relishing the subtle spicy smell emanating from the polished walnut panels, as well as the fragrances of the enormous vases heaped full of fresh flowers. The maitre d' approached them in a dignified manner and arched one eyebrow to the perfect angle of hauteur.

"Two for tea?" he asked.

Taro winked at Astrid. "Or tea for two," he quipped.

The maitre d' swiveled with a pronounced droop, beckoning for them to follow. "For god's sake, Taro. That tired old joke again?"

Taro shrugged. "I can't help it if I have a lame sense of humor. Don't be making fun of mental indigents now."

Once seated, Astrid leaned back in her high-backed, upholstered chair and took a deep breath. "Man, this is so relaxing. Thanks, Taro, for suggesting it."

"Hey—my pleasure." Taro paused and peeked into the sugar bowl. "Ah, thank god. Lumps. So—how are you, really? What did you think about that meeting the other night?"

She shuddered. "Horrible. I'm going to write an editorial."

Taro grimaced. "What? Another one?"

"Oh, shut up, asshole. I don't know that I've written all that many."

Taro sat up straight. "You mean you haven't heard?"

"Heard what?"

"That the newspaper is putting together a three-volume set of your collected writings."

Astrid kicked him lightly under the table, just as the waiter appeared. Taro stuck out his tongue.

"May I take your order for tea?" he inquired.

"Sorry, Kevin. We're having a little row here. My wife of twenty-seven years just told me she's in love with another man."

"I'll take Assam, please," Astrid announced, ignoring Taro.

"Sounds good—I'll have the same."

Kevin smiled, bowed and left. "Don't let that little scamp give you any trouble, Astrid," he called over his shoulder.

"See? Even he knows what a pain in the ass you are, Taro."

"Astrid, you wound me." Taro began building a pyramid with the sugar cubes. "But seriously, have you heard the latest from the grapevine?"

"I've been at the dairy all afternoon. It's sort of out of the way. What is it?"

Taro leaned forward, then paused as Kevin returned with the cart.

"Sherry?" Kevin asked.

"Oh, why the hell not!" exclaimed Taro. "Might as well be pigs about the whole thing. Right, Astrid?"

"Righty-o." Astrid waited until Kevin left, then fixed her gaze on Taro. "So what is it?"

"What is what?"

"Taro, you really can be exasperating at times! What you heard from the grapevine, of course."

Taro looked down suddenly. "Astrid if you haven't heard it yet, I think I should wait until after tea to tell you. Or I *would* be a cad."

"Oh, great. Keep me in suspense the whole time." Astrid glared while Taro thoughtfully lathered a crumpet with butter. Then she burst out, "Taro—"

"Okay, okay. How's your stomach? Strong?"

"I...suppose."

Taro laid down his crumpet, his normally mischievous expression replaced by one of such seriousness that Astrid blinked to reassure herself that it was indeed Taro who sat facing her. "A woman was murdered over by Mt. Shasta."

Astrid gaped at him, shaken to her core. "The murderer confessed?"

Taro shook his head.

"Then how can they be sure it was murder? It could've been an accident and the person too freaked to say anything yet."

"I'm afraid not. You see, the poor woman was raped. And mutilated."

All the breath went out of her. She wanted to cry or vomit—or both. Raped and mutilated! "But...but are people capable of such things now?" she quaked, swallowing to keep down the few bites of scone she'd eaten.

"Apparently."

"They're blaming the back mutations?"

"Yeah, I think so."

Astrid took a shaky sip of tea. She was reminded of her experience along the coast road and told the story to Taro.

"So, when I got away I began thinking that I imagined the whole thing," she told him. "You know, that I let my fears about everything that's going on now take over. And that I had projected them onto my environment." She pushed away her plate, casting a rueful glance at the succulent treats she no longer felt hungry for. "But now I don't think that so much. Whatever it was, it felt so…evil. That's the only word I can think of to describe it. Malevolent."

Taro regarded his tea plate glumly as well. "I keep trying to figure out what's going on, but it's difficult," he finally remarked. "I suppose it could be true that these atavistic behaviors are resulting from the mutagenic effects of old chemical dumps, but I don't know, my gut feeling is that somehow there's more to it."

"Yes, I feel it, too," Astrid agreed, nodding vigorously. "Lots of things are happening now, and I don't know that we can blame it all on back mutations. Have you heard that more people are disappearing?"

"Hmm. Until you mentioned it, no. What do you suppose that means?"

Astrid sighed. "That, my friend, is the million-dollar question." She drummed her fingers restlessly on the table top. "Maybe I can dream the answer. The problem is, when I'm uptight I can't tell the difference between what is really happening and what I fear might happen."

"Yeah, I know, I have the same problem."

They both regarded their mounded tea plates unhappily.

"See, Astrid? I warned you. Now neither of us has an appetite. And all this lovely food."

"Okay—we have to get a grip. Feeling depressed will only make things worse."

"You're right again, as always. Do you have to be smart as well as tall?"

Astrid ignored his last remark and gazed out one of the windows that opened onto a lush garden dotted with luminescent redbuds, flowering apple trees, and sleek azalea bushes cradling papery blossoms. She struggled to achieve a calm center, amazed to encounter such difficulty in accomplishing something that had become as unthinking as breathing over the last ten years. "In fact," she said, half-joking, "the best thing we could probably do right now is to enjoy this tea."

Taro laughed. "I can't believe *you* are reminding *me!*"

Astrid paused again as she finally managed to clear her thoughts. She relaxed and closed her eyes briefly, and when she opened them again, the items on the table beckoned temptingly. "Ah," she breathed, "this is more like it! How about you, Taro? Feeling better?"

"You know—doesn't take much to entice my appetite back. In fact, your mere suggestion worked wonders," Taro mumbled, his mouth crammed full of raspberry tart. "Oops, sorry!" he apologized, spraying more crumbs about as he attempted to whisk away his first emission.

They finished their tea pleasantly; in fact, they dawdled over a few extra cups of tea and glasses of sherry. And when they split up to go their respective ways, the sun was grazing the tips of the trees' topmost branches. Long, low beams slanted through Astrid's bicycle spokes as she rode home. At one point she passed a marsh so teeming with spring peepers that their eerie song surrounded her with an unearthly metallic timbre. She shivered, realizing only then that she still wore her chain-mail dress. Since she was between booths, she decided to change clothes in the woods.

She pulled off the road and retreated into the dense foliage, allowing a few leaves from a Christmas berry bush to tickle her face as she stepped out of her garment. She had just stooped over to open her bag and pluck out her pullover and jeans, when suddenly she felt her scalp tingle. She stiffened. Was she being watched?

Hastily she donned her clothes and boots, jamming her dress into her bag. She jumped onto her bike and sped swiftly away into the deepening dusk. It wasn't until she got home and threw herself into Nate's arms that it occurred to her that a leaf could have dangled onto the back of her head.

But still, she brooded, as she recounted her day's activities to a concerned Nate, a woman had been murdered. And for the first time in her adult life, she had begun to fear for her safety.

TEN

Judy hunched over her keyboard, positive that every Angel who worked in the office could tell that she was wearing a diaphragm. She would be hauled off and punished, of course, if anyone ever found out. Funny how the Right Hand of God hated the Muslim Power Blok so much, she mused—from what she knew, they sure seemed a lot alike in their thirst for punishment. She wasn't quite certain how an Angel would know her secret, but then it always amazed her what they seemed to possess in their informational arsenals. They liked to give the impression that the Lord had granted them telepathy in order to better police His servants. Judy, however, suspected that they were masters of intimidation capable of weaseling information out of people like her all the time, the minute they smelled something. And she feared that she must be exuding guilty terror right now and had been all morning. If it got any worse, she might as well get on the office intercom and make a public announcement.

She hadn't seen her super yet, and wondering what he would have to say about yesterday's absence added to her tension. Not to mention what he might have planned in retaliation for the little altercation in the stairwell the other night—assuming that it was him. He certainly hadn't bothered to give any of her work to anyone else. It lay stacked in discouraging piles all around her desk. But she didn't think she would take the chance of obtaining a cup of caffeine this morning. Anyway, the adrenaline from her fear and defiance was doing a good job of keeping her alert.

So she did her best to plow through her double load and not attract any attention, not to perspire too much, not to shake. In addition to the supervisory cadre of the Right Hand of God, a bonus incentive existed in the corporations, where regular employees who turned in other employees for proven misconduct received a reward. Since most people made barely enough to live on, the incentive plan proved quite lucrative, if only for a few incredibly snoopy people (most of the middle class, Judy believed, were drudges like herself who just wanted to be left alone)—and, therefore, most effective. But luckily, most of the workers near enough to her work station to notice her state didn't care or had received so many electric shock treatments that they wouldn't notice. Electric-shock treatments were a popular alternative to the crowded prisons, supposedly a more helpful, humane, psycho-logical approach to modifying criminal and antisocial behavior.

She finished a long, incomprehensible document in Bureaucratese concerning a chemical spill in nearby Arcata, then picked up a report on the dump site of Mt. Shasta. She entered the data into her computer, making the necessary computations on the mass of waste product accumulated and the amount deposited in the last three quarters, and then began tapping out the projections for future dumping capacity. To her surprise, she noticed that the stated amount of materials deposited had increased steadily over the last three quarters. The pattern had been running exactly the opposite, since just about every designated site had neared its legal capacity in the last few years. The figures on mass accumulation didn't make any sense, either; it was reported to be decreasing. Well, she sighed to herself as she put a request through her computer to have the data checked against its source, it wasn't as if this were the first time that somebody got the figures all screwed up. Honestly, everyone she had ever met always seemed so dull-witted. She didn't want to be too hard on people, but that was the only word that really fit. Because she felt so different from her peers, she had no friends—not that anybody had a lot. Standard work schedules didn't really leave any time for a personal life. And what was the point of making friends, anyway? she asked herself bitterly. They'd only end up suing you or turning you in for something.

While she waited for her data confirmation to come through, she decided she might as well go to the ladies' room, so she rose and walked as nonchalantly as possible past a little nest of Right Hand of God members who worked together on the regulatory aspects of the waste-management company. They tended to hold jobs in managerial or regulatory capacities, occasionally in personnel. Nervously, Judy wondered whether she walked differently because she was wearing a diaphragm. Did she look guilty, furtive? She definitely felt as if she were being watched.

Her heart fluttered as she tiptoed past them and into the ladies' room. There she stepped carefully into a stall and held her nose as she tinkled. The bathrooms happened to be particularly foul, as they were cleaned but rarely. Management claimed that regular maintenance was too expensive, especially when the employees abused them so. And surprisingly, as far as Judy was concerned, this was true. Rather than try to keep the restrooms as clean and neat as possible, given the irregularity of the cleaning schedule, people smeared shit on the walls and crapped on the floors, and left used tampons littered about as if they were roach pellets. Shaking herself dry (since toilet paper was too expensive to keep supplied), Judy listened as the door opened and someone else came in. An instinctive wariness caused her to wait for whoever it was to select a stall before she flushed and stepped out. But a sudden warning cry that shot through her brain came too late to prevent what happened next.

She heard the stall door swing open behind her, but before she could turn around, a knee jammed viciously into her right kidney. Emitting a thin bleat of pain and surprise, she fell forward heavily, cracking her head on the sink before collapsing onto the floor. She blacked out momentarily, but then came to as a hammer-like fist crashed into her eye socket. Through a blur of fists, she glimpsed the maniacally contorted face of her super as he straddled her, using her face for a punching bag.

"Put me off, will you!" he screamed, spittle spraying into her face, mixing with the blood that had begun to drip down her chin. "You stupid slut! Where do you get off thinking you can knock me down a flight of stairs? You think that feels good?"

Although it took what seemed like hours, she groggily managed to throw her arms in front of her face and she rolled, trying to wriggle out of his grasp. She'd been beaten before—by her caretakers when growing up, by gang members upon occasion, by boyfriends with regularity. It seemed as if everyone in her world were drunk on violence, as if violence were a new form of social intercourse, a new type of sex or religion. But it always hurt. She never got used to it. And she feared that as worked up as Mr. Egis obviously was, he might turn her face into porridge.

But somehow her newfound strength deserted her. When she tried to get away, all she did was flop helplessly while Mr. Egis successfully landed a brutal blow that sent her consciousness scattering. When she came to this time, he was raping her demoniacally; he seemed to her a mechanical manifestation of cruelty and depravity. But more horrible than that was the unshakable sensation of being watched. She couldn't see because Mr. Egis had her face down, but she would be willing to bet her life that a member of the Right Hand of God stood at the door, witnessing the entire act. So not only did she have to suffer through this beating, she thought fatalistically through a prickly red haze of pain, she probably had a flogging to look forward to as well. A curious double-standard existed where the sexual act, particularly the woman's role in the sexual act, was considered sinful and depraved. But birth and children were highly prized, to the point of religious reverence. So although a scarlet woman could be tortured, a repeat offender even killed, if she turned out to be pregnant she would be accorded a grim, dutiful respect. The church, however, wanted to get the message out about the evils of adultery, so they punished offenders with lightning rapidity.

When Mr. Egis finally withdrew with a satisfied grunt, she scrambled quickly to her feet so that whoever might be watching could at least see that she had been assaulted. Yet no one was there.

She peered up at the seeing-eye camera, but, as with her monitored television, there were so many of them, that they couldn't be watched all the time. At least if someone were watching, a corporation guard or a governmental employee, she could have some restitution. If witnessed by a member of the Right Hand of God, she couldn't escape some form of vigilante physical punishment, but the official governmental/military line was that rape was different from consenting fornication and therefore not punishable (although the rapist usually wasn't punished either, since the prisons and courts were groaning under their mountainous loads). Assault was not officially condoned, so if her rape had been recorded, she could have a case to take to court, maybe win some money from Mr. Egis. *If* the attack had been recorded. Fewer and fewer cameras made recordings these days, since the sheer volume of tape generated threatened to engulf the planet. Old records could not be destroyed fast enough to make room for new ones.

Judy looked down at herself, swallowing to keep down the gorge that rose in her throat. She was covered from head to foot with slime and muck. He had gratuitously ripped her nylons, one of two precious pairs that she had painstakingly patched and repaired with nail polish for almost a year now. And torn her panties—nothing fancy, of course, but they still cost money!

Fighting back tears, she washed up as best she could at the basin, with its little drizzle of florid, aquamarine-colored water. She donned her tattered underwear, and stuffed her stockings into the overflowing trash bin. Then she wobbled, wincing, out into the office. She was watched without question now. The little cadre of Right Hand of God members observed her suspiciously but did nothing, while the other workers cast quick, secretive glances her way. She groped back to her desk, her eyes beginning to swell shut. And there she sat, wondering what to do. She knew what was expected of her. She should just keep working, especially since she had just used up her one sick day. Up until a week ago, that's probably what she would have done.

But she straightened up, the knowledge that she'd at least prevented her super from impregnating her lending her strength. She wasn't going to do that now. She was going to take care of herself, she resolved suddenly, ferociously. A sob escaped her with the relief that her decision gave her. It flooded through her, energizing her, lessening even the throbbing, gouging pain that her face and internal organs were experiencing. I'll quit and go home, she thought, and bathe myself properly—lie down and rest, go to the Medimart. I'll get another job! Other jobs exist, damn it. I know I'm a better statistician than anyone in this whole stupid corporation. Surely other bosses exist besides this crazed sadist! I'll bet even the military is better than this.

Thus empowered, she stood up, painfully but with dignity. I'll just walk away, she decided rebelliously; what can they do, fire me? Her second act of defiance filled her with wild, uncontrollable glee. She even smiled, albeit only briefly, since it hurt. As she leaned over to switch off her terminal, she noticed that the data confirmation had come in on the Mt. Shasta dump site.

Now isn't that odd, she reflected as she switched off the power, the cathode ray squirting phosphorescent green squiggles over the screen as it died away; the data check out. I wonder where all that stuff is going?

ELEVEN

Astrid scowled and wiped away her tears, punched rerun on the dreamviewer and played through the rape scene yet again. Why on earth had she let Maria talk her into going against her instincts? She knew that something terrible was going to happen to that poor woman sooner or later. She had refrained from interfering at the critical moment, and look what happened!

"Damn it," she muttered. "Damn it, damn it!" She winced as she watched Judy's forehead slam unchecked against the sink, cringed as Judy helplessly suffered the rain of savage blows. At least her aid with the contraceptives had lingered in allowing Judy to protect herself from an unwanted pregnancy, Astrid thought guiltily. And had given Judy the strength she needed to take care of herself. That fact convinced her that Maria was wrong. The only saving grace out of the whole nightmare had come from a previous act of kindness. She would never, Astrid resolved, abstain from helping Judy again, no matter what Maria thought.

Sighing, she switched off the viewer and sat, mulling over different courses of action. While she mused, an idea occurred to her. An incredible one, but no more incredible than Maria's theories. If Astrid could travel to Judy's reality, what would prevent people from Judy's reality from coming to this one? Perhaps some of those awful gang members were somehow slipping through the dimensional windows and committing murder, not atavistically deranged members of her own community. And if this were true, then there would be no reason to impose a moratorium on births.

She jumped up, knocking over an end table in her haste to reach her computer. She logged onto the community bulletin board and then typed: Emergency meeting at 4 P.M., Town Meeting Hall—regarding recent violence. She signed her name and then scrolled through the other posts. To her surprise, she saw that an emergency meeting had already been scheduled for the exact same time and location—by Louise. But Louise's message gave no hint as to what her meeting concerned. Astrid shrugged. She hoped a lot of people would show up, anyway.

Astrid glanced at the clock and saw that she had six hours until the meeting. She headed out to her garden, which she had neglected lately, and soon she found herself relaxing. Plants had always charmed and soothed her, seeming almost magical in the way they sprouted from seeds and fashioned beautiful, nutritious bodies from sunlight, water, and air. In fact, they *were* magical, she decided—for if photosynthesis didn't represent magic, what did? Pulling a rabbit out of a hat seemed like nothing compared to the mysterious process of biological energy formation.

By the time she finished working in her garden, Astrid felt refreshed and fortified. Nate had gone to spend the day at one of the day-care centers, so she planned to meet him at the Town Hall. She took off absentmindedly, stopping at a public restroom along the way, one located at the end of an overgrown, tangled path that led into a grove of trees. It smelled of cedar and felt airy and cool, light filtering down through skylights. After using the facilities, Astrid tidied up and checked to make sure the composting system was functioning properly before leaving, very much at peace. She loved her community. It was so civilized, so pleasant. Then she shivered, the picture of the restroom in Judy's world slicing into her awareness. To think that people actually lived in Judy's world! Although, come to think of it, it hadn't been so long ago that her world had teetered on the brink of becoming what Judy's world had become. She had visited a few funky public restrooms in gas stations and rest areas before the release of the UFO virus, and although they hadn't seemed quite as bad as Judy's workplace facilities, they were pretty foul. Thank god her world had followed a different path.

When she arrived at the meeting, she saw that practically the entire three- thousand-member community had shown up for the proceedings. She also noted that an electric charge hung in the air from everyone's agitated emotions. Failing to spot Nate, she headed over to where Taro and Robin sat. As she lowered herself into her seat, she caught sight of Meagan and Louise chatting with Sharon on the other side of the room. Astrid thought she made eye contact with Louise, and smiled and waved, but apparently she was mistaken, for Louise didn't return her greeting.

Nate strode in just as the meeting came to order. He halted in the back of the hall to avoid disrupting everyone's attention, rather than join Astrid. She approved of his concern for the group but suddenly felt bereft. She wanted him beside her.

Nevertheless, she tore her gaze away from him to focus on the evening's speaker of the house, a member of the community over sixteen years old and chosen at random by the central computer at the previous meeting. Tonight Enid, a pragmatic, maternal woman in her early fifties, had the honor. The computer must know what it's doing, thought Astrid. Enid had a singularly calming presence on just about everyone, and she was often sought out to settle minor differences between community members. Until recently, those were the only kinds of differences that existed in Shasta City.

Because it was an emergency meeting, Enid dispensed with the usual opening formalities and went straight to the business at hand. "Louise, Astrid," she announced, "I believe both of you called this meeting. Which one of you would like to present your business first?"

Astrid looked over at Louise, noticing that she clutched a piece of paper covered with writing. She wondered what that was all about. Louise seemed to be hesitating, so Astrid spoke up. "Why not have Louise go first," she said. "She called this meeting before I did."

Louise appeared relieved and stood up, rather officiously, in Astrid's opinion. "Friends," Louise began, "these are difficult times. I imagine that by now all of you have heard about the grisly rape and murder of one of our sisters on Mt. Shasta. Unconfessed and, incredibly, still unsolved."

A troubled murmur rustled through the room.

"And that atavisms are on the increase." She sighed. Manipulatively, Astrid thought. She hadn't witnessed this oratorical side of her friend before and she didn't know what to make of it. "The Birth Center tells me that they have met with increasing resistance to their recommendations to halt reproductive activity until the source of the mutagens is cleaned up. We all know what unchecked mutagenic activity of this type can do to our civilization. The recent tragedy attests to what kind of horrors we face in our future if we do not cooperate in this! We could be facing societal suicide." She paused to let her last statement sink in. "So therefore, a group of us have put together a resolution, signed by the majority of the community, that we would like the community to adopt: that every individual, whether they've been cited for anti-social behavior or not, agree to refrain from reproduction until the danger is past."

A turgid silence followed. Then Astrid jumped to her feet, furious and dumbfounded. "What kind of shit is this?" she exploded. "I'll ignore the fact that no one ever showed me a copy of this resolution. But why should *everyone* refrain? You talk about societal suicide, Louise—what is total abstinence from reproduction but societal suicide?"

"It'll only be for a while, Astrid."

"Oh, great. For how long?"

Louise and Meagan exchanged pained glances. But it was Sharon who replied. "Only until we unearth the dumps and sequester them off-world. We're probably only talking one year—at the most, eighteen months. The more extra volunteer labor we can obtain, the shorter the time frame, of course."

Astrid felt light-headed, short of breath. "But I'm afraid the situation is more complicated than that," she said. "Surely you realize that there's increased activity at the dimensional windows."

Sharon waved her hand dismissively. "I hardly think that has anything to do with our current problem."

"Better think again. I have evidence that indicates otherwise."

An excited buzz filled the hall. Enid called for order, but it was a while before everyone quieted down. When they did, Enid pursed her lips and addressed Astrid gravely. "I assume, Astrid, that you're prepared to offer us your evidence."

Astrid sought out Nate's eyes before replying, knowing that he was observing her intently. Did he know about the resolution? she found herself wondering. Surely not. He would have told her about it; she would have sensed his anxiety. "Is Maria here?"

"Here, Astrid." Maria waved from the back of the room.

"Okay, Maria can back me up. It seems that several of us in this community have been dreaming about another alternate reality. Right?" She let her gaze travel around the room and saw several heads nod in agreement. "At first we thought we were dealing with a dream reality, but Maria feels that we're tapping into an actual physical reality different from our own. This possibility sounded a little bizarre to me at first, but the more I thought about it, the more true it felt. At any rate, this world is unbelievably awful. The closest I can come to describing it is that it's like a combination of an Orwellian nightmare and the worst areas of Eastern Europe before the clean-up. Now, I don't understand the connection between this world and our own, but if some of us are traveling there, what's to prevent some of them from coming here? Remember the urban gangs from the last century? Gangs overrun this place. Murder to them is a form of recreation. I think that's what we're dealing with here. Not people from our own community."

Pandemonium erupted. Enid didn't attempt to bring the meeting to order. She let the consternation run its course. When everything finally subsided, which took a full twenty minutes, Enid asked, "Can anyone else corroborate Astrid's theory?"

Silence. Finally Maria stood up. "Well, I can't actually back her up with specific information, but it seems possible to me. Several of my clients have been dreaming about this world, although no one has dreamed specifically about gang members. They are rampant in this society, however. And interdimensional travel is a distinct probability as far as I'm concerned."

"Anybody else? Anyone have any relevant information on this subject?"

It turned out that ten people had been dreaming about the world Judy inhabited, six of them in Maria's practice, three in another therapist's practice, and one community member not participating in dream or alternate-life therapy. Van, whom Astrid knew only peripherally, had been dreaming about a man in a military organization of some sort. He didn't have a dreamviewer yet, he said, although he had one on order, and as his recent recall was rather sketchy, he didn't have many clear details. But the man appeared to be a rebel—a member, perhaps of an underground movement. In his job, the man seemed to have access to highly prioritized military information and planned to make use of it in some fashion. The other community members dreamed of technodrudges like Judy, except for Rana, a prominent artist in the community, who dreamed about a shopkeeper. "A feisty old coot," Rana commented.

But no one had dreamed about gang members traveling to Earth. Meagan proclaimed that she had never heard anything so difficult to swallow and that it seemed like a ploy to keep from dealing with the real problem. Taro pointed out that she was mixing her metaphors. Louise retorted that the only hard evidence introduced was that an increase in mutagenic chemicals had, in fact, been observed, and what were they going to do about it? Then a frightened voice piped up that perhaps they should close the windows, no matter what the hard evidence suggested. Astrid turned her attention (along with everybody else) to Carly, who had made the suggestion. Having everyone's attention focused on her seemed to frighten her even more.

"P-people are disappearing and all—people who don't want to disappear, seems like. Those of us who want babies are being asked not to bear. Now there's murder." She shuddered visibly. "What if Astrid's right? Cleaning up the mutagens won't help. Are these windows necessary? Do we have to have them?"

A thoughtful quiet descended. Though seemingly innocuous, Carly's proposal chilled Astrid; she wasn't sure why. Then Enid spoke: "Van, you're a geophysicist. What function do the windows serve?"

"Well, as to function—that's still a matter of debate. They appear as vortices, possibly conduits in the fabric of our reality. Travel through them is evidently possible, as demonstrated by the disappearance of people, ships, and aircraft throughout history; although we have yet, as I'm sure everyone here knows, to understand the rules of travel through dimensional windows. The windows could be no more than side-effects resulting from magnetic anomalies in the Earth's electromagnetic field, analogous to whirlpools in a stream. Therefore, they may have no real 'function.' On the other hand, they may have a purpose we have yet to discern or understand. Now, I'm not certain that we have it in our power to close the windows."

"It's possible."

All heads swiveled in one direction toward the door at the sound of an unfamiliar voice. Astrid hadn't seen the person standing there for so long that at first she didn't recognize him: Cedric, an eccentric inventor who had retreated into the hills a few years ago in order to pursue experiments the community had judged as too dangerous to perform in inhabited areas. He had always been fascinated by Tesla's electromagnetic theories and by the rumored Philadelphia Experiment, which had purportedly taken place during the Second World War, an experiment designed to make a ship invisible, using a massive electromagnetic field. The ship had supposedly traveled instantaneously through time and space to another location and back again.

Cedric had always seemed a little scary to Astrid. He seemed even more forbidding now.

"Welcome back, Cedric," said Enid. "What can you share with us?"

"Well—just this morning I was in Weed. And the situation is even worse than you know. Another murder has taken place—the victim a man this time. But he was also raped, tortured, and mutilated."

The silence that had fallen deepened further, the gloom became palpable as even the light in the chandeliers dimmed.

"Are there—suspects, Cedric?" inquired Nate, who stood beside him.

Cedric shook his head. "None. And that is the really frightening thing—to think that a pathological mutant lives placidly in our midst without our knowledge. What I can't figure is how he or she manages so effectively to block their thoughts. That, I would think, would be impossible, given our new powers of telepathy. Which leads me to think that Astrid might be correct." He paused, took out a long, slender pipe, and filled it. "Although, as you no doubt know, the atavism for violent behavior carries with it the accompanying trait of decreased psychic abilities. This could explain the inscrutability of the murderer's state of mind. However, I tend to side with Astrid. And I believe that it is imperative that we act at once, before more lives are lost."

"You said there is a way to eliminate the windows?" asked Enid.

"Yes. In fact, through my studies and experiments, I believe that I am very close to developing a device that could disrupt the electromagnetic fields responsible."

"So what do you think about the nature of the windows?" she pressed. "Are they artefact, or do they have a purpose? Once destroyed, can they be created again?"

Cedric frowned as he lit his pipe and stepped closer to the open door to let the smoke waft outside. "As to their nature, we still have much to learn. I don't know, frankly. Nor do I know if they can be established again, once done away with. But I say we should give serious thought to getting rid of them. I see no point in allowing evil to come into our world, especially when we have already had one very close brush with it. There are other ways besides traveling through dimensional windows to explore the universe."

Astrid's nagging unease intensified. Why did this talk of eliminating the windows make her feel so peculiar?

Was it the concern she had come to feel for Judy? Or was it something else? She stood up. "I don't know, man—something tells me we shouldn't do that. What if they're important to the planet? What if they represent some sort of universal communication system?"

"Do you have another suggestion?"

"Well, not right at the moment. But—if we can travel to this reality, couldn't we effect some changes there?"

"It could take a long, long time, Astrid. Maybe more time than we have."

Astrid shifted her weight, fighting an inexplicable panic. "I still think we should research all possibilities. We don't want to make a serious error, do we? What do the prophets say?"

Enid replied. "I'm afraid, from what I've gathered recently, that there are conflicting fragments of visionary data available. Some see a period of long, withering decay, while others see a new, fruitful era of change and growth. I think we can assume that these visions represent two possible outcomes from the events we now face. Which fate we choose depends upon the choices we make now."

Astrid shivered. She had wanted quick, decisive steps to be taken, but it never occurred to her that eliminating the windows would surface as a solution. Hadn't she read something once about the dimensional windows serving as conduits for cosmic energy? Or had she dreamed this? It surprised her that apparently no one else seemed to think it was important, especially Cedric, of all people. "All the more reason to proceed with caution," she insisted, a bit desperately. "At least we could assign research groups and give them a week or two to come up with more concrete information before acting. What does everybody else think?"

An exhaustive round of debate followed, which eventually resulted in a decision to defer action for two weeks and to set up research groups. The groups assembled quickly along lines of preference, friendship, and expertise. Astrid, Nate, Taro, Robin, Van and Rana formed a group to explore the nature of the relationship between the two realities through their dreams and other studies. When all this was decided, many people stood and stretched, happy for the meeting to be over.

But before they could break up, Louise called out, "Wait—friends! We never decided the outcome of the reproductive resolution!"

Astrid plopped back down in her seat with an ill-tempered grunt. What tenacity! She responded irritably, "Well, since a resolution needs unanimous consent to be adopted, you can forget about it. No way do I support such authoritative tactics."

At this, Meagan leaped up and cried, "I don't see why our whole effort has to be sabotaged by one argumentative individual! Maybe you don't understand that we're in an emergency situation, Astrid, but don't stand in the way of those who do!"

Astrid regarded her with surprise. "Hey, I called this meeting, too, you know."

"Great! A meeting. Meetings and study groups. A lot of good those will do!"

"I thought you agreed to the groups, Meagan. You didn't veto them."

Meagan rolled her eyes. "I was trying to cooperate, Astrid. Have you forgotten that word? Can't you cooperate with us on this?"

"Damn it, I'm not getting pregnant on the Birth Center's recommendation. I don't know why we have to adopt a goddamned resolution!"

Enid cut in. "That's enough debate between you two. Astrid, would you be willing to adopt the resolution for two weeks until the results of the study groups come in?"

Astrid lowered her eyes. "I suppose so."

"Meagan, Louise, Sharon—would that be acceptable to you?"

They nodded.

"All in favor?"

A weary murmur of assent swelled from the crowd.

"All opposed?"

Astrid bit her tongue. No other dissenting voices arose. But as she made plans for a late meeting with her research group at Taro's house after a two-hour dinner break, she felt manipulated and bitter. She really hadn't wanted to agree to that stupid resolution at all, but she had felt pressured. Another new, unwelcome sensation. For god's sake, she pondered glumly, what is the world coming to?

TWELVE

Judy stumbled along the sidewalk, still not able to see very well, even though she'd given herself three days to recuperate and made a visit to the Medimart (where she used approximately one-third of her life's savings for the doctor's visit and the eye drops and ointment he prescribed). She spotted a hacked and dismembered body lying in the gutter as she made her way along, and felt thankful, for the first time, for her temporary (she hoped) disability. She couldn't see the stomach-turning details which, no matter how hard she tried not to look the other times she came upon such a sight, always indelibly imprinted themselves upon her memory. She couldn't see whether the body was male or female, although it was probably female and probably not another gang member. The gangs usually just carved the balls off of men and stabbed them to death. And even though gang members killed each other all the time, rumor had it that they had ritualized killings and cremations. In any case, their bodies were rarely to be found lying around in the gutters like the drudges'.

Judy felt a tug in her memory as she contemplated the gangs, realizing that she had dreamed last night about the punk who had given her back her glasses. He—at least, she assumed it was a he, despite that outrageous wig he wore and the blue freckles painted on his face—had been in an exquisitely beautiful, cavernous hall of some sort, surrounded by lots of other people just as peculiarly dressed as himself. She never knew where the gangs came up with their bizarre, tough costumes of rubber and aluminum. Tons of trash littered the streets, but she'd never found anything useful in it. No doubt the street people picked everything clean. But actually, it seemed to her that the outlandish costumes these people wore differed from most gangs, although it was hard to remember clearly. Maybe they wore different clothing when they congregated among themselves. Maybe she had glimpsed a ceremony. She blinked, shook her head exasperatedly. And maybe it wasn't anything at all, she lectured herself—here I am treating meaningless synapse firing as reality. Pretty fanciful dream to consider real. She frowned, perplexed by the appearance in her thoughts of the word "fanciful." Where did that come from? she wondered. Such an archaic word—she wasn't even aware she'd known it. Very little existed in her life that could be referred to as fanciful.

Judy was headed for the Statistics Division of the Military-Industrial Center, looking for a new job. She knew that by applying for and accepting a job with the military, she could find herself sent into combat any time troops ran in short supply, but she hoped that her gift for statistics, along with her wretched physical condition, would keep her from such a fate. And even if she did get sent, maybe exploding into oblivion would be better than living the life she led. From time to time she had considered suicide, a fairly common form of death among members of her class, despite its status as a major sin. But each time she had rejected it. Not only did it seem sinful and wrong, but it also felt nasty. And she certainly did not want to propel herself into worse circumstances than she was experiencing now.

Two blocks from her cubicle grid, a "Help Wanted" sign displayed in the window of a second-hand store snagged her attention. She halted. She didn't think she'd ever seen a "Help Wanted" sign in a retail store before. No small-business loans existed, and no one Judy knew had ever managed to save enough money from a job, after taxes and insurance premiums, to start a business. Most businesses were inherited, passed down through families. Anyone who worked in the business usually belonged to the family.

Hesitantly, she poked her head in the door. Although the idea of belonging to the eccentric, independent class of shopkeepers frightened her, it also appealed to her, more strongly than she had ever realized.

A frowsy little woman with rodentlike teeth, nose, and eyes, but no noticeable mutations, came shuffling from out of a dark corner in the back of the door. "What do you want?" she demanded gruffly.

Judy quailed. "Uh—well—I saw your notice in the window."

The woman cocked her head and narrowed her beadlike eyes as she gave Judy a frank and not very impressed once-over. "My name's Dorothy."

"Oh—I—I'm Judy. Pleased to meet you."

"What the hell happened to you? Gang member get ahold of you?"

Judy shook her head. "No, my boss. That's why I'm looking for a new job."

Dorothy snorted. "The nerve of some of those employers, huh? You'd never catch me working for one of those bastards. I'd live on the street before I subjected myself to that."

Judy stared at her sharply and decided she probably meant that. Not herself, though. The blurry image of those ravaged, bloody body parts in the gutter intruded into her mind's eye, nauseating her. "So what's the job?" she asked quickly. "What kind of help do you need?"

"Actually, it's just part time. Maybe I should have put that on the notice. I need somebody to help cart junk from my sources to here."

Judy looked around the room, which was absolutely crammed full of old car parts (despite the fact that no one but the rich drove cars any more—Judy had seen only one, not counting garbage trucks and police cars, in her entire life), raggedy used clothing, ancient furniture all falling to pieces, old bottles, cans, plastic dishes, ratty blankets, and busted luggage (although whoever went anywhere that required luggage, she certainly didn't know). Judy wondered where she would put more stuff.

"There's more space out back," Dorothy said. She led Judy into another room that seemed, if possible, to be even more crowded.

"What do people want used car parts for?" Judy asked.

"Don't know. I just know there's a demand for them, so I sell 'em."

"Who to?"

Dorothy shrugged. "Other shopkeepers. Drudges. Gang members."

"Gang members?" Judy gasped.

"Sure."

"Aren't—aren't you afraid they'll kill you and take all your stuff?"

"Nah—I'm more useful to them alive. They don't know my sources."

"But—they could torture it out of you."

"Not me," Dorothy replied smugly. "They tried."

"Oh." Judy shivered, wondering what they had done to her. She wished she could be that tough.

"It is conceivable, I suppose, that they could try to torture it out of whoever comes to work for me." She watched to see the effect of her statement on Judy. "Can you be trusted?"

"I don't know. I guess—I guess it would depend on what they did."

Dorothy grunted. "You strong? I need somebody who won't collapse on me. You don't look very strong—but on the other hand, that's quite some beating you took and you're up and around, aren't you?"

"So how much are you paying?" Judy inquired shakily, anxious to get away from the topic of torture and beatings.

"One hundred and fifty dollars a week. Under the table, of course."

Judy calculated quickly. Six hundred dollars a month. Her cubicle cost three times that to rent. And that wasn't taking into account her litigation payments to the burglar and her ex-boyfriend. If she tried to renege, either party could have her cubicle closed off to her by the police until she resumed payments. And then there was the price of food powder, which rose every three months as a built-in hedge against inflation. In fact, the price of everything rose automatically every three months (although salaries did not) in order, the corporations said, to keep up with inflation. They insisted that these practices were not in themselves inflationary.

"I'm, uh—I'm afraid I can't live on that," Judy mumbled.

Dorothy nodded. "I thought as much. Rent a cubicle, do you?"

"Yes."

"You don't have any place else to stay?"

Judy regarded her in surprise. "Well, of course not. Where else is there?"

"Oh, I don't know. I thought perhaps you knew another shopkeeper with some extra space. I'd let you stay here, but as you can see, I don't have a scrap of extra space. I myself sleep on top of my desk."

Judy's mouth twisted in disappointment. Even the potential threat of torture didn't entirely dim the attraction that this daring, independent position had begun to exude for her. The weakness of her heart and lungs she had decided to ignore for the moment.

But just as she started to ask Dorothy about the possibility of her checking with her shopkeeper friends to see if anyone had space for rent, she felt it again, that prickling sensation of being under observation. Could the government have this place bugged? Was dealing in car parts perhaps illegal? There were so many laws—millions, in fact—that it was impossible to know them all; but the citizenry was held accountable for them nonetheless. She reconsidered, her fear giving the whole situation a new light. She was trying to avoid physical pain; she didn't need any more—from gang members *or* the government. Physical punishment, along with electric shock treatment, was gaining popularity with the legal system in its futile effort to cut down on crowding in the prisons—thus, popular items from the Spanish Inquisition and Nazi concentration camps, as well as more sophisticated devices, were becoming more frequent in sentences meted out by judges.

Anyway, the more she thought about it, the more the idea of giving up her warm, safe—well, relatively safe— cubicle made her feel uncomfortable. She had already performed one illegal act. Maybe she should just leave it at that.

In the end, she told Dorothy she was sorry, but she couldn't take the job. Dorothy said she wasn't surprised, and besides, she added, with annoying and not entirely fair directness—since she had brought up the subject of housing—she hadn't actually offered her the job.

"Need anything while you're here?" she asked.

"Uh, no, I don't think so, thanks."

Dorothy shrugged. "Come by if you do."

"I will."

Judy scurried out of the store, crestfallen, feeling as if she had failed some sort of test. Not only that, but she couldn't shake the subliminal tickle of being watched. Did someone know about her cache of contraceptives? By some remote, awful chance had someone been watching through her TV monitor when she had carelessly dumped her booty all over the floor?

Cheeks burning, she quickened her pace to the Military Industrial Center, hoping—probably irrationally, she told herself—to outdistance whatever surveillance she might be under. But she quickly gave that up as she began wheezing and choking. Odd, it seemed that the air had been getting worse lately—another reason to hang on to her cubicle, with its filtered and oxygenated air. When she arrived at the massive doors of the MI Complex, the awesome power radiating from all its larger-than-life features sent any other thoughts flying. Dare she enter such a place? The doors alone scared her, towering over fifty feet at least, blank, smooth, impenetrable and invincible-looking. However, the minute she drew close her presence activated both the door and the conveyor belt, which she did not realize she was standing on. Immediately she felt herself whisked into a dark stillness, where she stopped. She waited. A cold, dim light gradually lightened the room.

"Please state purpose of visit," an electronic voice commanded.

"Job application," she responded quickly, afraid that if she did not she might be reduced to a smoldering pile of ashes.

"What category of job?"

"Statistics."

"Name?"

"Judy Johnson 1045."

"One moment."

She waited nervously. Then the voice spoke again.

"Please be seated in the lab chair to your right for mandatory tests."

"What—what kind of tests?"

"Drug tests. Venereal-disease tests."

She obediently removed her dress and underwear, glad nobody human was around to see the state of her

underwear, as pitiful and stretched out and full of holes
as it was. As she cautiously perched herself on the cold
Naugahyde chair and suffered the myriad jabs of needles
and insinuating slithering of a catheter that managed to
snake its painful way up her urethra, she wondered where
on earth they thought a drudge would be able to find the
money for drugs. On the other hand, drug use must be
wide-spread enough, despite the astronomical black-
market prices and particularly gruesome punishments for
possession and trafficking (eyes gouged out, tongues
severed, noses and ears lopped off), to mandate such tests.
They couldn't be cheap, not when eye ointment cost a
hundred dollars for a small tube.

After the lab tests had terminated, she was instructed
to give her personal and employment history into a
microphone that suddenly thrust itself into her face from
a slot in the wall. She didn't know whether to answer
immediately or to go over and put her clothes on, but she
was afraid to do anything wrong in such intimidating
surroundings, so she solemnly recited her history while
naked, feeling extremely uncomfortable and vulnerable,
wondering whether a hidden camera lurked somewhere.

Her mother had been a single mom who couldn't
afford to keep her, since day care for her daughter would
have cost more than she made at her minimum-wage job.
So Judy had been raised in an orphanage, euphemistically
referred to as a children's "camp." She hated it. It was an
awful, bleak place with mean old women for Mistresses
and a fierce, cruel hierarchy that existed among the girls
themselves. Judy, of course, with her health that was even
frailer than usual, her considerable overweight and
nearsightedness, had always occupied the bottom of the
pecking order, although she didn't give that information
to the microphone. She had had only one job, the one she
had just left, which she obtained immediately after
graduating from Vocational Training at the top of her
class. She stated that she had quit her last job, but did not

give the reason. Apparently the electronic voice didn't care about the reason.

Then up through the floor erupted a small computer terminal, whose characters, Judy felt relieved to see, were readable, even in her present condition. She hastily donned her clothes and then sat down to a six-hour battery of tests. At the end, she was thirsty and famished, but a conveyor belt whisked her into another room. She was glad she'd put on her clothes. She was deposited in front of a large, imposing desk set atop a raised platform. A tall, uniformed woman with square shoulders, a rectangular head, and crisp contours strode into the room and seated herself behind the desk. She scrutinized a file, which Judy assumed must be her file.

Before even looking up, the official barked, "Ever been involved in an illegal activity?" Then the woman fixed upon Judy the most terrible steel-gray eyes Judy had ever seen. She thought the woman could probably flay someone alive with that gaze.

Judy shriveled, but still couldn't imagine confessing to a crime, not with the punishments sure to be inflicted. They'd have to drag it out of her. "No, ma'am," she whispered.

"Ever had any contact with seditious persons, harbored any seditious thoughts?"

Judy shook her, head, hoping the woman would take her fright merely as a sign that the intimidation tactics were working effectively. She wondered why they didn't use lie detectors, as they did all the time on television, but perhaps they were unreliable, given the quaking, anxious state of most job applicants. Maybe it was more effective to have someone like this woman worm the information out of people.

"Would you willingly endure capture or give up your life for your country?"

Judy gulped and nodded. She certainly hoped it wouldn't be necessary.

"Has all the information given by you today constituted the truth, the whole truth, and nothing but the truth?"

"Yes."

"You will receive notification of acceptance or rejection by messenger tomorrow, unless you wish to sign on immediately as infantry." Serving in this way represented a societally sanctioned form of suicide, which a lot of drudges took advantage of, but not nearly enough for the needs of the military.

"Uh, no—thank you, ma'am."

The official stood up. "Dismissed."

The conveyor belt yanked Judy away so fast this time that she toppled onto her already bruised knees. Funny that the woman hadn't asked about her bruised appearance, but then beatings were common, after all. The Mistresses beat her as a child, police beat the citizenry, gangs beat the citizenry, employers had carte blanche to do whatever they wanted, and wife- and girlfriend-beating constituted the norm—at worst, considered an exasperating bad habit, like leaving clipped nose hairs in the sink or dirty socks lying about.

The conveyor belt spit her out onto the gray, smoggy street, the daylight just beginning to wane so that the light reminded her of her interrogation room. She hurried home, as best she could (could the air possibly have gotten worse in the last eight hours, or was it her imagination?), anxious to get home before nightfall.

When she eased herself into her cubicle and her panting slowed down a bit, she became aware again of that creepy feeling of being watched. This time she suspected that something had been planted on her during her interview at the MI Complex. She checked carefully, but if it had, whoever it was must have injected it under her skin. Well, the only illegal activity she had ever engaged in was wearing a diaphragm, and her cache of contraceptives was carefully hidden under a flap of her stiff, bristly carpet. They wouldn't find anything else on her.

To distract herself from worrying, she turned on her television. But she found that the routine violence in the shows bothered her more than usual, as if she had somehow become sensitized to it, or allergic. She could no longer watch the standard 15.2 murders per minute in bored fascination, even though rumor had it that to save money for props and materials, the producers and directors were beginning to actually injure extras and even to kill them, not on purpose, but sometimes it couldn't be helped. This apparently gave most members of the middle class a ghoulish thrill and had sent viewership and ratings soaring; and oddly enough, there seemed to be no shortage of extras willing to risk themselves for the money and the chance to become Somebody, even though fewer than .0001% of extras ever went on to join the privileged classes as actors and actresses. But Judy didn't find this new development to be exciting at all, even though she knew she was supposed to.

In the end, she switched it off and found herself fantasizing instead about the punk she had begun to consider "her" gang member. Did he ever go to Dorothy's store to buy car parts? she found herself musing. Who was he? Why had he been so nice to her? Oh well, she sighed, as she went over to the tap and rustled up a bowl of food powder, she'd probably never find out. Not when just asking around could cost her life.

THIRTEEN

Astrid laced her boots nervously. This was the first time she had ever gone in for job counseling. She just couldn't seem to settle on anything to do. Louise and Meagan's resolution had made it impossible for her even to consider continuing at GenFarm, and although she had intended to go work at the dairy, she never did. Somehow she just didn't feel like doing anything. She felt lethargic. She felt like her community wasn't allowing her to do the one thing she really desired, so what was the point?

And then Judy had to slither out of the plans that she had been laying with Rana in some dreamwork. They had wanted to involve Van and his rebel, but Van was offworld, engaged in the same toxin-relocation project that had taken Nate away again. But Astrid and Rana figured they could involve him later. They, along with Robin, were attempting to build a class of individuals in Judy's world who would put up resistance to being brutally treated and used. This seemed like a reasonable first step in effecting some kind of change. Rana's shopkeeper, Dorothy, seemed like a good bet, and Astrid had thought Judy not such a bad gamble, either. They had managed to create the part-time position—no mean feat—and guided Judy's path so she would know of it. But they had not counted on the economic realities they had to contend with, the going wages for that kind of position, the going price for a cubicle. Not to mention psychological aspects of Judy's makeup that Astrid had apparently glossed over: the strength of her desire to obey and conform, not to cause or get into any trouble; her fear, her paranoia. Was the woman really under surveillance? Astrid couldn't detect anything; neither could Robin or Rana.

The two-week research limit would be up in another week, and everything she had worked for in the past week seemed to have just gone down the tubes. Dream control had been more difficult to achieve than those two other spontaneous times when Astrid had returned Judy's glasses to her and fabricated the contraceptives in addition to the lizard to draw Judy's attention to them. Anxiety and the time limit weighed upon her mind and weakened her power.

In addition, Astrid didn't approve of Judy's choice. She knew the poor thing was desperate, but she couldn't help it—Astrid loathed the very concept of a military and everything it stood for: imposed will, rigidity, violence. Maybe Maria was right; she should back off and observe more so that she understood better. But there wasn't time, it seemed. Astrid could sense an odd feeling pulsing throughout the collective consciousness of the community —a potent fear, a vigilante mood.

Oh, things are in a mess, she sighed to herself as she pulled on a short dress, not even bothering to notice whether it complemented her boots or leggings. She rode off grimly for her appointment at the job counseling center, wondering where all the recent developments were going to lead. Not since she had left the East Coast for the out-of-the-way Humboldt University, sickened and fed up with all the environmental disasters and rampant crime— not to mention the former government's increasingly heavy-handed efforts to control crime—had she felt so confused and pessimistic. Just when everything seemed to be getting better and communities were getting back on their feet, why did all this have to happen?

The job counseling center occupied a well-kept Victorian house. Wisteria and honeysuckle dripped from the gingerbread trim like icing, and gardens of rosemary bushes, smoke trees and redbuds graced the grounds. Sunlight always seemed to shine here, fog never seemed to linger. Astrid had often passed by this spot with great pleasure. Today, however, it looked and felt different, now that she was coming reluctantly and with a heavy heart. The place actually looked a little spooky with its numberless nooks and crevices, its tall, dark windows. The cloudlike flower puffs of the smoke trees had waned, leaving a spiky network of petioles, and the redbud blossoms had passed their prime, drooping a little and turning brown in spots.

Inside, though, the place felt warm, cozy, and gracious. Refreshments had been laid out on one of the tables, for staff and for any community members having appointments or business at this time. Astrid ambled over and nabbed a slice of papaya before heading into the office of the counselor she'd made her appointment with, a woman who often attended the same parties as Astrid did. When Astrid strode through the door, she rose and gave Astrid a warm hug. Then she jumped back.

"Ugh, Astrid—you're all covered in goo!"

"Sorry, Nora. I just had some papaya."

"Warn a person next time, will you?" She whipped some tissues from a dispenser and handed them to Astrid.

"Sure. Sorry."

"Oh—no problem. So how are you, Astrid?" Nora settled back in her chair, scrutinizing Astrid appraisingly.

"Is that a loaded question?"

Nora laughed. "Could be."

Astrid shrugged. "Ah, not so good, to be honest. I'm having trouble finding meaningful employment."

"GenFarm isn't working out?"

Astrid made a face. "I'm not getting along so well with Louise and Meagan. Were you at the last town meeting?"

Nora shook her head. "I heard about it, though."

"So. We're on opposite sides. And they're pissing me off, to tell the truth. I thought about working at the dairy, but..." Astrid stopped, made a listless gesture.

"What about more time in toxic cleanup? We can always use extra labor for that."

"Too depressing right now."

Nora raised an eyebrow. "Maybe you need to see a therapist, not a job counselor."

"I'm already seeing a therapist." Astrid flung out her feet and studied them, noticing for the first time that her boots didn't match her leggings at all, not even in some humorous, funky kind of way. She burst out, "Look, the only thing I want to do right now is get pregnant and have a baby! And those assholes won't let me do it, with all their resolutions and regulations! And I don't feel like doing anything else right now."

Nora dropped her gaze, picked up a pen and began doodling. "Maybe you should get away for a while, what do you think? The tropics might be nice, you name the place—Hawaii, Costa Rica, Thailand...I can get you on a work-exchange crew. I know you've always liked construction work."

"I don't know." Astrid sighed heavily.

"Well, how would you feel about going to New York? I received a flyer in the mail not long ago saying that there's a genetics convention going on right now."

Astrid brightened. Why hadn't she thought of it before? Her parents had recently moved to New York from Boston, and it had been too long since she'd seen them. They found the West Coast a bit too flaky for their taste and came out but rarely. Astrid found the East Coast too crowded and felt so content in her community that she didn't like to leave it. "All right. Nate is offworld now anyway and I *am* feeling sort of stifled. Thanks for the suggestion."

"No problem." Nora straightened up and clicked her computer keys briskly, obviously happy to have come up with a suggestion that Astrid liked. "Will you need accommodations while you're there?"

"No—I'll stay with my parents."

"I didn't know they lived in New York."

"They just moved."

"Well, perfect, then." Nora stopped typing and gazed at the screen. "The convention is in Midtown, in the Chanin Building. Seminars start at 9:30 in the morning. When do you think you'll leave?"

"Tomorrow, maybe. No point in putting it off."

Nora smiled and nodded. "Okay, then. You're all registered. If you show up a day or two late, it's no big deal. It's somewhat informal—for the East Coast, that is." Nora typed up her final sequence and then made a print-out. She stood up to give Astrid another hug when she handed her the sheet. "Have a great time! At least you're not as slimy as when you came in," she teased.

"I'm glad," Astrid laughed, cheered by Nora's pleasant nature and the prospect of visiting her parents. She would like to see how New York had changed since the UFO virus, too.

Inspired by her impending visit, Astrid decided to stop by the day-care center to see Sara and Devin, two of her favorite children. She normally spent at least two or three afternoons or evenings a week at the center, but lately she had been avoiding the place. The sight of young children was making her breasts ache.

The day-care center in Shasta City was an exceptionally charming place—which both children and adults continually worked at making more charming. Most of the main buildings had doorways, ceilings, sinks, furniture and proportions that adults found comfortable, but there were two sets of doorknobs, sinks, and furniture, one for little people. In addition, all kinds of other places existed strictly for children—tree houses, playhouses, gazebos. Tiny boats could be navigated along the small, picturesque canal system, and ponies were available for riding, as were all manner of trikes, bikes, wagons, scooters and skateboards, not to mention rollerblades. Books, lots and lots of them, resided in the library and belonged to everyone.

The afternoon had gone from foggy to misty to rainy, but as Astrid noted when she rode into the center's grounds, that wasn't keeping anyone indoors who wanted to be out. Children in brightly colored rain smocks splashed energetically about in the puddles and nudged homemade boats down gutters. A few recognized Astrid and cried out greetings, which she returned affectionately. She didn't see Devin or Sara among them, though, so since it was still snack time, Astrid wandered into the main dining hall, hoping to find her friends there. She spotted them tucked away in a bay window, giggling over a plate of tea cakes and sporting large mustaches from their mugs of hot milk spiced with vanilla, nutmeg, and honey. She poured herself a cup of steaming black tea, added a little cream, and ambled over to their spot, blowing on her drink to cool it.

"Hi, you two," she grinned as she sat down upon the floor, attempting, unsuccessfully, to wedge her knees under the small table. "How's it going?"

"Astrid, hi!" they sang out delightedly.

"Where've you been?" demanded Sara. "We haven't seen you for a really long time! We thought maybe you went away without telling us."

Guilt wrenched at Astrid's heart. "Would I do a thing like that?"

"We didn't know," said Devin.

"Well—I'll tell you right now that I wouldn't. Okay? But actually, I am going away for a little while."

"Oh yeah?" Sara asked. "Where?"

"New York."

They both dropped their tea cakes, which they had been messily slathering with boysenberry jam. "Can we go with you?" they pleaded.

Astrid shook her head. "Sorry, guys. Not this time."

"Please!" Devin pressed. "We couldn't go on the San Francisco field trip last month because we were too young!"

Astrid bit her lip. "You're breaking my heart, do you realize that?"

They nodded happily.

"Well, thanks! But seriously, Sara, Devin—I just can't this time. I have too much business. Another time, I promise."

"Promise?" Sara regarded her solemnly. "Cross your heart and hope to die, stick a needle in your eye?"

Astrid shuddered. "Sara, ugh—where did you get that gruesome saying?" She thought such expressions had died out with the advent of the UFO virus.

"We're studying childhood history."

"I see. Tell you what—I do promise, but none of that other stuff. Yuk."

"Okay. But we won't forget. Will we, Devin?"

"Nope."

"All right, you two—you have fun while I'm gone, okay? What do you have going on now?"

Devin swallowed his cake eagerly. "We're starting a garden!" he exclaimed. "And building a new playhouse!"

"Sounds pretty fantastic."

He nodded vigorously.

"Now, see? You don't want to miss out on that."

"Yes I do!"

"Silly. C'mon—give me a kiss." They both smudged portions of their milk mustaches onto her face in their leavetaking. Not wishing to hurt their feelings, Astrid left their crumbs and jam sticking to her face until she had left the dining hall, her heart glowing fondly.

As she rode away, she decided to stop by and see whether Robin was free tonight for dinner. She would probably go on and leave for New York in the morning— no sense in dragging things out. Maybe Robin could let Taro and Rana know what she was up to and they could continue the research here while she was gone. Her parents might have some valuable insights, she mused. As East Coast intellectuals, they could always be counted on for an intelligent, if sometimes too cerebral, perspective. And New York should prove quite interesting itself, given the fact that it had practically come apart at the seams before the effects of the virus had set in. But from what she had heard, it had made a remarkable and encouraging recovery. It might put her in a more optimistic frame of mind to see how quickly things could turn around for the better.

FOURTEEN

When the electronic messenger arrived early the next day, Judy felt a sudden wave of misgiving. Had she done the right thing? She thought she had at the time, but last night had been filled with uneasy, foreboding dreams that she couldn't remember upon awakening. They probably didn't mean anything, just normal concern over a new job, but still, she hesitated a moment before letting the thing into her cubicle, painfully aware that if she had been accepted, she couldn't refuse at this point. The messenger slipped into her space with the lethal, insinuating grace of a Doberman pinscher, remarkable for something made out of metal, she thought. Doberman pinschers made frequent appearances in TV docudramas, although she'd never seen one in real life.

Sensing her body heat as it neared, a cable shot out from the robot's chest and wrapped itself tightly around her arm. Then it halted and an inflectionless voice bleated, "You have been accepted for service at the Statistics Division of the Military Industrial Center. Please come along."

"Okay," she assented nervously. "Just—let me get my purse."

The cable extended more of itself as she crossed the cubicle to fetch her pocketbook from her bed.

The thing slid along beside her with a smooth, mechanized whir as she walked apprehensively to her new place of employment. She'd heard rumors that the military implanted surveillance devices under the skin of all its employees, as well as a powerful magnetic device that could draw any AWOL employee to the center from a two hundred-mile radius. She wondered if they still did that—in any case, she hadn't rid herself of that weird feeling of being under observation, so perhaps they had already done something when they performed her tests. But then she remembered that the feeling had begun before she went to the MI Complex. Had Mr. Egis implanted something on her the day he raped her? That's when it first started, it seemed, now that she really considered it. But why would he do that? He wouldn't have any reason to stalk her. Unless—a cold sweat broke out over her entire body—unless he was a member of one of the secret satanic cults.

One of the side-effects of the success of the Fundamentalist movement was that it had spawned a converse increase in Devil worship. Although very, very secret, satanic cults possessed a widespread notoriety. Whenever someone disappeared and no body showed up anywhere, it was assumed that the Satanists had used the person. They kidnapped drudges for necromancy, sacrifices and rituals, and some people, it was whispered, were even bred with animals and demons, the women forced to bear monsters.

Mr. Egis was certainly evil enough to belong to such a cult, Judy affirmed to herself with a violent, prickling shudder. But why hadn't he used her before? Maybe he was just getting around to it? Suddenly the constricting grip of the electronic messenger felt comforting. At least if she were the property of the military, he'd have a more difficult time snatching her. The military didn't look kindly upon destruction of its property. Maybe if he discovered where she was working, he would back off.

Feeling relieved by this possibility, she relaxed a little—until her eye fell upon the body she'd passed yesterday. It hadn't been moved from the gutter, and it was becoming more bloated and hideous by the hour. She held her breath as long as she could, past the point where she gasped for air. Today the body brought to mind the first traumatic time she'd ever seen such a sight, the time her schoolmate Winnie had talked her into escaping from the Children's Camp for the afternoon. They had come upon a chopped-up body in the gutter and gone shrieking and crying back to camp, where they were promptly caught. Winnie convinced the Mistresses that it was Judy's idea, so Judy was the one who received the purification and obedience lesson while Winnie got off with two sharp cracks of a ruler. Judy had had to stand still while two junior proctors inflicted burns on her arms and legs with a device similar to a cigarette. Any time she shrank or flinched, she earned herself another burn. She still had the scars.

When she had stumbled back to her dorm barracks, her classmates held her down and rubbed corrosive cleanser into her wounds. Having tasted punishment so many times themselves, the children felt a burning need to impose it on others. Two traumas on the same day, and she didn't know which was worse: her first experience with violent death or the pain that Winnie had caused. Not the physical pain; Judy had to endure that all the time. No, it was the worse pain of betrayal by the one girl she had thought was her friend and the unfair, gratuitous censure by the crowd. Such beasts, she thought now, blinking back the tears that this memory always squeezed out—ready to judge and condemn at the drop of a hat.

Arriving at the MI Complex completely out of breath, Judy was dragged to the uniform dispensary by her mechanical guide. She was given two uniforms that she would have to pay for out of her salary. Although they were expensive, she was happy to have the new clothes, especially since they were far nicer than anything she'd ever owned. She was informed by the matron on duty that it was her responsibility to keep the uniforms dry-cleaned. A facility existed on the base where she could take them, but she was responsible for paying for the service. Since her salary was higher here, she could afford it, although once the uniforms and dry-cleaning were paid for she would end up with effectively the same amount as before to live on. But that was okay. Just the psychological boost of getting paid more helped.

As soon as she obtained her uniforms and heard the lecture on how to care for them, a series of conveyor belts took her to the implantation center where, sure enough, a magnetic device was inserted under the skin of her right forearm, also to be subtracted from her salary. Nothing was said about any surveillance aspects of the implant, but she assumed that she'd better watch her step from now on. After that, she was sworn in, subjected to a little torture to make sure she wasn't a spy or hiding anything, given a three-volume manual on conduct in the military (which she was supposed to memorize, although Judy wondered how many people on Earth had enough functioning brain cells to contain that much input), and then shunted to her new supervisor's office.

As she approached his door, she had a paranoid, nightmarish flash that she might find Mr. Egis here, in some bizarre twist of events. But when the door slid open, she caught her breath as she glimpsed the most handsome man she'd ever seen off the television screen. Deposited in front of his desk, she saluted weakly and stood trembling while he coldly assessed her. He might be handsome, but he appeared to have been chiseled out of ice. Just as well, she told herself, gulping with nervousness—at least he probably wouldn't try to rape her. Hopefully he wasn't overly fond of corporal punishment, even if the military itself was into it in a big way. Her fingernails ached where the cadets had shoved red-hot sections of metal wire underneath them to make sure she wasn't a subversive and holding something back.

He spoke. "I am Major Duncan. You, I assume, are Judy Johnson 1045?"

"Yes sir."

"I note from your file that you used to work at the Sunshine Waste Treatment Corporation. And that you reside at Merry Olde Highland Estates."

"Yes sir."

"Why did you leave your last place of employment?"

Judy hesitated, then decided she might as well tell the truth. "My supervisor assaulted me, sir. I feared for my health." When Major Duncan didn't reply right away, she appended hastily, "And I feared that I would no longer be of service to the country, sir."

"I see." He scrutinized her carefully. "Employers have the right to corporal punishment, you know."

Judy clamped her mouth shut. Not another one! "Yes sir, I know that, sir."

"Well. You will be relieved to know that I do not believe in unwarranted punishment. I think you will find me a fair, if demanding, superior. You scored quite high on our battery of tests, however, so I feel confident that you will be able to handle the job."

"What is my job, sir?"

He gave her a sidelong glance, his eyes hooded strangely. "You will be my assistant."

"Oh." Judy nearly fainted. She always knew that she could handle a job like this! She couldn't believe she'd waited so long to get out of the clutches of that horrible Mr. Egis and that repetitive, boring, stupid work. At the same time, now that she had this opportunity, it frightened her to death.

He stood up briskly. "Allow me to show you your new office."

She screwed up her courage and braced herself to confront fifty or a hundred new faces, none of them friendly, none of them interested in her. But when Major Duncan opened an adjoining door, she saw nothing but one desk, a telephone, and a computer terminal. She had her own office! She swayed, dizzy from her unexpected good fortune. Her gaze swept the room joyfully and she noticed a flat, rectangular object affixed to the wall. Her eyes narrowed as she tried to figure out what it was. She stepped closer.

"Like that, do you?" Major Duncan's voice carried a peculiar quality that Judy couldn't quite identify. She twisted around to look at him, but was met by his cool, bland expression.

"Yes. Yes, I do," she whispered. It was a painting. A beautiful painting full of the most vivid, vibrant colors she had ever imagined.

"That was painted by Bonnard, a nineteenth century artist."

"Why is it in here? Did it belong to your former assistant, sir?"

He shook his head. "No, it belongs to me." He paused. "The room needed something. The soul requires refreshment in order to work effectively, don't you agree?" Again that peculiar vibration in his voice.

"Yes sir," she replied wonderingly.

"As to your duties." His tone resumed its whiplike crack of authority as he explained what he expected of her. She would screen his calls, and she would input and organize all information and data that he gave her, which, from his description, sounded like it was a considerable amount. She was to keep an eye out for any interesting patterns and trends and to report these to him. She reported everything to him and only to him. She was not to release any information to any other member of the military or the citizenry. What she knew and researched would be top secret.

"Does that include your superiors, sir? I'm not to tell them anything, either?" Judy asked.

"It includes everyone," he stressed firmly. "We're dealing with a possible information leak of the gravest consequences. That is why my former assistant is no longer with us."

Judy swallowed, wondering if "no longer with us" meant no longer employed here or dead.

"Now. You will be working overtime many nights. In such cases, you will be accompanied by one of our mechanical messenger dogs. It will protect you from gang attacks."

"Th-thank you, sir."

"Don't thank me. It's policy. Under no circumstances are you to spend the night here. Is that clear? The first infraction will earn your dismissal."

"Yes, sir." The military provided housing only for the officers, she knew. Coming up with housing for everyone would prove too costly, especially with real estate prices so astronomically high.

"Do you have any questions?"

"Not at the moment, sir."

"All right, then. If you do have questions later, you may call upon me."

"Thank you, sir."

Again he seared her with his ice-blue gaze. "I have one order that I want you to carry out immediately upon finishing today's duties."

Here it comes, she thought fatalistically. Although why someone who looked like him would want her, she sure didn't know. At least if she got pregnant, it wouldn't be with a monster. She hoped. "What's that, sir?"

"I want you to see the medic for those bruises and injuries."

"All–all right, sir." His concern threw her off for a moment. First she felt pleased, immeasurably so. Then she drooped, thinking about her dwindling life's savings.

"Have them bill it to the office. I'll take care of it," he informed her, as if reading her last thought.

"Thank you, sir. Thank you!" she gushed, awed to the very soles of her tatty pumps.

He waved his hand in brusque dismissal. "As you said, you can't serve your country in inferior physical condition. Now, these are the preliminary data I want processed." He indicated a stack of papers on the desk beside the terminal. She noticed there was no printer. He gave her preliminary instructions to get her going and then left, shutting the door behind him. The quiet was almost unnerving. Although cars no longer thronged urban streets, a plethora of noise almost always existed: in her last office, the sounds of hundreds of keyboards clacking, phones ringing, chairs squeaking, printers chattering, shouts, coughs, sighs, rustles; in the street during rush hour, the number of people made a veritable thundering stampede; and the cubicle grids themselves produced noise, from the hum of transformers deep in basements to the roar of the air processors to the millions of televisions tuned in all at once to the fighting and screaming of couples co-habitating cubicles.

Judy tried to go over and sit down at the desk and start working right away. A seeing-eye camera was plainly visible in one corner of the ceiling. But somehow the painting on the wall drew her as strongly as if it were tuned in to the frequency of her new magnetic homing device. She walked over and stood in front of it, deeply moved by it. Those tall, graceful things outside the sunny window—they must be trees. She'd seen pictures of trees before, on television. Apparently urban areas had had some trees in the past, but once, a citizen had fallen over a tree root and sued the city she was living in, so most areas had cut down all their trees to avoid litigation in the future.

How amazing that Major Duncan had chosen to put this magnificent work of art in her office. A perplexing man. He seemed cold and stiff, but then he had given her the enjoyment of something that less than one percent of the world's inhabitants got to enjoy and ordered her to the doctor—on his bill! He didn't have to be so nice. Why was he being so nice?

Whatever the reason, she decided just to revel in her new good fortune—her boss who treated her like a human being, her new office, her nice new uniforms. She would devote herself to Major Duncan. She'd be the best assistant he ever had. She didn't care how much he asked her to do—she'd work twenty-four hours a day if he needed her to. She bent to her work gladly, noticing that the first group of data on her stack had to do with phytoplankton. How strange. What were phytoplankton?

FIFTEEN

"...So Robin and I are trying to help her out, right? And with the courage that she receives from us, Judy quits her job. But then what does she do but go join the military!" Upset, Astrid put aside her cocktail, which she had been eagerly guzzling only moments before. "I couldn't believe it, Mom! From the frying pan straight into the fire. And there she gets a job working as the assistant for this big-deal cold-fish militarist, who's obviously got some sort of weird trip going, and she decides to devote herself to him! All he has to do is refrain from raping her immediately, have the military pay for one crummy medical visit—so she can 'serve her country'—and put a painting in her office that he's probably looted from some poor, dead, defunct museum, a painting that lots of people should be able to enjoy, and she falls in love with him." Astrid shook her head in wondering disbelief for a long time before gloomily reaching for her drink.

Libby sat without speaking for a moment. Then she stirred and asked, "You dreamed this last night?"

"Yeah."

"And you honestly believe that there is some physical connection between this world and ours?"

Astrid frowned. "I don't know. I know it sounds wild. But why would so many people be dreaming about the exact same place? And Maria's no dummy. I mean, I know you think the West Coast holds some peculiar beliefs, but think about it this way—most of us possessed the atavistic genome before the UFO virus came along and we didn't all go around killing and mutilating people. That theory for the murders just seems a little facile to me."

"Perhaps. But maybe the murderer's genetic damage is more extensive than just the atavism. Have you considered that?"

"I have, as a matter of fact. But I don't know that you can blame pathological behavior solely on genetics." Astrid took another sip from her gin and tonic, made just the way she liked it with lots of ice and lime. But she barely tasted it. "Sure, I know that war and crime virtually disappeared with the UFO virus. But maybe mankind was ready for an evolutionary change. You know? Maybe the virus was just the physical manifestation. Ideas come first—then the physical reality. You can't invent something before you have an idea of what you want to invent. Even if somebody accidentally stumbles on a new development, they were looking in the first place—for something."

Libby regarded her daughter with affectionate skepticism. "So what is your point, dear?"

Astrid distractedly pushed her hair out of her face. "Well...I'm not sure exactly. Just that it seems to me more is going on than some random, impersonal genetic change."

"You never did like the idea of randomness, did you?"

"No," Astrid replied shortly. "It seems too lame an explanation for things we don't understand. I don't know. I just have this odd feeling of a connection between myself and Judy. Between her world and ours. The painting this Duncan character put in her office was created by a nineteenth century artist named Bonnard. For all I know her world could be our future if we don't handle this situation right."

"Now there's a sobering thought!" Libby exclaimed, laughing. She reached over and patted her daughter's knee. "Why don't you go take a bath and relax for a while. You seem keyed up, and I don't think the two of us are going to solve the world's problems this afternoon. Your father'll be here soon. He has a special dinner planned for you."

Astrid stretched, then drained her gin and tonic. "You're right. After that plane ride, I could use a long, hot bath."

"I thought so." Libby picked up Astrid's glass and started to leave the room, then paused. "I don't know what to make of this myself, but some group or other claims to have found a dimensional window in New York."

Astrid raised her eyebrows. "Really? In Manhattan?"

Libby shrugged. "I guess so. I didn't pay a lot of attention to it, to tell you the truth. It just seemed rather incredible. They can't pinpoint it, of course. It's not like it's in the back of Zabar's or anything. They say it shimmers in and out of existence."

"Interesting."

"Very!" Libby smiled. "But so far no aliens—or murderers—have been sighted, thank god. There are towels for you hanging up in the bathroom."

"Okay, thanks."

The bathroom, a spacious solarium filled with an effusion of healthy ferns and flowering plants, helped Astrid to feel right at home. The sunken tub resembled a tiny natural pool, fashioned as it was from small, smooth stones. She let the water run until it came almost to the rim, then lowered herself into the steaming water with a deep, heartfelt sigh. She let her gaze travel over the tops of the buildings in the neighborhood, admiring the stonework and brickwork, the copper and bronze adornments, the rooftop gardens and fancifully constructed windmills.

Her parents were lucky that a penthouse had been available when they moved to new York, although quite a few apartments went empty these days. A mass exodus had occurred from the city before the turn of the millennium as a race and class war had broken out. Housing had become all but unaffordable for the poor and middle class, and simmering racial tensions had finally exploded when a psychopathic white supremacist gunned down a group of mixed-race school children during their recess. He claimed retaliation for a string of gang incidents that had snuffed out the lives of several young white women. Then, when the UFO virus struck, what business and commerce still managed to carry on in the midst of guerrilla warfare had come to a standstill. Food had become scarce, heating-oil deliveries had dwindled away, and the boroughs had turned into an eerie, massive ghost town as the remaining residents flocked to nearby farming communities.

When the majority of the Northeastern population recovered, several blocks of buildings in Manhattan and most of the South Bronx had been demolished in order to create high-yield cooperative farms. The widespread lassitude had lasted long enough to destroy the complex, fragile infrastructure that highly urbanized areas had depended on for their sustenance. In the last five years, lots of people had begun to move back into the city, but the population density still hadn't reached even the halfway mark of the last century. Therefore, a great deal more space was available to the present inhabitants, a big improvement, in Astrid's opinion. The tiny cells that New Yorkers called home when she visited relatives during her prep-school years had appalled her, even though Boston wasn't much different.

Suddenly, the image of Judy's cubicle grid super-imposed itself on the building across the street. Astrid gasped and rubbed her eyes. The vision faded. But the uncomfortable feeling it produced did not. Astrid turned around in the tub so that all she faced was a tangle of ferns and moss and began to soap herself. Funny that she should have such a negative reaction to the major's assertion that Judy should maintain her health in order to serve her country best. A similar belief formed the basis for community service in Shasta City.

Certainly, no one could do his or her community any good if they suffered poor health, physical or otherwise. In Astrid's town, this approach truly seemed to promote the good and health of the individual as well as the community. But somehow in Judy's world this same belief seemed a pious mask for the underlying sub-belief that the health of the individual wasn't as important as the common need, that one should take care of oneself as a duty to benefit the community. In Astrid's view, it appeared even to imply that the individual good stood in the way of that of the group and should be denied if one cared about anyone but oneself.

At the same time, somehow this self-sacrifice actually conspired to benefit the few individuals who possessed all the apparent power. Such twisting of ideals—and pragmatic wisdom—was exactly what disturbed her about Louise and Meagan's approach. At least in their case it grew out of the best of intentions, but it was twisted nonetheless. Astrid did not want anyone with distorted ideals determining how she should live. A community is a collection of individuals, she affirmed to herself—and if the individuals who compose the group are not happy and thriving, the group cannot possibly thrive. Dissension and conflict would be inevitable under those borderline conditions, compromise a poor substitute for accord. Then would come dominance by a few in order to maintain a false, temporary harmony, just as before. Then, of course, would come dysfunction and the death of peace and true community. It would be as if the brain decided that the liver or kidneys would have to be sacrificed for the good of the body.

Astrid remained in the tub until the water began to cool. Then, toweling her hair dry, she headed into the guest room. A few of her childhood mementos had been preserved and brought along in the move, and her parents had put them in the room so that she would feel at home whenever she visited. A silkscreen she had made in prep school of a grove of beech trees hung over the neatly made bed, a pinch pot she had squeezed into shape as a small girl squatted on the bedside table next to the lamp. It had stood up rather well over time, she thought, pleased; the shape held a primitive, unselfconscious appeal. The coppery raku glaze had turned out well, too.

She appreciated these small touches on the part of her parents, since they both knew that her visits East would be infrequent. She had never felt at home in Boston. When she went to the West Coast to look for a university, she immediately felt that she had discovered her spiritual niche. During prep school, her East Coast friends had constantly teased her about her fascination with psychic phenomena, not always in a kind or charitable way, and even though now everyone possessed some psychic abilities, the people on the West Coast felt more comfortable with these new talents and put them to use more often and with more faith.

Tired from her journey, Astrid decided to rest before dinner; so she stretched out on the bed until she heard her father's voice in the hall. She got along well with her mother, who had always allowed Astrid to express herself however she wanted, even during difficult periods, but she possessed a special fondness for her father. It was his height that she had inherited, and his coloring, which derived from a combination of Irish, Welsh, and Sicilian ancestors. She bounded in to greet him, feeling a bit like a large, friendly dog, and he grabbed her up in an enthusiastic hug.

"Astrid, my girl, you'll never guess what I brought home for dinner!" he exclaimed.

Astrid put a finger to her lips in mock concentration. "Lobsters!" she replied with a grin.

He clapped his hand to his forehead. "I keep forgetting we're all telepathic now. No keeping secrets any more."

Astrid laughed. "I don't have to be telepathic to know you brought home lobsters, Dad." Her father had been one of the biologists who finally managed to grow lobsters in the lab through genetic engineering. All attempts to raise them in the past had met with failure since *Homarus americanus* possessed a wide-ranging migratory life cycle, part of which had never been documented or well understood. His group had short-circuited this part of the life cycle, spliced over it in a manner of speaking, so that a new, nonmigratory species resulted. Fortunately, this new lobster possessed all the delicacy of texture and flavor that the old species had possessed, and the original creatures were now left to roam and multiply in peace.

Arthur put his arm around his daughter and led her into the kitchen. "Has your mother told you about her new series of photographs?" he asked.

Astrid shook her head. "Actually, we haven't gotten around to it yet. There've been some weird new developments in the Mt. Shasta area, Dad. Some ugly new developments. That's what we've been talking about mostly."

His forehead creased in concern. "You don't say. You'll have to tell me all about it over dinner."

All three participated in putting the evening meal together. In addition to the lobsters, they fixed a hearts-of-palm salad (a special treat, as most imports had only recently resumed), light buttery popovers, and an assortment of sauteed vegetables garnered from the building's rooftop greenhouse. All the changes that Astrid had observed so far in New York seemed to her very positive ones, combining to make the city much more pleasant and livable—from the electricity-generating windmills on the tops of buildings to the demolition of several ugly black monolithic buildings for high-yield microfarming to the profusion of rooftop gardens, greenhouses, and window boxes spilling over with fresh herbs, produce and flowers. All the new plant life kept the air much cleaner and sweeter, and Astrid felt it probably also conspired to keep the vibrations in the city calmer and more peaceful. She believed that humans needed plants for more than sustenance and oxygenation —they soothed people's psyches as well.

She filled her father in on the events in Shasta City as they prepared their meal. And when they sat down to dinner, she finished up, feeling depressed all over again. Arthur wiped his mustache with his napkin and cleared his throat.

"You know," he said, "if you and Nate want to have a child, you could move here. There's no reason to let a bunch of wild-eyed hysterics keep you from doing what you want to do."

Astrid toyed with her salad, not wanting to meet his earnest gaze. "I've thought about that, Dad, but I really don't want to leave. We built our house with our own hands, all our friends are there...And I know you never thought a government without formal laws would work, but it's really important for me to make it work. If people like me leave and people like Meagan and Sharon take over, then it will fail. It'll be worse than a democracy."

Arthur and Libby exchanged amused glances.

"I hardly think a democracy is all that bad, honey," said Libby.

Astrid rested her chin on her hands. "I know you don't think so. The tyranny of the majority suits you now because you're in the majority. You never had people make fun of you and pick on you because your beliefs were radically different from the norm. But if what you are and what you want never matches up with the majority, then you might as well be living in a dictatorship as far as I'm concerned. I felt really comfortable in Shasta City until just recently. I don't understand why this is all happening."

Her father sighed. "I'm afraid that what's happening is a classic danger of an anarchistic system, sweetheart. Mob rule, vigilantism…It's exactly those kinds of things that cause people like us to opt for a government so those dangers are held in check. A formal government mitigates change so it doesn't happen too fast."

"Like the government prevented the changes from the UFO virus, right?"

"Well, that's different, of course."

Astrid shook her head. "I think change happens when conditions are ripe, government or no government. Look at what happened in Eastern Europe in the 1990s. But aside from all that, I also feel another responsibility. If I left Shasta City they might go on and tinker with the dimensional window, and for some reason, that possibility just fills me with an awful feeling."

"That's a very abstract thing you're talking about, Astrid," said her mother. "Has anyone even proved without a doubt that these dimensional windows exist?"

"Not directly with hard measurements. But a lot of people who are sensitive to electromagnetic fields definitely sense something. People in the vicinity of them often disappear."

"But could tinkering with them really do a lot of harm?" asked her father. "The magnetosphere is a pretty big entity."

"Yeah, right. So's the biosphere and look what we did to it."

"Hmm…you have a point there." Arthur picked up a lobster claw and gave it a vigorous crack. A thin stream of juice squirted out right into Libby's face.

"Good shot," she quipped, laughing, while her husband apologized, red-faced, and hurriedly mopped her cheek with his napkin. "I guess I'm lucky it wasn't that green stuff."

Astrid laughed, too, and for a moment the seriousness of the mood lightened. But their levity shattered in seconds as the quiet Manhattan evening was sundered by a heart-stopping, stupefying, blood-curdling scream.

SIXTEEN

Judy attached her shower hose to the faucet and stepped into her plastic basin, still positively glowing from the dream she had last night. No, she decided, it was more of a vision, as if she had glimpsed what her world could be if lots of things were different. It must have been inspired by the painting, she contemplated as she reached over and turned on the water—cold only—quickly wet herself down and soaped. In fact, it seemed like she had visited the world of the painting; everything had glowed and pulsed with such vivid, mouth-watering, entrancing color. There had been grids like hers, except they were beautiful—and every one of them different! Luscious, vibrant, exotic plants had been growing everywhere—in flower boxes, from hanging pots, on the tops of buildings and along the streets—exuding an intoxicating fragrance. It really felt almost as if she'd gone there; her whole being tingled with a sense of well-being she'd never experienced before.

So enthralled did she feel, Judy stood dreamily in her wash basin for several minutes before realizing that she was shivering and covered with harsh soap that was gradually eating its way into her allergic skin. Sometimes she wondered if the Right Hand of God devised the formula for soap; next thing she knew, hair shirts would become regulationwear. Probably, though, it was merely an economic thing: no doubt milder soaps cost more to produce and therefore the middle class couldn't afford them. No point in producing them if no one could buy them. She hastily rinsed off, shivering even more in the fresh blast of cold water, trying her best to keep from flinging or spilling drops onto the floor. But much to her frustration, the carpet always smelled a little mildewed no matter how much care she took in her bathing.

After she'd cleaned up and dumped the soiled water into the sink, she wedged herself into the cramped alcove which housed a chemical toilet. She always held her breath while relieving herself, since the combined smell and toxic quality of the cleansing fluid proved enough to practically knock her out every time she used it. While she sat, she realized, with a jolt, that the punk had appeared in this dream, too. Seemed like he lived in a cubicle—except that it was huge and absolutely gorgeous. Yes! He *was* in the dream, she felt sure of it.

She stood up, intrigued and amused. She must be getting pretty desperate if she was fantasizing about a punk all the time, someone who'd just as soon jam a spike through her as give her the time of day. But maybe— maybe she was dreaming about the rich; perhaps she was somehow glimpsing the way they lived. She'd seen simulated interiors of wealthy people's living quarters on television, but never the exteriors. It made sense that they would look like what she had dreamed. And that punk— perhaps he was an eccentric, bored sort who got his kicks from hanging out and doing bizarre, even good Samaritan- type things in the cubicle grids and unwalled parts of the urban areas. He didn't have that repulsive, slimy fungal infection from the sewers.

One thing didn't fit, though. This place she dreamed about—it didn't feel rife with the petty squabbling, ugly rivalry and unprincipled greed that the rich, at least on the TV shows, seemed to suffer from incurably. It just felt absolutely, marvelously, almost unbearably wonderful.

Which meant, probably, she thought with a sigh as she flushed distastefully, that it didn't exist, except in a dream. And she hadn't slept with anyone in so long—she certainly didn't count her rape, that's for sure—that she was having fantasies about one of the few people who had been nice to her. She couldn't deny that he was dazzlingly good-looking.

She dressed as smartly as she could in her new uniform (with her shape, she lamented, it wasn't easy), hoping that the blotches on her skin from leaving the soap on too long would go away before she got to work. She knew it to be hopeless and even ludicrous, but she wanted to appear as attractive as possible to Major Duncan. Then she gobbled down a bowl of food powder, slipping a packet into her purse for lunch, finding that, strangely, the stuff tasted better than usual. Perhaps a new batch?

Unhappily, though, her fresh, new-found feeling of well-being dissipated as she walked to work. She struggled for breath and her heart almost went into fibrillation before she reached the MI Complex. She had to walk a few extra blocks to her new job—that could be the problem, she wheezed to herself before gratefully reaching the conveyor belt and being whisked inside the complex. She stood still and rested as she was borne along, drew in great gulps of air, and by the time she arrived at her office she felt a little better. Was her respiratory and vascular state deteriorating, she wondered anxiously, right when things had started to go well for a change?

She collapsed into her chair and shakily tried to compose herself before greeting Major Duncan. He strode in, however, as if activated by her presence. When he caught a glimpse of her, his eyebrows lifted in alarm. He dashed over to a closet and whipped out some oxygen equipment, returning in a flash to press the mask urgently and firmly to her face. Then he fiddled with the knobs on the tank while he cradled her head in the crook of his arm. Judy felt faint, but whether from her physical condition, the oxygen, or the embrace—however inadvertent—of Major Duncan, she wasn't sure. She closed her eyes. Explosions of color drenched the insides of her lids.

When she came to, she found herself modestly arranged on the floor, Major Duncan's coat cushioning her head, a comfortable and revivifying concentration of oxygen flowing through the mask into her lungs. She gradually felt her strength return, and she sat up and looked around the room. It was empty. She took off the mask and extinguished the flow, then tiptoed over to peek into Major Duncan's office. She apparently caught him by surprise, for he instantly and reflexively covered up what he had been reading when he saw her. He scrutinized her so searchingly that she trembled. Had she done something wrong? Was he going to fire her?

"I'm—sorry if I disturbed you, sir. I just wanted to let you know that I'm okay now and to thank you for your help."

"Come in."

She obediently stepped forward.

"Close the door behind you."

She did so, a bit uncomfortably.

"Judy, did I make it absolutely clear to you yesterday where your loyalties lie here?"

"Oh, yes, sir. To you, sir."

"And are you completely comfortable with that?" His blue eyes, which seemed eerily colorless just now, glinted from the lamp on his desk.

"Yes, sir. Absolutely, sir. I—I would do anything for you, sir," she blurted, her face flushing.

"Good. I don't have to tell you that anything you read, see, or hear in this office goes no farther than this office."

"Oh, no, sir. I understand that, sir."

"Excellent. By the way, that was a very interesting report on phytoplankton submitted yesterday. Keep up the good work."

"I will, sir. Thank you, sir."

"Dismissed."

She turned to go.

"Oh—one more thing."

"Yes, sir?"

"I've hung an oxygen mask on your door, which you're to use when walking to and from work."

"Thank you, sir!"

"Close the door when you leave. I don't wish to be disturbed for the next two hours."

She saluted—smartly, she hoped—and did as he bid her. Back in her own office, she scooped up his coat, resisting the impulse to bury her face in it and inhale his scent. He might be watching her. She hung it up on the door beside her oxygen mask, and then turned to look at the painting before commencing work. Today the colors seemed to burn into her brain, to brand her with their very intensity.

She worked through reams of data regarding the composition of the atmosphere, a time-consuming task, since so many different compounds constituted significant proportions. Oxygen and nitrogen had dwindled from a historic level of 20% and 78%, to 16% and 70%, respectively. Sulfuric dioxide, carbon dioxide, and carbon monoxide together comprised a hefty five percent, biologically speaking. Good Lord, she thought, no wonder she was having trouble breathing! She was probably having more trouble than the majority of the population, given her congenital weaknesses, but if present trends continued at the same rate, it would certainly seem that soon everyone would start dropping like flies.

Yesterday she had learned all about phytoplankton. She discovered that they were microscopic, single-celled plants that inhabited the oceans. Her computer constructed three-dimensional representations of each of the species for which she logged data: location, density per cubic centimeter of ocean water, physiological requirements and photobiological needs, reproduction rate, and numbers of predators. Many of them constructed elaborate geometric skeletons from silica, intriguingly shaped, fanciful boxes in which the creatures zooted around, using streams of water pumped through specially constructed skeletal channels as a locomotion device. She found this awesomely fascinating. Touching, even.

And apparently, although she couldn't see this since her computer possessed only a gray-and-white screen, they arrayed themselves in a full spectrum of colorful hues. Many phosphoresced at night as well. What delightful beings, she had thought excitedly the whole time she plowed through the laborious data files—how wonderful that they even existed! Their historic predators, the baleen whales, had become extinct, so the plants had enjoyed quite a surge in population since then. Until just recently— Judy had noticed a slight dip in the numbers of most species.

Today's information definitely didn't prove such a delight. Nevertheless, she worked diligently for five straight hours before even leaning back wearily in her seat—not nearly so uncomfortable as the one she had occupied at Sunshine, although corporations and businesses had succeeded in passing legislation that dictated the existence of a hard, knotty protuberance somewhere on all seats in order to prod the occupant into safe alertness—to avoid litigation. She realized, then, that Major Duncan had not opened his door the whole time she had been working. Was he all right?

She feared interrupting or bothering him, but at the same time a protective devotion stirred her heart. He could have had a heart attack or something. Once again she tiptoed to the door, but she listened this time. The door whipped open so fast that she sprawled clumsily into

Major Duncan's office. A faint acrid odor stung her nostrils as she scrambled to her feet. Sulfur?

"Yes?" he asked coldly.

"I was just checking on you, sir," she babbled nervously. "You said two hours and it has been five. Sir."

"Next time, use the phone."

"I will, sir. It was stupid of me, sir."

"Do you have something for me?"

"I do. At least, I will in a few more minutes."

"Have you eaten?"

"Why, no, sir—that is, not yet."

"Eat before you finish the report."

"Aye, sir." Judy spun on her heel, a little too vigorously, and ended up not quite facing the proper direction. She bumbled into her office and extracted her food-powder packet from her purse with shaking hands. Darn, she didn't have a bowl and spoon here—she'd forgotten and left her extra set at the waste-treatment company. What should she do? Major Duncan had ordered her to eat, but she was afraid to be so bold as to ask him for eating utensils. In the end, she tore off a small corner of the package and tipped back her head as she poured small amounts onto her tongue and attempted to mix the powder with her saliva.

Suddenly Major Duncan loomed in the doorway. "What are you doing?" he demanded.

Judy choked on her last bite and squirted powder all over her face in a futile effort to hide her activity. "Eating, sir," she said, snapping to attention.

"I hardly call that eating. Don't you have a bowl and spoon?"

Tears pricked at Judy's eyes. "Not yet."

He sighed. "I'll get you one from the dispensary. On second thought—I'll order you something from the mess hall."

"Oh—that's not necessary, sir, thank you all the same," Judy protested.

"I'm perfectly aware that it's not necessary."

"Yes, sir. Sorry, sir."

"Now—which would you rather have, ham loaf or chicken loaf?"

Anticipatory saliva flooded into her mouth with a painful rush. "Chicken loaf, please," she murmured reverentially.

He gave a curt nod and dialed the mess hall from her phone. When the food came—complete with instant mashed potatoes and tinned gravy!—she had to use every ounce of self-control she possessed not to gobble it down like a garbage truck. She ate every bite, although she wasn't used to such generous portions and her stomach ached. Then she finished up her report and handed it in to Major Duncan. His face darkened when he saw it.

"Thank you, Judy. You may go home now. And take your oxygen mask with you."

"Sir? It's a little early, sir. I could start something else."

"I told you to go home. I want that order obeyed."

"Yes, sir," she barked, twirling around with a little better aim this time and charging out the door with enthusiasm to show him that she wasn't questioning his orders.

He certainly was a strange man, she reflected, as she shut down her computer and gathered up her things to go. He sure liked to give the impression that he was hard-hearted and went strictly by the books, but she'd never known anyone to look after her so well. She licked her lips, thinking about her tasty meal.

On her way home, she decided to stop by Dorothy's shop to see whether perhaps she had a nice plastic barrette among all that other junk. It would be splurging to buy such a frivolous item, but she felt like doing something frivolous. When she reached the shop, however, she found it closed, even though it was still light outside. The bar across the street caught her eye and she ambled over and peered in. Didn't look *too* bad. She signed the customary legal waiver upon entering, then sauntered over to the dark and dingy bar. She perched herself on the bar stool—shifting to find the least irritating spot upon which to flatten her bottom—and ordered a draft beer. The bartender, an odd-looking man who had an extra, distracting set of lips embedded in his left cheek, nodded and served up a thin, sour, tepid brew with only the barest scum of a head floating on top.

"That'll be twenty-five dollars," he said.

Judy took out her bank card nonchalantly, although she hadn't realized that beer had gone up another five dollars, it had been so long since she'd had one. Probably another sin tax or a spectacular lawsuit that had managed to circumvent the waiver. She hadn't been watching enough television lately.

As her eyes grew accustomed to the darkness, she realized that one of the other patrons huddled over the shadowy bar was Dorothy. But since Dorothy wasn't acknowledging her presence, Judy decided against greeting her. Judy had just put her glass to her lips when a horrid, ear-splitting scream pierced the very walls and practically shattered the window. Everyone rushed to the door in time to see a woman returning from work being dragged off by a gang member. He'd already knifed her once, and blood streamed onto the sidewalk as he hefted her onto a small dumpster and began the grisly process of raping her.

Judy wanted to help the woman, but she knew that no one else would come to her aid and she would only succeed in giving the punk a second body to desecrate and destroy. She had no weapon.

She turned away, sick at heart, although everyone else stayed glued to the door, even, presumably, throughout the part where the serious slashing began. After that one first surprised shriek, the woman remained quiet and passive. More screams might bring on increased torture by more gang members and besides, drudges were trained to submit. What was the use in fighting? Everyone else had all the power.

Judy remembered her little pledge to herself to confound the powers-that-be after she had stumbled across her cache of contraceptives and smiled ruefully, embarrassed. What could have made her think that? She picked up her beer and downed it in one long, gurgling swallow. She wiped her mouth and shivered. Did she feel any better? She didn't think so.

All of sudden she found herself weeping, blubbering, crying out of control for that poor woman on the street, for all the people who'd been murdered, for the people watching and not helping, for her mean, hopeless, hardened world. Much to her surprise, she felt a hand rest upon her shoulder. She looked up to find Dorothy's rodent face peering down at her in sympathy.

"Hey, that's life, kid," she said.

"But *why* is that life?" Judy demanded, her lips rubbery from grief. "That's not life—that's death! And a horrible one at that!"

Dorothy sighed. "Yeah, you're right. But what can we do?"

"I don't know," Judy sobbed. "I don't know."

Dorothy shifted uncomfortably. "Ah, buck up, now. Come on. I'll buy you another beer."

Judy regarded her, astonished. "Can you afford that?"

"Nah, not really. But what the fuck, right? Albert owes me one anyway, don't you, Albie?"

The bartender nodded, rather stonily, it seemed to Judy. Nevertheless, he served up two more drafts.

Dorothy held up her glass and clinked it into Judy's. "Here's to life, shitty as it is."

Judy didn't exactly relish that toast, but she drank down the beer. She thought she felt a lot better after the second one. However, daylight was beginning to wane, so she stood up to go, unsteadily. Thanking Dorothy for her kindness, she started for the door, then realized that the gang member—or another one just like him—could still be out there. She became paralyzed with fear, and her feet refused to budge. A whimper escaped her lips.

Dorothy drained her glass and jumped up. "Hey, Judy! Wait up and I'll walk you home."

Judy gaped at her. "You'd—really do that?"

"Sure! Come on."

"But—what about you? Then you'll have to go home alone."

"Huh! Those gangs know better than to fuck with me."

Judy didn't know what made Dorothy so fearless, but she decided to accept her offer. How peculiar that someone else was treating her kindly. Was this her lucky week or something? Maybe God did exist? A different one, that is, from Their god. Her own god. One who looked after her and cared about her.

"Don't look!" Dorothy admonished, shielding Judy's gaze from what was left of the murdered woman as they stepped outside. "Hey, what do you say to joining me for dinner?"

"Why, sure! Thank you!" Judy exclaimed, completely bowled over.

"Don't thank me before you see what we're having," Dorothy chuckled, steering her around the piles of trash that dotted the street like an obstacle course.

"Food powder?"

Dorothy stuck her fingers down her throat and pretended to gag. "You kidding? I wouldn't eat that stuff if you paid me. Well, depends on how much, I guess. Nah, I've got some K rations. And some dog food. Fucking guard dogs eat better than the middle class." Dorothy halted in front of her place and pulled out a key ring bristling with keys. She fiddled impatiently with the myriad locks and chains that barred the door.

"Where do you get these food items?" Judy asked, blinking in the musty gloom of the shop as they crossed the threshold.

"Black market. I trade for them." She kicked a plastic dish out of the way and it went skittering into a rubbishy heap of tattered lampshades. Who had lamps, Judy wondered, that they would want shades? "Okay, where did I put all the stuff? Oh, yeah—here it is." Dorothy ransacked an ancient, dented file cabinet. "Ta da!" She held up the K rations and dog food with a flourish. "Let's see, now, where'd I put the can opener?"

Judy watched in fascination as Dorothy rooted about her piles of junk and set up a little feast on the lid of an old, beat-to-shit suitcase. She couldn't believe that she, a cubicle-dwelling technodrudge, was sitting in this wild shop getting ready to dine with one of the most unconventional segments of society.

"Dorothy?"

Dorothy gave a small grunt, carefully placing a fork and spoon at each place.

"Have you ever been out of the city?"

Dorothy rocked back on her heels and shot Judy a sharp, appraising glance. "Yeah. Why?"

"Well, I—I just wondered. I wondered what it was like other places."

"Depends on where you go. A lot of places look just like this. No different. Now, the survivalist camps aren't like here 'cause they all live underground, like termites. You won't find any cubicle grids in one of those camps. And there's stuff growing there, too—food plants real close and handy. I wouldn't want to live there, though. Those survivalists are really uptight. Now, the government farms are kind of pretty, actually—pretty little bunches of leaves all growing in rows."

Judy tried to imagine what a survivalist camp or a farm would look like. They were never shown on TV. She found it surprising, actually, that the government allowed survivalist camps to exist, but most of them were religious in organization, and as such, must have had some sort of exemption from normal civil status, like the Right

Hand of God. "What about the ocean?" she asked. "Have you ever seen that?"

Dorothy shook her head. "Can't say that I have. There's a big wall around it, you know."

"Yes, I know." Judy fell silent. Then inquired, eagerly, "How...how did you get to these places?"

But her question produced a tangible barrier. The shopkeeper turned her back as she fussed with the dog-food cans, sliding the contents onto the plates with a sucking plop so that they stood up in quivering cylinders.

"Oh, I have ways," she finally responded coolly, lips set thin and flat. "You planning on going somewhere?"

Flustered, Judy shrank down onto an overturned bucket and clasped her hands between her knees. "No—of course not. I just wondered, since, you know, there aren't any buses or anything. Do you have a car?"

"Nope. Well, I guess everything's ready." Dorothy rubbed her hands together in anticipatory satisfaction. "You hungry?"

Judy nodded and struggled to her feet, burning with curiosity; but, clearly, Dorothy wasn't giving out any more information.

"Might as well bring your seat," she said, though, pleasantly enough.

Judy stooped over to grab the bucket, and as she did so her eye fell upon a tattered paperback. She seized it greedily.

"A book!" she exclaimed in delight.

"Oh yeah? What book?"

Judy brushed the dust from the cover. "It says, 'Developing Your Psychic Powers.'"

"So that's where it got to," Dorothy muttered. "Bring it over here, will you?"

Judy walked over and placed it on the suitcase next to Dorothy. Since Dorothy seemed disinclined to talk any more, Judy said nothing until they'd polished off the dog food and K rations and washed it all down with bug juice.

("Really high in protein," Dorothy remarked.) After the meal, Dorothy offered her a plastic toothpick that looked rather grubby, in Judy's opinion, but she accepted it anyway, in the spirit of camaraderie. She decided to approach Dorothy again.

"So, Dorothy," Judy began.

"Yeah?" she growled, immediately suspicious.

"Do you—well, that is, could you believe in psychic powers?" Judy stammered nervously. "You don't think they're powers of the Devil?"

Dorothy snorted. "Powers of the Devil! Do you know what I consider to be the powers of the Devil?"

Judy shook her head.

"The fucking ass-backwards repressive church, that's who! And that goddamned military which thinks nothing of wasting millions of people in the name of so-called right! If they're the good guys I'd rather consort with the Devil, that's for damn sure."

Judy paled at hearing this heresy. And yet, it rang true. She had never quite understood why her country was right when as far as she could tell, it used all the same tactics that its enemies did.

"Take the book home! Take it and read it—see if you think it's from the Devil."

"Oh, no." Judy blushed. "No, I couldn't!"

"Why not?"

"I—well—I should pay you for it, shouldn't I?"

"It's not for sale."

"Oh."

"But take the fucking thing. You're not going to get arrested, for God's sake."

"This isn't—seditious literature?"

"Are you kidding? The government doesn't take that shit seriously enough to consider it seditious. Anybody who believes in that stuff is soft in the head as far as they're concerned."

"But—what about the Right Hand of God?"

"Oh yeah. I forgot about them. Better not let them catch you with it."

Judy turned to go, leaving the book lying on the suitcase. "Wait! Wait, for Chrissakes," Dorothy protested. "I'll walk you home. I'll carry the book, okay? And if we get stopped by the Fundies, they'll haul me in, okay?"

"But—I wouldn't want that to happen, either," Judy squeaked.

"Don't worry!" Dorothy insisted, standing up and tucking the book under her arm. "Everything's gonna be fine." She gripped Judy's hand under her other arm and gave a sharp nod.

When the two reached Judy's apartment grid, Judy invited Dorothy up (for what, she didn't know—a glass of water? a bowl of food powder?) but Dorothy declined, explaining that cubicles gave her the creeps. She thrust the book into Judy's hands and took off.

Interestingly, when Judy turned to say one last goodbye after unlocking the grid door, she noticed that Dorothy was heading in the opposite direction from her shop. Even more strangely, the way the mercury-vapor lamp illuminated her figure, it made her seem as if she trod the air a few inches above the sidewalk. Judy rubbed her eyes, which were obviously overtired, and slipped quickly inside. She didn't want anyone to see her with the book. Although now that she had it, she couldn't wait to take a peek.

SEVENTEEN

Astrid skated briskly down Park Avenue, trying her best to keep from glancing over her shoulder every three seconds in fear of the elusive Uptown Slasher. He'd not likely attack a roller-blading person, she had tried to convince herself as she set off for the convention early this morning, after a night of jumbled nightmares triggered by last evening's incident. Goaded by that terrible scream, every occupant on the block had poured into the street to come to the person's aid. They found a woman sprawled bleeding and unconscious and five traumatized, bewildered passersby who had tried to catch the assailant but failed.

"I don't even know where the attacker came from," one man said, in complete shock. "It was as if he suddenly materialized."

"And we couldn't hold him, either!" added a woman who was even bigger than Astrid and who looked perfectly capable of holding onto anyone she had a mind to. "It was as if he was covered in oil. He just—slithered out of all our grasp."

"And cut a few of us in the process!" exclaimed a teenager, pale, wide-eyed, blood dripping from a cut on his hand.

However, only the woman attacked from behind had suffered any serious injury. Luckily, a health hospice was located just a block away. An ambulance showed up within minutes of the incident and took the victim to a care facility, while one of the healers stayed and tended to the more superficial wounds of the others. Astrid had watched the proceedings with sick, shaky horror and could not take her eyes off the injured woman until she was finally borne away. Astrid had never seen so much blood, even though several people had been trying desperately to stanch the flow before the health-care workers arrived. She couldn't believe the human body could contain so much blood, let alone lose that much and still live.

And that scream! Astrid couldn't rid herself of the sound of it. She must have listened to it fifty times over in her dreams. Even now it echoed in her ears, louder than the smooth, tearing roll of moving skates, louder than the sibilant swoosh of the solar/electric buses and occasional taxis, louder than the murmur of conversation.

But when she came to Ninety-second Street, she halted, and finally the scream stopped, too. Astrid loved the view that swept down Park Avenue all the way to Grand Central Station and beyond; now it was even better than before. A massive, black, blockish building used to lurk behind the train station, spoiling the view. It was one of the graceless monoliths that had been dismantled—sacrificed for recycled materials and inner city farmland.

She could see only one new building nearing completion in Midtown, a light, airy, soaring structure, built from shimmering glass and smoothly sculpted marble. New construction had resumed only recently, and then very slowly. For the longest time after the epidemic, only the necessities, activities that related directly to sustaining life such as producing food, distributing energy sources, and providing shelter and clean water, had labor available to them.

Fortunately, not everyone had succumbed to the illness at once. There always existed enough people either recovering or waiting to exhibit symptoms for the population to remain more or less stable, although the effect of relatively sparse numbers of three- to ten-year-olds had yet to be felt reproductively, and the world population was decreasing already. The twentieth century had generated so much stuff that North America had subsisted quite well once extensive and well-organized recycling efforts got under way. Americans had enough surplus so that, even during the height of the epidemic, they were able to distribute goods to other parts of the world in need.

A peculiar disease and not entirely unpleasant, in Astrid's experience. The major negative side-effect consisted of feeling so tired she could barely lift her head from the pillow to sip a drink of water. But she never felt feverish or achy, like with the flu, and there was no cough or sinus infection. In fact, she cherished one wonderful side-effect, which was that it stimulated dreaming to an incredible degree.

Actually, when she thought about the content of her dreams, it seemed understandable that she felt so tired. At first she dreamed that she swam endlessly in a soft, vast ocean, an ocean so astonishingly clear that she could see all the way down to the mountains that loomed in the depths, an ocean filled with great clouds of squid, pods of whales, and fragile, crystal-globed coelenterates. Then she dreamed that she, and others, were building an ancient city, as if in ancient Egypt, or a Mayan civilization. Rich plant life crowded around the buildings, and the structures gleamed with a dazzling golden glow. She almost felt sorry when she finally recovered. The enchanted city beckoned so lusciously, so powerfully, and after she recovered, her dreams muted a bit, seeming not quite so vivid and startlingly real in recall; but they remained greatly enhanced.

On the other hand, the newly enhanced psychic abilities that developed after her recovery had taken some getting used to. When her increased telepathy first manifested, she had experienced it as a welter of confused emotions that *she* was feeling. It took awhile to sort out other people's emotions, almost as if by scent—each person's unique energy emanations carried a distinctive tang that Astrid could never really put into words. Then she had to learn to screen them, shut them out when necessary, availing herself of them only when she wanted to, as she had done with sound in the past.

The telekinetic abilities also required considerable training and assimilating, even though she had exhibited some minor poltergeistic phenomena during her adolescence. Even now, the ability scared her a little—she had seen enough horror movies during her youth to associate a dread and creepy sort of feeling with invisible forms of power. Responding quickly and adaptively to the situation, however, Humboldt University had organized a new branch of psychic arts and sciences in order to help their students cope with their new traits. It helped a lot, and after a while Astrid didn't think that her life felt much different, really, except that her impressions and sensations seemed richer and deeper, and nuances stood out in greater relief.

Astrid waited at Ninety-second Street through three lights before starting up again, weaving considerably through the other skaters and pedestrians on the sidewalk. Traffic in Manhattan had become much, much lighter than the last time she had visited here, and it pleased her to see that the space allowed more room for bicycles and roller bladers. Manhattan was so flat and well paved that skates made perfect sense. The pace seemed just right, too, for getting around most of the island, and reasonable rental places had sprung up all over, just as video stores had done before the turn of the century. In addition, the streets and sidewalks gleamed with cleanliness. Years before, she had never liked to look down at the pavement in New York for fear of what she might see. It was only dread of what she might step in that drew her unwilling gaze to rest upon particularly repulsive globs of spit, fluorescent dog shit, and other stomach-turning visual horrors that she preferred not to identify. Now she could skate along, completely at ease. That is, she could if the slasher hadn't destroyed her peace of mind.

Astrid passed a pastry shop along her way and stopped to pick up a warm cheese danish; then she ducked into the produce market next door and selected a fresh, ripe peach. She nibbled as she skated, thoughtfully considering Judy's two revolting meals that the poor thing had found so exciting. Interesting that Dorothy was giving her books on psychic power. Perhaps some avenue for action might lie in that direction. One person she certainly planned to keep an eye on was that fishy Major Duncan. She didn't trust that man. Obviously, he was intentionally building up a fanatical trust in Judy. But to what purpose? Nobody in that world was nice to anyone else unless some ulterior motive lurked. Maybe he had a coup in mind and wanted to use Judy as some sort of sacrificial pawn. Maybe he was a Satanist. Astrid wished fervently that she could see into his mind, watch his actions in private. But so far, she could apparently enter into only Judy's thoughts.

Astrid didn't have the same feelings of distrust for Dorothy's kindness as she did for Major Duncan's, but that was only understandable, she thought. That fascist Major Duncan had something up his sleeve, some hidden agenda. He'd just better not make the mistake of trying to take advantage of Judy, Astrid asserted to herself, licking peach juice off her fingers and dropping the pit into a bio-can along her way, her napkin into a paper recycling bin. He doesn't know he'll be dealing with two of us.

Thirsty after her cheese danish, Astrid breezed into a dairy bar that occupied a spot on the ground floor of the Chanin Building and drank a large glass of cold milk.

Then she took off her skates and changed into her boots, heading over to the elevator bank.

While waiting for the next available elevator, Astrid's eyes traveled around the lobby, a classic, well preserved Art Deco design. The polished granite floor contained inlaid brass medallions, the elevator doors were faced with bronze bas-relief. Moss-green marble wainscoted the walls and wrought brass trim ran around doors and shop windows. Even the stylized, frosted glass and bronze lights that flashed on to indicate the next car struck a pleasing and whimsical note. The civilized beauty of it all conspired to soothe and calm her, so when she stepped into the elevator she sighed with relief.

Strolling into the suite of rooms hosting the convention, she brightened even more when she spotted an old friend. Milo had grown up in Brooklyn, but Astrid had met him as her math tutor her freshman year at Humboldt State. Even though Milo was a good deal shorter than Astrid and even charitable friends described his nose as a beak, he nonetheless exuded tremendous sex appeal, which, she felt, derived from an ingenuous and appealing appreciation for women. The two had eventually become lovers until they went separate ways after Astrid's graduation. Astrid wanted to be part of a genetic engineering lab, and Milo had always wanted to fly medical rescue planes in Alaska. They parted on extremely amicable terms, but had gradually lost track of each other. To run into him here was a terrific, unexpected bonus.

"Milo!" she cried with delight, making her way across the crowded room filled with schmoozing geneticists. "What are you doing here?" she asked, as soon as she reached him.

Milo's face lit up when he turned and caught sight of her. "Astrid! My god, what a surprise!" he beamed. They hugged enthusiastically. "Hey, I could ask you the same thing."

Astrid shrugged, puckering her face into a grimace. "It's a long story. I'll tell you about it later. I guess you could say I'm visiting my parents."

"Libby and Arthur live here now? I didn't know that. I'll have to look them up." Milo possessed a strong Brooklyn accent, which Astrid found endearing and charming. She had no accent, since her mother was a transplanted Midwesterner.

"You should, they'd love it." Astrid reached over and touched her fingertips to his face. Milo caught her hand and smiled at her. "I can't believe you're here!" she said. "Since when did you become a geneticist? Last time I saw you, you were going to be a pilot in Alaska."

"I was. But then when I was picking up people for rescue, I started wanting to do more for them than just fly them somewhere. You know? And hey, my mother always wanted me to be a surgeon. I figured I would be good at it—which it turns out I am. I got into NYU's medical school and did my residency here. I ended up in genetics through surgery. The thing is, if you can stimulate a person's own body to do something for a problem, it's going to be a lot more effective than doing something from the outside."

"I've always thought so," Astrid agreed.

"So I've become obsessed with finding out how our genes are read—what decides which ones will be transcribed and when, how often, all that sort of thing."

"Are you getting anywhere?" Astrid asked, interested.

Milo lowered his voice. "I'm giving a paper today. I've gotten some amazing results. I think the electromagnetic fields of our brains and bodies have a direct effect on how our chromosomes are read."

"Hmm...sounds entirely plausible to me," she said. "But what will our august colleagues say?"

Milo laughed. "I'm getting ready to find out. But listen—what's going on with you? Are you still living in Northern California?"

Astrid nodded. "It's been great. We started that lab I was always talking about. It's been a big success—we came up with that fiber Woolex—"

"No kidding!" Milo interrupted, obviously impressed. "Everything I own is made of Woolex!"

Astrid smiled, pleased. "Yeah, it's really taken off. We're working on meat substitutes now. Not your cup of tea, I would think."

Milo shook his head. He had occasionally taken time off at Humboldt to go hunting, either with a spear or a bow and arrow. To Astrid, this had seemed an odd pastime for a native of one of New York's boroughs, but perhaps it provided some sort of balance for him.

"Do you still hunt?" she asked.

"Oh, yeah."

She found it interesting that the effects of the UFO virus hadn't caused a demise in hunting, which seemed to indicate that hunting and violence were not genetically related. "Actually, though," Astrid continued, "I'm not working at GenFarm any more."

"Oh yeah? Why is that?"

Astrid sighed heavily. "That's part of the long story." Briefly, she filled him in on the situation. She told Milo about the reproductive ban, the murders, the mood she felt developing in the area. She told him about the dreams, the theories about the dimensional conduits, and about Cedric's proposal. When she mentioned Cedric's name, Milo started. Astrid asked whether he knew him.

Milo glanced at his watch and then laid his hand on her arm. "I know of him, you delicious strapping prize example of womanhood." Astrid chuckled at his flattery. "And I want to tell you something about him, too. But I've got to go give my slides to the projectionist for my talk. I'm on in half an hour."

"Hey—great. I want to hear you speak, of course. I'll come along and we can go out for lunch after—we can talk some more."

"How about if we tack on a make-out session in the park?" he suggested mischievously.

"Milo, you rake," Astrid laughed. In fact, she didn't feel that anything she did with Milo would compromise her relationship with Nate. Milo was an old friend, one of her first lovers, and he had a historical precedent, so to speak. Nate was her main man, the future father of her children, her partner and best friend and primary responsibility in the relationship category. But Astrid saw no reason to allow having one really fine relationship spoil the chances of developing or keeping others. Or to pass up a chance to nuzzle up to Milo, who happened to be outstanding in the nuzzling category. She had missed him, she realized.

What a cute beaky nose he has, she thought, as they made their way down the hall to the room where Milo was going to speak. Most of the other participants seemed to be heading to the same room. Astrid hadn't had a chance to look at a program yet, so she didn't know what else was being presented. She wondered whether Milo's paper could be generating most of the interest.

It turned out that it was. After two fairly routine papers about some specific gene-engineering breakthroughs, Milo gave his paper to an intensely attentive audience. Everyone had at least one question or comment afterward, running the gamut from outrage and accusations of mysticism to enthusiastic support from researchers who wanted to report their own unofficial findings. Astrid found the evidence difficult to dispute, and Milo's theories confirmed her own personal beliefs and experience anyway. While wrapping up his talk, he spoke of the fact that currently, the control of conscious thought over gene expression seemed clumsy, if not haphazard; but if we learned how to use this latent power, we could play our genome as a pianist produces music from a keyboard— and that more than one piece could certainly be coaxed from the keys.

The implications were obvious. People could "think" cancer away. They could play around with their physical appearances, alter the aging process, draw out latent talents, further enhance psychic abilities. Some participants in the conference clearly found the idea frightening and didn't want to believe it could be possible. Others, however, took delight in the idea, and it became evident that many had suspected the same thing for years but didn't want to be the first one to bring it up.

Although psychic abilities had become unmasked by the virus, this didn't necessarily mean—to Astrid's surprise at first—a change in everyone's thinking. The species had become more spiritually and mystically oriented, and new religions were replacing old ones, but those people with a strong analytical orientation still applied that particular way of thinking to the new traits. They finally had the physical proof that had always eluded them before as far as psychic abilities went; now they had it, and they would concede their reality. But they would continue to balk at believing in new unperceived forces until handed "irrefutable" physical evidence. Astrid found such people mulish, limited, and irritating, but Milo obviously relished sparring with them and enjoyed the question-and-answer session thoroughly.

Afterward, at lunch, they had a good time mimicking some of the more pompous responses, laughing themselves silly over wine. They chatted to catch up over the intervening years, flirted and joked with one another. Nate didn't flirt, it wasn't his style. He expressed all his emotions simply and forthrightly—one of the things Astrid loved most about him. He loved like a good parent, a protective gentle bear of a father, like a huge, solid oak tree that lovingly shades a family's house. She did enjoy flirting, too, however, and Milo was a big bundle of fun.

"I think instead of making out in the park I should get us a room at the Plaza," Milo suggested after dessert, a tasty chocolate-strawberry pie. He reached across the table to touch Astrid's fingertips. "There's nothing very exciting at the conference this afternoon. Certainly nothing to compare with your company."

Astrid blushed. "That's awfully extravagant, Milo," she said.

"Hey, it's not every day we get together, right?" Besides—you know me, I'm a workaholic. I have credits out the ass. You gotta use them up or they go bad."

"You're right. They think you don't want them and they go away." Astrid smiled warmly at Milo, then hesitated. "But listen, before we go, you have to tell me what you know about Cedric."

Milo leaned back in his chair. "Oh yeah. Weird guy. Really nuts about Tesla, right?"

Astrid nodded.

"He was a faculty member at Humboldt; he left a couple of years before you got there. He was in the physics department, teaching electromagnetics and working on theories about interdimensional travel. I took one of his classes." Milo paused and took a swallow of wine. "One day I stopped into his lab to ask him some question about class. It was really weird. I walked in there and it felt like he was around, but I couldn't find him. Some of his machines were on, using juice and making readings and so forth. I called out and didn't get an answer, so I started to leave. But as soon as I got out in the hall, something made me turn around and there he was, standing in the lab."

Astrid shivered involuntarily and her eyes watered, the way they always did when she heard ghost stories. "Had he been there all along?"

"To tell you the truth, it seemed like he'd materialized, for god's sake. But that isn't even the weirdest part. There was this creature standing next to him. A really horrible-looking slimy thing—sort of human but almost not, if you know what I mean. When Cedric saw this thing standing next to him, he went berserk. He started screaming and grabbed some sort of stun gun from his lab coat and shot it. But instead of falling down or anything, the fucking creature disappeared!"

"Oh my god!" Astrid exclaimed, with another long, deep shudder. "Milo, why didn't you ever tell me about this before?"

"Well, he spotted me then and called me into his office. He told me not to tell anyone what I'd seen or he would see to it that my worst nightmares became reality. I don't scare easily, you know that, but I'm no dummy, either. That's a pretty scary guy we're talking about."

"So why do you feel comfortable talking about it now?"

Milo shrugged, pushed his dessert plate away and rested his elbows on the table. "He's on the other side of the continent. And besides, this was before the virus. I figure maybe he's mellowed out since then."

Astrid stroked her lower lip, pondering. "He's still pretty intense," she said finally. "I wonder if he's so hot to wipe out the dimensional window in the Mt. Shasta area because he feels responsible for what's coming through there now. That thing you described sounds a lot like the gang members in that world I've been dreaming about."

"Could be. He left after semester and sort of dropped out of sight. I hadn't heard about him again until you brought him up."

Astrid fell silent. If it was true that Cedric had stumbled into Judy's world through his experiments, and that he had set up an electromagnetic "bridge" between this world and that one, how odd that he should pretend to know so little at the town meeting. He had acted like it was her idea entirely that interdimensional travelers were coming through and committing the atrocities.

She reminded herself, however, that even the new age ushered in at the turn of the millennium hadn't perfected everyone's faults. People didn't kill each other and make war any more, but that didn't prevent them from making mistakes, behaving badly, and wanting to save face and avoid censure.

Suddenly, a horrible thought occurred to her. If Cedric had set up a bridge between Judy's world and this one in Northern California, might she have done the same thing in New York? Did the Uptown Slasher somehow "follow" her here, traveling on a current of probabilities that she had generated in her dream activities? She certainly hoped not. More likely, the separation between the two worlds was becoming thinner and more veil-like as their probable paths converged. Astrid had to believe that a connection had developed between the two worlds for a reason. She just wished she knew what it was.

Fortunately, the rest of the afternoon with Milo took her mind off most of her worries. He thoughtfully took care of the contraceptive responsibility and proceeded to ravish her with skill and caring. How like the universe to provide such a rejuvenating respite, right when I really need it, she mused as she in turn ravished her friend; I should remember that the universe knows what it's doing even when I don't. As she caught herself thinking that, she found herself also hoping, a little desperately, that this was a universal truth that had just occurred to her, and not the false optimism of wishful thinking.

EIGHTEEN

Judy walked stiffly, trying not to jump at every little sound, trying instead to focus on the streamlined metal body that padded before her in the inky night. Her oxygen mask comforted her, too, despite its awkward bulk, since she always felt better and stronger when she had it on. Unfortunately, it made the air in her cubicle seem not so wonderful any more, although perhaps her air processor needed to be serviced. She should put in a request now, she thought worriedly, since it would take three months— at least—for anyone to get to her.

As soon as she reached a working street lamp, she paused and peered once again at the map Major Duncan had drawn for her. Her route seemed to be taking her into the heart of the industrial area, a place she'd visited only once before in her lifetime, and that was on a camp field trip. The place had dismayed and terrified her with its frantic, shrill whines, its alarming roars, choking stench, and smoky fires belching ceaselessly into the air. At the time, Judy had thought, this is hell, and the caretakers have brought us here to show what awaits us if we're not obedient and good. Later, of course, she found out that it was merely an industrial park.

Nevertheless, she had avoided it ever after. And it didn't appeal any more now in bleak, gritty silence than it had then. From one smokestack a noxious orange-and-green flame billowed in sputtering, intermittent bursts. A big rat—almost half as big as Judy—slithered out from a crack in the fence ahead of her and regarded her with phosphorescent red slits. It took in her robot guard as well and retired to its hideaway, apparently deciding to leave her alone. Judy shivered in revulsion. She hated rats. Packs often attacked humans these days, although single rats rarely attacked, as it seemed this one might have if she hadn't possessed a guard. Sometimes rats appeared to her smarter and more cunning than humans, and the sight of such a one made her wonder whether they might be planning an eventual takeover. She quickened her step, her skin crawling in disgust.

One more block and she started looking for the I.V.C. Corporation, whatever that was. Major Duncan hadn't told her and she didn't ask. She felt important and flattered that he had ordered her to undertake this mission, even though it was dangerous. She just hoped she wouldn't mess it up. Another rat poked its head out of a hidey hole and examined her, the flickering of the industrial flame causing its eyes to dance and grow larger with every guttering flare.

Judy swallowed nervously. What she wouldn't give to have Dorothy with her right now! Or the spiritual guide that the psychic power book had told her she supposedly had at her command. She had read through the first few chapters, one of which dealt with summoning up a guide; and she tried the procedure outlined. Twice. But nothing had happened, probably not so surprisingly. If psychic powers really existed, why didn't everyone have them or practice them? Why didn't the government use them to control people? It would sure be a lot easier than having to have police and military and surveillance. Probably only special people had psychic powers. On the other hand, maybe Dorothy just wanted to show her how harmless the ideas were.

"I.V.C. Corporation, I.V.C. Corporation, it should be around here somewhere," she muttered to herself, hoping she hadn't taken a wrong turn. But soon she spotted its faded, dingy lettering on a gate, which, if Major Duncan were correct, should be open, only appearing to be locked.

She unwrapped the chain, finding it loose per instructions, trying not to make too much noise as the heavy links clinked against the metal fence. She pulled the gate open a crack and tiptoed in, wincing as the hinges emitted a treacherous, accusing shriek. She glanced around wildly, sure that at any moment the night watchman and a pack of slavering, out-of-control guard dogs would come racing into the yard.

Look for a dumpster, Major Duncan had told her. To her relief, she spotted it squatting truculently nearby. She tottered over to it, rigid with fear, and reached underneath, praying that she would encounter the smooth metal of a capsule and not something furry or slimy. Her hand groped around for what felt like eons before finally locating the capsule. She strained to cram her arm farther under the bin in order to get a good grasp. It would be just like her to accidentally push it so far away that she wouldn't have a chance of retrieving it.

Finally, though, she managed to wrap her fingers around it and she pulled the capsule to her, panting a little. Under no circumstances was she to open it or examine the contents—Major Duncan had made that part quite clear. And she had no intention of disobeying him. She hugged the capsule close to her body as she made her exit and wound the chain back around the gate, securing it this time.

When she turned to retrace her steps, she froze, then shrank whimpering against the gate, which she now wished she hadn't locked. Five grinning gang members confronted her. One held a thick chain, much like the one she had just secured, one brandished a tire iron, two flashed wickedly long switchblades and one theatrically carved up the air with a butcher knife, an insinuating promise of things to come.

So unused was Judy to having a guard at her disposition that she waited a fatal instant before screaming the attack command to her robot as Major Duncan had instructed her. In that second, the tire-iron punk had leaped forward and smashed its head in with a small grunt of pleasure. He stayed crouching and reached up to savagely rip off Judy's oxygen mask.

"Hey look, guys," he shouted with goonish glee, "the fucking thing's so horny she's taken to stealing dildos!"

They all laughed uproariously at this as Judy glanced down at the metal capsule that she still gripped against her with all her strength. One of the punks tore it out of her grasp and she cried out hysterically. She howled like a maniac while they threw her to the sidewalk and sliced off her panties, causing a substantial blood flow in the process. Two of them held her down while two others roughly parted her legs and the last swung his chain around his head in an apparent decision to tenderize before carving. Judy wailed, she screamed, she begged and pleaded.

"Help!" she shrieked, struggling wildly while the gang members laughed and told her to shout all she wanted. "Help!" she screamed. "Somebody!"

She closed her eyes when the chain finally descended, and braced for the blow. But it never came. Instead, the night exploded into brilliant, searing light. The gang members all stopped their activities, momentarily blinded. Judy opened her eyes wide to see a person or being of some sort standing in front of them, bathed in light of all colors. She gasped when she realized that it was the punk who had given her back her glasses, the one she had been dreaming about. It took a while for the gang to gather its collective stupefied wits and decide to transfer its malicious intent in the intruder's direction. But when they did, they made a big mistake. Every weapon flew out of their hands, and suddenly they found themselves confronted with their own bristling arsenal as it hovered protectively around the newcomer.

The gang turned and fled at this (after they finished bumping into and falling all over one another, madly clawing and tearing and cussing and snarling), not so dimwitted that they couldn't comprehend a terrifying force greater than any they'd ever encountered. Their weapons chased them all the way down the block but then came back and clattered harmlessly at Judy's feet.

The being (for Judy recognized now that this could not possibly be any ordinary gang member or any member of the wealthy class) frowned and bent over Judy, muttering and shaking his head as he examined her wounds.

"I'm sorry," he apologized. To her amazement, Judy saw that his eyes brimmed with tears. "I couldn't get here any sooner. But lie back and relax, okay? I'll see if I can't fix you up, all right?"

Judy nodded, speechless, and did as the being bid her. She felt his cool touch on all the places that the gang had cut or mishandled. Not only that, but he did some peculiar manipulations that didn't even involve her body but instead affected the energy fields all around her—she could actually feel them! When he helped her to sit up, she realized that she'd never really felt good a day in her life, because now she felt good: relaxed, tingly, strong. She glanced down at her wounds and, astonishingly, saw only clean, shiny lines of healing scar tissue.

"Are—you an angel?" she squeaked, when she could find her voice.

He shook his head. "I'm—I'm—uh…"

"My guide?" Judy demanded eagerly.

He seemed to consider the idea, which puzzled Judy. "Sure," he said finally. "That's as good a term as any, I guess. Or I suppose you might say I'm a helper and a messenger."

"A m–messenger? Who from?"

"Oh, the universe. Or your future, perhaps." When he saw that she had recovered, he began gathering up her things—her oxygen mask, capsule, and poor smashed robot. He rounded up the weapons and melted them into lumps of metal merely by holding his hands over them, using some of them to repair her guard.

"So—what's the message?" Judy inquired wonderingly.

The being switched on the robot, which promptly began to nuzzle him affectionately. Judy's eyes grew wider still. "You're not alone, okay?" he said, gazing into her eyes with intensity. "You do have your own god who cares about you and looks after you. You don't have to feel afraid and powerless because you're not—do you see what I'm saying? But—you have to follow your own heart and impulses. And look after yourself. You don't need to sacrifice yourself for the good of anybody or anything— that's not right. The true health of your country lies in the health of every individual— does that make sense to you?"

Judy nodded, although he was going so fast she wasn't sure whether it all made sense. He looked at her and sighed.

"Okay. So think of me as your guide or your guardian angel. Just remember that God talks to you through your deepest yearnings and impulses—the religious leaders in your world would have you think that those are the promptings of the Devil and that you need to listen to their dogma instead. They're wrong. Keep praying for what you think is right. Pay attention to your dreams, especially the ones that carry the greatest emotional import. They come from God. A loving God."

Judy blinked, awed, and wondered whether she should get on her knees. But before she could do so, he rose about three feet into the air. Her jaw dropped.

"Your guard will see you back safely."

"Thank you—sir." She tacked on the "sir" lamely, not quite sure what to call him. Your worship? Your holiness? Your guideship?

"Just call me Astrid. And by the way, Judy, I'm a she, not a he."

At that, she flew away into the night, leaving Judy standing with her mouth agape, eyes bulging, heart hammering away. As soon as Astrid disappeared, Judy found herself wondering whether she had hallucinated the whole thing, but she glanced down and saw that she still had the scars from where the gang had had its fun. She donned her oxygen mask and clutched the capsule, starting back to the MI Complex and Major Duncan. Should she tell him what had happened? If she did, he might think she was crazy or a heretic. Either way, she could get fired. Perhaps she should just keep it to herself.

As she trudged along the deserted streets with her robot, Judy found herself wishing that her guardian had left her one of those weapons to protect herself with, but she got the feeling that he—she, Judy corrected herself— didn't want her to have anything to do with them. She wouldn't know how to use a weapon anyway. And what better protection could she have than a guardian angel?

Assuming, of course, that Astrid was what she said she was. She could have been the Devil in one of the many guises the preachers were always warning about. After all, she'd hesitated when Judy asked her whether she was her guide and then had come up with the guardian angel thing later. The being had told Judy exactly what she wanted to hear, it seemed, and that in itself was a little suspicious. Judy had been taught since childhood that the truth was obscure, difficult to divine, especially by someone like herself. But would the Devil go to such lengths to capture her paltry little soul? Probably. She had been brought up to believe that the Devil would stop at nothing to claim even one wretched soul.

Her intellectual mind usually rejected such rubbish, yet her fear always whispered, "But what if the preachers are right?" If they were right, the consequences of not believing them would be eternal damnation. By telling her to follow her impulses, was Astrid trying to trap and trick her? She didn't know.

She did know, however, that she was alive and not cut up into little pieces, that she felt better than she had ever felt, and that she was about to accomplish her first mission for Major Duncan successfully. She would take things one day at a time. And for now, she couldn't imagine anything more wonderful than believing she had her own personal deity who would come to her aid whenever she really needed it.

NINETEEN

Astrid skimmed along in the opaque darkness, so startled to find herself actually flying and disconnected from Judy's point of view that she barely had any conscious idea of where she was heading. It wasn't until she had risen high enough to glimpse the twin cones of a mountain—which, eerily enough, looked just like Mt. Shasta in the moonlight—that she realized she was trying to gain her bearings. My god, she kept thinking, I'm really here! Wherever "here" was. Did the Mt. Shasta look-alike, like the Bonnard painting, indicate an alternate Earth? And how had she gotten here? Through some sort of direct psychic/emotional connection with Judy? Or had she somehow gone through the window in New York?

First she had started dreaming, then Judy got into trouble, and Astrid felt an intense desire to help her. The next thing she knew, she was in this other reality (although not soon enough—she hadn't wanted a drop of blood to flow, nor all that terrifying psychological torture), fully functioning. In fact, as in a dream, she possessed even more powers than she did in her own world: an added dimension to her telekinetic characteristics that allowed her to heat metals to the melting point and to heal Judy's wounds on the spot, in addition to the ability to levitate.

It seemed to represent a hybrid environment between her world and a dream reality. It wasn't a standard symbolic and/or learning dream where she could control all the elements; but the psychic and physical rules were different from those on her Earth in that she could actually perform these special deeds when ordinarily she could do so only in her dreams. Assuming she wasn't dreaming. Could this be some type of super-real, multi-layered and advanced dream?

She wished she could drop in on Major Duncan, but if she actually occupied space in this world and Maria's fears were correct that someone could find their way here and not necessarily return, she probably shouldn't linger or waste time on something that seemed a comparative emotional extravagance on her part. She had thought about warning Judy against him but feared that such specifics might be meddling, going too far. And she had no proof that he represented anything other than a firm, fair boss of this other world's warped variety. As it was, she hoped her little speech about not sacrificing oneself might penetrate. God, but she had felt like a pompous asshole delivering her encapsulated philosophy with such didacticism. But Judy seemed to respond reasonably well to that approach, even to expect it.

Astrid wished she could run across one of the ruling class on her way, collar the bastard and blast him or her with exactly the opposite message: Better start making some concessions, nanobrain; if you think your fate is unrelated to those poor, pathetic drudges, think again.

Of all the misconceptions in this backward, dreary place, this one mystified Astrid the most. People honestly believed that some people had to suffer in order for others to live well; both rich and poor alike believed that. Somehow the idea of the planet as a living whole had not occurred to anyone. No one viewed the biosphere as a single organism, one made up of many parts, as a body is composed of organs, tissues, and cells. If the stomach or muscles or blood cells suffer, the whole body suffers. It doesn't pillage the kidneys so the lungs can function more effectively. The vascular system didn't obtain its health by preying on eye tissue. So why did classes and nations form, why did people in this world (as well as her own species in the past) try so doggedly and ferociously to use, trample, manipulate, and vanquish the others? Even now, despite the behavioral advantages that the UFO virus had bestowed, people such as Meagan, Louise, and Sharon seemed to have lost sight of the fact that everyone's true best interests all lay together.

Flying to the flanks of the mountain she had spotted took longer than she thought it would. At first Astrid had looked down curiously to see what things looked like on the ground, but she soon gave that up, since it depressed her immeasurably. On her way out of Judy's city, Astrid had caught sight of an impossibly high wall that shielded the coast from her view, the one that protected the rich, presumably. Apartment grids and industrial centers went on forever, then she crossed a huge, mechanized tract of farmland, probably most of which went to feed the wealthy, although farms for the ingredients of that disgusting food powder had to exist, too, Astrid reckoned. Waste-treatment plants abounded, although not enough to deal effectively with the copious amounts produced, obviously, as did dumps and military installations. Sizable areas of bombed-out, charred, radioactive wasteland pocked and pitted it all. No trees existed that she could see, none at all.

But when she reached the volcano and alighted on a tumbled boulder field, she cried out in utter dismay. The white-capped mountain didn't appear to glow from within, as it often did in her world, nor did it sparkle from the snow in the moonlight. Apparently, it had been turned into a radioactive dump site, smoldering fiendishly in the smothering night. Could this be the source of toxins surfacing in her world?

If so, she should probably keep her suspicions to herself, she decided. This would just give Cedric and his supporters one more reason to close the dimensional windows. Even if Cedric's experiments had established the link, even by accident, it would seem that the connection was meant to take place. If they succeeded in breaking the link between the worlds now, her world might fail some sort of cosmic test—perhaps one that the collective unconscious of mankind had even designed for itself in its spiritual evolution. Turning their back on a problem in callous indifference, trying to isolate themselves from a less fortunate population whose fate might be inextricably connected to theirs in an attempt to save their own skins—that couldn't be the right action to take. Hadn't the human race already learned that lesson? Or had they only learned it in the microcosm of their own world and had yet to apply it to the universe at large?

She looked around and tried, with her enhanced telekinetic powers, to turn the radioactive material into harmless isotopes. But she found she could neutralize only a couple of grams a minute. At that rate, it could take her a million years to get rid of all of it. And if her physical body had really made the journey, she should hightail it out of this radioactivity. It was time to go back.

She felt a little nervous, though. Maria's warning about possibly getting stuck here nagged at the back of her mind, and she wondered whether she needed to be near Judy in order to have a conduit back. If she left from here, would she end up in Shasta City, on Mt. Shasta, or in New York? Any place would be fine, as long as she ended up in her own world. When she had come here before to give Judy her glasses, she had believed she was dreaming and had no problem at all. But now that she had to think about getting back, she wasn't sure how to do it. She thought about flying back to wherever Judy was, but discovered to her dismay that she could only bump along, her feet dragging the ground.

Fighting panic, she sorted through her astral-projection lessons and remembered that her teacher had always maintained, "If you find yourself in a place you don't like, just wish yourself back to your body and you will return instantaneously." Unfortunately, if her body had come along this time, she wasn't sure she'd have anything to wish herself back to; but surely some portion of her being waited for her back on her own world. She relaxed and cleared her thoughts. Closing her eyes, she thought longingly of her parents' comfortable apartment. She waited. She peeked through her eyelids. Still in this awful place! She imagined herself flying home, stimulated her pineal gland by rubbing her forehead ferociously, tried every trick she knew. Nothing!

Desperately, Astrid screwed her eyes shut tight and envisioned every detail of the dark, pleasant room she had been sleeping in, down to the smoothness of the clean sheets and the musky aroma of the eucalyptus that spiced the flower arrangements. A loud, roaring *whooosh* pummeled her ears. She experienced a jarring thud that knocked the wind out of her. When she anxiously pried open her eyes this time, she found herself, to her vast relief, sprawled on the bed in her parents' guest room.

She remained motionless for a while, her pulse fluttering. Then she sat up and looked around in the early lavender wash of first dawn. She felt exhausted but was wide awake, so she arose, rumpling her hair as she ambled into the kitchen to make some coffee. She made as little noise as possible, but the coffee grinder awoke her father, who came in yawning.

"Rather early for you to be up, isn't it?" he asked.

Astrid sighed. "Yeah, I guess so. I just had a...weird dream. Actually—at this point, I don't know that I can even tell the difference any more."

Arthur frowned and crossed the room in order to put his arm around his daughter. "Do you want to tell me about it?"

She recounted her experience while waiting for the coffee to brew, then they both sat down with a cup at the breakfast table. When she finished, her father leaned back in his chair.

"You know, honey, I'd like to be able to advise you, but I'm afraid this is just out of my area of expertise."

Astrid laughed, tweaking her father on the shoulder. "Dad, I know this isn't your area of expertise. I know you can't fix everything for me—some things I have to figure out for myself."

He sighed. "I know. I just want to help. But…it all seems so fantastic—so far outside of my own personal experience. I can't help but think that you've blown some unusual dreams all out of proportion."

Now it was Astrid's turn to sigh. "I know, Dad. And you didn't believe in poltergeists until you had one in your house and it repeatedly conked you on the head with a metronome in time to the music that was playing. Three different times."

"Look, sweetheart—I couldn't ignore the physical fact that something real was going on with my daughter's psychokinetic abilities. But where's your physical proof that these dreams are any more than that? I realize it's very tempting and appealing to think that these murders are being committed by phantoms from another reality—"

"Why tempting and appealing?" Astrid interrupted.

"Well, because then it's not us, it's something else that we can objectify and project away from ourselves. We don't have to take responsibility for it."

Astrid bristled. "Well, *I'm* not relinquishing responsibility. I'm the one who's saying this world is connected to our world and that we should keep the conduits open."

"I realize that. But still…"

"Still—you can't accept anything that doesn't fit into your twentieth century, preconceived notions of reality."

Arthur raised one eyebrow. "I think you're being a little hard on your old dad."

Astrid relented. "You're right," she said. "I'm sorry, Dad."

He smiled at her, then gave an exclamation of surprise as the phone rang. He turned to answer it. "It's for you," he said, handing her the phone.

Wondering who would call so early and expecting that it must be Milo, she experienced a jolt when she recognized Taro's voice. "Taro!" she exclaimed. "My god, it's four in the morning your time. Or are you in New York?"

"No, I'm in California, Shasta City, to be exact," came the reply. "I've been up all night trying to decide whether to spoil your vacation and let you know what's going on or whether to leave you in peace."

"What is it?"

"Two things. Cedric announced yesterday that his device for disrupting the windows is ready to do its thing. He's putting a lot of pressure on everybody to let him go ahead—a *lot*. Some people think he might just go on and do whatever it is he wants to do, with or without approval."

"Oh, great!"

"Wait—there's more. Louise and Sharon are pushing for approval of their original resolution—that a moratorium of indeterminate length take effect for having babies."

"You're kidding!"

"Nope. It's the old two-pronged attack. Either way, if you don't get your Amazonian butt out here and throw your considerable weight in with the oppositional forces, you're not going to be happy with the results."

"I can't believe this!"

"Believe it."

Astrid exhaled sharply, distractedly threading the phone cord through her fingers. "I'll see if I can catch a plane out of New York this afternoon. Can you meet my train in Shasta City?"

"Just give me a call. Either Austin or I will be in all day."

"Okay. Thanks. Thanks for calling, too."

"Hey—I just don't like to see a bunch of bullies ganging up on my favorite giant."

"Ho, ho, ho."

"Jolly Green Giant, circa—oh, I'd say, 1960s." Taro and Astrid occasionally liked to play the Advertising Edition of Trivial Pursuit, for basically the same reasons that they liked to go the library and look up old twentieth century tabloids.

"Very good, Taro. I'll catch you later."

The phone had awakened Libby, and she now stood in the kitchen pouring a steaming mug of coffee, her hair tangled and uncombed. Astrid thought she looked best that way.

"What was that all about?" she asked.

Astrid exasperatedly blew a stray lock of hair out of her face before answering. "The hysterical factions are getting out of hand in Shasta City. I need to get back."

Arthur and Libby exchanged uneasy glances. "Astrid, sweetie, do you really think that's wise?" her mother inquired, a squiggle of worry creasing her forehead. "It sounds like things could be getting a little dangerous there."

Astrid swallowed a smile. Only a mother would worry about a six-foot woman who rode her bike twenty to forty miles a day, she mused. Libby caught the gist of her thought.

"Look, I know you're not exactly a fragile flower, Astrid, but mob violence is nothing to take lightly."

Her words shot tendrils of alarm through Astrid's limbs and heart. "Who said anything about mob violence?"

Once again her mother and father glanced at one another uneasily. "Well, no one—yet," replied Arthur.

"But honey, don't you see? It's almost inevitable under these circumstances."

"Wait a minute, wait a minute," said Astrid. "You're forgetting we've all had our behavioral repertoire modified by the UFO virus."

"We haven't forgotten," Libby replied. "It's just that— behavior is a very complex thing."

"The UFO virus didn't extinguish poor judgment and shortsightedness, sweetheart," her father added, echoing thoughts that she had mulled over herself. "It didn't phase out fanaticism or well-intentioned but misguided desires to force everyone to do what one group sincerely believes is best for everyone. They might not hurt you physically, but what's to prevent them from locking you up if you become enough of a threat? Violence takes more forms than direct physical harm."

Astrid stared, disbelieving, at her parents. "I know you've never liked the West Coast, but you don't honestly think someone would incarcerate me, do you? The Northwest is an anarchistic organization. We don't do that sort of thing."

"Anarchies have been known to forcibly sequester individuals perceived as a threat to the society," Libby told her, anxiously reaching up and smoothing Astrid's hair back to take the sting out of her words.

"Well, all the more reason that I should get back," Astrid replied stubbornly. "To make sure things like that don't happen."

Libby and Arthur fell silent. Libby picked up a spoon to stir her coffee, and in her agitation fumbled and dropped it into the space between the counter and the stove. "Damn!" she exclaimed.

"Don't worry, Mom—I'll get it." Astrid mentally maneuvered the spoon back up through the crack and, with an added flourish, somersaulted it into the sink.

Libby tapped the side of her mug with a well manicured fingernail. "I must say, Astrid, that having your psychokinetic abilities under conscious control is a big improvement."

Astrid laughed, then bent to give her mother a kiss. "Don't worry about me, okay? Listen—if they try to throw me behind bars, I can just pick the lock telekinetically."

Arthur cleared his throat noisily. "Don't underestimate the power of fear, Astrid," he said. "We know you're an unusually capable young woman, but fear has induced as many drastic measures as anger or hatred ever has. Don't take this situation lightly."

Astrid sobered immediately. "I'm not, Dad. Believe me."

After breakfast, Astrid got on the phone to find an afternoon flight to San Francisco. Once she had secured herself a seat, she posted a couple of inquiries to the global village on the Internet to see whether other areas on Earth had been experiencing what Shasta City and now New York seemed to be undergoing. Then she packed up her belongings and gave Milo a call. His phone machine answered, so she left a message, trying also to reach him at the conference. He was in a seminar, however.

Her father came into her room to say goodbye before leaving for the lab. Astrid avoided looking him in the eye, since she knew he was worried about her and it made her feel guilty. He told her to be careful and reminded her that she and Nate were welcome to come and stay for as long as they liked, any time. Astrid gave him a bone-cracking hug in farewell, experiencing an odd, fleeting sense of misgiving as she did so. She wondered whether the situation in Shasta City was even worse than Taro had indicated. Oh well, she thought, she was never one to avoid an unpleasant or difficult situation.

When it was time for her to leave, Astrid found her mother in her office, sorting through proofs for a show she was putting together on doorways, a subject she had found fascinating for several years now. Libby leaned back from her desk.

"If you want to come here to have your baby, you're more than welcome, you know."

"Thanks, Mom. I really like the midwives in Shasta City, though."

"Well, if you want either or both of us there for the birth, we'd love to come. It's been much too long since we've seen Nate."

"I know. He misses you, too. Well, listen—when all this weird stuff is over, you should come out for a visit."

"I'd like that," Libby smiled. She patted her daughter's hand. Again, Astrid felt a shiver of misgiving. "So—you're taking the subway?"

"Yeah—I'm dying to see the new improved system."

"You won't even recognize it," said her mother, standing up to give her daughter a heartfelt squeeze.

Libby's prediction turned out to be true. The only aspects of the system that looked familiar were the green-globed lamps that marked the entrances—everything else had been refurbished and cleaned. The subway trains were composed of gleaming new electromagnetic cars that whispered into the station. The walls along the waiting platform had been tiled over and looked immaculate as well as pretty, and the person at the token booth smiled at her in a friendly way. The passengers waiting for the train looked relaxed, well nourished, and well clothed, every one of them.

As she boarded the train and took a nice, comfortable seat, Astrid thought back to her last rather daring journey on New York City's underground transit system when she was visiting from prep school. Most everyone on the train had looked poor, shabby—and either blank and hopeless or mean, hardened, and hostile. The interior was filthy, as was, of course, every other aspect of the system, even down to the glistening, torpedo-shaped rats that squeezed and scuttled along the rails between arrivals of roaring, deafening trains, boldly nosing about the tossed garbage in search of sustenance. Just about everyone carried a weapon of some sort, whether poorly concealed or flagrantly displayed. The air stank, too, due to the presence of several homeless people riding around to keep warm on the frosty winter day.

What was it about the UFO virus, she wondered, that had changed so many details of the scene here? Lack of aggression would have eliminated the weapons and muggings, but how did the virus also help to clean everything up, solve the homeless problem?

Perhaps, she mused, the UFO virus had been a great equalizer. No one was spared, from the wealthiest financier to the poorest ghetto dweller. Everyone—black, white, brown, red, yellow—had to work together and cooperate for civilization to get back on its feet again, and past prejudices didn't seem so important any more, not when every single individual's efforts counted. For another thing, everything had slowed down considerably while everyone recuperated—in fact, lots of things had come to a virtual halt and everyone had been able to see, clearly, just what was and was not indispensable for survival.

The insular ultra-rich came to realize that even their quality of existence deteriorated when so many desperate poor roamed urban streets, so that going out to a nice restaurant, theater, or ballet became an exercise in guerrilla strategizing. Accordingly, they became more philanthropic and less acquisitive, as anxious as everyone else to create a healthy, livable planet to occupy. The poor stopped destroying their own neighborhoods and dwellings—in fact, they energetically improved them—and the middle class gained a galvanizing new hope, a new sense of purpose. Real estate and housing no longer represented investments, but became places to live and call home. Vacant dwellings were awarded to people who had no homes and could take care of them, and, given the overbuilding in most of North America, plenty of them existed. The UFO virus had had a decided ripple effect.

What could she possibly precipitate in Judy's world that would have the same far-ranging consequences?

She fell to thinking about the gang members, wondering what created them, what they represented. The more she thought about it, the more she came to feel that they represented the dark side of the more repressed, pious, powerful members of Judy's society. Religious leaders and members who truly believed in good and evil, who believed that they (and everyone else) could be only one or the other, might have created alternate selves embodying the characteristics that they so vehemently denied in themselves. Astrid believed that good and evil represented perversions of the concept of yin and yang, that both the light and dark sides of humanity had to be embraced in order for a healthy psyche to develop. Labeling certain emotions and urges as "bad," striving to suppress them and then punishing them when they inevitably surfaced, usually produced grotesque and deformed behavior as a result of so much guilt, repression, denial, and heavy-handed judgment, whether from the individual himself or the society at large. Tell teenagers not to have sex because it's "bad," and what results? Teenage pregnancies and high rates of venereal disease. Make mind-altering substances illegal, refuse to address any root cause of drug abuse, and what happens? A raging, out-of-control drug problem supporting a wealthy, violent criminal elite.

Things had started to improve in her world, she felt, because rich and poor, black and white, "good" and "bad" came to realize that they all constituted the human race of the planet and that all must thrive for the whole to thrive, and tautologically, for each individual to thrive. Judy's world exhibited all the pathology that her world once had, because everyone lived splintered, separate lives, looking out only for themselves and willing to trample on others to achieve their goals. Through fear of violence and aggression, they had turned their societies into prisons;

through belief in individual powerlessness, no one roused themselves to challenge the odious status quo, even to try to change things for the better.

Which meant, thought Astrid, that if she could change the way everyone viewed reality on that other planet, if she could somehow get them to recognize that they all, individually and collectively, determined the health of the planet, then maybe it could begin to heal. The toxins could begin to get cleaned up, no longer spilling into her world; perhaps the murderers could start to disappear from the societies.

So excited was Astrid about her new plan, and so absorbed in spinning details and favored scenarios, that even her psychic senses failed to pick up on the passenger who stepped onto the subway car at the next stop. If her back hadn't been turned toward him, his appearance would have snagged her attention and alerted her. As it was, however, the frightened looks on the faces of the passengers opposite her gave her the first warning. Before she could even turn to look, their expressions had changed to ones of horror, and Astrid heard behind her a wet, gargling, choking sound, like nothing she'd ever heard before. What met her eyes when she focused on the scuffle caused her to grow faint, then sick. A man lay gasping on the floor of the car, garishly bright blood pumping from the gash where his throat had once been.

After a shocked second, which allowed the attacker to run into the next car, pandemonium erupted. Some passengers rushed to the victim's aid, trying futilely to stop the flow of blood and save the man's life. Others, with Astrid in the lead, tore into the next car in pursuit, while someone grabbed the emergency brake, throwing Astrid and everyone in her wake into a bruised, jumbled pile. Astrid scrambled up and ran the entire length of the train, but whether the assailant had managed to force the doors open and flee the subway or whether he had simply dematerialized, he was nowhere to be found.

Glumly, Astrid returned to the first car, where several people sat sobbing and others crouched in stunned silence, whiter even than the poor man who lay dead.

"Who got a good look at the murderer?" asked Astrid.

"I did," said an elderly woman, her voice shaking. "He was dressed in black—in some kind of rubbery fabric. He was the ugliest thing I've ever seen in my life! He— he hardly looked human, if you want to know the truth."

"Yeah, and he had a shadow about him," added a stylishly dressed young man. "There was darkness all around him—it almost looked like he was wrapped in melting black cellophane."

Astrid began to shiver and couldn't stop. She plunked herself down on the bench and tried to keep her teeth from chattering. I need Nate, she thought miserably; I need to see him—right now. She wrapped her arms around herself, tightly, tears trickling down her cheeks. She would see whether she could get on one of the shuttles to the space station; now that the novelty had worn off and toxic clean-up had slowed down, one could often find a vacant seat. She didn't care how many credits she would have to use, she couldn't possibly wait for him to come home.

Astrid remained hunched in misery until the healers came and bore the body away. Then another team of workers arrived to clean up the blood. The train started up again. Only now the soft sibilance of the train took on an eerie, mournful, ominous sound, and the passengers looked anything but relaxed. Dear God, please help us through this mess, Astrid prayed, sick with fear and grief. Help us.

TWENTY

Judy sat motionless in her seat for Silent Prayer, briefly raising her eyes to the looming crucified Jesus with His crown of thorns dripping simulated blood, the gash gaping graphically in His side; then she dropped her gaze humbly and prayed in standard form, as did all the congregation. Church comprised one of the few quiet experiences in her life, although microphones were scattered throughout the gothic beams like sprinklers, amplifying every cough, whisper, and rustle emitted by each member of the flock. If you fidgeted too much, you earned a good sharp thwack across the back of your shoulders from a crook-wielding deacon. Since some zealot in a religious fervor had decided to design the pews and kneeling benches to be as uncomfortable as possible for penance's sake, it wasn't easy, either, to refrain from fidgeting.

Judy hated going to church and had missed the last few Sundays, showing up today only because she feared a vigilante church group might appear at her door. Church attendance was not officially mandatory, but brown-noses, interfering old battleaxes, and pious fanatics kept track of the records and forcibly dragged anyone who had fallen from the path back to the ways of the Lord. No need to incur such an unpleasant experience, in Judy's opinion.

Besides that, she had had a most disturbing dream last night. She had dreamed that she had become some sort of special person, a religious figure—she might even be tempted to say a messiah of some kind, if the thought itself weren't heretical. She didn't see how this could happen, given her lack of fervor for the church and her general unremarkableness, but the dream had been so intense, so vivid and compelling that, especially on top of her guardian angel experience, she had felt she must attend church, to see if she could gather some clue to its import. She didn't know where else to go. Other churches and denominations existed, sure, but Judy had attended several in her search for spiritual guidance and they were all the same. This one happened to be the closest and, therefore, the least hardship on her lungs.

Up until recently, Judy had more or less pretended to herself that she held conventional beliefs, tempered only somewhat with a statistician's skepticism. Her early childhood indoctrination had been extremely intensive. She knew that an official God existed, the one with a capital "G," the one belonging to the religious leaders and the one Who the political and military establishment claimed supported all their endeavors. This God was an angry, stern, jealous God, one Who knew absolutely everything, one Who required exacting punishment for every minor infraction, including heretical or sinful thoughts. She wasn't quite sure, however, whether this God was a colossal, gigantic male, a light, or an invisible force.

Then there was the Devil, more personified, a sly, oily character who was always the opposite of what he seemed. He was a trickster, a tempter. He would promise all sorts of wonderful things but if a person listened to him and succumbed to seduction by Satan, one's soul would be lost for all eternity.

Then there were God's angels, whom one always heard about but never saw, and there were the demons.

They were invisible, too, but more present, since they went around possessing people all the time.

Judy had been brought up to believe—with tireless proselytizing, conditioning, and even brainwashing by the caretakers at Children's Camp—that the Earth was a testing ground for human souls, the ephemeral, transitory period of suffering that determined whether a soul went to heaven or hell for all eternity. The more one suffered on Earth, the better chance one had of getting into heaven, which was why it was better to be a drudge than a member of the ruling class, why it was better to be punished in this lifetime than the next.

But lately, despite her deeply entrenched fears, Judy had begun to entertain all kinds of notions: like maybe suffering wasn't the way to exist after all. Like the existence of her own god. And just as she had begun to postulate the existence of such a being, he—she—had appeared! Maybe the preachers insisted so vehemently that only one god existed because the other gods had to be thought of first in order to come into being. Religious leaders didn't want other gods around because it might take away some of their power—they wanted their god to be the biggest and strongest.

On the other hand, she thought uneasily as Silent Prayer ended and one of the circulating Elders gave her a particularly sharp glance, her savior the other night definitely did fit one of the many descriptions of Satan: seemingly wanting nothing but to help, possessed of supernatural powers, telling her anything and everything she wanted to hear, promising the entire universe. And telling her to ignore the religious leaders.

She eased cautiously onto the kneeling bench for the Confirmation of Man's Lowliness, wincing as she put all her weight onto her kneecaps. The worshipers on either side of her gave her sidelong glances, causing her back to break into a sweat. Wincing wasn't allowed, either. One withstood one's suffering cheerfully, or else one questioned God's goodness and set one's judgment higher than His own.

When the preacher mounted the steps of his gilt- and fur-covered podium to give the sermon for the day, it was all Judy could do to keep her eyes from rolling back in her head from conditioned boredom. Despite the fact that most preachers shouted, screamed, pranced, wept, slavered and drooled, the subject matter of sermons always sounded so standardized and predictable that maintaining the required attention proved a real challenge. But today, as Judy allowed some of her excitement to surface about her meetings with Major Duncan—both the one that had taken place last night when she brought back the capsule and the one he had set up for today after church—it tinged everything with more interest than usual.

He had been delighted when she walked in with the capsule, that was obvious. And then when he asked her if she had kept her word and refrained from examining the contents, and she said yes, he looked at her long and searchingly. Then he had said a peculiar thing. He said, "Judy, if you could have anything you wanted, what would it be?" He probably expected her to say a baby, that's all any woman was supposed to want. But Judy had a different answer. "I'd like to live in my dreams," she told him.

Judy practically jumped out of her skin when the pacing preacher roared out the title of his sermon for the day. "Dreams!" he thundered contemptuously, spittle spraying the first few rows of shrinking parishioners. "Satan's Secret Passageway into the Subconscious!"

Good Lord, Judy thought in sudden terror. Maybe the religious leaders *were* telepathic. Had they picked up her thoughts about...about...she was afraid now even to conjure up the image of her guardian for fear that the preacher could see it, too. She trembled in her seat.

"My dear flock." The preacher dropped his voice and addressed the congregation softly, draped forward over the podium. "We all have dreams. All of us. And not all of them are evil." He paused for effect, catching the eye of a few parishioners, including Judy, and glaring at them balefully. "But lately, friends, lately, the Father Confessors tell me that there are new varieties of dreams afoot, beguiling, enchanting dreams, false dreams, ones that seek to make the dreamer dissatisfied with his lot in life." He gathered himself up like a puma preparing to pounce. "Sinners!" he barked. "Pay no heed to these dreams, for they are the work of Satan! Seek not to change thy station in life; God put you where you belong. And with good reason! Would thee give up the kingdom of God for a few baubles and material comforts? Would thee disrupt the natural order of things? Worship false gods and false values at the everlasting cost of your soul! Defy God almighty at your own peril! For the eternal scorching fires of hell await those who do!"

Judy sat quaking and hyperventilating, too frightened to contemplate the fact that apparently others had been having unusual dreams. So worked up did she feel by the end of the relentless, two-hour sermon that she began even to suspect Major Duncan. Come to think of it, why *had* he invited her over to his quarters? What did he have in mind? And that time she had smelled sulfur in his office—everyone knew that sulfur was the smell of the Devil—she had just felt so overwhelmingly in awe of him that she had ignored it. Was the whole thing with the capsule just a test to see whether she would obey him blindly, do whatever he told her? "Oh God," she prayed, "help me to do the right thing!" She had a mind now to miss her appointment at Major Duncan's quarters—but she also felt afraid not to go. What would he do, what would happen if she didn't go? She huddled miserably, passively accepting the discomfort of the kneeling bench now, feeling she probably deserved it, and anyway, maybe some punishment could help her position at this point.

When mandatory confession came, the last item on the service's agenda, Judy felt so scared that she almost blurted out everything: her dreams, her possession of illegal contraceptives, her sinful use of them to prevent conception, her consorting with Satan. However, her instinctive fear of punishment prevented her. She just couldn't seem to get the words out as she sat in the monitored booth of the Father Confessor. She had to say *something*, though. If she didn't confess anything at all, they'd figure she was lying and would punish her for that, particularly as she hadn't had good attendance lately.

"Forgive me, Father, for I have sinned," she began. The shadowy figure behind the curtain was bathed eerily in the green light of a cathode ray tube. He said nothing, merely tapped her name and number into the All Souls Computer and waited. "I...I've lusted in my heart, Father," she stammered. "And—coveted the lifestyles of the rich and famous." Two minor sins. Hopefully her penance wouldn't be too great.

"Is that everything you have to confess, my daughter?" he droned.

"Yes, Father. Please forgive me."

"My child, you must atone, as you know. I sentence you to an hour in the stocks as penance. Go now."

Judy stood, relieved. As penance went, the stocks weren't so bad, although it would delay her meeting with Major Duncan. But maybe that would be better, she pondered. Maybe by the time she got there he would be gone and she would have a good, verifiable excuse for her tardiness. For she realized she would probably go. Obedience was too strongly instilled in her not to.

She exited out the side door of the church where the stocks and flogging pillories stood, took a number and then her turn among the crowd of parishioners, half of whom also had penances to perform, half of whom came to watch the whippings and throw stones and rotten tomatoes at the people in the stocks. Judy always wondered where all the rotten tomatoes came from, since she'd never seen any except for here. She could let fly a few herself; in fact, she was expected to. Most people, since they had suffered similar sentences in the past, threw themselves into the practice with vigor, hurling insults and rocks and tomatoes with savage glee, occasionally breaking a bone and putting out an eye here and there, the tormented enjoying the role of acting as the tormentor for a change. But the same impetus that drove most of her fellow men to inflict humiliation and pain, it seemed, produced exactly the opposite reaction in Judy. She hated having things tossed maliciously at her; she didn't feel one iota better in reversing the process.

Once she had actually hit someone (a consequence of her terrible aim), a tired-looking, deflated woman who just hung there in the stocks. The tomato had splotched right into her poor old hopeless face. The woman couldn't wipe the stinging stuff out of her eyes, and juice slowly drizzled into the trembling, down-turned corners of her mouth. Judy felt so sorry and so awful that she had wanted to run up to the stocks and wipe it off the woman's face with her own dress. But she knew that, although such action would be approved of if undertaken by Jesus himself or one of His apostles, such behavior on her part would be construed as interfering with God's judgment, setting herself above God.

She looked down at herself, realizing that she had worn her best dress for her meeting with Major Duncan. She wished she hadn't done so—it would be ruined. Not only that, she would arrived bruised and covered with putrid tomato goo. Oh well, she sighed dejectedly, it couldn't be helped. She fiddled with her plastic number, fighting a wave of sudden fear that drenched her as she thought of her assignation. She sure hoped she wasn't waltzing blithely and stupidly into a really odious situation.

TWENTY-ONE

Gazing moodily out the window of the space shuttle, Astrid prickled with relief as she passed out of Earth's gravity. Man, but it felt good to leave the planet and all the problems and crises. She was exhausted. She had had to lay over at the airport overnight, and she felt so traumatized that she had barely slept. When she did drift off, giving Judy encouraging messianic suggestions as she did so, she ended up instead witnessing Judy being terrorized by that disgusting church service, watching all the progress she had made in the previous episode (and at no small risk to herself) degenerate into subservient fear. She couldn't believe it when Judy meekly accepted her punishment—took a number and waited for it, for god's sake—and then her main concern revolved around her dress.

Astrid gnawed at her lip and flung out her legs impatiently, bobbing gently within the restrictions of her harness. She had clearly overestimated Judy's daring streak. What was it that made that odious, unappealing religion so compelling? Was it just because it *was* so awful, the consequences so dire? She had the impression that Judy didn't really believe the version of reality presented by this form of Christianity; rather, she felt afraid not to believe it: What if they were right and people's souls really did roast in hell for all eternity if you didn't play by the rules of their game?

It was unfortunate that Judy's socialization had taken so well, embedded itself so deeply. Everything in that damned warped world conspired to undermine the individual, to convince everyone that they were powerless in the face of other, more massive forces. The religions convinced the people that they were unworthy sinners by their very nature, deserving of constant punishment and suffering. Their sciences told them that they were nothing but accidents of enzymatic affinities and the biochemical properties of deoxyribonucleic acid, that their Earth represented nothing but a random coagulation of particles destined to become cosmic dust one day. Their society viewed them as insatiable masses, as economic burdens by the very fact of their unfortunate, swollen existence, yet it insisted on their frenzied propagation. And their economy perceived them as nothing but markets to be manipulated en masse, as consumers, and not very impressive or intelligent ones at that.

The problem was, Astrid reflected, that no one had any real choices. All their choices were fake choices, distinctions in appearance only, just like the thirty-seven different brands of food powder.

In Astrid's own lifetime, right before the close of the millennium, voter turn-out had dropped to thirty percent at best, nationwide. Journalists and political pundits speculated on this phenomenon endlessly, but Astrid always felt convinced that no one voted because no one felt they had a real choice. Which image-obsessed, corruptible, self-seeking, self-satisfied proxy for powerful vested interests did you want to vote for? Why bother?

Judy's world needed more choices, real choices, just as hers had before the turn of the millennium. Astrid needed to let those people know that their societal structures were not invincible or infallible. Or immutable.

She didn't want to hurt or kill anyone, but she did need to make dramatic gestures in order to affect as many people in as short a time as she could. Perhaps, with her enhanced psychokinetic abilities in that world, she could cause significant sections of edifices that represented power there to collapse—unpredictably, inexplicably, inexorably. A nice, obvious symbolic gesture. But would anyone get it? Someone like Judy was a necessary key player to interpret these events in no uncertain terms for others. Maybe she could find some way to reward Judy whenever she allowed her daring, earnest, messianic side to emerge. The fact that she didn't immediately embrace Astrid's tactic did, in fact, argue for a stubborn, determined self, who contained the wherewithal to become her own person—even if that self had almost been socialized and brainwashed into extinction.

Astrid absentmindedly selected a floating tendril of hair and slipped it into the corner of her mouth to nibble on it, a habit she hadn't indulged in since childhood. Maybe she just needed to temper her own sense of urgency with a little patience and not underestimate the power of Judy's desire to conform, to keep from doing the wrong thing, to avoid punishment—no matter what form it took, whether administered by God or a person. What if, besides protecting Judy, she provided her with a magic table or purse, like the ones in fairytales, that supplied the owner with everything she could possibly want? Astrid smiled for the first time in twenty-four hours. It would cheer Judy up so, as long as Astrid could convince her that the miraculous gift came from God, not the Devil.

Astrid leaned back in her seat and stretched to unkink her muscles. She could see the space station now, as a silvery mercuric drop orbiting the Earth, the solar-sensitive sheath giving a dazzling reflection in the sunlight. The Earth below looked so lovely and perfect that it almost didn't seem real. Cumulus clouds lay scattered across land masses like handfuls of fluffy popcorn; fresh water flashed in tangled, ribbonlike rivers and shiny, coin-shaped lakes. Viewing the spiraling arms of a storm system from this height gave it a planned artistic quality, as though some colossal entity had hand-painted the orb the way one might an Easter egg, and the heart-catching cobalt blue of the vast oceans seemed magical in itself. Everything about the planet sang with life, with vitality and sentience.

Just about everyone these days perceived Earth as a cognizant, living entity with a will, a set of powers that protected and enhanced Her survival, and a destiny. The recently moribund conception of a mindless, "dead" hunk of rock that just happened to have the right conditions to support a thin film of life encircling it seemed amazingly ignorant and primitive now. But it was the one, obviously, that everyone in Judy's society shared. How much harm did that belief inflict in and of itself, she wondered. For actions follow from beliefs, and people will certainly take different actions if they believe something to be alive rather than dead.

Astrid checked her watch, impatient for the flight to be over and to snuggle down in Nate's arms. She knew she had to work quickly in finding a solution to the current crisis, but she needed some emotional sustenance first before she could go on. Nate had sounded tired when she talked to him on the radio phone, worn out from work and disheartened by Astrid's news about the murders. She pressed her hands together, trying to ease the ache in her heart. No good. A tear squeezed from her eye, she wanted to see Nate so bad—it balled into a tiny globe that floated away from her.

Without being aware of it, Astrid slipped into a deep, dreamless sleep. She didn't awaken until the shuttle docked at the space station, sending a gentle, rippling shock wave throughout the craft. Astrid unbuckled her harness and leaped to her feet, even though it would be at least fifteen minutes before she could disembark. Anxiously, she peered out the window to see whether she could catch a glimpse of Nate on the waiting platform, but machinery and gizmos blocked her view. Finally, all the docking procedures were complete, the passengers free to exit. It was all she could do to keep from climbing over the people in front of her who shuffled off at a maddeningly slow pace. When she emerged from the shuttle, Astrid anxiously scanned the small crowd of people gathered around the gate. At first she didn't see Nate's curly head, which should have towered over everyone else's, and she feared she might break down into uncontrollable sobs. But then she spotted him sitting on a crate, looking smaller than normal and rather despondent.

Astrid rushed over to him and practically knocked him off the crate by throwing herself into his arms. She covered him with desperate kisses, wanting to assuage not only her unhappiness but his as well. He held her tight and kissed the tears on her face as they fell.

"Oh man, Nate, that trip was torture—I couldn't believe it!" she wept. "I wanted to see you so bad—it felt like I'd entered a time warp that stretched every second into an hour!"

"Well, it's okay, baby," he soothed, smoothing back her hair from her face. "We're together now."

"Thank god for that, at least!"

Nate cradled her against his chest, then gently disentangled himself and stood up. "Do you have any luggage?"

"Yeah—my dreamviewer and an overnight bag. I shipped the rest of my stuff back to California." She spotted her cases squatting among the other luggage, which had been disgorged onto the platform by conveyor belts within minutes of the shuttle's docking. Ambling over to the collection of suitcases, she handed Nate her overnight bag and picked up her dreamviewer.

Barely glancing at the striking spectacle of the mammoth shuttle resting in its cavernous enclosure, a rare, futuristic sight that normally would have captivated her, Astrid clutched Nate with her free hand and buried her nose in the arm of his jacket as they walked along, eagerly inhaling his scent. The air smelled surprisingly fresh, actually, since the halls and rooms were crowded with healthy, hydroponic plant life; and a comforting though frolicsome lightweight gravity had been induced on the spinning, wheel-shaped station.

Astrid did notice these things, but as heartsick as she felt, they didn't delight her the way they usually would have. Even the majestic, expansive space and views of Earth that filled the viewports failed to lighten her mood. Observed from this height, the Earth looked so serene. The fact that all the contention and panic seethed in her community struck Astrid as an affront to the gracious entity that supported them all.

If nothing else, she thought, everyone should relax and try to get along out of mere politeness and gratitude to the Earth. She thought guiltily about the fact that Meagan and her group considered herself to be the fractious and difficult one. But they're such fascists, she asserted to herself. Why did they have to come up with such an extreme solution? Why did they assume that unless they forced everyone to follow the path they perceived as the correct one, everything would fall apart? Couldn't they just trust everyone to act responsibly?

"So Meagan and Louise are pushing their stupid resolution again," Astrid grumbled.

Nate remained silent.

"And Cedric is all hot to start screwing around with the dimensional window."

Nate shook his head.

"You know, just when I start to think that humankind is evolving and getting its act together, something like this happens."

"Maybe we just need to be patient—wait and see what happens," said Nate. "Maybe we're not aware of all the factors in this situation. You know, sometimes good can grow out of seeming bad."

Nate's response irked her, even though usually she would have agreed with him. "What do you mean?" she demanded, stepping back and withdrawing her arm. "Just stand by and let hysterics legislate our behavior, tell us whether or not we can even have children, for Pete's sake?"

"Astrid, we can always move someplace else. My parents would love to have us come stay with them in Berkeley."

"I don't want to move! Anyway, why should we let Louise and Sharon and Meagan think they can get away with stuff like this? What if another toxic hot spot develops right where we move? They'll probably think they have the right to march in and tell us what to do there, too."

"That's not very likely," Nate responded mildly, infuriating her even more.

"How do you know?" she snapped. "I think those toxins are leaking in from that other dimension. I think there's starting to be less and less separation between our worlds. I think that the more totalitarian we become, the closer we draw to that world. The more our fates have in common."

"Hmm," said Nate. "That's an interesting idea."

"Nate, it's more than an interesting idea! It's a highly likely possibility. I *went* there the other night. That world has a Mt. Shasta! And they're using it as a gargantuan dump site."

"Really?" Nate gazed at her with a troubled expression. "Interesting. We've been getting inexplicable increases in the toxins emanating from Mt. Shasta. We were thinking that somehow wastes had made their way into the magma and that they were leaking upwards, but without anymore volcanic activity than we've had, I couldn't quite figure out how it was doing that." He scratched his beard absentmindedly. "But if that's the case, maybe we should let Cedric go on and see if he can disrupt the connection."

Astrid sighed. "Yeah, logically that seems to be what we should do, but then I keep asking myself why the connection exists in the first place."

"And?"

"Well—I think that we're supposed to help somehow. We're in much better shape than Judy's world. That's how the universe works. The more fortunate help the less fortunate. That's part of our gig as sentient entities, don't you agree?"

"Sure I do. You know that."

"So I think that's what's going on here. To break the connection now would be irresponsible." Astrid caught the tip of a philodendron that dangled overhead as they passed by, then let it go. "You know, I saw my old friend Milo in New York at the genetics conference, and he told me that Cedric could have been in contact with that other dimension as many as ten years ago."

"That's bizarre. Why is he so anxious to undo his work, then?"

"He must feel responsible for the murders. In fact, I think I might go talk to him when we go back to Shasta City. I'll tell him that the connection was supposed to happen. He shouldn't feel guilty."

"But I thought you said totalitarian measures were drawing us closer in a negative way. And that our destinies were converging dangerously."

"Well—I think they are."

"So—I don't quite understand. On the one hand you think it's irresponsible to break off our connection, but in the next breath you imply a pejorative relationship," Nate protested, puzzled.

"Look, we're supposed to help them! We're not supposed to get all mired down in the muck with them and become like them!" she cried, causing two passersby to look up, startled.

"I see," Nate responded soothingly, grabbing her hand and smoothing it over his arm.

"Don't try to placate me!" she burst out, snatching her hand back.

"What do you want me to do?" he exclaimed. "Get you more upset than you already are?"

"You can't do any worse!" she declared angrily. "Don't you realize how infuriating it is for an angry person to be talking to some kind of super-calm, reasonable... zombie?!"

Nate clamped his lips together in a flat, unhappy line. "I didn't realize that zombies were reasonable," he said.

For a moment, Astrid didn't laugh. But then she couldn't help herself. "Oh, god, I'm sorry, Nate." Astrid turned to face him, grabbed the lapels of his rumpled jacket, and stood on tiptoe to give him a kiss. "I shouldn't be picking a fight with you. I'm just—so freaked out. I'd like to let patience play a part, but it seems like everyone else is rushing toward unacceptable solutions. Let me tell you about the plan I'm working on."

So she filled him in on her plan, slipping her arm back through his, feeling guilty for allowing her tension to create strife between them. What she really wanted to do was fight with Meagan and Louise, she realized, and here she was taking it out on the person who least deserved it. Her guilt kindled her passion, so that when they reached Nate's sleeping quarters, a one-room apartment flooded with light from the moon that lay on every surface like powder, she dropped her dreamviewer to the floor and melted against him in a fervid, smoldering kiss.

They tore off their clothes as they kissed, and they sank down onto the soft carpet, unable to get enough of the other's lips, skin, and scent. They made love hungrily, as though this represented their last chance, as though the fate of the world depended on their love-making. And when at last their passion subsided, and they lay mute in one another's arms, Astrid realized, with a jolt, that Nate had just impregnated her. Should she tell him? Would it worry him with everything else that was going on? But her heart refused to listen to her mind. Her heart was bursting with joy and excitement and she wanted to share every morsel.

"You've not been taking herbs, have you?" she finally murmured.

Nate shook his head, not raising it from her damp breast.

"How do you feel about space babies?" she asked softly, feeling him stir as she posed her question.

He raised himself and gazed at her now, his face filled with longing. "We may have done wrong, but it feels like the right thing. I want this baby, too, Astrid."

"I know," she whispered. She paused, tangling her fingers in his luxuriant chest hair. "What do you think they'll do to us?"

"I don't know."

"I guess we'll have to deal with it, whatever it is."

"Yeah."

"They don't need to know for a while, anyway."

"No."

"Maybe, when all this mess clears up..." Astrid halted, unable to finish her sentence as she broke down into helpless weeping. Nate gathered her close and held her tightly. "God, Nate—what if it doesn't clear up? What will we do?"

"Maybe all we can do is pray to Spirit."

"Yeah, I—I should trust the universe to take care of us—work something out," she choked.

"Sounds like a good idea," he murmured comfortingly, kissing her hair.

What else can we do? she thought mournfully. And soon she found herself dropping into a delicious, seductive sleep, remembering too late that she hadn't activated her dreamviewer or donned the transistor electrode. I'll remember my dreams anyway, she reassured herself drowsily, too tired to get up. And even if she didn't, the world wouldn't come to an end, surely, if she went one night without remembering her dreams.

TWENTY-TWO

Judy straightened her dress nervously as she stood before the door to Major Duncan's quarters, flicking off as many tomato seeds as she could reach, hoping she didn't look as disheveled as she felt. She didn't know whether she wanted to find Major Duncan at home or not. Her head ached from the rock that had caught her right above her glasses, and in fact, all she wanted to do was go home to her cubicle and lie down. But there was no way that she could purposely miss this appointment, even if her doom waited on the other side of the door.

She felt supremely uneasy, although she couldn't say why exactly, except that it was most unusual for someone in Major Duncan's position to invite someone like her to his private quarters. Either he had another secret mission in mind or—she couldn't avoid this possibility, given the irregularity of the situation—he was a Satanist and she was his intended victim. He had set her up pretty craftily, she had to admit, as she raised a trembling hand to ring the buzzer. By being so nice to her, he had made sure she would do anything he told her to do, even during her off hours.

The door opened so quickly she gave a little jump of surprise. Major Duncan stood in the foyer, looking more brutally handsome than ever. His eyes traveled over her as he invited her in, stepping back with a formal click of his heels. She saluted, wincing as she accidentally tapped her swollen eye. He sighed.

"Been to church, I see."

"Yes sir, I have, sir."

He shook his head, his lips pursed in distaste. He probably thinks I'm revolting, Judy thought, tears pricking her eyes.

"I need to discuss some important matters with you, Judy, but I'm afraid I can't bear even to look at you in such a state." He led her to a small room which opened off the living room. "Take your dress off and give it to the maid. It'll clean it for you. You may wash up in the restroom." He took down a clean, fluffy terry-cloth wrap from a wall hook and handed it to her. "While you're waiting for your own garment, you may wear this. Please join me in the living room when you're ready." Much to her surprise, he ran his finger softly along her bruise. "I'll dress your wound for you."

Judy was so flabbergasted by his attentiveness, that she remained rooted to the spot. He gave her a push and closed the door, whereupon a robotic maid approached. Judy stepped out of her dress, handing it, with considerable embarrassment even to a mechanical device, over to the robot. Her head was absolutely whirling when she reappeared in the living room, the robe tightly belted around her. He might rip it off her in whatever scenario he had in mind, but before that happened, she didn't want to offend him with any of her unsightly bulges.

"Ah!" he exclaimed, when he caught sight of her. "Much better. Sit down next to me, please, and I'll take care of that nasty bruise."

Wonderingly, she eased herself down onto the edge of the sofa where he sat. He cleaned the broken skin with a medicated pad, then applied a soothing ointment. He handed her a small rubber bag filled with ice and instructed her to hold it to the injured area in order to minimize the swelling.

"Sit back and relax," he insisted smoothly, earnestly. "You have nothing to fear."

She did so, the nagging unease returning for some reason. Why was he being so nice? Was he trying to lull her suspicions? If he wanted to rape her, why not just go on and get it over with? Suddenly she noticed a screen in front of the two-way television. Then her eyes fell upon a book lying upon the coffee table. Panic shot through her and she gasped in alarm, dropping the ice bag. A Satanist symbol was imprinted on the front cover! "Satan!" she choked. "My God! Help!"

She sprang to her feet but tripped over the coffee table as she attempted to flee, and sprawled clumsily onto the floor. Scrambling up, she perceived Major Duncan reaching for her anxiously, exclaiming, "Judy, it's all right! Judy, listen to me—it's not what you think! It's not a Satanist symbol, it's the symbol of the Tao!"

She stopped in her tracks. For some reason she felt infinitely relieved, so relieved that she found herself sobbing, even though she had no idea what he was talking about. Nevertheless, she allowed him to help her into her seat on the sofa.

"What—what's the Tao?" she quavered, once her sobs had quieted.

"It's life. The mystery of life. It's an ancient religion that arose in the Orient over two thousand years ago."

"A primitive religion?"

"No, not primitive. It's quite sophisticated, in fact. What we have now, Judy, is a primitive religion. Very, very primitive."

Judy blanched and glanced apprehensively at the television. "But that…that's heresy!" she squeaked.

"Don't worry. They can't hear. I've installed a device that produces white noise and creates the illusion of silence. All they can see is what I have on the screen. If anyone monitors these quarters, they will see me reading and moving about the room, engaged in innocuous activity."

"But what about my homing device? Can't they hear through that?"

"It's a homing device, nothing more, although the old devices had a tracking feature. Surveillance has become too expensive to keep up with the level the government would like. Besides, the fear of surveillance has proven almost as effective. But you should remind me, next time we're in the office, to have that objectionable device neutralized."

Judy regarded him, speechless. He smiled wryly at her, the first time she'd ever seen him smile. Her heart and every other contiguous organ melted on the spot. Could this be the same man she worked for?

"I suppose you wonder what I'm up to."

She nodded, dropping her gaze to her twisting fingers. To her astonishment, he reached over and gently lifted her chin, locking her eyes with his.

"Judy, what I'm about to tell you is of the utmost secrecy. It's treason. I know I can trust you, that's not the problem. Your performance on my little errand proved that. But I have to warn you that if you agree to help me, if you even acquiesce to listen to what I have to tell you and don't turn me in immediately, you could lose your life. Not only that, you could lose it in a hideous manner. You would assuredly be tortured to death. Please know that I will understand if you choose to leave now. I want to feel that if you join me, it is completely of your own free will."

Lord! Judy lamented; why did this have to happen? She wanted to serve him, yes, but why did it have to be this way? She didn't want to die! She didn't want to be tortured, either! Should she leave? Should she explain to him how very much she wanted to help him but couldn't? For it seemed clear, as she shyly observed his frank and compassionate expression, that he wouldn't hold it against her.

And then she realized that she wasn't, in fact, free to choose. She knew that she was bound to help him from love, even if all he had in mind was to use her in this new cause. Her eyes swam with tears.

"I...I agree," she finally choked, tears falling as she spoke. "I—want to help you, sir. I don't care what I have to do."

Major Duncan seized her hands and gave them a squeeze. "I knew I could count on you, Judy!" he declared. "You have strength you don't even know you have. I'm glad you made the decision you did," he said, "because in point of fact, it may well be that we will all die if something isn't done." He spoke soberly, rapidly. "In fact, we are all dying as I speak, and very little time remains. That's why I had to bring you in, Judy. We have dire need of your excellent capabilities."

"My capabilities?" she peeped.

"Yes. Now, the situation is this: the phytoplankton are dying. Once they go, the oxygen in the atmosphere will quickly disappear. In times past, the rain forests help to produce the world's oxygen, but as you may know, they are all gone, vast deserts of hard, baked clay now. Farms exist, of course, but the biomass of the plant life that they compose is far too insufficient to carry the load for the entire planet."

Judy nodded dumbly, wiping her perspiring palms on Major Duncan's robe without thinking. Had it really come to this?

Major Duncan continued. "The top brass and insurance executives, of course, know all about his. They've begun construction on underground tunnels provided with oxygen generators, which will be fueled by geothermal energy sources. They have begun cultivation of underground fungus farms. They are hoping that in this way they and their families will be able to survive." He paused, searing her with the intensity of his icy gaze. "However, regardless of the grotesque immorality of such a solution, they may be too late. The oceans are dying much more quickly than they had anticipated. Instead of dying gradually, the oceans have reached a critical point and are expiring at an exponential rate. Not just humans are in danger. Every living thing on this planet is threatened."

Judy swallowed, trying to ease the gigantic lump that had formed in her throat. "So what do you plan to do?" she whispered. "How—how can anyone stop it now?"

Major Duncan expelled a short breath. "All we can do is try. We have only a rather desperate plan, I'm afraid. And this is where we need your help."

Judy removed her glasses and wiped them on the hem of the robe, blinking nervously. What if she couldn't come up with what he wanted? It was one thing to want to help and another thing entirely to be capable of helping.

"I hope to set off the western edge of the Ring of Fire."

"The Ring of Fire, sir?"

"Yes, it's a system of volcanoes that runs along the rim of the Pacific Ocean. Resonating devices are being put into place on every volcano in the Americas, devices that will heat up the underlying magma to the eruption point."

"But…wouldn't that create havoc with the world climate?" she protested. "Wouldn't that cause a winter that lasted for years?"

"I'm hoping that it will do far more than that."

"You—you do?"

"Yes, I'm hoping for a somewhat significant displacement of the Earth's crust over the Earth's core."

"You are?"

"It should work. A liquid-like layer underlies the lithosphere. Such intense geologic activity all at once could easily effect such a phenomenon. It's probably happened before in our Earth's history, in fact."

"And what would that do?" she inquired hesitantly, wondering whether she had just pledged her allegiance to a madman.

"Oh, massive tidal waves, of course. The poles would melt, if they shift from the axes of the planet. Massive areas would be flooded, submerged under tons of water. Rapid, catastrophic tectonic activity would result, surely. Some areas will uplift while others will sink, probably all within a couple of days. Violent storms will no doubt rage for weeks."

"But, sir—wouldn't that kill everybody?"

"Not everyone. Not the phytoplankton."

"The people, though. The humans. Would they survive?"

Duncan cocked his head. "Many would die. Some would probably survive, though. Those who happened to be in the right place at the right time."

"The military and the survivalists," she said flatly.

"Not necessarily. The military hasn't relocated yet. The underground structures aren't finished. Not only that, the tectonic activity could easily destroy them—and the survivalists' camps. But those psychically attuned would probably be in just the right spot at the right time to survive. If that were their purpose and desire, of course."

Judy stared at him, horrified, unable to believe what she was hearing. "Those psychically attuned, huh?" she burst out. "I suppose that's you and your underground. It's okay for everyone else to perish!"

Major Duncan whitened, the muscles in his temples flexed. "Fair enough," he replied shortly, his voice sharp. "But you forget—the human race is killing itself anyway. If we poison our planet to the extent that we destroy not only life but the very capacity to provide life, I see no humaneness in such a solution. Do you?"

Judy shrank away from him. "No, sir."

"But you think it's better to allow our species to murder an entire planet."

"Of course not, sir," she responded, tears swimming into her eyes.

He briefly pressed his thumb and forefinger to his eyes, then glanced over at her, his expression softer. "I'm sorry. I didn't mean to use that tone with you. But you do see, don't you, that we are all dying anyway, taking the entire planet with us? Once we've ceased our destructive activities and discontinued pumping billions of gallons of toxic waste and untreated sewage into the oceans, there is a chance, still, that the phytoplankton could survive and continue to oxygenate the planet. And a catastrophic event is bound to happen sooner or later. We just want to make sure it happens in time—before it's too late and all the phytoplankton are dead."

He glanced at her again, then bent his head and gathered her small, damp hands into his. "I'm so sorry that I ever involved you in this, Judy."

She sighed. "Don't apologize, sir."

"Judy," he replied with a glimmer of amusement, "you may drop the 'sir' when we're in private. I realize that my...very necessary, I assure you...facade at the MI Complex has given you the wrong impression of my true character. And probably intimidated you out of your wits. But please, there are no subordinates and superiors here. You are a highly intelligent, very caring, loyal and compassionate woman. We're equals. Both humans. Both living creatures. Please, call me Robert."

"Okay," she acquiesced timorously, shaken to hear herself described so flatteringly. Still, it was fine for him to say they were equals. He was beautiful. She certainly didn't feel equal to him in that regard. "Say—say I wanted to help you. Where would I fit in?"

Major Duncan leaned forward eagerly. "I need you to check over my calculations," he explained earnestly, "make sure they're correct. Mt. Shasta is the keystone of the plan, the first to go; if I don't have the right resonance frequencies and it fails to erupt, nothing will happen. And obviously, we don't want an explosion so severe that we cause irreparable damage to the biosphere."

She marveled at how Major Duncan managed to love the biosphere so well and at the same time to think nothing of considering mass murder. Did that make him a psychopath, or a savior? She didn't know. She did know that his touch was plunging her into a mesmerized state of dazed desire. She would do anything for him; she didn't care if he was only trying to seduce her to his cause with his affection. What was she doing with her life, anyway? Why not sacrifice it for a cause, even if the cause was mad? Nothing could be worse than what the overwhelming majority on the planet suffered already. Perhaps a clean though painful cauterization would be better than a dead world or one covered in running sores of warfare and extreme toxic irresponsibility.

"I'll—do whatever you want, like I said," she heard herself murmur. "You—realize, though, don't you," she blurted, "that theoretically you're asking me to kill not only myself but you, too?"

"Yes, I do. You can still back out, Judy. I won't hold you to your promise. I know that what I'm asking you to do is monumentally difficult."

"And, uh, you see, my expertise is really in statistics. I mean—I didn't take a whole lot of physics or geology courses."

"I know. I checked out your background thoroughly, believe me. I also know that you graduated from vocational training with the highest cumulative score ever recorded."

"Are you kidding?" Judy gasped. "Why didn't anyone ever tell me? Why did they stick me with that stupid job at Sunshine?"

"Out of fear, most likely. A repressive society always fears its most gifted members. I imagine the powers that be didn't want you to gain too much power."

"Power? Me?"

"Yes, you," he mocked her gently. He rose to his feet, drawing her with him. "Your dress should be cleaned and pressed by now." He leaned over and tapped out a command on his personal computer and the maid appeared instantly, dress in hand. "Please, use my room to change in while I obtain us some refreshment."

"All right, sir—Robert," she amended hastily. She reddened. Great, call him Sir Robert, she castigated herself as she retreated into his room; he must think I am such an unbelievable idiot!

When she came out, he was waiting for her in the living room. A pitcher, two glasses, and a plate of something were laid out neatly on the coffee table in front of him.

"Milk and cookies?" he inquired as she seated herself timidly on the sofa beside him.

"Y–yes, thank you," she stammered, tears rushing into her eyes. He was being so kind to her! She'd never had cookies in her life, ever, and milk only when she was in Children's Camp. She nervously wiped the back of her hand across her lips, afraid that she might start salivating excessively.

"So, Major—um, Robert," Judy began, as she selected a cookie from the plate he proffered.

"Yes?"

"Did you—I mean, I don't want to pry, but I—I assumed you grew up wealthy, right?"

Duncan nodded, gravely pouring them each a glass of milk. Judy's taste buds quivered, but she didn't want to start before he did. Fortunately, he bit into his cookie.

"Well, what was it like?" she asked eagerly, unable to stop herself from cramming the entire cookie into her mouth at the end of her question.

Major Duncan laughed and offered her another cookie. She decided to take two this time. He leaned back on the sofa and clasped his hands behind his head. "Not nearly so wonderful as you would imagine."

"Really? Why not?" She couldn't imagine it otherwise, what with wonderful food, beautiful clothes, comfortable furnishings, private education, and real showers. All those things they had on "Rich People, the New Generation."

"The fact is, Judy, there's a void in the center of each person in my class. No one believes in his or her spirit. Religion, as perhaps you perceived, is only for the lower classes, and a highly distorted one at that. That means that in my class, a black hole exists where the wellspring of each person's psychic and physical sustenance should be. They try to allay this lack with possessions, phony power, drink, or drugs. Of course, nothing ever satiates them. They never supply the void with what it really wants, so they end up sucking energy from everyone and everything around them." He exhaled wearily. "Like vampires."

His choice of words made Judy shudder. "You mean, everyone is like that? Didn't you ever have…a lover or fiancee?"

"I did. A beautiful creature by modern physical standards. I say 'creature' because I found her morally repugnant. The wealthy try to fill their spiritual abyss with activities far more degenerate than you could ever imagine."

Judy swallowed, her curiosity piqued. She wanted to know what sorts of activities he referred to, but felt that it would be impolite to ask. He probably didn't want to talk about it. But he had used the past tense in referring to this woman! Did that mean he was unattached? Surely not. Surely he kept or visited some poor but exotically beautiful mistress.

"Since that depressing liaison, I have dedicated myself to my work. And to my spiritual search," he remarked, as if answering her unspoken question. "By the way, I believe that you're acquainted with my colleague, a fellow member of our organization."

"Who?" Judy asked, mystified. Who on earth could it possibly be?

"Dorothy," he replied.

"Dorothy!" Judy considered this bit of information in amazement. Somehow Dorothy just seemed too independent to devote herself to a cause, too amoral. But then, she ruminated, what was morality, anyway? She felt confused.

Major Duncan reached over to the end table and picked up a small black cylinder that Judy hadn't noticed before, she had been so focused on him—and the plate of cookies. "This contains a set of microfilm and lenses so that you can study my equations."

He handed it to her and she accepted it with trembling hands.

"I don't want to rush you," he said, "but unfortunately, time is rather short. If you've finished...?"

Judy hastily downed the last of her milk and bolted to her feet, causing Major Duncan to laugh yet again.

"We're not in that big a hurry!" he chuckled. "I'd give you the cookies to take home, but you might get mugged for them and I wouldn't want that to happen." He arose also, and handed her an elastic band, which he instructed her to use in strapping the cylinder to her thigh for concealment and safety. She did so nervously, yet, she had to admit, with irrepressible excitement.

"Just—out of curiosity, sir," she inquired as he ushered her to the door, his hand resting lightly upon her waist, "what was in that cylinder I obtained for you the other night?"

He hesitated before answering. "Actually...nothing," he told her.

"Nothing?!" she exclaimed. "I risked my life for nothing?"

"Not for nothing," he responded uncomfortably. "I had to know whether I could count on you—depend on you. I'm sorry. It had to be done." He gave her a sidelong glance as he opened the front door and stood aside to let her pass.

"Waste no time. I want you to sleep on what I've said," he told her, rather contradictorily, Judy thought. "And perhaps," he mused, "when we all wake up from this terrible nightmare, we'll find ourselves living in the land of our dreams."

TWENTY-THREE

Astrid bounded down the steps of the Shasta City train station, two at a time, spying Taro's sporty yellow car waiting for her in the parking area. Astrid and Nate didn't own a car, since they got around on bikes and public transportation, but Taro had designed and built this car himself, an ethanol-assisted solar automobile of which he felt extremely proud. When she slid into the passenger's seat, tossing her bags into the back, he gave her a peck on the cheek and started up the engine.

"I see you got my message," she said.

"I did. How was your trip?"

"Oh—fine, I guess. If you don't count that subway ride."

Taro grimaced as he turned onto the street. "Grisly business. I'm afraid there's been another murder in Shasta City," he sighed.

Astrid looked at him aghast. "Are you serious?" she exclaimed.

Taro nodded glumly. "Afraid so." He pulled up to a stoplight and put on his blinker. "There's a meeting at Robin's house. I thought we could go there right away."

"Uh...Taro, I think I'd like to change clothes, if you don't mind. I'm wearing the same clothes I had on the space shuttle."

"I wondered what that smell was."

"See? It's in your own best interest."

"Okay. I'll call Robin from your house and let her know we're on the way." Taro ran a slim hand through his short black hair. "By the way, did you see anybody at the train station?"

"What do you mean, 'anybody?'"

"Anybody you know?"

"I don't think so. Wait—I saw Zach and Brittany. Why?"

"Just curious."

Astrid expected him to say more, but when he didn't, she decided not to press him. No doubt she would learn everything she needed to know at the meeting. She noticed that he was driving faster than usual—also glancing about apprehensively in an uncharacteristic fashion. She chalked it up to the murders and settled back in her seat, buzzing from an odd blend of exhaustion from her travels and exhilaration from having conceived a baby. She wondered whether she should tell Taro about her new passenger but decided to wait.

Soon they were driving up the road to her house. A few manzanita bushes still flowered, their creamy pink blossoms hanging in clusters among the frosty, oval leaves, their spicy fragrance suffusing the air. Astrid caught a glint of metallic fuchsia as a hummingbird flashed by, sipping nectar from the pearly blooms; a few bees droned in the bright sun. How odd, she thought, that murders could occur in such beautiful, peaceful settings.

"The person who was murdered," she said suddenly. "Did we know them?"

"No, thank god. Although that's little consolation to the people who did. Well—here you are. You scamper in and I'll bring your things. Bring your dream videos with you to the meeting."

"Okay," she replied guiltily. What were her dreams the night she conceived? It seemed she dreamed about

Judy, but for the life of her she couldn't remember any more than that—and some urgent, ominous emotion associated with it. The next night on the space shuttle to San Francisco, she had used her dreamviewer, but she hadn't dreamed about Judy. She'd dreamed instead about Meagan and Louise, some paranoid fantasies about them locking her up in a hospital-like place.

She had also, for some reason, dreamed again about the golden city, the one she'd visited so often during her bout with the UFO virus. In that dream, she could fly, and she flew all around the city, which was filled with a lush, healthy, sentient plant life; and the city, although seemingly devoid of people, emanated the most inviting, welcoming feeling. That dream had really rejuvenated her. She wondered whether her oversoul had sent it to her after her prayer for help or whether it had something to do with the new child she carried. Perhaps during its embryologic development, it went through the stages of "infection." She wondered also whether conceiving in space would have any noticeable effects on her baby.

Astrid showered quickly and changed into a soft, rose-colored flannel dress while Taro phoned Robin. Astrid had noticed when she came in that her message machine was blinking, so after Taro made his call she played her messages back.

The first message was from Maria. "Hello, dear—this is Maria," it said. "I just wanted to tell you that I hope you had a good trip to New York and that I look forward to seeing you when you get back. You can have your usual time if you want it. And by the way, I thought over what you said about needing to help people. I think you're right. We can talk about it when I see you. Call me, okay?"

Astrid smiled and made a note to call her while waiting for the next message. The voice was not one she recognized.

"Atavistic bitch," it hissed, sending a shock through her. "Don't interfere with things you know nothing about."

Taro, who was standing by a set of bookshelves, leafing through one of Astrid's art books, jerked his head up. "What was that?" he exclaimed. "*Who* was that?"

Astrid shrugged, chilled, trying to decide whether to play it back to see if she could identify the caller. She wasn't sure she wanted to hear it again. She started to erase it, but Taro came over and punched the play button. Astrid walked away as it played, cringing at the malice in the speaker's voice.

"Whoa, pretty heavy," said Taro when it finished. "Lovely voice. I wonder if he's ever considered a career in radio broadcasting?"

Astrid tried to laugh but couldn't.

"Hey, listen—don't let that person upset you. Whoever it is is obviously a cretin. On the other hand..."

"On the other hand, what?"

"On the other hand, things are getting a little weird here."

"Weird how?"

Taro sighed. "I was going to let Robin break the news to you. She's so much more tactful than I am."

"You tell me," Astrid demanded bluntly.

"Well—certain members of the community are rounding up other members of the community for investigation purposes."

"Investigation purposes?"

"Yeah. Genetic screening. Looking for the hypothetical atavisms."

Astrid sank down into a nearby chair. "I can't believe it," she whispered.

"I know. That's why I asked you whether you saw anyone you knew at the train station. As far as I know, Zach and Brittany are okay, but I prefer the safety to be found in numbers. So if you're ready, why don't we hotfoot it over to Robin's? When is Nate due back?"

"In the next day or so."

"Good. We need more giants on our side. Ready?"

Astrid nodded and got up to follow Taro to his car. "What—happens to these people who get 'rounded up?'" "Actually, no one knows."

Astrid folded herself back into the car, drumming nervously on the dashboard and trying to scrunch herself up even more so that no one they passed would recognize her. They reached Robin's house without incident. When they let themselves in and Robin caught sight of Astrid, she rushed over to her with a glad cry and grabbed her up in an embrace.

"I am so glad to see you!" she exclaimed.

"It's mutual," beamed Astrid, leaning back to admire Robin's creamy complexion and coppery hair. Why Joshua wouldn't want to have a baby with such a wonderful woman, she would never understand. A look of comprehension and delight dawned on Robin's face.

"Astrid!" she whispered. "You're—" she stopped.

Astrid nodded happily. "Yup."

"When? When did it happen?"

"Two days ago on the space station."

Robin grabbed her hands and gave them a squeeze. "Congratulations!" she said.

"I don't suppose you two could stop your female bonding long enough to tell me what's going on," Taro complained.

"Oh, sorry, Taro," giggled Robin. "I thought perhaps you knew."

"Know something that Ms. Telepathic Strongbox here didn't want me to know? I'm afraid I didn't take Psychic Sleuthing 101."

Astrid turned to him. "I'm pregnant."

An odd look crossed Taro's face. "Hey, that's great, really." He smiled briefly. "But…it's not going to go over real big with the community at large."

Robin's expression changed to one of distress. "That's true, Astrid. I'm afraid that last night Louise and Meagan managed to get their resolution passed."

"What? Didn't you block it?"

Robin clasped her hands together and glanced at Taro.

"Well—we tried, Astrid, but—we were outvoted."

"Outvoted? What happened to unanimous consent?"

"Well—they're going by majority rule now."

Astrid gaped at her friend. "Majority dictatorship, you mean. How did that happen?"

"The majority decided."

"Oh, man." Astrid dropped wearily onto the couch. "So what do I do now?"

"Right now I think you should relax," Robin ordered her briskly. "I'll make a pot of tea and we'll go over our options. Rana should be here soon and Van, too, if she managed to locate him."

"Van's offworld," Astrid said.

"Oh, really?"

"Yeah, he's gone from the space station to mining on the asteroid belt. Although why he chose now to do something that makes him so unavailable, I don't know."

"Avoidance," remarked Taro dryly.

"No doubt," muttered Astrid, thinking that the asteroid belt sounded pretty good to her at the moment.

Robin disappeared briefly into the kitchen and then returned with a tray rattling with a teapot, cups and saucers. "I made chamomile tea so we can feel relaxed," she said.

Astrid gratefully accepted a cup and leaned back on the sofa, inhaling the delicate flowery aroma of the tea. Sunlight streamed in through the bay window in Robin's living room, warming her back and brightening the lovely, soothing colors that Robin had chosen to decorate with: cool mint green, deep forest green, light mauve and deep, luscious rose.

"Astrid, you go perfectly with my living room in that dress," Robin commented, smiling. "I think you should stay right there and never leave."

"Or change my dress, right?" Astrid replied, reaching over to squeeze her friend's hand. The doorbell rang and

Robin jumped up to answer it, ushering Rana into the living room and serving her a cup of tea. Rana, looking more disheveled than usual, nodded a greeting to Astrid and Taro, then took her dreamviewer out of its case.

"Maybe we should get started," she said.

"Good idea," agreed Taro, sitting up attentively.

"I thought I'd just run through some clips of recent dreams about that other world, although to tell you the truth, I think Dorothy is holding out on me," Rana said.

"Holding out on you?" echoed Robin.

"Yes, it appears that she's involved in some sort of subversive activity, but she has amazingly effective blocks set up around that whole aspect of her thoughts and experience. The only way I got wind of it was the fact that my dreams kept getting chopped off abruptly. I'll show you."

Astrid set her cup down on the coffee table and leaned forward with interest as scenes began to flicker across the video screen.

Interestingly enough, Rana had also dreamed about Judy's dinner with Dorothy. The book on psychic powers precipitated some interested murmurs from Robin and Taro, as did the provocative visual effect at the end of the dream where it looked as if Dorothy were floating along. There the dream ended abruptly.

"See?" said Rana. "My dream ends right there. Now watch this."

The next dream began with Dorothy rummaging around in her back room for parts, consulting a diagram she had spread out on her desk. At one point she reached for the phone, but the minute she began to punch the numbers the screen went blank.

"Now look at this one."

In the next clip, Dorothy sat at her desk with some sort of instrument assembled in front of her, a wild, eccentric-looking device whose purpose no one present could even guess at. A knock came at the office door, but before Dorothy answered it, everything went black yet again.

Rana switched off the viewer. "She's definitely hiding something. Even from me. I was hoping that you might have some more information, Astrid."

Astrid shifted uncomfortably. "I'm afraid I don't have much on Dorothy," she replied. "I'll show you what I have on Judy. I'll warn you, one of the dreams is a little disheartening, but actually, I don't think it's as bad as it looks, and it helped me to develop a great idea. I think I'll show them out of sequence, get the depressing one out of the way first, and then I'll show you another one." Astrid ejected Rana's video and inserted her own. Taro groaned audibly throughout the entire church service, then started in on simulated retching noises near the end. By the time Astrid had finished showing this dream, Taro was hanging limply over the side of his chair.

"God, how can you stand it?" he exclaimed. "That entire world is so pathetic! Rana, it would seem you have tabs on the only creature with a backbone on the entire planet."

Astrid stiffened resentfully. "I'd like to know how you'd stand up, given the kind of life Judy's had to live," she snorted. "Judy has more going for her than you give her credit for. Watch this next clip and see whether you think you'd have the nerve to do what she did."

Astrid rewound the tape to the previous dream in which she saved Judy from the gang. When Astrid appeared onscreen, Robin gasped. "My god!" she breathed. "I dreamed about this!" The dream ran all the way to the end, where Astrid flew to the mountain. It stopped when she transported herself back to New York. As Astrid stood up to eject the video, Taro uttered a pitiful moan.

"Do you realize what this means?" he said.

"That I am actually able to travel to Judy's world," Astrid answered grimly.

"No, not that—although that is fairly apparent. What I mean is, from the logistics I've gathered from your dream, Judy's city must be an alternate San Francisco!"

"Oh, you're right, Taro. How...unfortunate," Robin sympathized.

"It's worse than unfortunate! It's a tragedy! My god, how could they do that to such a jewel of a city?"

"Robin, you said you dreamed about this last dream," said Astrid. "What else have you dreamed about?"

Robin poured herself another cup of tea, shaking her head. "Not much," she admitted. "At least, not much about that other world. I don't seem to have as strong a connection to it as you do. When you're not around, I usually dream about other things."

"Taro?"

He shrugged. "For some reason, I've mostly been having sexual fantasy dreams."

"Oh, that's a big help."

"Well, I'm sorry! What do you expect me to do?"

Astrid ignored him. "Rana, have you been able to have any effect on Dorothy—on events in her life?"

Rana sighed. "It's hard to say. It seemed like it when we created that position for Judy at her store, but now, with whatever Dorothy has going on, it seems that she's set up a barrier of some kind. Maybe now that you're back, we can have more of an effect together. You're our strongest dreamer, you know."

Astrid didn't reply. She carefully smoothed her dress over her knees, feeling frustrated and guilty for having left town.

"So what's this wonderful plan you've got brewing?" asked Taro.

Astrid perked up. "Well, it's a bit of a long shot and somewhat indirect, but if it works, it could be very powerful. I think we should create an invincible messiah. I seem to be able to protect Judy, so I could make it seem as though she has divine protection. I thought she could promote some radical societal changes." Astrid explained her theory about the gang members representing repressed aspects of the dark side of Judy's society. "At the same time, I thought perhaps I could level a few institutional buildings, encourage people to see that these institutions are not as impregnable as they've always thought. It's a sick, ailing society that needs healing. We can help, but they need to do the majority of the healing themselves." Astrid nodded to Rana. "I thought Dorothy could be a key figure in all of this as well."

Taro reached over and slapped Astrid on the shoulder. "Bravo, Astrid. Good plan! Don't you all agree?"

Rana and Robin did agree, so the group busied themselves with hammering out ideas, following through on different possible developments and outcomes. When they were all talked out, Robin slipped back into the kitchen and returned with slices of a sour-cream cinnamon coffee cake she had baked that morning.

"We all need to keep our strength up," she said as she passed around the plate.

Astrid's eyes filled with tears. Even in the midst of all the strife and turmoil, Robin was still baking coffee cakes and managing to coax Astrid to relax with a cup of chamomile tea, Taro was his usual rascally, entertaining self, Rana still briskly straightforward. Man, but she loved her community. It was worth any risk, any personal sacrifice she could make to save it. There was absolutely no way that she could simply turn her back and move some place else.

When she had finished her cake and brushed the crumbs from her lap, she suddenly remembered her conversation with Milo about Cedric. She recounted it to the group. Everyone's expression became very grave.

"Now, I know this might sound strange, but I'm starting to think that, even though Cedric's meddling might have set up the initial probability frequencies, this connection was meant to take place. Cedric was merely the agent of implementation. He hasn't succeeded in getting his plans through Town Meeting yet, has he?"

"No, we convinced them to wait on that proposition, at least until you got back. You think we're meant to help this world?" asked Robin.

"I do. Not only that, but in the same way that the gang members represent a fragmented dark side of Judy's world, maybe this whole world represents the underside of our own. Our past, perhaps, or a possible future. It could be an aspect of our nature that we no longer want to own up to, now that our world is doing so much better—our submerged fears, our history of destructiveness that the UFO virus has managed to keep in check. The UFO virus might constitute sort of an outside solution, so to speak. Perhaps only a temporary one, unless we come to grips with the destructive side of our nature in the deepest part of our psyches. In our dreams. In our hearts."

"Interesting concept," murmured Taro. "Rather subtle and slippery. Do you think you can get the foaming-at-the-mouth faction to listen to you?"

"Well, I don't know. All I can do is try."

"Try how?" asked Rana. "I assume Robin and Taro told you about community members getting picked up for investigation. A couple of people have been asking around as to your whereabouts. And I don't think they wanted to invite you to a party. If they know where you are, they might sequester you."

Astrid shivered involuntarily. Her parents hadn't been so far off the mark after all. She considered. "Maybe I could hide out and broadcast this stuff from my computer."

"That's a good idea!" exclaimed Robin, who had been gazing worriedly at Astrid.

"I also thought I'd go talk to Cedric."

Taro and Robin glanced at each other in dismay.

"I'd nix that idea if I were you," said Taro. "He is definitely a major foamer at the mouth. Major. And ugly besides."

"Look, I've got to talk to him. If somebody doesn't reach him and talk some sense into him, he could screw up everything!"

Taro didn't reply. Robin and Rana looked down at their plates.

"Does anyone know where he's living these days?"

Rana sighed, fingering the string of cinnabar beads she wore around her neck. "I think I heard that he's been staying at Sierra's old place. But if you go, we should go with you. I don't like the thought of your seeing him by yourself. He's gotten weirder by the day."

"Okay. Fair enough. Is everybody ready to go?"

"Right now?" asked Taro.

"Yes, right now. I don't think we have a minute to lose. Didn't you tell me his device is ready?"

"Yes, but…"

"But what?"

"Well, here Robin has fixed this lovely coffee cake and I've barely finished my first piece, and—"

"Why don't you wrap up a piece for Taro, Robin?" Astrid interrupted.

Robin smiled and reached for the cake to comply.

"Oh, never mind—don't bother," Taro grumbled. "It's just going to be rather crowded in my car, you know. I mean, it wasn't really built for giants."

"Stop complaining, Taro," scolded Astrid. "You didn't have any trouble coming over here."

The four headed outside and squeezed into Taro's car. It was, in fact, close quarters, made even closer by the tension emanating from each passenger. When they reached Sierra's place, the rundown condition of the house appalled Astrid. Shutters hung askew, the boards desperately needed paint, and a couple of windows had broken panes, patched carelessly with sheets of clear plastic and tape.

"It looks like a haunted house!" said Robin. "I had no idea that Sierra had let it get so bad before he died."

"Or that Cedric was content to live in such a pig sty," added Taro.

Astrid caught a glimpse of movement in one of the upstairs windows, but when she looked up, she didn't see anything. They rang the bell and the door wrenched open immediately. Astrid swallowed nervously upon seeing Cedric. His hair looked matted, his clothes filthy. When he stared at her, she felt as if he were X-raying her entire being. She shrank away from him, wanting to protect herself from his gaze. Cedric, she knew, possessed awesome psychic abilities.

"What's this all about?" he growled.

"Uh, well—I needed to talk to you about something," stammered Astrid.

Cedric gestured at the rest of the group. "What are they doing here, then?"

"We came along for the ride," said Taro.

Cedric glared balefully at him. Taro fell silent.

"Listen, Cedric—I just came from New York where I ran into an old friend of mine. Milo Defiore. Does that name ring a bell?"

Cedric tugged at his beard, contemplating. Then he stood aside and opened the door wide. "Come in," he said. When he shut the door behind him, Astrid thought she heard the click of a lock but decided it must be her frayed nerves playing tricks on her.

Inside, it appeared as if Cedric had settled into a symbiotic relationship with the spiders. Virtual ropes of webs hung slackly from the ceiling and beams, beaded with clumps of dust. When the group sat down on the sagging furniture, clouds of dank-smelling dust poufed into the air, causing both Robin and Rana to sneeze. And the windows hadn't been cleaned in so long the light that penetrated had a dim, clotted, yellow cast.

Cedric lowered himself onto one arm of the sofa, his knotted fists shoved under each arm. "What did Milo have to tell you?" he asked quietly.

"Well—he told me about some experiments you were conducting at Humboldt. Apparently he saw you in the company of something strange once. Listen, I haven't come here to accuse you or anything. I just want to say that, despite these unfortunate murders, I think we were meant to come in contact with this world. You didn't do anything wrong. But I think disrupting the connection at this point could have disastrous consequences."

Cedric didn't respond for a long time. Then he stood up and walked over to a blinking digital clock, fiddling with the reset mechanism. Finally he said, "You've seen this world. Correct?"

Astrid nodded.

"Then you know the kind of filth we're talking about."

Taro caught Astrid's eye and raised an eyebrow. She looked away.

"I do, Cedric, but—I think they need healing on that world. If we don't help them, who will?"

Cedric banged the clock down. "They got themselves into this mess," he snarled. "They can deal with it themselves. I'm not about to stand by while they drag us down into the cesspool with them."

Astrid bit her lip, then tried again. "Look, what if the UFO virus hadn't come along to help our world? We could have ended up just like them."

Cedric waved his hand dismissively. "It was our destiny not to, obviously."

"Maybe it's their destiny not to either, Cedric. Maybe we're destined to help them."

"They need to be punished!" he roared, eyes and veins bulging alarmingly. "They need to know that they can't foul their nest so outrageously and have somebody else come in and get them out of it. They must live with the consequences of their actions!"

"And what about us, then? We have to live with the consequences of knowing we refused to help when we could have. You want to live with that?"

Cedric strode rapidly across the room and seized Astrid by the shoulders. "You have no right to meddle with things you don't understand," he hissed, his face inches from hers. All of a sudden Astrid knew who had left the anonymous message on her answering machine. "This world is hopeless. It's evil! I breached the barrier; now I intend to rectify my mistake."

"Two wrongs don't make a right," piped up Taro. "On the other hand," he mumbled, when Cedric whirled around to train his scowl upon him, "what do I know?"

Cedric straightened up. "It's unfortunate, Astrid, that I can't make you understand what kind of a threat we're talking about here. You're young, of course. Too young to remember, really, what the twentieth century was like."

"I'm not that young, Cedric."

Cedric continued as if she hadn't spoken a word. "Too young to have any real grasp of the danger. You realize, don't you, that I'm going to disrupt that window whether you and your...little band here approves or not. This is too dangerous for know-nothings like yourselves to decide."

Robin stomped her foot and jumped up. "That's it!" she exclaimed. "I can't take another word! Who are you to be passing judgment?" She gestured wildly at the shambles surrounding them—the stacks of mistreated, broken-spined books, the desiccated apple cores and orange rinds littered about, furniture in various stages of becoming kindling. "You live like a pig! Where do you get off calling the inhabitants of the other world filth, and us know-nothings? What makes you the final authority on what we should do? I wouldn't ask you what movie to see, much less let you decide the fate of our future!"

Astrid stood agape, amazed at Robin's outburst. She had never seen her like this. Cedric turned to her, obviously amazed as well.

"Fortunately," he replied, smiling frostily, "none of you will have anything to say about it."

"Well, we're taking it to Town Meeting, at the very least," Astrid stated flatly.

"Oh, you go right ahead," he retorted smugly. "I doubt they're going to be highly receptive to anything you have to say."

"Why not?"

"Someone who deliberately defied the recommendation of her community by becoming pregnant? I don't think that will impress anyone, Astrid. By the way, I'm placing you under citizen's arrest. The whole lot of you."

"On what charge?" gasped Rana.

"Atavistic chromosomal arrangements."

TWENTY-FOUR

Judy sat perched on a set of rusted car-seat springs in the back of Dorothy's shop, feeling such a complex mixture of emotions that she wasn't sure just what she felt. Frightened, definitely, but amazed, too—awed, flattered, excited. But as she became uncomfortably aware of Duncan's and Dorothy's tense expectancy, she decided she mostly felt frightened.

"Well," she said at length, after carefully examining the device that Major Duncan had designed and Dorothy had constructed, primarily from a carburetor taken out of a souped-up 1956 Chevy and ham-radio parts, "I know this will sound strange, but I had a dream last night that this thing needs a part made out of a special synthetic crystal that doesn't exist."

Major Duncan regarded her intently. "No, that doesn't sound strange," he remarked slowly. "But...did you get any more information than that? Any clue as to how to synthesize the crystal?"

Judy ground her teeth. "I think so, but it's so hard to be sure it's for real, you know?"

"Think you could give it a whirl?" Dorothy asked jauntily in an obvious effort to pep her up. "You took chemistry at VoTech, didn't you?"

"Yes, but only four years—and it's been a while. Besides, it would take extremely sophisticated equipment. I can't imagine where we'd get all that stuff."

"Bob knows, don't you, Bob?"

Duncan gave a short, weary sigh. "Yes, I do. I'd been hoping to avoid anything like this, though. It adds immeasurably to the risk."

Judy eyed him shakily. "What would we have to do?" she asked. "Because you see, this...this was only a dream. I mean, I hate to pin all our hopes on something like that."

Duncan came over and joined Judy on the car-seat springs, calmly resting his hand on her knee. Her eyes riveted on his hand. "But what are your feelings about the dream? What did you feel when you first woke up?"

"Really good," she admitted, having no trouble in recapturing the confident feeling she'd had. "I felt like, this is it, this is the answer."

"So? What's your problem, then?"

"I—I don't know," she faltered. "I mean, I think there's more to dreams than what the psychologists tell us. But how can anyone prove it? And—and," she trembled, "I don't want to be the one responsible for the failure of this enterprise. I'm not a chemist or an engineer, I'm a statistician." She gulped, unable to voice her other fear: that her help would guarantee success and kill everyone on the planet, including herself and Major Duncan. She struggled to bring her feelings under control. She'd had about as many shocks as a person could handle in a twenty-four-hour period.

First, there was her meeting with Major Duncan and all the earth-shattering revelations that had taken place, then that dream last night—that distressing, disquieting dream in which her guardian appeared to be in some kind of serious trouble while going on at length about the power that Judy carried inside her. Not exactly an auspicious omen, even if Judy had felt that she had indeed come up with the correct solution in a second dream. She felt reluctant to mention Astrid to Robert and Dorothy, for some reason, so she kept that part to herself. Then her stint at work had tortured her, forcing her to pretend as if everything were normal so as not to give anything away. Now here she sat in Dorothy's shop, a surprised new member of a subversive underground resistance. A tiny underground resistance. How had she gotten herself into this? Surely things couldn't be as bad as Major Duncan and Dorothy thought. People still lived, business was going on as usual.

And Major Duncan! Did he not have any idea he was tormenting her, or did he just not care? Why did he have to be so affectionate with her, so damned appealing? She already said she'd help, she *would* help; honestly, he didn't have to seduce her any more. Sometimes she wished she had the nerve to say that to him. But then every time his hand brushed hers, she felt completely on fire and all she could think was that she never, ever wanted him to stop touching her, not for an instant, whatever his reasons for doing so.

"You're a brilliant statistician," Duncan reminded her, withdrawing his hand and bringing her back to earth with a jarring thud. "A gifted mathematician. At any rate, I have more faith in your dreams than you do. I say we try making this crystal of yours."

"But—where?"

"There's a lab at the MI Complex. I think it should have everything we need." He fell silent for a moment. "It clears out after seven. What time is it now?"

"It's about that," said Dorothy, without, as far as Judy could see, consulting any timepiece.

"Good. We need to move fast. Dorothy—you should stay here. We don't have a uniform for you. So I'm afraid you'll just have to work with what we bring back to you."

Dorothy shrugged. "No problem."

Duncan turned to Judy. "Do you have a clear idea of how the crystal works?"

She nodded miserably, picking up the device to scrutinize it once again, marveling over the accuracy of her dream about this instrument when she'd never even seen it before. And helplessly wondering if she were not, in fact, playing into the hands of the Devil, even as perhaps Major Duncan or Dorothy were, whether from design or well-intentioned, duped fanaticism. All she had to go on about that symbol on Major Duncan's book was his word for it. And if her guardian was entirely good, why was she in trouble? Oh God, what to do?

"Let's be off, then," Major Duncan urged her softly, grazing her cheek with the tips of his fingers.

She stood up obediently, cursing her dilemma.

"We'll eat when we return," said Duncan. "Dorothy, do you suppose you could prepare a meal for us while we're gone?"

"Sure thing, boss."

Robert paused, a smile playing about his lips. "I think we both know, Dorothy, who's the boss here."

She cackled delightedly. "That's for damn sure!"

Major Duncan activated the two guards as he and Judy went out, bringing the Dobermans to sinuous life. As they stepped out into the night, a warm, balmy mist enveloped them, creating a strange—and false, no doubt about that, Judy knew—sensation of coziness and safety. Luckily, the guard dogs possessed infrared vision and extremely keen chemoreceptors. They would know of any other presence on the street long before their little party was spotted. And Duncan carried a gun.

Hurrying behind Major Duncan, clutching his arm as he had instructed her, Judy tried to think of nothing but each step as she took it. She tried not to think about any possible confrontations with gang members, about what sneaking into the MI lab would involve and what would happen to both of them if they were caught. But she couldn't refrain from contemplating the fact that Major Duncan positively oozed virility and sex appeal and that holding his arm was making it difficult to concentrate on anything except the exceptionally beautiful curve of his jaw.

They arrived at the MI Complex far too soon for Judy. They passed through all the computer access points with no evident trouble, finally making their way into a vast room filled with the most awe- inspiring equipment Judy had ever seen.

"This—this is magnificent," she breathed, turning around to feast her eyes upon every bit of it.

"Yes," Duncan replied, his voice shaded with irony. "Amazing that man can produce all this and still not figure out how to keep from killing himself on a planet custom-designed for him. So. Reagents are over in those bins along that wall. Special items can be ordered and delivered by computer, although the fewer the better. Glassware there, furnaces over here. Anything else?"

Judy shook her head and began to gather up the things she needed, glad for the first time in her life that she'd had such broad and thorough vocational training. Once involved in her project, she worked happily, absorbed in the problem-solving process, reveling in using her mind to full capacity for once. The necessary information came to her easily, in bursts of inspiration, and she began to feel that perhaps their mission was in fact divinely guided.

But when another officer, Captain Gregory, eventually showed up to investigate their activity, she cringed, desperately hoping that she wouldn't break out into her usual incriminating sweat. She worked as casually as possible, even when the man strolled by and peered over her shoulder. Try as she would, she couldn't keep her hand from trembling as she pipetted her solutes into solution. She felt relieved when she could shove the whole thing into the furnace for a while. Much to her discomfort, he stayed the whole while, determined to view the final product. Judy didn't know whether to weep or shout for joy when she removed the compound and realized that it didn't resemble at all the crystal structure she'd beheld in her dream: a graceful polyhedron. What she drew from the furnace looked like spiky lumps of mold. Captain Gregory cast a disdainful though curious glance at the crystallized compound, then left. Major Duncan strolled over to take a look, and Judy started to ask him about his interaction with the man. But he anticipated her and shook his head warningly.

"Is that how it's supposed to look?" he asked.

"No, it's not," Judy replied, torn between keen regret at disappointing him and vast relief that she had failed. Now maybe she could turn everything back over to him and Dorothy.

Duncan stood and stared at the compound, rubbing his chin in a thoughtful fashion. Then he said, brusquely, "Do it over again."

"Sir?"

"I said, do it over again."

"But, sir, it didn't work! It doesn't look anything like it's supposed to. It—" Glancing up desperately at Major Duncan, Judy found her voice dying in her throat. An exceptionally fanatical expression had frozen on his face. "Yes sir," she muttered, clenching her teeth to keep from sobbing in shame. How could she have questioned him? she asked herself fiercely. Things must have gone to her head with all his flattery and attention. Of course he was right, she had probably done something wrong the first time and now she had to do it over until she got it right. After she worked silently for a while, Duncan approached her again.

"You are keeping firmly in mind the structure of the crystal you want to attain, correct?"

Flustered, Judy started automatically to defend herself; then she realized that her mind was, in fact, a moiling knot of turbulence in which the form of the crystal danced amid visions of a world in chaos and burning fantasies involving Robert.

"You do remember, do you not," he reminded her, "that new crystal formations are particularly sensitive to mental templates?"

Judy bit her lip. How had she forgotten? Crystals could assume any number of myriad molecular arrangements. The first time a new crystal was formed, it rarely achieved the desired configuration, since apparently the molecular matrix was unsure how to express itself in the face of so many possibilities. Geophysicists in the last century had discovered that mental projections, in the form of distinctive wavelengths produced by the minds of scientists or workers, had a dramatic and specific effect on the formation of seed crystals, the microscopic physical templates upon which the macroscopic crystals fashioned themselves.

From then on, Judy kept her attention firmly locked on the crystal structure she sought. And this time, when she pulled the compound from the furnace, she had a trayful of waxy, amber crystals, the sides cleanly faceted as if sliced. She could almost swear that a flicker of incandescence pulsed from within them, bathing her in a triumphant, golden, syrupy glow.

Duncan swooped down upon her from behind, grabbing her up in a fierce embrace. "I knew you could do it!" he beamed, smiling and smiling at her.

"We don't know that it works yet," she cautioned, her limbs turning to liquid at his touch.

"It will. You'll see."

"I hope so," she sighed.

"I have every faith in you, Judy. Now—we need to get going. We don't want to overstay our welcome."

Judy held her tongue until they were back on the street. And then she was prevented from asking Duncan about his conversation with the other officer by his halting abruptly. Judy plowed into the back of him.

"Damn!" he muttered.

"What?"

"That's the second time I've forgotten to neutralize your homing device."

"Can we go back?"

He shook his head, glowering as he resumed his brisk pace. "No. Too risky. It would look suspicious. I'm still not sure that I completely fooled Captain Gregory. He didn't seem satisfied when I told him I was working on a crystal that would spontaneously turn oxides back into oxygen. But remind me tomorrow at the office without fail. It's important."

Judy felt too apprehensive to ask him why it was important, for fear she might not like his answer. One step at a time, she instructed herself. And don't look at his ass while you're taking it, either, she added sternly, despairing over her hopeless obsession with the mysterious man who strode in front of her. What could be worse, she mourned, tears gathering at the corners of her eyes, than falling head over heels in love with someone—with no hope, not even the slightest, of that person returning her passion. She might as well be in love with the moon and the stars. Once again she stumbled into Duncan as he stopped abruptly in the thick, dampening fog.

He twisted, the strangest look on his face as he stretched out his hand and grasped her by the nape of the neck. He drew her roughly to him and she buried her face in his chest, too startled to pull away.

"Ah, but Judy," he murmured, ever so softly, "we should love the moon and the stars. And when I look at you, I see a gorgeous, radiant sun of love and affection."

TWENTY-FIVE

Judy had no sooner drifted to sleep, still warm and tingly from Major Duncan's caresses, than she was jarred into a panicked consciousness by a thunderous pounding that threatened to demolish the door. Her first thought was that it must be Robert, and she sprang to open it without a moment's hesitation. But instead she found herself confronted by a garishly outfitted female gang member. Judy opened her mouth to scream and the woman neatly stuffed a wadded-up sock into it. She had shoved Judy back into her cubicle, kicked the door shut, and smashed the television with a truncheon before Judy realized that her visitor was Dorothy.

"Sorry about the disguise," Dorothy apologized as she plucked out Judy's gag. "And the sock. I just didn't want to attract any attention. I'm sure you understand."

Judy nodded mutely as she picked the lint off her tongue.

"Okay. Here's the deal. Christ." Dorothy sighed. "Fuckface Gregory blew the whistle on Bob. Told the authorities he didn't know what he was up to but that it couldn't have been anything good if he was working after hours without prior authorization. Fortunately, I had my scanner on and we were listening to it when he put the transmission through. Bobby's split already; I'm meeting him on the outskirts of town. You can stay or you can come, but if you stay you'll probably be hauled in and tortured to spill what you know about Bobby's activities."

Judy stared at her in shock.

Dorothy fidgeted. "Obviously, it makes more sense to come. Besides, we can use your help."

"I—I—" Judy stammered. "I, uh…"

"He asked me to tell you he wants you to come. But the decision should be up to you. We may all get our asses fried, you understand. Me, I'd rather take the risk. Anything to keep those goons from laying a hand on me."

"I'll come," Judy replied quickly. "I…let me see, what should I bring? I'm sort of befuddled. I just woke up."

Dorothy gave her a sharp glance. "Oh yeah? Any dreams?"

Judy shook her head. "No, I don't think so."

"Too bad. Well, I brought you some clothes to travel in." Dorothy held out a pile of chains and black rubber. "They should fit."

Judy gaped at the clothes Dorothy proffered. "But— those are gang duds! Couldn't some member kill us for wearing them under false pretenses?"

Dorothy shrugged. "Maybe. I doubt it. Not with me along. Anyway, it'll hide us from the police and military. If they spot us out at this hour in civilian or military clothes, they'd nab us for sure. C'mon, put 'em on. We don't have a lot of time. There's probably a squadron on its way to your cubicle right now. And if there isn't, there will be."

With trembling hands Judy doffed her nightclothes and put on the gang outfit, embarrassed to find that the studded rubber halter top had cut-away, peekaboo nipples and that her tight-fitting rubber pants had a zippered crotch—not to mention chains around the ankles. Gratefully she accepted a metal studded jacket from Dorothy, relieved to find that it covered her exposed areas.

She snatched up one of her dresses and crammed it into her handbag, much to Dorothy's amusement. She'd absolutely have to change, though, before she saw Major Duncan. She would rather die than for him to see her in this get-up.

"You look great," grinned Dorothy.

"Oh, right." Judy reddened.

"You do, seriously. Here put this helmet on. It'll offer some protection. Pull your hair through the top, like this. Dorothy stood back to survey her, then doubled up laughing.

"Dorothy, this is hard enough," Judy retorted.

"Oh, don't be such a spoilsport. You look great. All you need now is some makeup."

"I thought we were in a hurry!"

"We are. We are," Dorothy agreed. "But you got to take time out to have fun along the way or nothing ever turns out right. Haven't you noticed that?"

"I can't say that I have," sniffed Judy, still smarting over Dorothy's insensitivity and fun at her expense.

"Yeah, and your life sucks, doesn't it? Here, smear this oil on your skin so we'll look like we got that fungal infection from the sewers. And don't forget your oxygen mask," Dorothy reminded her, not giving her a chance to parry that last little thrust.

But actually, Judy mused, as she scooped up her mask and bag, throwing in a few packets of food powder for emergency use, she had to admit her life had sucked. Right up until the last few weeks. Even if she got zapped the minute they stepped out of the grid, she could die happy. Major Duncan actually cared for her! For the first time in her life, something wonderful and exciting had happened.

They hit the street not a moment too soon. Judy and Dorothy hadn't even reached the end of the block when a military van came screeching past them, squealing to a lurching stop in front of Judy's building. A SWAT team swarmed out, carrying machine guns and long-range rifles.

Judy shuddered, fighting the overwhelming urge to reach over and clutch Dorothy's arm.

"Just keep walking," Dorothy muttered. "They probably won't take any notice of us—this is a big deal for them."

"What is?"

"Your arrest."

Judy's head began to sweat and itch, but she couldn't scratch it with her helmet on. They made it around the corner and into the shadows, away from the sight of the military, only to stumble on a gang in the midst of banging one of their female members, whom they had casually chained to a row of garbage cans.

"Hey guys," shouted one, "more meat, coming our way!"

Everyone except the woman, who had a bag over her head, and the member presently engaged turned to spy them in slavering anticipation.

Dorothy emitted a low, nasty chuckle. "Don't even think about it, boys."

"Shit, it's Dorothy," someone muttered.

"Sorry, Dorothy."

"Hey, didn't see it was you, Dorothy."

Judy gaped at her.

"Just keep walking," Dorothy prodded.

But when they were out of earshot, Judy burst out, "Dorothy, what is it with you? Lord!"

Dorothy smiled with obvious pride. "Ah...might as well tell you. We're probably gonna be dead in a couple of days, anyway." She sailed on, oblivious to the terrified expression on Judy's face. "I've got me a guardian angel, see. Always have, from the time I was little. And she protects me."

"Really?" Judy's eyes opened wide. "What does she look like?"

Dorothy gave her a sidelong glance. "I haven't ever actually seen her. I just hear her telling me what I should do, or I feel her working through me. She arranges events sometimes."

"That's—amazing, you see, because I have a guardian angel, too!"

"You don't say."

Judy nodded eagerly. "But she's just appeared recently."

"Interesting. I thought you had something about you. Now I see I was right. Anyway, it's like magic, you know? When I ask for help, it's incredible what happens sometimes. I feel like a superwoman."

"Yes," Judy murmured, thinking about her own experiences.

"Sometimes I look at things and I feel like I can see right through time. Atoms are mostly air, you know. At least in this crappy little dimension."

"Yes, I know."

"You may not believe this," Dorothy continued expansively, "but sometimes I can make things move just by thinking about it. Small things, sure, but big things, too. You'd be surprised."

"Is that how you protect yourself from the gangs?"

Dorothy nodded, pleased. "Mostly. I squashed a couple of them with a street light one night. Squashed them like roaches. Didn't kill 'em, though. That goes against my principles. But you know, it's amazing how quick information like that gets around on the street. No one's ever bothered me since. Uh-oh, here comes that military van."

Judy's legs locked and she came to a complete standstill, her heart hammering wildly.

"Better duck behind this dumpster. C'mon, hurry," Dorothy hissed, "make yourself scarce!"

Judy had to consciously lift each leg to make it move, she felt so frightened. She scrambled madly to hide herself, smacking her head on a corner of the dumpster in the process. The van cruised by slowly.

"Oh, God," Judy wept, teeth chattering. "How are we ever going to make it?"

"Hey, it's like I told you—we're protected. Don't worry!" insisted Dorothy as she crawled forward to check the progress of the van. "It's okay. They're gone," she announced. "See? Like magic."

Judy didn't want to tell Dorothy, as they resumed their trek, that her guardian appeared to be in some sort of trouble. Hopefully Dorothy's wasn't. Hopefully they didn't have the same guardian.

They made it to the outskirts of town with no further confrontations, but as they neared the city limits Judy began to feel an alarming panic at the thought of leaving the city. She felt, in fact, that going outside the city might end up being one of the most foolish things she could do in her lifetime, and she experienced an overwhelming desire to rush to Major Duncan's office.

"Dorothy," Judy gasped, "I have this terrible feeling that Major Duncan may not have made it out of the city. I think they might have caught him and taken him to the MI Complex!"

Dorothy stopped and cocked her head to one side. "What makes you think that?"

"It's—just a feeling I have. But it's so strong it must be right! I—I think we should turn around, don't you? We ought to try to rescue him if they've got him!"

Dorothy shook her head. "Uh-uh. No way, doll. Our agreement was that I should go on, even if something happens to him. I've stashed the device, see; we're all ready to go."

"But—"

"Sorry."

"I'll go then," Judy begged, on the verge of hysteria. "We'll meet up with you."

"It's up to you, I said that from the beginning. But frankly, I think you'd do better to come with me. The thing is...oh, shit!"

"What?" demanded Judy, unable to keep from sniveling and wringing her hands in desperation. "Did Bob ever neutralize your homing device?" "My what? Oh. No, he didn't. But what does that have to do with anything?" Judy cried. "I'm not going another step, Dorothy!"

"Oh, Christ." Dorothy exhaled heavily. "Shut up and listen. They've addled your brain, Judy. That's the homing device talking. They've activated it. They want you, sweetheart."

"That's not it! I know it! Let me go, Dorothy! Damn it!" Judy swore as Dorothy dropped to her knees in a flash and fastened the chains on Dorothy's pantslegs. Before Judy could collect herself, Dorothy had whipped out some rope and tied her hands behind her.

"Sorry, babe. You'll thank me for this," Dorothy grunted, dragging Judy into a hidden spot behind the rusting hulk of a car. "Now you just sit tight while I go locate the Major. Oh." She fished in her pockets and pulled out the sock. "Just in case." She forced open Judy's mouth, since she was crying and squirming and gnashing her teeth in despair, and crammed in the sock. "Be right back."

When Dorothy left, Judy nearly went insane. She considered rolling to the MI Complex, but discovered that Dorothy had hooked her chains onto something under the car. "Damn you, Dorothy," Judy bawled in muffled agony, then stopped, as she thought she heard something moving in a nearby rubbish heap. Could be a rat or a gang person or one of the crazy survivalists who were rumored to live on the edges of town.

She spent the next two hours in abject fear and silence, perspiration pouring off her even in the chilling rain that had begun to fall. Parnoid thoughts began to foment in her mind, and she began to believe that Dorothy had planned this whole thing for some unfathomable reason, that she had never intended to take her to Major Duncan. Maybe Dorothy was a government spy!

Judy had herself so worked up by the time Major Duncan finally appeared, that she didn't realize who it was. She nearly passed out from fright. When she did recognize him, she began to cry in helpless embarrassment and shame. Her jacket had flapped open during her struggles, her peekaboo nipple cutouts exposed for all the world to see, and her zippered crotch somehow managed to glint from something, though how it did in this inky blackness she surely didn't know. And here she lay with a sock stuffed in her mouth, all trussed up like a roast pig in one of those TV shows about wealthy people's dinner parties.

Duncan knelt beside her and tenderly removed her gag. He drew her jacket snug about her and smoothed back her damp curls, murmuring, "I'm sorry, Judy, I'm sorry. This is my fault. And I'm afraid there's nothing we can do until we get out of the range of your homing device."

"When will that be?" she wept, unable to look him in the eye.

"Several hours." He took her chin in her hand and turned her head towards him. "Look at me, Judy. Don't be embarrassed."

He smiled. "In fact, Dorothy was right, you look good."

Judy laughed despite herself, splashing tears down her cheeks.

"If I unbind you and assure you that you have more to fear if you return than if you go on, will you be able to make it? Obviously, I stand before you. Fears about my safety were unfounded, correct?"

Judy nodded, allowing her gaze to linger on Major Duncan's finely chiseled features. God, he was beautiful. The fact that he didn't recoil in distaste from her filled Judy with a deep gratitude—to whom, she didn't know. Him? God? Her lucky stars? But to have him treat her with such loving kindness instilled in her a joy so profound that it seemed to be something else for which she knew no name.

"I'm going to untie you, then. I hope you don't hold this against Dorothy. She truly was acting in your best interests."

"I—I understand," she said, although she did feel that Dorothy had enjoyed cramming that sock into her mouth just a bit too much.

"If you feel yourself becoming frightened, hold tight to me, all right?" he instructed her. "If you feel you can't go on, tell me."

"Okay," she whispered, blushing as he unfastened her chains, glad that he couldn't see her so well in the dark. Lord, but I want him, she lamented. For the first time in her life she wanted to make love to somebody. But she knew that no matter how much he cared for her as a friend, he certainly couldn't want her as his lover. She stood up, rubbing her wrists where the rope had bound them. "Sir? I mean, Robert?"

"Yes?"

"Do you suppose I could change before we go? I brought a dress with me and...and we don't need to be disguised any more, do we?"

Duncan frowned. "I think you'll find, Judy, that the clothes you wear now will be more practical for the type of traveling we'll have to do. They'll keep you warmer, for one thing. Protect you from scratches and scrapes, for another. And besides," he leaned over and breathed in her ear so softly that it tickled, "you really do look quite...exotic."

She turned to him in surprise.

"Come." He held out his hand. "We have no time to waste."

Judy accepted his help and stumbled behind him to the road, where Dorothy stood guarding their belongings. Duncan advised everyone to use their oxygen masks sparingly, since they had a long trip in front of them. They hiked out of town, Judy's desire to rush back to the MI Complex growing stronger with every step. Aware of her struggle, Duncan firmly gripped her hand in his. Amazingly, though, it seemed to Judy that she breathed easier than she ever had before.

Five kilometers out of town, Duncan led them to a survivalist settlement. Low concrete bunkers squatted in the still, damp darkness. A sentry burst from one of them, armed with a machine gun, a real Rottweiler writhing and frothing at his side.

"State your business," he snapped.

"Name's Boyd. Arthur Boyd," said Major Duncan. "I made arrangements with a man named Mike to buy a four-wheel drive. He around?"

The sentry eyed them suspiciously as he flipped out a walkie-talkie and spoke into it, muffling his speech with his hand. The dog kept them at bay, teeth bared, a low, menacing growl rumbling deep in its throat. Judy tried not to look at it for fear it might attack her, but she couldn't keep her eyes from straying to its sharp, pointed teeth.

"Okay," the guard announced, with obvious disappointment. "He says it's okay. He'll be out in a minute." The man made no move to quiet the dog, which seemed more and more likely to attack the longer they stood there. Finally Mike appeared, roaring up out of nowhere with a battered, beat-up jeep. He jumped out, leaving the motor running.

"Got the money?"

Major Duncan nodded, handing over a small, zippered pouch. "Count it. A hundred thousand dollars in thousand-dollar bills."

Mike riffled through the bills, while Judy wondered how on earth Major Duncan had come up with so much money. The man flashed a moss-toothed grin. "She's yours, then—full tank and everything. The starter code is 4359. Don't forget it or you won't be able to start her up again."

The party scrambled into the jeep, Dorothy hopping into the driver's seat and gunning the vehicle for all it was worth, peeling out of the settlement. Judy gripped the dashboard, terrified by the tremendous speed. She'd never traveled in a conveyance before.

"Charming fellows," Dorothy remarked as they bounced wildly along the pitted road. "Hey, and what a deal, eh?"

"At least we have transportation."

She laughed. "True. Where'd you get all that money, Bobby?"

"It's family money."

"Well, excuse me, Mr. Moneybags. You never told me your parents had a lot of dough."

"That was the last of it."

"Not saving it for your retirement, then?" Dorothy inquired.

Duncan laughed, hollowly, it seemed to Judy.

"So have you two been in on this plan from the very beginning?" Judy asked, trying to quell her gnawing anxiety, as well as to turn the conversation away from their probable demises.

Dorothy shook her head. "Nah. This guy was coming to me to buy parts and finally I asked him what he was up to. Good thing, too, 'cause he'd gotten it all screwed up."

"I'm a designer, not a builder," Duncan demurred. "Dorothy, though, is a mechanical wizard. She's a designer's dream."

"Ain't he a sweetheart," Dorothy chuckled.

Plagued by a nagging unease, Judy twisted around to look behind them; however, she glimpsed nothing but a sheet of rain lit a lurid crimson by their tail lights. Judy found that she was growing to like the sensation of speed; if only the roads were not in such an alarming condition. As fast as Dorothy was driving, and with all the unguarded precipitous drops off the curves they were whipping around, Judy fully expected that at any moment they would find themselves poised in midair. She turned around again to look behind them, unable to shake the sensation that someone was following them. Not that she could necessarily see anything in this driving rain, not to mention the tendrils of fog that had begun to snake their way across the road. But she thought she saw—although when she blinked, it disappeared—she could almost swear she saw ripples in the rain, as if an invisible something pulsed in the space behind them.

"Um, Robert?" she quavered.

"Yes, Judy," he replied, inclining his head in her direction.

"Do you—do you see anything behind us?"

Duncan twisted about, narrowing his eyes to scan the road. Then he turned white. "Oh, my God," he whispered.

Dorothy threw him a worried glance. "What the fuck is it?"

"It's the secret police! My God, how did they find us so quickly?"

Dorothy craned her neck to look in the rearview mirror. "I don't see shit."

"They're using a cloaking device. We've got to do something!"

No sooner had he spoken than a bead of light glowed on the dash.

"Dorothy!" he shouted, "do something!"

Dorothy gunned the engine, wrenching the wheel hard to the right.

Judy opened her mouth in a soundless scream as she found herself, just as she had feared, plunging off into an abyss.

"This isn't what I had in mind, Dorothy!"

"Just—hang on," she snapped.

"Hang on to *what*?" Above them, rocks exploded and showered down on them.

"I need to nudge us over to that shoulder over there..."

Judy covered her eyes. She didn't want to look.

"Exactly how do you plan to do that?" shouted Duncan.

"Shut up!" Dorothy bellowed. "You're distracting me, asshole!"

Judy couldn't believe how long this was all taking. They seemed to have entered some bizarre time warp where every second stretched into an eternity. Suddenly her head snapped back as the car crashed to a halt; then a great rush of air buffeted them as the police car plummeted past them to the bottom of the rocky crevasse below.

No one moved for a long time. Judy realized she tasted blood in her mouth. She must have bitten her tongue when they landed. Finally finding her voice, she gave a short, shrill scream.

"Yeah, my sentiments exactly," agreed Dorothy. She leaned on the steering wheel for a minute, breathing hard. "Man, that shit really takes it out of you." She cut the engine and climbed out to survey the condition of the jeep and the lay of the land. Silent and grim-faced, Major Duncan got out as well. Judy found she couldn't move. She rested weakly on the seat while they moved about in the darkness. After a few minutes, Dorothy came back and poked her head back in. "You okay?"

Judy nodded shakily.

"Have some oxygen, why don't you?" Dorothy offered, thrusting a mask in her face. Then she popped out again and disappeared back into the underbrush. A few minutes later Major Duncan emerged, but Dorothy didn't. He strode back to the jeep, where Judy had begun to fret.

"Did Dorothy come back?"

"No, she didn't."

"That's odd." He rubbed his chin, his eyes eerily catching the light from the instrument panel as he stared searchingly at the thicket that enveloped them. "Well, I guess she's trying to find a route out of here. It won't be easy." He paused. "I certainly would like to know how those agents found us so quickly. Perhaps I've been under closer surveillance than I realize." He shook his head.

"Robert?"

"Yes, Judy."

"Do you mind my asking just how Dorothy pulled that stunt with the car?" She shivered in the chill night air. "I mean, no offense, but that—that's just not human, is it? What are you guys really? You can tell me. I—I won't be afraid."

Duncan laughed, a startling sound amidst the tense silence. "We're human, Judy, just like you. But special mutations have given us...special powers. Although some only come out under great stress. Dorothy possesses the ability to levitate and an impressive psychokinetic ability, as you just witnessed. Although, I'll tell you—for a minute, I didn't think she was going to pull it off." He rubbed the bridge of his nose wearily. "I myself possess the traits of telepathy and the ability to perceive people's electromagnetic fields, sometimes referred to as auras. Obviously, we represent the lucky five percent, mutants who benefit from our genetic alterations. The other ninety-five percent on this planet aren't nearly so fortunate, as I'm sure you know."

"Do you...have a guardian like Dorothy does?" Judy asked in awe.

"Yes," he answered slowly, "in fact, I do. But I don't really think of him as a guardian. I think of him as a portion of myself, as someone I have yet to become reaching back and helping me to evolve into what I will someday be." Duncan twisted to scan the area anxiously. "What do you suppose could have happened to Dorothy?" he exclaimed.

"Should we call for her?"

"Better not. This is mountain-gang territory. I've got a machine gun, but I'd rather not use it if I don't have to. They could outnumber and overwhelm us."

A huge explosion shattered the air, propelling Judy out of the car and into the arms of Major Duncan.

"It's okay, love. It's the police car that went off the cliff behind us. I'm surprised it took so long for the gas tank to catch fire." He sighed, stroking her shoulders abstractedly. "You know, it has always been a lifelong puzzle to me just how the powers-that-be convince the very people they mistreat to risk their lives in doing their dirty work for them."

He sighed. "I wouldn't think that's all they have in store for us, but then the powers of the military are stretched so thin these days that half of the equipment doesn't work. The other half is already tied up in one of our countless, mindless wars." This last word he spit out bitterly.

Aware that her nipples were beginning to harden from his touch, Judy extricated herself from Major Duncan. He remained silent for a moment, then spoke.

"Judy," he said quietly. "You mustn't think that I don't want you, because it isn't true. I would like nothing better than to make love to you as you never have been before, believe me. But this isn't the time."

Judy's pent-up emotions finally broke loose. She clenched her fists and screamed at Duncan. "Don't lie to me!" she shrilled. "Damn it, you don't have to say stuff like that to me! As a matter of fact, I can't stand for you to say things like that! Do you think I haven't ever looked in a mirror? You couldn't possibly want me, don't you think I know that? So just—don't give me that line of bullshit, okay?" She broke down sobbing. Duncan hesitated.

"You're wrong, Judy. The mirror doesn't reflect what I see. When I told you I saw a beautiful, blazing sun when I looked at you, I wasn't using a figure of speech. When I look at people, I can see their physical bodies, yes. But don't forget, I can also see their energies, their essences. You have one of the most entrancing auras I have ever encountered. Spiritually and emotionally you're quite evolved, Judy. I find that exquisitely attractive."

Judy stared at him. She stood motionless, trying to assimilate what he had just told her, when she felt a slight sting on her neck. She put her hand to the spot. It came away sticky with blood.

Major Duncan's expression changed instantly to one of horror. "We've got to get out of here!" he exclaimed. "Right now!

Judy's eyes rolled back. Her knees buckled. And then she plunged headlong into a soundless, suffocating darkness.

TWENTY-SIX

Astrid sat in her makeshift cell, a locked room in a defunct hospital, gloomily picking at the fabric of her dress. Her arm ached from where two of her friends—at least she had thought they were her friends—had taken blood for a genome analysis yesterday, but what hurt the most was the thought that her community had degenerated to the point where they were forcing people to do things against their will. She tried not to despair, because her trial was coming up and she needed to keep her wits about her. But waves of dread washed over her whenever she thought about the impending meeting. It certainly seemed that the hysterical faction had won out, that people were no longer willing to listen to reason.

Ironically, Astrid could easily pick the makeshift lock installed on the door—unlike the situation at Cedric's house where his psychokinetic abilities had overwhelmed her own, keeping her and all her friends captive until a van full of thuggy individuals had arrived to haul them away. But now she had no desire to escape. She wanted to attend her trial, to make one last-ditch effort to win the community over to her side. She wondered what had happened to Robin, Taro, and Rana. Of course, the charge of atavistic chromosomal arrangements was spurious—

just an excuse to lock up anyone who didn't agree with they way things were going. Astrid's mouth twisted miserably. She hadn't even been able to dream about Judy last night, since all her tension and anger had given her insomnia. Nevertheless, she had tried, as she tossed on the musty, medicinal-smelling cot provided for her, to send empowering thoughts to Judy. She would just have to hope that it did some good.

Astrid heard footsteps in the hall and stood up uncertainly, wondering whether someone was coming to see her. When she heard the key in the lock, she braced herself, wondering if the time had come for her trial. But then she saw Nate ducking through the door. Sobbing aloud in relief, she rushed to embrace him, ignoring Sharon, who had accompanied him.

"My god, did they arrest you, too?" she cried.

"For Pete's sake, you're only being held for investigation, Astrid," replied Sharon.

Astrid glared at her. "That's not what Cedric said."

Sharon blew an exasperated breath through pursed lips. "Cedric's a little overdramatic."

"So what do you call locking someone up against their will?" Nate asked gravely.

Sharon's gaze faltered. "Look, we have an emergency situation here. What do you expect us to do when people won't cooperate?"

"I expect you to leave us alone!" Astrid cried, clenching her fists. "I expect you to know that you're not the only one with the best interests of society at heart!"

Sharon folded her arms and leaned against the door jamb. "Fine, Astrid. You'll have the chance to convince the community of that. Although how you could get pregnant at a time like this—"

"It just happened!" Astrid shouted. "I never did agree with that goddamned resolution anyway. And we didn't know that your fascist fear tactics had managed to get it extended while we were gone."

Sharon flushed angrily. "Name-calling won't help your case, Astrid. At any rate, it's time to go. Are you ready?"

"As ready as I'll ever be," muttered Astrid. "What about you, Nate?"

He sighed. "Sure."

When they reached the town meeting hall, what little bravado Astrid possessed melted completely away. She and Nate took their places on the central platform, surrounded on all six sides of the amphitheater by a seething mass of people, all of them anxious and upset. As she looked around the room, Astrid noticed Taro, Robin, and Rana huddled in a group near the front, apparently not on trial. But then none of them were pregnant.

Sharon joined them on the platform. Louise and Meagan, Astrid noted, sat in front of a computer, ready to enter the proceedings of the trial—one grim, the other prim and haughty. She didn't see Cedric anywhere—not a good sign.

She felt light-headed from the emotional turmoil that filled the hall. It seemed as though the agitation had sucked all the air right out of the room. An angry buzz circled about them, but when Sharon called for order the noise ceased abruptly, leaving a vacuum in its wake. Astrid thought she might throw up, she felt so nervous. She sought Nate's hand, dropping her gaze to a scuffed spot on the floor.

"The trial of Astrid Zefferelli and Nate Buford will now come to order," Sharon announced. "The charge against them is threefold: unlawful propagation, deliberate refusal to comply with a resolution passed by the community, and a willful disregard for the good of the community. Said defendants have conceived a child, and at least one of the defendants possesses anomalous genetic sequences. The community seeks to impose an abortion on the defendants, or at the very least, a lifetime ban from the community. The community will now hear arguments from the defense."

Astrid found herself speechless. An abortion! My god, what right do they have to take away my baby? she asked herself, shocked. Giving her hand a reassuring squeeze, Nate spoke up first.

"Friends," he said quietly, "I believe that most of you here know us—know us well. In the heat of all this confusion and heartache, it might be that some of you have forgotten the service that Astrid has performed for this community. So I would like to remind you.

"I imagine that just about everyone here has benefited, either directly or indirectly, from the lab that Astrid established. The prosperity of the community rests in large part on genetic breakthroughs that she's accomplished. She chose not to patent her organisms so that everyone could stand to gain. She's put more time into toxic cleanup than just about anyone I know, and she's volunteered hours and hours of her labor and talent for civil artworks that everyone enjoys.

"Her resistance to this resolution and to the efforts to disrupt the dimensional window doesn't come from selfishness, as Sharon would have you believe, but from concern for the good of us all. Anyone is free to challenge that if they want, but I urge you to look honestly and fairly into her heart before passing judgment." He stepped back to allow Astrid a chance to speak.

A heavy silence followed, in which Astrid finally found her voice. Trembling with emotion, she lifted her chin and gazed around the packed hall. "I'm not about to apologize for getting pregnant," she said. "Or to defend my actions. And if anyone wants to abort my baby, they'll have to kill me first. As for quitting the community, if this is what lies in store for the future, I'll leave gladly. But not until I've made one last effort to make you see what you're doing and address an issue even larger than my pregnancy. Fear has caused you to go along with this simple-minded, shortsighted reproductive ban. And fear has led you to consider disrupting our connection to another, more unfortunate world. A world, in fact, that is dying from its own poisons, excesses and fears—as ours almost did before the UFO virus came along and saved us. Let me ask you this: If something had not come along to help us, where would our world be now? All of our well-being depends on helping each other."

Her eyes traveled the room and came to rest on one of her neighbors. Adam—what about the time you broke your back? There's no insurance any more. If all your friends hadn't pitched in and taken care of you, worked for you and donated their credits to you, what would have happened?"

She held his gaze until he looked away, then she caught sight of the person sitting directly behind him. "And you, Erin, what about those masked defects that your daughter Marina ended up expressing after birth? What if we had demanded that she be destroyed because she turned out less than perfect? What if, instead of rallying around you both and helping her to overcome these defects, everyone had turned a cold shoulder?"

Erin's face contorted and tears gathered in her eyes. "You're right, Astrid," she whispered. "I haven't forgotten."

"And you, Ben, what about the time your house burned down? No insurance. If the community hadn't come to your aid and helped you rebuild your house, what would you have done?"

Ben muttered something unintelligible and bent over to tie his shoe.

"We see ourselves as superior, don't we?" Astrid continued. "As superior people in need of protection from an outside threat—whether it's toxins or another, inferior people. Us against them. Did we really learn the lessons of the last century so poorly? Have we already forgotten that our continued survival and prosperity depends on our ability to reach out and encompass a world larger than our own back yard? Our world almost destroyed itself— and not that long ago, either—by nations all fighting and warring with one another.

"We finally evolved to the point where we understood that our whole planet must thrive for each individual to thrive. But we can't stop there! Earth is part of a larger universal system. We never live in isolation. If suffering exists, it is our responsibility to help alleviate it—not to close in on ourselves and try to save our own skins at all costs. When there was continuing famine in the Sudan, Shasta City sent food and aid. When a hurricane destroyed towns on the Gulf of Mexico, we hurried to provide temporary shelters and clean water."

"Yes," came a loud voice from the back of the room, "but when these disasters struck, they didn't send out murderers to harm us!"

Astrid strained to see who was speaking, but couldn't locate her. "Good point," she conceded. "Why are these murderers showing up in our world? Are they here to remind us of our own intent toward this other world? If I were to tell you that breaking this connection to the other world might result in its death, would you change your minds? Or would you think, better them than us? They're already in horrible shape, they're nasty people—we have to protect our superior world. Are these murderers here to remind us of our past, or to let us know what we have the potential to become, virus or no virus?" Astrid paused to let her message sink in. Another voice piped up behind her.

"But is this other world real? If it doesn't really exist, what harm would Cedric's plan inflict?"

Astrid turned to face the speaker. "It seems, doesn't it, that this world is real enough to you to try to do it harm, but not real enough to try to save it. Look," she pleaded, "at the very least, all I want is to try one thing before letting an obsessed madman put a potentially globally destructive device into play. Let's all take just fifteen minutes, right now, to bow our heads and send healing intent to this other world. There are some good people in that world. Everyone is worth saving, no matter how damaged, twisted, or misguided. If we turn our backs, we're no better than the morally bankrupt elite on this other world who are willing for everyone else to suffer so they can enjoy a privileged existence. What do you say?"

Maria leaped to her feet. "I say we try it. What do we have to lose? And if I may say so, we should all be ashamed of ourselves. We shouldn't need Astrid to remind us of our most basic ethical responsibilities."

Astrid allowed herself a smile. "Thank you, Maria," she sighed, suddenly weak and drained from her speech. Sensing this, Nate moved closer beside her, slipping his arm around her. To her surprise, Van stood up next.

"We shouldn't lose any time, either," he announced. "In my most recent dreams, I've learned that this world is on the brink of death as we speak. If the phytoplankton don't perish, then a desperate plan to ignite the Ring of Fire and displace the lithosphere might destroy human life there."

Once again, the room became abuzz with talk. Astrid sneaked a glance at Sharon, Louise, and Meagan, who all sat stony-faced. Meagan whispered something to Louise and started to rise, but Louise yanked her back down, shaking her head.

"When did Van get back?" Astrid whispered to Nate, wondering just where Van had obtained his information. Who was the rebel he visited in his dreams?

"Same time I did. Except that he didn't get arrested. Excuse me—'investigated.'"

Robin jumped up then, pulling Taro and Rana with her. "I move that we all act on Astrid's recommendation," she said.

"I second the motion," Taro declared.

"I move that we make it unanimous," said Rana.

"All in favor?" asked Nate. And to Astrid's everlasting and gratifying surprise, the room resounded with a deafening chorus of "Aye!"

Everyone bowed their heads. At first the room remained quiet, as still as dawn, but then a chant began to swell. It started as nothing but a rippling murmur, then it gained strength, purity, and clarity of tone. It rang throughout the hall, it vibrated the very stones that made up the bones of the building. It pierced the skies, it caused the crust of the earth to shift and sigh. When it was over, everyone turned to their neighbors and gave them heartfelt, enthusiastic hugs.

On the platform, Nate and Astrid grinned at one another, embraced and kissed.

"Hey, Nate."

"Yes, Astrid."

"Where's Cedric? I don't see him anywhere."

"Hmm." Nate scanned the auditorium. "You're right."

Astrid grabbed Nate's hand and dashed down the aisle. "Hurry—we've got to find him!" she cried. "Before it's too late!"

TWENTY-SEVEN

When she opened her eyes, Judy found herself lying in a meadow of some sort, a meadow covered in spiky clumps of grass in which glowworms nestled, softly casting their milky phosphorescence. Her glasses were gone, so she couldn't see quite clearly, but it seemed infinitely lovely. She heard sounds nearby, and music, and she strained to catch it, wondering whether, by some incomprehensible chance, she might have awakened in the land of her dreams. A lock of hair fell into her face from a sudden breath of wind. She started to sweep it back when she realized that, once again she was bound hand and foot. Very tightly. And with no sock stuffed in her mouth this time. She squirmed in panic, blinking desperately to resolve her surroundings. Her movements earned her a sharp kick in the stomach from a figure who suddenly loomed over her.

"Be still!" a gravely voice commanded.

Obediently she lay still, terror beginning to ooze into her from the very ground on which she lay. She heard footsteps and more voices, and then rough hands began tying her to a stout pole. They hoisted her up when they were through and dangled her, swinging, above the ground as they marched through a thicket. Branches whipped into her face, stinging and smarting. But she had a terrible feeling that this was nothing compared to what they had in store for her.

When they burst into another small clearing and propped her up against a twisted tree, she cried out in anguish. For there in front of her hung Major Duncan, bound in exactly the same way, except that his right leg had been hacked off below the knee. Blood dripped from a filthy tourniquet into a small puddle in the dirt. Sickened, she turned her gaze to the disgusting fellow squatting in front of the fire, roasting something on a spit. She froze. Surely it wasn't…surely they weren't…Horrified, her eyes flew to Major Duncan's face. His skin was ashy pale, his mouth tight in pain. He nodded, understanding. Cannibals! The realization brought the taste of vomit to her lips and she spat. This earned her a brutal slap across the face with a studded glove.

Of all fates, she asked herself in despair, what could be worse than falling prey to cannibals? Astrid, help me! she pleaded, her eyes turning toward the murky heavens. Help me, Astrid, God, Jesus, anybody! But she heard nothing, only the crackle of the fire and the tinny rasp of a nearby tape box. And what now filled her sight was the grotesque and disfigured body of the mountain man advancing toward her.

Apparently self-mutilation was big among these dirt-bike gangs, since all of them were missing an ear or nose or lip, chunks of tissue swiped from limbs and chests, sunken tubs of white scar tissue reflecting in the fire. The deformities and cancers of the age must not satisfy them, Judy decided, shrinking every cell in her epithelium away from this creature; they had to glorify ugliness and take it to an even greater extreme. Or maybe, when times got tough, they snacked on each other.

The man picked up Judy and her pole as if together they weighed nothing, raising them above his head and then jamming the pole a full half-meter into the earth.

MICHAELA CARLOCK

With a grunt of happy anticipation, he sliced off the thongs that tied her feet, then tugged at her zipper. It stuck. Judy bit her lip, tears streaming down her cheeks. He yanked and swore. She held her breath, praying to every deity in the universe.

Suddenly the camp erupted into chaos. Missiles of incendiary plastic whizzed through the air in sizzling globs, driving her tormentor off in agonized screams. A few stray drops landed on one of Judy's arms, burning her, but also melting enough of her bonds so that in her frenzy she could wrench free. Without even thinking, she grabbed up the knife her would-be assailant had dropped in his flight and dashed over to Major Duncan, cutting him free. Military agents began to swarm into the camp, spraying machine-gun fire everywhere, while the mountain men began to fight back with automatic weapons of their own.

Judy pulled Major Duncan into a standing position and they hobbled for cover behind one of the nearby hovels. Judy plastered him with frantic kisses while bullets splattered into the thickets and structures around them. Duncan caught her by the wrists.

"Judy, my love—I'm afraid we haven't much time. You'll have to go without me from here."

"Without you?" she gasped in terror. "But—but—but—"

"No buts," he said firmly, a faint smile hovering about his mouth. "I have to stay here, of course. I'll only slow you down with this one leg I have left."

Tears rushed to Judy's eyes. She couldn't speak.

"It's all right, Judy. Listen—if all goes well, I won't be alive to miss it."

She shoved her knuckles into her mouth to prevent the wail that rose involuntarily within her. "Don't—don't say that," she begged.

"As you wish," he sighed. "Now. You must get back to the jeep—it's very close. The computer code, in case you don't remember, is 4359. Go through the thicket behind us and keep the noise and gunfire to your back. If you're lucky, Dorothy will be there waiting for us. If she's not, you'll have to go by yourself. Did you pay attention to what Dorothy did when she drove?"

"Well, sort of."

"You'll figure it out. Be sure to switch to the reserve fuel tank, it's marked—the one we drove on will be getting low. Maps are in the glove compartment. You want to go to Mt. Shasta. Do you know how to read a map?"

Judy nodded affirmatively, unable to stop the tears that gushed down her cheeks.

"The device is under the seat. Snow and ice gear is in the back. The gang was so delighted to get their hands on us that they didn't even bother looking in the jeep, so everything should still be there, unless they sent someone back to loot it. Our people have infiltrated the guards on duty at the Mt. Shasta dump site, so your way should be clear. All you have to do when you reach the mountain is set up the device and flip the switch. Any questions?"

"Only about a thousand!" she moaned.

"Listen to me, Judy. You have all the strength and knowledge that you require within you. Believe in it, trust in it. Otherwise it will elude you." He reached over and tenderly brushed away a tear. "Now—one more thing. A rather painful one, I fear."

"What is that?"

"Your homing device. It's possible that yours is one of the few that possesses a tracking function. They might have suspected you of something for some reason. That may be how we were traced so easily. I may also be bugged, of course. Another reason why I should stay here. But yours needs to be cut out. It's the only way."

Judy swallowed, keeping her gaze fixed on him.

He dropped his eyes. "It's horrible, I know. Do you want to do it or do you want me to? Whichever you choose, we must act quickly."

"You do it," she decided, thrusting her arm toward him and clenching her eyes shut. She felt a slicing sting, like a paper cut, and then it really began to hurt. She opened her eyes to see Major Duncan wrapping a torn shirtsleeve tightly around her arm. He took the homing device and tossed it into the bushes.

"You must go."

"I know." Still she hesitated. "I—I love you, Robert."

"And I love you, Judy. Never forget that."

She stood and gazed at him longingly, miserable. A bullet went zinging past her ear. Panic-stricken, she plunged into the thicket, running like a creature gone mad. She ran until she thought her heart would explode and when she finally burst into the area where the jeep sat, she collapsed on the grass, not even having the strength to pull open the jeep door and grab her oxygen mask. Luckily, there was no guard at the jeep. Perhaps it was close enough to the mountain gang's encampment that they felt they didn't need a guard. Or maybe the guard left when he heard the gunfire.

When at last she caught her breath, both arms began to ache ferociously from the cut and the burning plastic, but nevertheless, she staggered to her feet.

"Dorothy?" she whispered cautiously. No answer. That certainly would have been too much to hope for, she thought savagely: somebody to help me. Of all things, the future of the world in her hands, hers alone. And the man she loved—she swallowed, trying not to think about him. Dear...whoever, she prayed, please don't let him be killed.

She gritted her teeth and hugged her arms tight about herself as a chill wind whistled down the canyon. Unsettled, she ran for the jeep.

She spotted the computer lock with no problem, thank God. Checking under the seat, she was happy to find the device still stowed there. She did find maps and a compass in the glove compartment, but without her glasses she had a miserable time trying to read them in the weak, watery light of the flashlight. Anyway, they wouldn't do her any good until she reached a road, whenever and wherever that might be.

Taking a few deep breaths from her oxygen mask, Judy let her gaze sweep her surroundings: a plunging cliff on one side and dense thicket on the other. Her lips quivered, she felt so poorly qualified for this task. Just how and why had the fate of the world come to rest in her incapable hands? Was this the gods' idea of a joke? Not for the first time, she found herself wondering about Astrid's affiliation. Why hadn't she shown up at the cannibals' camp? Was she, Judy—or Dorothy and Major Duncan, for that matter—a pawn in a game played by superbeings? In fact, was setting up this device the best thing to do? It was up to her now, to decide.

But whatever she decided, she knew she had better leave right away. She caught a snatch of sound from the altercation behind her. One of those military men had surely seen her when they raided the camp. And they wanted her as much as they wanted Major Duncan. She flipped the switch for the reserve tank and timorously entered the computer code, jerking back with a cry as the engine turned over. Cautiously she eased out the hand brake, pressed the button that said "Drive," and lurched forward as she stepped unevenly on the gas. She stopped, wondering which way to go. A sudden flash of lightning illuminated the thicket in front of her.

Odd—there seemed to be a clearing, a thinning of branches in one spot that she hadn't noticed before. She inched forward, surprised to find that the thicket actually opened up there. She gazed around her as she picked up speed and confidence. It was hard to say, given the blurry edges that her vision smeared over everything, but it didn't appear to be a groomed path. It felt instead as if the thicket moved back as soon as she got to it. There just always happened to be a space, and then another one—and then one beyond that. Small tufts of radioactive moss glowed on the brambles' branches, and once she drove over a glistening sheet of giant slime mold.

By the time she reached a highway, the skies had begun to lighten with the approach of dawn. She checked the compass and once again squinted over the maps. She wanted to go northeast to get to Mt. Shasta, that much she knew, so she got pointed in the right direction and started driving before she even remembered that she didn't feel certain she should go ahead with the whole mission. But what else could she do at this point? Go back to the city to get arrested? Give herself up to a mountain gang or survivalist colony? From what little she'd heard rumored about those places, women got treated worse than the dogs, which were considerably abused to keep them mean. No, she might as well do her best to go through with it. She would do it for Robert. Whether she could actually accomplish anything, she thought grimly, remained to be seen.

She passed very little traffic on her way, which was just fine with her. Supposedly bandits liked to run cars off the road to rob and kill the occupants. And motorcycle gangs would probably love to play cat-and-mouse with her. She passed a few bombed-out, scarred areas, some waste-treatment plants, tracts of military land. When she dropped down into a vast, gigantic valley, she drove by mile after mile of cultivated farmland. She marveled over how many different things seemed to be growing, since she never saw anything for sale in the food stores except for food powder. Probably for the wealthy classes, she figured. She sure would like to try some of those things she saw people eating on television. That meal Major Duncan had treated her to sure had been wonderful, and the lard and beans Dorothy had fixed—just last night, was it? Judy's stomach growled insistently, reminding her that she hadn't eaten since then. She reached over and shook the contents of her purse onto the seat as she drove. Ugh.

Food powder. On impulse, she reached into Dorothy's bag and came out with a dogfood-and-potato-chip sandwich. Elated by her good fortune, Judy gobbled it down, guiltily considering Dorothy the whole time. What could have possibly befallen her?

Thirsty after the sandwich, Judy groped around for some liquid, but all she could find was Dorothy's whisky flask. She took a swallow anyway, attempting to calm her anxiety over the rising sun and increasing traffic. She reassured herself that, ensconced in the safety of the jeep in broad daylight on a major highway, no one was likely to mess with her. Except the police or military. She wondered whether the secret police had broadcast a description of this vehicle. At least with her homing device gone they couldn't track her, and they had no idea of her destination. Unless, she shuddered, they managed to torture it out of Robert.

After two hours of surprisingly uneventful driving— Judy feeling so comfortable at the wheel now that she leaned back and steered with one hand—she began once again to climb into the mountains. The farms disappeared, replaced now with more waste-treatment centers, more tracts of military land, ravaged and desolate, bristling rows of barbed wire drawn tight along the peripheries. At one point a squadron of military jets screamed overhead, giving her major heart palpitations, but apparently they were on other business. She passed a few police cars going in the other direction, but since only the wealthy and the survivalists owned cars, the police didn't seem prone to bother anyone on the highway unless there was an obvious problem. Or unless they were looking for somebody. Judy always craned her neck as unobtrusively as possible to follow their movements in her rearview mirror. Yet none of them came after her. She began to feel as if she were invisible.

Judy ascended higher and higher into the mountains, the weather becoming wilder with each meter she climbed.

She cursed her poor vision as the day went from gray to black and the rain fell in heavy, intermittent squalls. She fought a strong cross-wind for kilometers, only to come within a hair's breadth of driving off a sharp drop when the wind suddenly stopped. Fewer vehicles appeared on the road, giving the area an unpopulated feeling, although presumably somewhere off the highway there were underground army barracks and survivalist camps. Judy reflected on the paradox that although the Earth was dying from the excesses produced by a massive population, so much of the time it felt empty, desolate. The only time she had been around people was when she was walking to and from her jobs and working at her office at Sunshine. Otherwise, everyone was compartmentalized, put away, shut in. And even when she had been surrounded by a sea of people, she had still felt compartmentalized, isolated. Until she met Robert.

As the shock of her flight from the cannibals' camp wore off, or perhaps deepened, Judy began to experience strange sensations. She started to feel as if she were moving in a dream, as if her environment were not real. She hovered in a twilight state of consciousness, driving automatically, now taking in each new sight as if she had gazed on it many times before. She felt as if she traveled on another planet, and yet this alien planet was in fact her home. When the swirling clouds parted for an instant, and she caught sight of the blazing twin cones of Mt. Shasta, she felt almost as massive and ancient as the mountain itself. She drove through the gate, which was open and apparently deserted, as Major Duncan had anticipated. She drove until the road wound up the flanks of Mt. Shasta, until the copious amounts of drifting, blowing trash made driving impossible. She came to a halt.

She slowly gathered up the gear she would need to hike to the top, although the wind screamed maniacally around the jeep and she caught a faint, acrid whiff of sulfur from the outside. She picked up the device. Dreamily, she fastened her crampons. Swathing herself in the woolen blankets provided with the jeep, she jumped out and started up the mountain.

Odd creatures that subsisted on the dump refuse scuttled and sidled behind her as she went, but she paid them no mind. She realized that trudging through this radioactive wasteland was probably killing her, but somehow it didn't matter. She walked and walked until the rain turned to snow and piled in soft, glowing mounds about her. Her feet and hands turned numb, then her face and legs, yet she churned onward like a mindless, mechanical contraption. But when the ground began to heave and rumble beneath her feet, she hesitated. She cocked her head and listened. Louder and louder it grew, until the very air trembled and shook. Deliberately, she placed the device in the snow. She flipped the switch. And the last thing she saw was a pillar of fire streaming straight into the heavens.

TWENTY-EIGHT

Halfway down the aisle, Astrid realized that she and Nate needed a car. She turned to run back to Taro and Robin, colliding with them as she did so.

"Not so fast!" said Taro. "Don't you even want a little congratulatory hug from your friends?

Astrid leaned over and threw her arms around Taro, picking him up off the ground. "I sure do," she replied, setting him back down and turning to give Robin a big squeeze as well. "But I don't see Cedric anywhere, and I'm afraid he might be planning to use his device."

"Oh. You may be right."

"Can we borrow your car to drive to Mt. Shasta? I promise we'll take good care of it."

"Sure. Go right ahead. Be careful, though. Do you want Robin and me to go with you?"

"No, that's okay. Thanks, though."

Taro handed her the keys. "I mean it, Astrid. No heroics."

"Listen to him, you two," said Robin anxiously. "Cedric is definitely dangerous."

"I'll keep an eye on her," said Nate, stooping over to kiss Robin and Taro on the cheek.

"You big lug," murmured Taro, batting his eyes.

"Let's go, Nate. Every minute counts."
They raced out of the hall, waving to various friends who called out to them. Jumping into Taro's car, they tore off toward the highway to Mt. Shasta. The twin cones gleamed a bluish, brilliant white in the sunlight from a recent spring snowfall.

"I hope we don't need crampons," said Nate.

"I hope not, too," said Astrid, silently cursing her captors for allowing things to get to this point. "Maybe we can use our telekinetic powers to improve our footing if necessary."

When they arrived at the Bunny Flats trailhead, Astrid parked the car hastily and leaped out. Two other cars sat in the lot, but whether one of them belonged to Cedric, Astrid didn't know.

"We don't have any jackets," commented Nate, as he climbed out of the car.

"No."

"Let's hope we don't get hypothermic."

"Well, if we move fast enough, maybe that will keep us warm."

They set off on the trail, scanning the tree-tufted landscape for any signs of Cedric.

"You know, he might have taken a different route," Nate puffed.

"True."

"Looking for him on this mountain could be like looking for a needle in a haystack."

"No, he's around here somewhere. I can smell him. His aura reeks."

Nate fell silent, and the two of them concentrated on hiking the steep trail. Soon patches of snow began to dot the woods around them, and the trail turned to slushy mud. Once a deer sprang across their path, giving them both a terrible start. The snow became thicker and deeper, until they were struggling to keep their footing, and the air thinned progressively, making Astrid a little breathless and dizzy. Before long, however, they cleared the forest and emerged into an alpine meadow, smeared with a thick icing of deep snow. Shattered walls of frozen lava formed a mammoth backdrop, rearing up to 11,000 feet. The peak, 3,000 feet higher, floated above like a mirage.

"There's the Sierra Club hut," said Astrid, pointing to a stone cabin half-buried in snow.

"Think he might be in there?"

"If he's not now, he was. I don't see any tracks, but he'd make sure to cover them, knowing him. Let's go check it out."

A tremor that began beneath their feet caused them to halt. Then, as quickly as it came, it quivered away.

"What was that?" gasped Nate.

"I don't know, but we haven't a moment to lose. We need to keep moving."

They floundered through the snow, occasionally glancing overhead to keep an eye on the weather. Mt. Shasta had a notorious reputation for whipping storms up out of thin air, for generating its own savage weather, which claimed the lives of several hikers and mountain climbers every year. Today, a single smooth lenticular cloud hovered above the mountain, but little else.

When they reached the hut, Nate wrenched open the door and they both burst in, panting. Nothing. No sign of Cedric. Astrid walked over to one of the metal bed frames and plunked herself down. "Damn it!" she swore. "Where the hell is he?"

Nate shrugged. Another tremor began, this time accompanied by an eerie roar from the mountain, a shriek of rock and stone.

"Oh, god, you don't think the mountain is going to blow, do you?" cried Astrid.

"I don't know. Could Cedric be putting his device into play?"

"Christ, I hope not!" Desperately, Astrid broadcast a blast of mental energy in all directions, hoping that she might interfere with whatever Cedric was doing. Everything became deathly still. Wide-eyed, Astrid gripped her elbows and gazed questioningly at Nate.

Without further warning, brilliant rays of crimson, blue, gentian violet and phosphorescent green blazed in the skies and spilled through the windows, bathing everything in a luminescent kaleidoscope of glowing hues. The room appeared to warp sickeningly, this way and that, giving Astrid a ferocious headache. And the last thing she remembered, before she plunged into a cool, limitless darkness, was lightning, more lightning than she had ever seen in her life: a net of lightning, a sheath of lightning, polarizing and galvanizing every molecule in the atmosphere.

TWENTY-NINE

Judy stirred languidly, drops of sunlight tickling her face. She felt warm, elastic, tingly; pleasant pulses of energy coursed through her. She lay for a while without opening her eyes, so wonderful did she feel, so relaxed, so content; but finally her eyelids fluttered open, coaxed by the dancing, quivering light. I'm dreaming, she decided, her eyes so filled with glimmering photons that she could scarcely make out little else. But then she became aware of a discomfiting cold, a prickly, nettlesome sensation that caused her vision to adjust. She found herself nestled in a cavelike drift of clean, powdery snow, gazing out on a vista that overwhelmed her. Apparently she lay atop a mountainside that overlooked a valley, a valley so verdant, so fertile and impossibly green that she felt that she could almost smell it—bursting with life, rich, fresh, and tangy.

The cold prodded her to get up and start walking, although she felt like all she wanted to do was go back into that velvety, comforting sleep she'd been enjoying right before...right after...She froze in her tracks, suddenly remembering: Right after she'd set off the device that Robert had entrusted her with—the one that was supposedly going to destroy the world. The vital, entrancing Earth spread out around her certainly wasn't destroyed. Which meant what? That she'd died and gone to heaven? But, she pondered, was it cold in heaven? At least she wasn't roasting, thank God.

She continued to walk, slipping and skidding on the snow despite her crampons. Going up had been easier than coming down. *Would I be this clumsy in heaven?* she wondered. Glancing down at herself, she saw that she still wore that same awful gang outfit that Dorothy had given her, not a plain, white robe. Twisting around to examine her back, she saw that no feathery wings sprouted, either. Oddly enough, the contours of the land gave her a sense of deja vu, as though she'd been here before. *I must be dreaming,* she decided. *My body is in a coma and I'm dreaming.* She reached over and pinched her forearm, hard. Yelping in surprise from the pain she managed to inflict, she felt her feet going out from under her and she sat down with a bump. *I'm not in heaven and I'm not dreaming,* she mused thoughtfully; *so where am I?*

After falling a few more times, she discovered that she could make better progress if she just plopped down and lifted her feet, allowing herself to slide down the snowfields. It was a little scary at first, and some sections looked steep enough, with no visible leveling-out place, that she walked them, as gingerly as possible. But after awhile, she enjoyed the glissading, grateful for her rubber clothes and boots, which kept her relatively warm and dry. The terrain passed so quickly in this fashion that it wasn't long before she found herself out of the snow and picking her way through a dense, muddy forest. This proved more tiring, so that by the time she stumbled across a road, hungry and thirsty, she collapsed beside it, a limp pile of tired flesh and wet rubber. Amazingly, though, her breathing didn't bother her at all, despite the altitude and her exertion.

The approaching whine of a vehicle caused her to perk up warily. She considered running for cover, but before she could move, the car—a gleaming red one, peculiarly shaped like some sort of gigantic, fantastic insect—burst over the rise. Judy stood up when the car came to a screeching halt. Two occupants jumped out and she bolted. When she heard them call her name, she nearly fainted. Her knees buckled from fear and exhaustion. Crying, she struggled to get up, but it was too late. These people ran so swiftly that they were already upon her. They seized her and hoisted her up to a sitting position.

"Are you okay?" they asked her anxiously, two of the most beautiful people she'd ever seen: one a copper-haired goddess, the other a diminutive, dark, elfin creature.

"Who are you?" she whispered. "How do you know my name?"

They looked at each other. The woman said, "That's...a long story. Too long for right now. But don't worry, we won't hurt you. I'm Robin and this is Taro. We're friends of Astrid's. You know Astrid?"

"Astrid?" Judy cried. "My guardian?"

The man smiled. "Get a load of this. Astrid, the guardian angel."

So she was an angel! Did that mean this was, in fact, heaven? Judy gazed upon her benefactors with new interest. Were they angels as well?

Robin shook her head. "I think you're confusing our guest, Taro. Look, I've got a suggestion. Why don't I take Judy back to my place, and you go see if you can find Nate and Astrid. You can come back and meet us at my house."

"You're the jock!" exclaimed Taro. "Why don't I take Judy to my house and you look for Astrid and Nate?"

"Taro, don't give me this bullshit. I think the regional freestyle ski champion can do a little cross-country. It'll be good for you. Besides, I think I can do a little better job filling Judy in. Okay?"

"Okay," grinned Taro, who obviously had always intended to go. "Let's go on up to Bunny Flats and see if my car's up there. You can drop me off."

Judy watched this exchange with puzzled curiosity. They didn't speak the way she imagined that angels would. The two helped her up and escorted her to the car, a clean, well-cared-for machine. She climbed into the back, noticing that the seats looked brand new and smelled good. The interior was warm and toasty, too.

When they reached the parking area for Bunny Flats, they spotted Taro's car. He jumped out, gathering up an assortment of skis, crampons, and snowshoes. Shoving everything except his skis and poles into a big backpack, he gave Robin a kiss and Judy a wink.

"Listen, I love your outfit," he said to Judy in parting. "When we get back together, maybe we can talk clothes. I'm making an outfit for my boyfriend, and I think he'd look dynamite in what you've got on."

"Uh...sure," said Judy, thoroughly confused.

"Goodbye, Taro," groaned Robin, leaning over to push the seat forward. "Here, Judy, why don't you come sit up front."

Judy clambered into the front seat, blushing as, instead of driving away, Robin stayed and examined her intently.

"This is just incredible," she murmured finally.

Judy didn't know how to respond, so she said nothing, glanced down nervously at her gloved hands.

"A visitor from another world! Judy, your presence here is...is just astounding!"

Judy's head snapped up. "A visitor from another world? Is that what I am?"

Robin nodded.

"Well—how on earth did I get here? And where am I?"

Robin leaned back in her seat and loosely gripped the steering wheel, letting out a short, staccato breath. "Okay," she said. "Here comes the long story..."

* * *

Taro hoisted his pack and tightened all the straps, flicking a glance at the mountain that loomed above him, eerily mute—especially considering what had just happened. Balancing his skis on his shoulder and grasping his poles, he started up the trail, trying, without success, to shrug off a growing sense of panic that he hadn't wanted to share with Robin. She was worried enough as it was.

All the data was just now starting to come in from surrounding areas, but it appeared that an ionic blast had emanated from Mt. Shasta yesterday afternoon. Taro, along with Robin and Rana, had been watching Van's dream videos after the trial, where Van's rebel was revealed as none other than Major Duncan. Extraordinary, coming upon Judy like that, less than twenty-four hours after watching her on Van's videos. If ever he needed proof for Astrid's theories, there she was, in living rubber.

But then, right after the last clip, things started to get weird. First, he had felt odd and uncomfortable, so much so that he mentioned it to the others. Then they all heard a strange, grinding roar, and the next thing they knew, the whole world had turned into colors, the most exquisite he had ever seen. He and the others rushed outside to glimpse an aurora borealis gone sensationally wild before the impact of the storm had sent him to his knees and then on his back, where he lay and hallucinated for sixteen hours or so.

This morning, computer bulletin boards were starting to report similar effects in other areas as the storm traveled throughout the magnetosphere. Everyone in Shasta City was more or less okay, although some people kept seeing more colors than usual, but the town lay somewhat removed from the blast. Nate and Astrid could have ended up right in the middle of the onslaught. Not only that, they had probably left in such a hurry that they hadn't taken proper clothing. Since they hadn't come back yet, he sure hoped he wouldn't find his friends blasted to death or frozen to death. Or murdered.

Anxiety kept his pace up, and when the snow became deep enough to ski he fairly flew. He had no trouble following their tracks—clearly, they had not brought the proper gear—and soon he was traversing the field to the Sierra Club hut. If they had any luck or sense at all, they should have holed up there, but the lack of activity inside and out didn't bode well. He skied up to the entrance and fumbled frantically to get out of his bindings, then threw open the door. Nate and Astrid lay crumpled and inert, Nate on the floor, Astrid on a cot. Neither wore anything more than a Woolex shirt and jeans, and their lips looked positively blue.

With a cry of dismay, Taro ran from one to the other, slapping their hands and faces, shaking them desperately.

"Wake up, wake up!" he shouted, almost to the point of tears when they finally began to stir.

"Taro, Jesus, what's all the fuss?" mumbled Astrid. He rushed to her side.

"Astrid—wake up, dear. You're freezing to death. You, too, Nate."

Nate groaned and brought his fingertips to his lips. "You're right, Taro. I'm freezing."

"Well, get up then, you big stupe!" he scolded, wrapping Astrid's arm around his shoulders and trying vainly to stand. "Astrid, you're going to have to give me a little more help here…"

At last, he managed to get them both moving, stamping their feet, slapping their arms. He rummaged about in his pack for some extra pullovers and tossed them to his friends.

"Never underestimate the power of Woolex," observed Astrid, as she struggled into her sweater, her cheeks and lips barely pliable enough to work.

"Amen!" agreed Taro. "You gave me quite a start, I'll have you know. What were you pinheads thinking, rushing up here without so much as a windbreaker between the two of you?"

"We were in a hurry," Astrid retorted. "Which reminds me—what in the world happened, do you know?"

"As far as we can tell, a massive magnetic storm originating from Her Highness here."

"Mt. Shasta?"

"None other."

"So that's what the colors and lightning were all about. I guess it must have knocked us out, huh, Nate?"

"I guess so."

"I wonder where Cedric was and what he was doing when the storm hit."

"An academic question at this point, Astrid," said Taro. "We'll send out a search and rescue team to look for him. But right now, you two need to get warm. Unless you want your limbs and digits to fall off."

"Such a pleasant prospect, Taro!" Astrid exclaimed. "Say…"

"Yes?"

"Have you always been so colorful?"

"I beg your pardon. I've always done my very best to exhibit a colorful personality. Are you telling me it hasn't been working?"

"Oh, shush." Astrid turned to Nate, slipping her hand into his. "You, too, Nate. You look…extremely colorful."

"So do you, Astrid," he laughed.

"Is this left over from the storm? Is the magnetosphere still in an excited state?"

Taro shrugged. "Maybe. Other people have been noticing the same thing. I know I'm excited. But listen—how about it? Are you ready to go? I've got a big, big surprise for you at Robin's house."

"Really?" Astrid raised an eyebrow. "Don't play games with me, Taro. Tell me what it is."

"Nope. Sorry. This is just too much fun as a surprise. You'll have to wait until you get to Robin's. I'll give you a hint, though—it's a person. Now, that's all I'm going to say." He giggled mischievously.

Astrid sighed and turned to Nate. "I think my lips need a kiss before I can feel warm enough to go."

Nate smiled, pleased. "You got it, babe." He planted a full, sensuous kiss on her lips.

"All right, all right!" declared Taro. "You can make out in the back of the car on the way home. Can we go already? I'm about to freeze to death!"

The three sorted through the gear that Taro had brought, donned snowshoes, and made their way down the trail. Vibrant colors and wispy shapes continued to crowd into Astrid's vision, making it a little difficult to see. She felt as if she had swallowed some psychotropic plant substance. It was primarily pleasant, actually. A vitalizing hum pierced her every pore and radiated back out, drenching and energizing every molecule in her body. It felt as if something or someone had turned up her aura. Much of the color swirling about her must belong to her.

She wondered what kind of a welcome she would receive back in town, how Meagan, Louise and Sharon would respond to her—both in private and in public. She was also dying to know what had happened to Cedric and where he had been during the magnetic storm, whether he had anything to do with the blast. Somehow, she felt he was no longer a threat. She wouldn't have left the mountain if she hadn't felt that the crisis had passed, frostbite or no frostbite.

And Judy—Astrid let out a heavy sigh. She sure hoped Judy was okay. Had the healing thoughts that her community sent her way done any good at all? While Astrid slept in the frosty embrace of Mt. Shasta, she hadn't dreamed about Judy, she had dreamed about…about aliens, she realized with a start. But they didn't look like modern visions of aliens, they more closely resembled fairy folk: beautiful, golden-eyed creatures, gracefully attired and surrounded by rays of sumptuous color. As I must be now, she mused: as I must have always been except that now I can see it.

She said a little prayer for Judy, hoping with all her might that she remained safe and sound. She certainly would like to see Van's dream videos, if he had any. At the very least, she wanted to talk to him. Hopefully, Cedric hadn't severed the connection with Judy's world and she could still dream about her and visit her. If Van's claims were true, that other world would need her help for a long time. Somehow, though, she had the strange feeling that a catharsis had taken place on Judy's world, just as it had on her own. Maybe she did dream about Judy but just didn't remember it.

A melting clump of snow splattered unexpectedly onto her head from an overhead branch, startling her out of her reverie. She inhaled the rich, sharp smell of pine mixed with late spring snow and damp earth, grateful to Taro for having saved her life—not to mention Nate's life, as well as that of her budding little one. What in the world was Taro's surprise, she wondered suddenly. Or more properly: Who?

THIRTY

Judy sat plopped in the middle of an enormous, steaming tub, sobbing her heart out. Now that the reality of her situation had sunk in—a marvelous one, that was for certain—other considerations had come crowding in. Sure, she might have somehow crashed into paradise, but what about her poor world? What about Robert? Was he even alive any more? Anything could have happened to him. Those filthy cannibals could have finished him off if they ended up winning their skirmish with the government agents. Or the government could have captured him, hauled him off and tortured him to death to learn what he had done. Or—and this was the worst to contemplate, even though in many ways it was the kindest fate of all—had he died after she put the device into play?

The tempting tray that Robin had heaped with food and drink and placed on the shelf beside the tub looked and smelled more delicious than anything she had ever known, and she felt so famished it made her feel faint. But how could she eat, not knowing what had happened to Robert? Tears slid down her cheeks, falling like drops of crystal into her bath. How long would the charm of this world sustain itself without her true love? For it was most definitely charming. Everything she glimpsed during her ride to Robin's house absolutely dazzled her, from the shaggy, graceful trees to the incandescent green meadows dotted with brilliant orange flowers—poppies, Robin had called them—to the lovely, luxurious dwellings, every one of them different and unique. But was paradise truly paradise if she couldn't share it with Major Duncan? She felt as if her heart were crushed. Crushed and bruised, aching, bleeding. And how could she ever find out what had happened to him? Not knowing his fate tortured her almost as much as fearing he was lost to her forever.

Licking away the tears that had gathered in the corners of her mouth, Judy fingered the bottles of subtly scented shampoos, oils, and who-knew-what-else that Robin had lined up on the shelf behind the snack tray. Knowing that she would feel better if she ate something and cleaned up, Judy ducked her head under the water and began to soap herself.

Robert wouldn't want me to spurn the gift of this world, she thought; he would want me to rejoice. Easier said than done, but when she was all clean she began to sample some of the dishes Robin had prepared for her. Soon she was wolfing them down as if there were no tomorrow. She had never realized that so many different, wonderful flavors existed; they made her dogfood-and-potato-chip sandwich seem like industrial waste.

Before long she was stuffed, and every part of her glowed with energy and new life. She couldn't bring herself to get out of the bath, though. What if Robin noticed she had been crying? Anyway, it felt safe in the tub—wonderfully warm, private, sympathetic.

Robin told her to use all the hot water she wanted, as it was heated by the sun. Remarkable! In her own world, water had been so expensive to heat that she never used it. Her world had a sun. Why couldn't they have used it for energy, too, like in this world? These people even ran their cars on sunlight.

Lounging away in the bathtub, alternatively mourning Duncan and marveling over all the incredible things that Robin had attempted to explain to her on the drive home—dimensional windows, dream videos, viruses that actually performed beneficial functions, Astrid's struggle to help her toxic, doomed world in the face of rabid opposition from her own—Judy completely lost track of time. Not until she heard the slam of car doors and the murmur of voices did she stir. She hoped Taro had found Astrid and that she was okay. Judy felt profoundly grateful to Astrid for all the risks she had taken on her behalf—and that of her world, even though in her opinion it didn't deserve it. Judy felt mortified that, according to Robin, gang members from her planet had taken advantage of the conduit between worlds to come and inflict their crazed thirst for death and violence on this peaceful dimension. Why did things like that happen? She felt almost embarrassed to face Astrid, knowing this. But on the other hand, she was dying to meet her in these different circumstances, and the hope that one of the voices in the driveway might be hers propelled Judy out of the bath.

She burrowed into the soft, thick bath sheets Robin had laid out for her, quickly toweling her hair dry. She started to open the door into the bedroom when she caught sight of herself in the mirror. What she saw transfixed her. She looked absolutely stunning. She was still recognizably herself, but everything had taken on an enhanced, enchanting quality. Her mousy curls had turned a rich nut-brown, her eyes sparkled a clear and dappled gray. Her skin gave off a rosy, healthy glow and her body had somehow rearranged itself into that of a most appealing, voluptuous woman. She touched her face. Were the changes for real? Or was this the way she looked in this world? Just what was real any more, anyway?

In the bedroom, she found her gang outfit neatly folded on the bed, but Robin had also laid out a lovely gown fashioned from a deep blue fabric. She attired herself in this instead, dazzled by her own beauty when she caught her reflection again in the wardrobe mirror. Of all her dreams, this was one that she'd hardly ever dared to hope for: that she could be so pretty! If only Robert could see me like this, she sighed sorrowfully. Odd how one's dreams changed according to one's circumstances. Before, she had wanted only to live in the land of her dreams. And now that she was here, all she wanted was Duncan beside her. Did that make her ungrateful? Would the gods take this away from her for thinking such ungrateful thoughts?

* * *

Astrid stepped out of the car, cramped up and finally starting to feel the cold from the night before. She couldn't wait to jump into Robin's hot tub—preferably with Nate, of course—and she was dying for a hot beverage. Her curiosity over Taro's surprise had by now taken a back seat to these other considerations. Robin ran out of the house to greet them, hugging them and fussing over them, bringing with her the sweet, cinnamony aroma of hot spiced cider.

"Come in, come in, you poor frozen things!" she exclaimed. "I've been heating some cider for you, although I can make coffee if you'd rather, and the hot tub is waiting for you. I guess Taro told you who's here."

"Nope!" Taro broke in. "I didn't. I thought this would be more fun as a surprise."

"Hmm. Come to think of it, you might be right, Taro," Robin replied, smiling. "Let me go fetch her from the tub while you three serve yourselves some of that cider. I should make sure she hasn't drowned, anyway."

So the surprise guest was female, Astrid reflected. Who could it be? Her mother? But her mother wasn't particularly fond of soaking in hot tubs; she had dry, sensitive skin.

Planet Dreams

Taro brought a couple of blankets in from Robin's sunroom, while Astrid and Nate ladled themselves mugs of the fragrant, steaming cider. They wrapped themselves in the blankets and then sank into kitchen chairs, sipping their drinks gratefully.

"By the way, thanks for saving our lives, Taro," remarked Nate, sucking a few drops from his mustache.

"Hey—don't mention it." Taro settled at the table to join them after filling a cup for himself and spiking it liberally with some dark rum that Robin had left on the counter. He grinned at Nate. "On the other hand, I was rather gallant, wasn't I?"

Voices in the hallway caused Astrid to sit up with interest, wondering who could possibly get Taro so excited. When her eyes fell upon the pretty young woman who stepped shyly into the room, she felt puzzled. The girl looked very familiar, but Astrid couldn't place her. Then she gave a yelp of recognition.

"Judy!" she cried, jumping to her feet and bounding across the room to throw her arms around her. "My god! How did you get here?"

Judy flushed with pleasure. "Well...I'm not sure, exactly. Robin was trying to explain it to me, but I'm not sure I understand it."

Astrid grabbed Judy's hands and stepped back to take her in. "We can talk all about it later. You look wonderful! This is just incredible! In all my wildest dreams, I never imagined that you would show up here."

"Believe me, neither did I," Judy laughed, thrilled to pieces to find Astrid alive and well and to have her so delighted with her arrival.

"So what's going on in your world? Did Robin tell you we sent a healing transmission and prayers to your world?"

"She did," Judy replied. A lump suddenly rose in her throat. "I hope—I hope it did some good." Tears began streaming down her cheeks.

∞ 288 ∞

Concerned, Astrid glanced at Robin. Robin bit her lip
and shrugged. "Here, come sit down. Tell me what
happened."

So Judy proceeded to tell her about the desperate
ecological plight of her world, about the dying oceans
and Duncan's drastic efforts to save the biosphere. She
told Astrid about the device that she and Robert and
Dorothy had constructed, about their flight from the city
and capture by the cannibals, about her subsequent escape.
When she got to the part of setting the device into play,
she cried so hard that everyone in the room crowded
around her and stroked her hair, patted her on the shoulder
and squeezed her hand.

"So...so I don't know what's happened after that,"
she wept. "I don't know whether it killed everybody or
not." She wiped her eyes ferociously with her free hand.
"I might have even killed Robert," she gulped.

Everyone in the room remained silent for a moment.
Then Nate spoke up.

"Listen," he said, "why don't we locate Van and Rana?
See if we can prevail upon them to take a nap."

Judy regarded him doubtfully. This sounded like a
bizarre suggestion to her. But everyone else in the room
embraced it enthusiastically.

"Great idea, Nate," declared Robin. "Why don't you
and Astrid go on and take your bath, get nice and warmed
through, and Taro and I will track down Van and Rana.
Besides, Astrid might want to take a nap, too."

Astrid nodded. "Couldn't hurt. Although I'm afraid
with Judy here, I might not have a link to her world any
longer."

"A nap would feel welcome in any case," said Nate.
"Is it okay if we take it here, Robin?"

"Don't be silly!" she exclaimed. Of course it's okay.
Just use the guest room. When everyone wakes up, we'll
rendezvous back here in the kitchen. We can watch the
videos and then all have dinner together. I have a freezer

full of spanakopita and stuffed grape leaves that need to be eaten."

"Great!" said Astrid. "So...we'll jump in the tub." She leaned over to give Judy another squeeze. "We'll do whatever we can to help, Judy. Don't despair—miracles can happen. You're here, right?"

"Right," echoed Judy, trying her best to buck up. She didn't want all these kind, generous people to think she was ungrateful. But when everyone wandered out of the kitchen, Robin urging her to make herself at home and do whatever she wanted, she hugged her arms to herself and allowed her misery to overtake her. Sure, miracles could happen; but maybe she had already used up all that were coming to her.

THIRTY-ONE

"Well, whaddya know. It's gone."
Major Duncan nodded, his face drawn in pain and exhaustion. "Let's hope that means Judy has it."
"Yeah, no shit. Whoever's got that jeep also has my sandwich." Dorothy plopped herself down with an irritable grunt. Gunfire and fighting could be heard in the background. "C'mon, Bobby—rest your weary bones. Take a load off."
He expelled a long, shaky breath. "I'm afraid that if I sit down I won't be able to get up again.
"Christ. I'm not going anywhere, are you?"
"Well—"
"I'm not hauling a gimp around in this thicket any more. No way. Either Judy's got the jeep or she doesn't. She's the only other person with the starter code, so I think the chances are good. Either way, though, we can't do anything except wait, since we don't have the jeep or the device. We gotta just trust our fate now. Right?"
Major Duncan sighed as he dropped his makeshift crutch and eased himself down next to Dorothy. "You're right. As usual."
Dorothy reached over and patted his injured leg, her expression softening. "I'm sure sorry about what happened

to you, Bobby. I just couldn't figure out a way to get you two out of there without getting caught myself, especially since they had your gun. I thought about trying to levitate you out, but they could've shot you down, easy. And that wouldn't have done us any good."

"Don't blame yourself. We were vastly outnumbered."

"Still." Dorothy sighed and shook her head regretfully in the pale phosphorescent darkness. "Bastards. I'm glad they're getting theirs. Who do you think'll win?"

"Oh, the government, no doubt. Eventually. Someone has probably called in whatever reinforcements can be spared. There's been intensified fighting in the Middle East, you know."

"No, I didn't. I never follow that stuff."

"Ah."

"Makes me tired."

"I see."

They fell silent.

"You getting cold, Bobby?"

"A little."

"Shit." Dorothy chewed savagely on a fingernail. "I wish we could build a fire. You know, if I hadn't have been so goddamned anxious to check out that cannibal's camp, I would've gotten back sooner. We could've all been outa here. And you would've still had that leg of yours."

"Soon it won't matter, Dorothy," said Duncan.

"And you know," she continued fretfully, "if I hadn't have been on the opposite side of the camp when the agents showed up, I could've probably gotten us all on the road, goddamn it." She yanked up a clump of glowing moss and threw it angrily into the thicket.

"I thought we were trusting to fate now."

"Oh, yeah," Dorothy muttered. "I just want my sandwich is all." She rose wearily. "I'm gonna build us a little shelter, so you just sit tight. Something to keep us out of sight as well as warm. Don't you budge now, okay?"

"Don't worry," responded Duncan. He leaned back against a rock, his face haggard. "I'm not going anywhere."

"Don't die on me, either, cocksucker."

Suddenly the screen went black. Judy cried out in disappointment.

"Don't worry, Judy," Rana assured her softly. "There's more. I spliced two dreams together."

Judy clenched her fists, her eyes trained on the screen. Soon the darkness began to lighten again, and she heard ragged breathing. When the scene brightened to full daylight, she could make out Dorothy and Major Duncan huddled in a small blind made of twigs, branches, and leaves.

"I could sneak back to the camp and score some water," Dorothy said.

Duncan shook his head. "I don't know, Dorothy."

"Look, they're probably all dead. I haven't heard a peep out of anybody for hours."

"What about that party that came by looking for us?"

"Shit—they weren't looking for us. They're not stupid—they were looking for a way out of here."

"Do whatever you want, Dorothy."

"You'd feel a lot better if you had some water to drink."

He didn't answer. Judy cursed herself, wishing she'd taken the time to find the water bottles and left them for her companions. She strained to make out Robert's features in the gloom, wondering how much time had passed since the other dream. He sounded weaker than in the last video.

"Judy ought to be on the mountain by now," Dorothy remarked after a long silence. "That is, of course, if she didn't run into any trouble."

Duncan didn't reply, and Judy froze. Had he died?

"Bobby? Are you okay?" Dorothy inquired anxiously.

"I'm...okay," he responded, his voice strangled.

"You in pain?"

"I'm—concerned about Judy."

Judy clutched her elbows in anguish. She wanted to be able to leap into the screen and assure him that she was all right. She couldn't bear for him to grieve over her on top of everything else that poor man had suffered. Tears streamed down her face, and Rana reached over to stroke her shoulder. She cried even harder.

Then, without warning, a blinding light seared the night sky. Blossoms of fiery incandescence illuminated Robert's and Dorothy's faces. A deep, muffled explosion pummeled the air. Judy gasped and covered her face, but then she peeked through her fingers, unable to bear the suspense. Onscreen, Dorothy and Duncan regarded one another.

"Must have been Shasta," Dorothy remarked.

"Yes. If everything is working properly, we should see the area around Lassen go off next."

"And Crater Lake will soon be nothing but a bowl of steam." Dorothy paused. "Why is it I don't feel more excited?"

Duncan sighed. "Because this is a hell of a solution. I wish man had chosen another course."

"You think he chose this, huh?"

"Well, obviously. Don't you? Who made our species follow this destructive path? No one. We couldn't race down it fast enough."

Dorothy snapped a twig from the interior of the lean-to. She placed it between her lips, observing with satisfaction, "I've always wanted to do this. No need to worry about chemical poisoning now, is there?" She chewed on it for a moment, tossing it back and forth with her tongue. "I don't know, Bobby, it seems to me like blaming the lemmings—you know, those animals that committed mass suicide by rushing into the sea?"

"They never rushed into the sea, Dorothy."

"They didn't?"

"No, they migrated in huge numbers and sometimes got swept downstream when they forded streams and rivers."

"Oh." Dorothy nibbled thoughtfully. "Well, anyway, same thing, basically. They couldn't help themselves. It was a mindless, blind-instinct type of thing."

Duncan snorted. "God gave us minds. And eyes."

"Okay, fuckface—so she gave them to the lemmings, too. The point is, if they could've helped it, don't you think they would have? Christ! Who would have chosen this? It just happened, Bob. It's too bad, it's a drag really, but we're gonna do our best to fix it and hope things improve. You know?"

"Fine, Dorothy."

She threw her twig down. "Jesus, don't go caving in on me like that. It's insincere, Bobby, it's not worthy of you."

"Shh!" he hissed abruptly. "What is that?"

"What is what? Oh."

Judy gripped her seat, wide-eyed. Even she could feel it, a faint vibration, a gently amplifying oscillation of the earth and air.

"Shit," said Dorothy. "Here it comes."

No sooner had she spoken than the dusky, overcast sky erupted into blinding light. An explosion to the east roared in lurid, murderous fury, looking all the world like a nuclear explosion. Lightning sizzled and crackled about them, standing their hair on end, practically illuminating their skeletons in its violent intensity. The earth began to tremble, to shake noticeably, then Judy watched in horror as Robert and Dorothy were tossed about their shelter like crumpled bits of paper. Rana reached over and gripped her hand, hard. The tremors lasted a full five minutes, which seemed an eternity to Judy as she observed her friends buffeted about by invisible sources, their bodies eerily lit in bright, erratic flashes. Finally, miraculously, everything quieted, although Judy imagined that she could feel the echo of the Earth's massive shudders rippling throughout the entire globe.

"Is that it?" Dorothy asked cautiously, voicing Judy's own burning question.

Duncan shook his head. "Not by a long shot. This is the lull before the storm. Fortunately, we appear to be located in the opposite direction from the two nearest volcanic blasts, so the ash won't reach us for a while, nor in its full force. Not only that, but we're in the mountains and away from the coast, so we shouldn't be affected by the tidal waves. They'll devastate every coast in the world if the lithosphere is, in fact, slipping over the mantle and core."

"Wouldn't we know it, if it is?"

Duncan squinted up toward the sky, where lightning and garish streaks still seethed and flickered in the turbulent atmosphere. "Not with such thick cloud cover. If we could see the sun, it would appear to move in the sky. But as it is, it would be difficult to distinguish the lithospheric movement from the earthquakes associated with all the volcanic activity." He paused. "Hurricane-force winds are probably building on the oceans right now," he remarked, "and more shocks and aftershocks are due. We should brace for them as best we can." He returned his gaze to his companion. "But tell me, why didn't the earthquakes knock our shelter down? How did you build this thing, anyway?"

Dorothy cackled gleefully. "I used a little bit of magic. I forgot to tell you—I thought I might just see if we could survive this little shindig."

At this point, the tape flickered and went dark once again. Judy whipped around to look at Rana, hoping she had another segment spliced on here, too. But Rana gave her an apologetic glance.

"Sorry, Judy," she said. "That's where my dreams end. With any luck, Van or Astrid should be waking up soon. And they should have more recent information since my dreams were recorded this morning." Rana stood up. "Do you want some coffee while we're waiting?"

"Oh—sure." Anything, Judy thought, to keep the suspense at bay. And she could use a pick-me-up. Interesting, she mused, that they used such an old-fashioned word for caffeine when everything else appeared so advanced.

Rana flicked on the lights and opened the blinds to the kitchen windows so that sunlight came pouring in once again. When she made the coffee, a rich, dusky aroma permeated the room, setting Judy's mouth to watering.

"Is that the caffeine?" she inquired.

"Uh, yes, Judy. Caffeine is a component of coffee. You haven't ever had coffee before?"

Judy shook her head. "I guess not."

Rana gave her a troubled glance filled with pity and compassion. "Would you like cream or sugar in your coffee?"

"Everything. Put in everything," Judy murmured. She gazed delightedly at the cup of creamy mocha-colored beverage that Rana placed in her hands. Liquid caffeine on her planet had been clear, watery. Medicinal. Sipping her drink now, she found, to her surprise, that it tasted just like it looked.

"Man, does that smell good! Any more where that came from?"

Judy twisted in her seat, relieved to see Van ambling into the kitchen. He carried a tape in his hand.

"Did—did you dream about Bob?" she blurted, unable to contain herself.

He nodded gravely, accepting the cup of steaming coffee that Rana offered him. "I did. I imagine you'll want to see this right away."

Rana darkened the room again while Van placed his tape in the dreamviewer. Judy held her breath. When the dream came onscreen, Judy was surprised to see that the scene had changed. Dorothy and Duncan now struggled through the forest, which was covered by several millimeters of powdery gray ash, and they wore strips of dirty cloth across their noses and mouths. Duncan leaned heavily on Dorothy, his face pale.

"You doing okay?" Dorothy mumbled through her mask.

He nodded, but Judy could see even that effort cost him. She wrung her hands in distress, more anxious than ever to crawl into the screen and rescue him. Just then Astrid and Nate stole softly into the room and settled into the seats next to her. Astrid sought her hands in the dark and gave them a squeeze.

"Boy, those were some winds, huh, Bobby? I thought they were going to blow our shelter away for a while there."

Duncan didn't reply.

"It shouldn't be much longer," Dorothy told him, not sounding as cocky nor self-assured as usual. The elapsed time (however much that was, Judy wondered in frustration; one could never tell in dreams, since time there could accordion, telescope, and jump all over the place) had obviously taken its toll. "I'm almost positive that I visited a survivalist camp around here at some point a while back. They had some toaster ovens they wanted to trade. Of course, none of them worked—anyway, who could afford the electricity?—but I ended up with some great parts."

"What did they want in exchange?" Duncan inquired through clenched teeth, his voice raspy through the cloth.

"Now this'll surprise you," she said. "They wanted music stands! Isn't that the weirdest? I know for a fact that hardly an instrument exists to be had. I've looked for them, ever since I found that book on music. What happened, did all you wealthy people hog them up and hoard them?"

Duncan shook his head. "They must have been making some instruments. What the military didn't melt down for the metals, the Right Hand of God destroyed in the Purge Against Satan. You knew that, didn't you?"

Judy wanted to tell him not to talk, to conserve his strength, but then she realized he was probably trying to distract himself.

"To tell you the truth, Bob," Dorothy remarked, "I try to know as little about the church as I possibly can." Suddenly she gave a whoop. "There it is! There's the gate! I knew it was around here. Okay, we'll need to be cautious. They're one of the friendlier camps, but still—you know how they are. If their strategy for survival worked, they may still be alive. And now is when they'd have most of their defenses up." She stopped, then let out a harsh caw. She called four times. But nothing stirred.

"Hmm," she pondered. "Coulda changed their password. Nothing else to do, I guess, except keep going. Keep your eyes peeled for punji sticks."

Dorothy and Duncan edged closer to the encampment, and as they did so the dwellings came into view on the videoscreen. They were in a shambles, nothing but caved-in hills of rubble. A chill, brooding quiet pervaded the place. Dorothy clucked her tongue.

"Uh-oh, doesn't look good for the survivalists. They must have miscalculated when they built their shelters."

Duncan dropped weakly onto the ground and leaned against a chunk of concrete while Dorothy continued to prowl. "I'm going to find us some food and water, maybe even some medical supplies," she called over her shoulder. "Doesn't look like anyone's going to stop us." Then she came to an abrupt halt and ripped off her face cloth in disbelief. She whirled and jogged over to Duncan, hoisted him up and dragged him through the rubble.

"Sorry," she panted. "I know you're ready to drop, but this you gotta see."

They burst into a clearing and looked out onto the vast central valley spread out below them. Except that now it was a vast, inland sea. It churned a turbulent and foamy gray-brown full of mud, ash, and chunks of pumice. A rustle in the brush next to them caused them to jump, instantly on guard. Two children, a boy and girl, stood clutching one another, their faces streaked with dirt, blood, and tears.

"Oh Christ," said Dorothy, shaking her head regretfully. "Somehow I hadn't thought about all the orphans this situation would create. Now what do we do?"

The picture faded, and Van switched off the dream-viewer. Judy turned expectantly to Astrid, and Astrid, knowing what Judy hoped for, shook her head.

"I didn't dream about your world, Judy. I guess now that you're here, my link is severed." She hesitated. "At least...you know he's alive."

Judy nodded, wondering why she didn't feel any better. She fiddled with her coffee cup, pretended to drink the last swallow. At a sign from Astrid, everyone discreetly withdrew from the room, clicking the door shut behind them. Judy remained at the table, blinking back tears.

I should feel happy, she ruminated; why don't I? He's alive. He's still alive. So why don't I feel happy?

Because, she thought, as she laid her head on the cool, smooth surface before her and wept, as far as a life together is concerned, he might as well be dead.

THIRTY-TWO

Astrid flicked off her dreamviewer and leaned back thoughtfully in her chair. In the last few days her dreams about her beautiful planet with all the pastel moons and brilliantly striated canyons had resurfaced, except that now she knew this to be the home planet of the exquisite golden city she had dreamed about so often before. She was taking classes in the city from the graceful alien folk who lived there, classes in how to manage her new ability to perceive certain wavelengths of the electromagnetic spectrum. She was not alone in possessing this new trait. According to information coming in from computer bulletin boards, just about everyone in Shasta City and any other population center located next to a dimensional window (New York City, for example, the Bermuda Triangle, Nepal, Machu Picchu, Northern Scotland, and Egypt) had begun to express the trait. In addition, so did a decreasing percentage of populations in increasing distances away from the hot spots.

Intriguingly, according to her alien mentors, the magnetic storms had represented the final step in a multi-tiered evolutionary leap, put into motion by the UFO virus. The virus had laid the groundwork for the changes, and toxins leaking in from Judy's world had introduced tiny chromosomal breaks, inversions and translocations to prepare the genome for the effects wrought by the storms. If any of these steps had not taken place, the entire scheme would have collapsed, and serious genetic deterioration would have set in.

Last night Astrid's tutors had begun teaching her how to go into a particular trance state and perceive the electromagnetic emanations produced by the electrons of her DNA. In this way, she could learn how to "read" her chromosomes—but as a whole, not as a complicated linear series of discrete units. It would seem that Milo's dream of consciously manipulating the human genome had realized its first step.

When she asked the aliens if they had, in fact, released the UFO virus and orchestrated the evolutionary saltation, they said no—but they had helped. The Earth and every creature who resided upon it had devised the plan; the aliens had merely tried to help behind the scenes at every juncture. Sentient beings possess free will, they reminded her, so that we may choose our fate at any step of the way. So although the evolutionary jump was planned—on a scale Astrid couldn't begin to comprehend yet—it was not predestined. You can plan to go on a picnic, they said, but that didn't mean you had to go.

She caressed her belly absentmindedly, seeking communion with the little spirit who had taken up temporary residence inside of her. She had a feeling that this baby would turn out to be very special, perhaps possessing some unusual traits, given her conception in space and proximity to the ionic storm. Thankfully, genetic damage was not a problem—she had seen that a couple of nights ago when her instructors took her into the baby's genome. These last few days, she had been sleeping and dreaming a lot—a relaxing regimen, especially after all the hoopla of the past two months. What a lot had happened in a short period of time! She felt it was definitely time to sit back and assimilate all the changes. She stretched languorously, luxuriously.

Hungry, she arose and ambled into the kitchen, spying the note that sweet Nate had left her. It said Judy had awakened early and needed to talk. Not wanting to disturb Astrid's sleep, they'd gone off on a bike ride. A couple of days ago, Nate had rented Judy a mountain bike. She loved it so much that they had obtained her one of her own. Astrid's heart glowed fondly as she thought of Judy and the transformation that had occurred since her arrival in this world. She had absolutely blossomed, each day bringing her new thrills and delights.

Astrid just wished that Robert were faring better. From dream videos passed on by Rana and Van, it was clear that he was not doing so well. The world itself, actually, had fared amazingly well, although civilization had come to an abrupt halt from all the earthquakes, volcanic eruptions, and tsunamis. No summer would take place this year—at least—and the ash circulating in the atmosphere would block a good deal of sunlight for years to come. An ice age was on the way.

The lithosphere had apparently remained in place, however, and Astrid felt convinced that the healing prayers directed to that other world had minimized the damage and casualties. Duncan, though, had developed a serious infection in his severed leg. Frustratingly, if he could come here or she could go there, he could be healed easily; but Astrid no longer even dreamed about Judy's Earth. She hesitated to attempt travel via the dimensional window on Mt. Shasta, since probability functions at the windows were fluctuating wildly after the storms. Astrid couldn't count on ending up in Judy's world, nor on returning to hers even if she did. Van and some other scientists around the globe had been working on developing inter-dimensional travel devices, but they were still in the experimental stages. If only Robert had been able to accompany Judy to Mt. Shasta. As it was now, moving him just a little, let alone making a dangerous, arduous trip over quake-ruptured roads, could conceivably kill him. A boat could get him up the Central Valley, but not up the side of the mountain. And although Dorothy had made several scouting forays from the survivalist camp—which, in fact, turned out to possess far more survivors than originally thought—no functioning aerial craft had turned up. She could only hope that in time, Judy would manage to get over Robert and concentrate on her newfound happiness in this world.

Sighing, Astrid opened the fridge and saw that Judy had gathered more strawberries from the patch behind the bathhouse before leaving on her ride. The gardens and bathhouse held as much of a thrill for her as bike riding did. Plucking a handful of berries from the bowl, Astrid selected a container of yogurt as well, then mixed them both with honey from Robin's bees and plump, meaty walnuts from a neighbor's tree.

Sighing once again, this time with pleasure, Astrid settled into the sun-warmed breakfast nook, happy to see that the local newspaper had resumed publication. Everything had slowed down after the storm, which basically suited her just fine. She regretted the fact, however, that periodicals had missed issues. Up-to-date information could always be gleaned from a computer news service, but Astrid preferred the sharp, clean smell, smooth feel, and crisp look of a newspaper. At this point, too, her new abilities made it harder to read her computer's monitor.

She scanned the pages as she ate, looking for any information on Cedric. She had heard only rumors so far. A search-and-rescue team had found him sprawled unconscious on Mt. Shasta—his device lying melted beside him, some of the more colorful reports maintained. But no one seemed to know whether he was dead or alive. Her search was rewarded on page three, where a short article announced that Cedric lay in a coma at the Hill

Country Hospice. He had not regained consciousness since being rescued from Mt. Shasta. No mention was made of the device, but then it could have been blasted to smithereens or catapulted to God knows where. Obviously, he hadn't managed to screw things up, and that, as far as Astrid was concerned, was the most important thing. Not that she wished a coma on anybody.

Leafing through the rest of the paper, savoring her berries, Astrid's eyes fell on a letter to the editor. "A Public Apology to Those Wronged," read the headline. She dropped her spoon into her bowl and read the letter eagerly. All the members of the community who had taken in other members for mandatory genetic testing were apologizing for their actions. It warmed her heart to see it; she admired the writers for admitting a wrong. Before the turn of the millennium, everyone had always sought to lay any blame elsewhere, a pathetic and embarrassing approach to life. At the end of the letter, she saw that it mentioned her by name as particularly deserving of an apology. Then, much to her surprise, it wound up by announcing that a community baby shower would be held for her a month from now at the Town Center.

"See?" she whispered happily to the soul nestled snugly inside her, "everyone thinks you're special."

Saving the comics for last, Astrid had just begun to peruse them when she heard a knock on the front door. She went to see who it was, wondering who could be calling so early. Robin had left yesterday on a raft trip and Taro had zipped off to Tahiti with Austin. His nerves were shot, he said; he needed a rest and a beach cure. When she opened the door, she was surprised to find Louise and Meagan, looking sheepish and apologetic.

"Mind if we come in?" Louise asked.

Astrid stepped aside, jerking her thumb back in awkward, eager welcome. "Not at all! Come in!"

She led her friends into the kitchen and they all sat around the breakfast table. To put everyone more at ease,

Astrid cut slices of the banana bread Nate had baked yesterday and poured them each a cup of coffee. She settled down into her seat and propped her chin on her hands, trying to separate the dancing aureoles of colored light from their physical features.

"So," she said. "What's up?"

Meagan looked down and traced the grain of the tabletop with her finger; Louise met Astrid's gaze.

"We've come to apologize in person," she replied, her flickering colors full of honest regret. "We behaved very badly."

"Ah, that's okay," Astrid muttered gruffly.

Louise shook her head vigorously. "No, it's not okay. We were wrong. I'm afraid we let fear and prejudice take over."

"Well, it all worked out," replied Astrid, glad, in fact, to hear these words.

Meagan glanced up abruptly. "If I may say a word in our defense, the preliminary changes in the Earth's electromagnetic field didn't make things easy for some of us. It scrambled a few impulses and made it hard to see things clearly, you know."

Astrid laughed and laid her hand over Meagan's. "I know."

"And you know, Astrid," she blurted, "you did make me angry a lot."

Astrid raised her eyebrows but took no offense. "I guess we're even, then," she responded softly. "You put me off too, sometimes."

"But I had no right to legislate your behavior, I realize that."

Astrid smiled. "I agree. I guess that's one thing at least we can agree on."

Meagan nodded, smiling back.

Astrid and Louise both started to speak, then stopped and laughed. Astrid motioned for Louise to proceed, breaking off a corner of her banana bread.

"I just wanted to say that everyone at GenFarm misses you," said Louise. "It's not the same without you. We'd be really happy to have you working back there any time you like."

Blotting her lips with her sleeve, Meagan nodded emphatically. "We would, Astrid. And, uh, actually, Louise has been talking to me about the importance of developing a sense of humor. So—your animal fruits don't really bother me so much any more. I think they're sort of cute, actually, now that I look at them differently—like animal crackers."

Astrid laughed with delight. "I'm glad you think so," she replied.

Meagan drained her cup, then turned to Louise. "We'd better go. We're supposed to meet the rest of the crew in twenty minutes."

Louise smiled mischievously at Astrid. "We've decided to do something frivolous for a change. We're working on a film."

Astrid escorted them to the front door where, surprisingly, Meagan reached up and gave Astrid a hug. Louise then caught her up in a fierce embrace and murmured, "I just know you'll have a beautiful, strong baby."

Tears sprang into Astrid's eyes. She kissed her friend on the top of her curls. "Thanks, Louise," she whispered.

She stood in the doorway for a few minutes to watch them go, soaking up the warm, toasty beams from the sun. No sooner had she turned to go inside than she heard Nate's bicycle chime. She stopped and waited for them to ride into the clearing, Nate poised and comfortable on his bike, Judy still a bit wobbly and prone to screech on the brakes if even a leaf floated into her path. When they drew close, Astrid noticed that Judy's face looked all blotchy from crying and her aura was drenched in sorrowful hues.

"What's the matter?" she asked anxiously.

"I've got to go back!" Judy blurted, screeching to a halt and letting her bicycle clatter to the ground.

"Back?"

Judy nodded, tears breaking out afresh. "Robert's critically ill!" she sobbed. "and he's going to try to find me. I've got to go back and stop him before he kills himself!"

Astrid looked at her, then Nate, in dismay. "Did you see Van or Rana?"

Nate shook his head. He parked his bike and walked over to her to give her a quick kiss. "No, this was from Judy's dream."

"Really?"

"Yes," Judy gulped, trying to stop crying long enough to explain. "I had it last night." Unfortunately, she didn't have a dreamviewer yet, to give her more solid proof. DVs had to be specially calibrated to the individual and a series of brain wave readings performed. But she remembered the dream as clearly as day, her first memorable dream since arriving in this world. Her voice breaking, she told Astrid what she'd dreamed: Robert lying on a cot, alarmingly gray and drawn, demanding that Dorothy take him to Mt. Shasta, even if she had to drag him there. He insisted, rather deliriously, that he had to know what had happened to Judy. Dorothy tried to persuade him to stay put, saying that it was too dangerous—who knew whether Mt. Shasta had finished doing its dance? He should at least wait until he felt better. But Judy sensed from Dorothy that she didn't think improvement would be any time soon—if ever.

"If—if he's dying," her voice caught at the word, "I've got to see him once more," she wept. "And I don't have much time. Nate said you could take me to Mt. Shasta."

"I tried to talk her out of it, but this was the decision she reached while we talked," he said glumly.

Astrid gathered her up into her arms, holding her tightly. "We can do whatever you want—you know that."

She remained silent for awhile, then spoke hesitantly. "Are you absolutely sure this is what you want? I mean, I certainly understand wanting to see Robert before he dies, but if you go there and he does die, you could be stuck there for the rest of your life—without him and without this world, which, honestly, Judy, loves you very much."

"I know." Astrid's words caused tears to spout from her eyes. "But…I can't leave him there to die without me."

Astrid heaved a sigh. "I understand. Okay. We'll help you get some things together."

Judy wiped her eyes and gazed up miserably at Astrid. "You know, maybe somehow I can even bring him back with me."

"Sure," said Astrid, swallowing to ease the lump in her throat. "You never know." She blinked back tears of her own and headed into the house, Judy trailing behind her, Nate behind Judy. "I'll call the pharmacy and have some herbs and homeopathics sent over for you to take with you. Nate—do you want to put together a little survival kit for Judy?"

"Sure," agreed Nate, reaching down briefly to massage Judy's shoulders. "You know that the area around Mt. Shasta is a disaster area right now, don't you? You'll have to be on the lookout for hot spots and tremors and downed trees. If she blows again while you're there, you won't have a chance."

"I know," she quavered, not wanting to think about that part.

Nate exhaled heavily. "And it might not be possible to get back there at all. The dimensional windows have become highly unstable. I know that Van's been working on a gizmo to create the necessary probability functions to travel interdimensionally at will, but all he's got is a prototype. It hasn't been tested on living creatures yet."

"I guess I'll be the guinea pig, then," Judy replied, her expression grim. "Let's not talk about this any more, okay? My mind's made up."

*   *   *

Judy watched while Astrid put some food together for her, too traumatized to do anything else. The thought of going back to her poisoned, damaged world after having spent a week in this one filled her with fear and despair. Maybe she could come back. Surely the probability functions at the windows would calm down again someday, reestablishing a regular conduit. She refused to think very carefully about a third possibility: that the dimensional window would snatch her up and spit her out into neither her world nor this one, but into a world totally inhospitable to her form of life. Or into the vacuum of deep space. Astrid had tried to explain her own perception of how the windows worked, something to do with the fact that matter is really clumps of energy, a density of wavelengths and probabilities, she said. Certain kinds of other wavelengths could cause matter to rearrange its composition, defy the "logic" of space and time, and travel nonlocally through them as if they didn't exist. Which, in certain dimensions, they don't.

The explanation made sense on the surface, but Judy had decided to shelve a deeper understanding of it for later. Earlier, she had been too busy trying to assimilate Astrid's world. And now she had more immediate concerns. Apparently she could make use of the phenomenon even if she didn't understand it. She hoped so, anyway.

She felt a sudden wave of misgiving as she watched Astrid stock the pack intended for her, Astrid's forehead all crinkled up in concern. Both Astrid and Nate possessed more psychic abilities than she did, although her own had increased considerably since coming here. Did they know something they weren't telling her, knowing that she had her mind made up? At that moment, Astrid glanced up at her and flashed her a reassuring smile. Judy smiled back uneasily.

"I guess we're ready to go," Astrid announced when Nate showed up in the kitchen, carrying a small pouch clinking with tools and the package from the pharmacy, wrapped in cream-colored paper. Astrid slipped them into the pack and zipped it up noisily. He also held a small electronic device, apparently the one that Van had been working on. "How about you?"

Judy nodded and stood, stiff from the conflict that seethed inside her—desperation to race to Robert's side warring with complete and total dread of leaving the closest thing to paradise that she had ever imagined.

"You can still change your mind, Judy," Nate reminded her.

"I know," she muttered, clenching her teeth to maintain her composure. "Let's go."

Taro had left his car with Nate and Astrid while he vacationed in Tahiti, so they all trooped out to it and piled in dispiritedly. Judy tried to memorize every luscious leaf, every charming, eccentric doorway and weathervane, every cheerful, healthy person who strolled easily along in the most vibrant, beautiful colors she had ever seen— fuchsias, rich purples, deep greens and clear, light-hearted yellows. Every color in the spectrum, as a matter of fact— a fitting expression of the colorful richness of their lives. She had never, ever imagined that so many people could be so kind, so contented with their lives, so spontaneously and effortlessly productive. Happiness ran in rivulets throughout the entire psychic current of this world, as bitter vitriol and cynical hopelessness had permeated hers. How did things get that way? Was her world simply unlucky and this one lucky? Bad things just happened in her world and things went downhill from there?

Or was it the fact that the inhabitants of Astrid's world had decided to seize their own destiny—without cynicism, greed, or fear? If so, perhaps hope yet existed for her poor world. Perhaps a cataclysmic event was what they needed to change course, to jolt them out of the nightmare they had all been living before. Superstitiously, she crossed her fingers and prayed to whoever had gotten her this far. Make everything work out, she prayed. Save Robert, save my world. Protect me.

Long before she felt ready, they had pulled into the trailhead parking lot. They all donned snow boots and checked their packs to make sure they had all their gear, then started silently up the trail. The day had dawned clear, fortunately, although a few wisps of blowing snow and cloud had begun to wreathe the mountain. Judy swallowed nervously, wondering what sort of mood the Shasta in her world occupied at the present moment.

Astrid and Nate were able to sense the direction of the dimensional window once they left the forest, almost as if by scent, they commented to each other—scent that also possessed glimmering streams of color and temperature differences. Judy sometimes envied them this remarkable new ability, but on the other hand, she had her hands full with a budding telepathic sense and indications of a latent psychokinetic ability. Instead, she marveled at the magnificent sights that were available to her, from the haze of blue-green valley that shimmered below to the massive features of Mt. Shasta: precipitous rock cliffs, wind-carved cornices of snow, walls of blue ice as smooth as gelatin.

Much too soon, Astrid and Nate halted, saying that they had arrived at their destination. Judy gripped the straps of her pack, so frightened she felt faint.

"So." Judy swallowed unhappily, pushing her dark curls out of her face with a mittened hand. She didn't want to leave. She was scared to go back. But she couldn't live happily without Robert. She wished she could look like she did now when she went back to her world. "I guess I should just go on and go, huh? What do I do, now that I'm here?"

Astrid eyed her sorrowfully, then hugged her close. "I'm going to miss you, Judy. I wish you could stay. But

I understand why you have to go back. If I can ever help you, I will. You know that, right?"

Judy nodded, unable to speak.

Nate leaned over and gave her a kiss. "That makes two of us. You always have a home here. Don't ever forget that."

"I won't," she choked.

"Okay." Astrid sighed and stepped back. Nate got out the apparatus that Van had provided, fiddling with the gauges and settings. He took some sort of reading from her with a small gaussmeter, then set the device on the ground next to her and made his final measurements and adjustments.

"This is what you need to do, Judy," he told her. "Close your eyes. Relax. Think of where you want to be and who you want to be with. Picture it clearly in your mind, okay? And don't try to make it happen. Try to let it happen, all right?"

"Yeah." Judy drew in a deep breath and closed her eyes.

Nate flipped the final switch and retreated. Astrid bit her lip, reaching over to grab Nate's hand for support. They waited. Nothing happened.

Then a blinding, freak bolt of lightning seemed to arc from the peak itself, accompanied by a simultaneous clap of deafening thunder. Astrid also became aware of an ear-splitting whine, which seemed to be coming from Van's device. The two blinked to regain their vision, expecting to see that Judy had vanished off the face of the earth. But she still stood before them. And next to her sprawled Robert, limp, but very much alive.

Judy gaped at him in astonishment, then whirled around to take in her surroundings. "My God!" she cried in disbelief, dropping to her knees to throw her arms around him. "You came here instead! How did that happen?"

Astrid and Nate stared, equally amazed.

"Judy's superconscious must have known where she really wanted to be," mused Astrid.

Nate rubbed his chin thoughtfully. "Think so?"

"Well, there's another possibility..." She nestled amorously into Nate's arms, waiting to give Judy and Robert a few private moments before offering their assistance.

"What is that?"

"Magic really *does* exist."

THIRTY-THREE

Dorothy sat on the step of her plane, placidly picking her teeth with an ivory toothpick she'd found during one of her foraging trips. Things were really not that bad, once the dust had settled a bit. Sure, she wished Bobby hadn't up and disappeared like that on Mt. Shasta. She had turned her back for one second, practically, and when she turned back around he was gone. She'd waited around for an entire day, but when he stayed disappeared, she had to give up. Who the hell knew where he'd gone or what had happened to him, the asshole. Besides, there was work to do, lots of it. And Mt. Shasta had always been a freaky place, even more so after its eruption, all covered with black ash and glowing lava flows, smoking ominously and looking pretty ornery still. She didn't want to hang around too long. She missed Bob, missed his company. But all in all, things were really all right. At least his pigheadedness had prodded her into finding this plane, which had come in really handy ever since she managed to appropriate it from that air force base.

Anything she wanted she could just go and take. No one was going to stop her, that's for sure. The surprising number of survivors she'd discovered on her trips to scope things out were all in shock. Besides, she was the only one who knew what was going on. All she had to do was act important and officious, like she was in charge, and everybody let her do whatever she felt like, even in their own camps and grids. She enjoyed telling everybody what to do, too.

She had to admit that everyone seemed to have undergone a definite improvement in attitude. She had yet to come across anyone who wanted to threaten or harm her. Most of the people were eager to pitch in and do whatever needed to be done, like taking care of the injured, gathering together whatever foodstuffs, water, and warm clothing could be found, or making radio broadcasts to contact other areas that might have some extra resources.

Very few of the military had survived, but mainly because of their own practices. The earthquakes, eruptions, hurricanes, and tornadoes had wreaked havoc on the arsenals. The occupants of those bases with poisonous gases, like the first one she'd visited, had died from escaped gas. Those were the handiest, as they yielded up planes, jeeps, and helicopters, not to mention synthetic fuels and batteries. Others had exploded, leaving nothing but craters and huge pockmarks. Still others—and these were the really disgusting ones—had perished from unleashed microwave weaponry, with everyone splattered all over the place. Those Dorothy just flew over; any survivors could find their own way out.

Fortunately, biological warfare had not been employed for a long time, ever since it had backfired on every country that used it. Somehow the diseases would always come back to those who had propagated them. So she didn't need to worry about that, thank God. Infection was going to be a big enough problem as it was. But as of now, it seemed to be under control.

She placed her toothpick in her breast pocket and climbed into the plane. *I wonder how Earth's privileged classes like the latest developments,* she mused, fastening her seatbelt and flipping the switches to her instruments.

She should check out a few of those short-sighted assholes one of these days. But this morning she was in the mood to make another scouting foray. Earth, right now, was a scavenger's dream, a pack rat's paradise.

Oh yeah, this is the life, Dorothy reflected happily as she taxied briskly down the runway and caromed into the sky. Where would she go today? Oregon? Idaho? Utah? There were rumors of a particularly fat survivalist camp in Utah. Maybe she should check it out. She made a wide arc and then headed east, squinting into the climbing sun, which was made brilliantly colorful by the volcanic ejecta and ash in the air.

"Wherever you are, Bobby," Dorothy said aloud, "I hope you're having as much fun as I am." She leaned back expansively and let out the throttle, full blast. Yeah, life was sweet. Life was good.

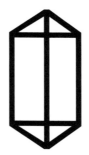

About the Author

Michaela Carlock has worked as a carpenter in the high country of Colorado, as a professional shopper for a millionaire in Dallas, as a writer-in-residence in Escazú, Costa Rica, as a hospital technician in a large teaching hospital in Arkansas, and as a versatile office temp in Manhattan. She studied genetics and biology at Wellesley College, where she obtained her B.A., and the University of Massachusetts, Amherst, where she received her M.S. Currently, she resides in northern California.

If you would like to obtain additional copies of PLANET DREAMS, check your favorite local or on-line book store, or send your name, address, and daytime telephone number, along with a check or money order for $13.95 plus $3.50 shipping/handling (California residents add 7.25% sales tax) *per book* to:

KESWICK HOUSE
P O Box 992535
Redding, CA   96099-2535

For more information about our press, authors, or other titles, check out our Web site at:

www.snowcrest.net/keswick